DEEP STATE STEALTH

VIKKI KESTELL

NANOSTEALTH | BOOK 4

Faith-Filled Fiction™

www.faith-filledfiction.com | www.vikkikestell.com

DEEP STATE STEALTH

Nanostealth | Book 4
Vikki Kestell
Also Available in eBook Format

BOOKS BY VIKKI KESTELL

NANOSTEALTH

Book 1: *Stealthy Steps*
Book 2: *Stealth Power*
Book 3: *Stealth Retribution*
Book 4: *Deep State Stealth*

A PRAIRIE HERITAGE

Book 1: *A Rose Blooms Twice* (free eBook, most online retailers)
Book 2: *Wild Heart on the Prairie*
Book 3: *Joy on This Mountain*
Book 4: *The Captive Within*
Book 5: *Stolen*
Book 6: *Lost Are Found*
Book 7: *All God's Promises*
Book 8: *The Heart of Joy—A Short Story* (eBook only)

GIRLS FROM THE MOUNTAIN

Book 1: *Tabitha*
Book 2: *Tory*
Book 3: *Sarah Redeemed*

The Christian and the Vampire: A Short Story
(free eBook, most online retailers)

DEEP STATE STEALTH

Copyright © 2018 Vikki Kestell
All Rights Reserved.
ISBN-13: 978-0-9862615-7-2
ISBN-10: 0-9862615-7-2

DEEP STATE STEALTH

CONSPIRACIES. COLLUSION. PLOTS. Secrets within secrets and plans within plans.

Thanks to Gemma and the nanomites' timely intervention, President Jackson survives Vice President Harmon's attempt to assassinate him and seize the presidency. Back in Albuquerque, Gemma makes a difficult decision: She allows the explosion that killed her identical twin sister to serve as the cover-up for her own "death."

Half a year later, Gemma emerges from hiding as Jayda Locke. Soon after, the President's sole contact within the NSA, an old and trusted friend, vanishes. Did the President's friend learn the identities of Harmon's co-conspirators in his plot to assassinate the President? Was the President's friend found out and eliminated because of what he uncovered?

The President calls upon Jayda (now married to Zander Cruz) to infiltrate the NSA and, with the nanomites' assistance, identify the remaining traitors. But is the sedition within the government more widespread than either Jayda or the President believed? More importantly, will Harmon's confederates stage another coup, a second attempt upon the President's life?

As Jayda and the nanomites breach the NSA's security and begin to untangle the web of treachery, no one can conceive how deep the corruption runs—or how close it stands to the President himself.

DEDICATION

To all those who have sworn an oath
"to support and defend
the Constitution
of the United States of America
against all enemies,
foreign and domestic,"
and who have held to their oath
with both honor and sacrifice.

REMEMBERING

Wayne

ACKNOWLEDGEMENTS

I have acknowledged and thanked
my wonderful team many times,
but they deserve every kudo I can apply.
Thank you,
Cheryl Adkins and **Greg McCann**.
I am honored to work with such
dedicated and talented individuals.
I love and value both of you.
Our *gestalt* is powerful!

COVER DESIGN

Vikki Kestell

FOREWORD

THE DEEP STATE:
The unelected "fourth branch"
of the U.S. government.

"A BODY OF PEOPLE, typically influential members of government agencies or the military, believed to be involved in the secret manipulation or control of government policy."

—Oxford English Dictionary

⌘

"A HYBRID ASSOCIATION OF ELEMENTS of government and parts of top-level finance and industry that is effectively able to govern the United States without reference to the consent of the governed as expressed through the formal political process."

—Mike Lofgren, former Republican U.S. congressional aide, 2014

⌘

"THE DEEP STATE DRAWS POWER from the national security and intelligence communities, a realm where secrecy is a source of power."

—Jason Royce Lindsey, *The Concealment of the State*, 2013

⌘

"THE ENTRENCHED BUREAUCRACY composed of political appointees and career government employees engaged in coordinated attempts to undermine the authority and legitimacy of the democratically elected President of the United States. Civil servants opposed to the President's political beliefs and agenda, pulling strings in the background to obstruct the executive branch through regulation, procedural red tape, weaponized national intelligence actions, a complicit media, and the judicial overreach of like-minded allies in federal courts. Unelected officials able to thwart the will of the voters and effectively impose their values and objectives upon the American people. Sedition and treason. A 'soft' coup."

—Vikki Kestell, *Deep State Stealth*

⌘

PROLOGUE

I WAS DREAMING—and it was not a sweet or pleasant dream.

The thing is, I *knew* I was dreaming, but I couldn't wake myself up. If you have ever been caught up in a nightmare, you get what I mean: I twitched and tensed, tangling my feet in the bedsheets, but I was powerless to pull myself from the events unfolding before me. I was reliving that evening—and my anxiety levels had already spiked through the roof.

I was with FBI Special Agent Ross Gamble in his apartment. He'd invited me there for dinner (ostensibly), but my gut knew in advance that there was more to his summons than food and a friendly chat between friends. When I'd knocked on Gamble's apartment door, he'd eyed me with mistrust. Well, it *was* the first time he'd seen me in my new persona as Jayda Locke . . . you know, *Gemma Keyes being dead and all.*

Gamble's wariness had been so strong that I'd been obliged to ask the nanomites to temporarily dissolve my disguise. Only then had Gamble, with a begrudging shudder, conceded that the stranger at his door was truly me. He had allowed me to enter and, in my dream state, we drifted through a meal of homemade pizza and salad.

Odd.

I could smell the warm pepperoni and spicy Italian sausage pizzas—right down to their yeasty crusts and still-bubbling cheese. The memory was so true to life that my stomach clenched as Gamble worked up to what our meeting was really about.

Like I said, I knew what was coming, but I couldn't jar myself awake or wrench myself from the inevitable. In perfect detail, my subconscious replayed our conversation, starting with me slicing through Gamble's pretense.

"The pizza was great—thanks for making two, by the way—but why did you ask me here, Agent Gamble? What do you need?"

Gamble exhaled and eased into the point of our meeting. "You'll never guess where I spent the early part of this week."

"Cut the guessing games, Gamble."

I hadn't been in the mood for his stalling tactics that evening, and I wasn't now.

He rubbed his jaw. "Fine. All right. Here it is. I got an interesting call last week and flew out of Albuquerque Monday." He slanted a look at me to gauge my reaction. "I spent Tuesday at Camp David."

I said nothing, only stared at Gamble. The same jolt of panic I'd experienced at that moment stabbed me as I sank deeper into my dream.

"I met with the President and the lead agent of his protective detail, Axel Kennedy."

I slowly and methodically folded my napkin, trying to delay what was coming. "What . . . did the President want?"

Gamble leaned toward me. "He wished me to convey his thanks to you for your assistance in December. He didn't elaborate on the specifics of the assistance you provided, only that your aid averted a national crisis— a crisis that had something to do with the Vice President. From that, I took it to mean that Harmon's death wasn't from natural causes, after all?"

Gamble searched my face, probing for answers. What he found was the poker face I'd perfected as Gemma Keyes—the old Gemma Keyes, *Gemma BN* (Before Nanomites), back when Gemma had honed the art of fading into the background like so much white noise.

"The President asked me to tell you that, although the head of the snake was severed, he has uncovered evidence of co-conspirators in the NSA who continue to plot against him. The evidence suggests that intelligence gathering is being weaponized to use against the President's key allies in the government—all with the purpose of taking down his administration."

I squirmed in my sleep. Co-conspirators in the National Security Administration. *Great. Super. Nothing better than knowing your enemies are smiling in your face while sharpening a shiv to stick between your ribs.*

"The situation has grown particularly dicey. The single contact whom the President trusted—an individual placed high within the NSA—has disappeared. This means the President is now without eyes or ears on the inside. Meanwhile, every move he makes is watched—perhaps by treasonous elements within the intelligence community. The President doesn't know who he can trust, and Axel Kennedy is wound tighter than a drum. I think he fears for the President's life."

I'd met the President and his wife just the one time—when I'd snuck into the White House to warn them of the Vice President's intent to assassinate Robert Jackson, our second African American president. I found that I liked Robert and Maddie Jackson very much. Within the dream, concern for their safety harried me. Apprehension chased after me, and I tossed and moaned.

"The President is growing desperate, Jayda. He needs someone who can infiltrate the NSA, penetrate their bureaucracy, and get inside their secrecy—someone who can provide him with the evidence he needs to clean out that nest of vipers. Someone who can defeat every kind of security, go wherever she wants, search every air-gapped computer, and listen in on the most private of conversations."

"H-he wants me?"

No, I protested in fretful sleep. *Not me.*

But Gamble continued. "Yes. He proposes providing you with a bogus identity and slipping you inside the NSA in a low-level position. He said you and your unique 'skills' could handle the rest from there. But I think—" and here Gamble hesitated. "—I think Jayda Locke is the perfect bogus identity. You even have the right mix of employment skills and experience the NSA might desire."

I said nothing to Gamble, but I felt the bottom falling out from under my perfectly reconstructed world. And now, within my dream, his previous words lodged in my mind: *Although the head of the snake was severed, the President has uncovered evidence of co-conspirators in the NSA . . .*

The head of the conspiracy had been Vice President Harmon.

The *dead* VP.

I shivered in my sleep. *The head of the snake.* Something about that phrase disquieted me. Could snakes regrow their heads like some reptiles or amphibians could regrow limbs and tails?

No, I assured myself. Of course not.

Gamble's voice droned on, "The President was stumped, however, at how to ensure that the NSA would hire you—especially within a tight time frame. I told him to leave that to you, that you and your little friends could manage it. Am I right?"

"If. If I were to agree to the President's plan."

"Let me lay it out for you, er, Jayda. The President wants to transfer me to the D.C. area. Special assignment. We—you and I—would work together."

"We? How?"

"I would be your handler, convey instructions to you, provide whatever logistics you needed, and communicate your information to the President. You and I have worked together; I think we make a good team, don't you?"

I stared at the floor—anywhere but at him. "I'm not looking to make a career change, Gamble. I just started a good job, and Zander and I . . . well, we've been talking about getting married."

"Congratulations. I'm glad you guys finally figured it out."

"No. No, we haven't. That's the problem. We're trying to work out how to deal with my 'condition.' Frankly, it's a total wet blanket on our relationship. A deal breaker, so to speak, for multiple reasons."

I must have looked as morose as I felt, because the kind and compassionate Gamble had shown himself.

"I'm sorry. I hadn't thought about the relationship problems your, uh, 'condition' might create."

"You have no idea. And I've just established myself as Jayda Locke. If my cover is blown, do you have any idea how difficult it would be to start over? Again? Right now, only a handful of people know my new identity. I want and need to keep my ID and 'condition' confined to that small group. It's the best way to keep me and those I care about safe. You know that old saying, 'The only people I trust are you and me—and I'm not sure about you'?"

Gamble was empathetic. "The President agrees with that proverb. That's why he called me himself. Outside of him and Agent Kennedy, not a single other person will know that we've planted you in the NSA. Nor will anyone suspect your ability to turn invisible and penetrate their most secure areas, hacking the NSA from within."

In my sleep, I shook my head. "Nope. Sorry, Gamble, but no. I can't run off on Zander. We . . . we're praying about our relationship and waiting for God to answer. Besides, what you propose is way out of my league."

My recollections of that night petered out, and Gamble wafted away, leaving me alone in the dream, no longer in his apartment but in a damp and dim place where thick mist puddled about my feet and legs. I didn't recognize my whereabouts, so I turned, slowly, looking for some marker or clue as to where I was.

I found nothing—only emptiness in every direction.

With tentative steps, I advanced, hoping to spot a door—or even a wall. Anything to indicate the boundaries of this strange place. I counted off fifty paces, encountering more nothingness and more of the ubiquitous mist.

"Hello?" I whispered.

No response.

I raised my voice. "Hello?"

Had I gone in a circle? Without a fixed position to orient myself, I supposed it was possible.

Pointing my eyes straight ahead, I counted off another fifty steps.

When I stopped, I called, much louder than before, "Hello? Can anyone hear me?"

My words faded without echo or amplification. No, perhaps "faded" is the wrong descriptor. My shouts thudded to the ground as soon as they left my mouth. They dropped as though weighted or robbed of impetus, adding to the weird impression of vacuity around me.

Wherever I was, the laws of physics did not seem to apply. This place was unnatural.

Creepy.

Wrong.

Aloud, I said, "It's okay. I'm just dreaming. When I wake up, all this will be gone," but I felt my pulse quicken and throb in my throat.

Within the dream, Gamble's words repeated: *Although the head of the snake was severed, the President has uncovered evidence of co-conspirators . . .*

That phrase stuck in my craw. Vice President Harmon had been the *head* of the plot, and he was dead. Since Harmon was dead, why did those words bother me so?

The head of the snake. The words made me itch; they gave me the heebie-jeebies. I shivered and kicked at the soupy fog that obscured the "floor" and my feet. The fog was so thick, I couldn't tell if I was standing on stone or tile, only that the substance was hard and cold. I stretched my hand down into the mist—and changed my mind. Maybe fumbling around in the mist with bare fingers wasn't the smartest idea. Instead, I decided to keep walking, to try to find my way to the "end" (or the beginning) of wherever I was.

"Any exit will do," I whispered.

I started forward and walked for quite a while, gradually growing drowsy. Lethargic. I couldn't focus. My eyes drifted closed.

I may even have sunk into a deeper sleep, leaving the dream behind.

I only know that I was much more relaxed when I heard it: the faintest rasp—small, whispery, similar to the sound a sheet of soft tissue paper makes when it is drawn slowly across the smooth surface of a desk. Up until now, I hadn't heard anything in the shadowy void except my own breath, words, and footsteps.

I halted, forced my drooping eyes open, and listened.

There it was again. Faint. Subtle. Intermittent. Hardly the breath of a sound.

Yeah, like I said—a sheet of gauzy paper slowly pulled across a smooth surface.

I blinked, still stupid with sleep. The thick mist eddied off to my right and, within the mist, I thought I caught movement.

When I turned and focused on the shifting haze, it—whatever it was—stopped. I squinted through the gloom, trying to figure it out. Then I picked up on the sound again.

The tiny hairs on the back of my neck prickled and stood up and, well, I realized it wasn't paper I heard.

A gliding form—scarcely discernible through the swirling fog but recognizable for what it was—slithered in my direction then paused. Motionless.

"Snakes," I whispered. "Why'd it have to be snakes?"

I swallowed the thick wad of fear stuck in my throat.

Well, no worries, right? I'd cooked up snake before. Cajun style.

If it's smokin', we're cookin'; if it's black, it's done.

Time to fry me some snake!

I grinned, took a step back, and brought my hands up, palms facing each other, anticipating a tongue of sparking, flashing electricity to bloom and build between them.

Not a blessed thing happened.

The smirk dropped from my mouth. "What the hey, Nano? What gives?"

The nanomites did not answer. The "warehouse" in my mind—that place where the nanomites and I often communed—felt as forsaken as the emptiness around me.

"Wait. How is that even possible?"

The nanocloud and I were indivisible and inseparable. They couldn't leave my body without killing me—and I was fairly certain that *I wasn't dead*—so where were they?

"Nano? Talk to me."

Nada.

The form hiding within the mist inched forward, so I again held my palms toward each other. To my chagrin, I could not activate the electrical current that should have leapt effortlessly from my fingertips to build within the cradle of my hands.

Although the head of the snake was severed, the President has uncovered evidence . . .

More movement. The swirling miasma out in front of me undulated in telltale coils. Wow, *huge* coils! Mounds knee-high and as wide as my hips. The vaporous body weaved side to side, closer with each turn—and beneath the murky, obscuring haze, the hint of something broad and flat . . . pointed toward me, leading the way, advancing with every turn of those winding mounds.

The mist swirled, for an instant disclosing the gleam of a golden eye.

"But the head! We cut it off!"

I was babbling. The nanomites had deserted me—and my defenses had failed me.

Not taking my eyes from the monster's approach, I backed away, thinking I should make a run for it—but I did not relish the idea of turning my back on the serpentine creature concealed in the mist.

I screamed aloud, "Nano!"

No response.

"Nano? Where did you go? I need you!"

I scurried backward in quick, panicked steps, on the verge of "losing it." If I turned tail and ran, I *knew*—with horrifying certitude—that before I gained enough distance, the creature would fling its massive body forward and loop its constricting, crushing coils about me.

A pair of flared nostrils, followed by two glittering eyes, lifted above the mist, and the head revealed itself. I could not look away: The eyes—intelligent and cruel—were mesmerizing, no doubt how he beguiled his prey into immobility.

The beast's tongue flicked once, twice . . . then the body of the snake gathered itself and shot forward.

I bolted and ran.

Only pure survival instinct and nano-imbued reflexes saved me—but for how long? I could see nothing ahead of me except more shrouding haze. I had no sense of direction, no avenue of escape. Still, I sprinted for all I was worth, terror fueling my flight, all the while shrieking, "Nano! Nano!"

The nanomites did not answer me, but another Voice did.

This is not a physical enemy, Jayda. You cannot combat a spiritual foe with natural weapons, nor will your Help come from what you know or can do yourself.

I felt the serpent's presence closing. Legs pumping hard, I planted one foot and jinked to the right, hoping to win some ground, but I already knew I could not outrun the beast.

A heavy weight slammed against the back of my knees; I stumbled and went down. Immediately, thick rings looped around me. The steely coils flexed and wound more tightly. The rings pinioned my arms, so I kicked and thrashed with my legs.

It was a futile exercise. The more I struggled and screamed, the more the snake's muscles contracted until they were crushing my ribs. The pain was excruciating, the pressure on my lungs so great that I could no longer draw a full breath.

The serpent was killing me.

I kicked out for all I was worth, a last ineffectual effort.

"Jesus . . . Jesus, please help me," I wheezed.

⌘⌘⌘⌘

PART 1:
DEEP STATE
INCURSION

CHAPTER 1

"GEMMA! GEMMA! Wake up!"

I couldn't move my arms; they were pinned to my sides, but I twisted as far as I could within my restraints and broke free. I hauled my knees up and kicked out with every bit of my waning strength. My feet connected . . . with my husband's chest.

"Ooof!"

Zander's arms let go as he flew across the mattress, sailed off the edge of the bed, and smashed into the bedroom wall. When the fetters binding me dropped away, I sprang from the bed, throwing my arms wide as I did. One hand connected with the cute little bedside lamp on my nightstand. The pitiful thing exploded against the wall—about the same time Zander's impact rattled our room and likely the apartment below us.

Oh, dear. Our neighbors are going to be really unhappy with us.

My eyes snapped open. "Zander?"

He groaned.

"Zander! Zander, are you all right?"

His reply was muffled. "Dang it, Gemma!"

My automatic response was, "Jayda. Don't call me Gemma."

"Fine. Dang it, *Jayda!* What in the world?"

By then I'd switched on the overhead light. "I had a bad dream."

"Ya think?" Zander picked himself up, massaging the top of one shoulder as he stood. "I'd been trying to wake you up for a while before you used those jackhammers you call legs to launch me out of bed and just about put me through the wall."

"I'm sorry, Zander. It . . . the dream. It was so ugly. Scary."

My voice shook.

I shook.

I could see the serpent's head rising from the mist, fixing its eyes on me. Evil. Malevolent. Lethal.

Jayda Cruz, we, too, attempted to interrupt your REM state when we detected your abnormally elevated heartrate and shortness of breath. However, you did not respond to our attempts to wake you.

Zander and I heard my nanocloud "speak," and we looked across the bed at each other, puzzled that the nanomites' efforts to wake me had been as ineffectual as Zander's had been.

Jayda Cruz, your vital signs indicate that you are quite shaken. Do you wish us to stimulate calming endorphins?

"No."

Your heartrate is still uncharacteristically rapid. Are you certain—

"No. Thank you."

Very well. However, we—

"Oh, stuff a sock in it, Nano!"

I was so peeved with the nanomites for "abandoning" me in my dream that snubbing them felt weirdly gratifying. And, yes, I get how stupid that sounds—it was a *dream*—but the terror of that shadowy place clung to me the way the murky fog had adhered to my feet. I shivered in its grip.

"Hey. Come 'ere, babe." Zander opened his arms, and I went to him— until his arms closed about me.

I pulled back. "Don't. Please."

"Don't what? Don't hold you?"

I teared up then. "I dreamed a stupid, ginormous snake was chasing me. It caught me and twined itself around me and was squeezing me to death. When I woke up, you had your arms around me and-and-and—"

"And I got catapulted from the bed."

"Uh-huh. Pretty much."

"Are you okay now?"

"I-I don't know," I sniveled. "It was different from any kind of nightmare I've ever had."

The bizarre, ultra-vivid dream was stuck on repeat behind my eyelids, and my legs felt like so much soft rubber, incapable of holding me up.

"Maybe we should make some coffee, and you can tell me about it?"

Zander glanced around for the clock. He found it on the carpet with the broken remains of the cute lamp. The clock's glowing red numbers stared at the ceiling.

"Well, well. Four o'clock on a Saturday morning. What lazy bums we are."

His little joke bombed. I tried to chuckle for him anyway, but I couldn't pull it off. My attempt fell as flat as his joke.

He arched his brows. "So, coffee?"

"Coffee. Yes, please."

We fumbled for our clothes, pulling on shorts and t-shirts to accommodate Maryland's June weather. The eighty-something temps were no big deal, but the humidity was brutal—us coming from Albuquerque's normally bone-dry climate.

A trip outside in Maryland's high humidity felt like hot yoga while breathing through a thick, wet blanket. Within minutes, crisp, freshly laundered clothes clung to our skin as though coated with damp, gummy paste. The muggy air did weird, inexplicable things to my hair, too. I mean, how can hair be limp and frizzy at the same time?

20

While the coffee was brewing, we sat on the sofa, and I relaxed enough to lean against Zander and let him drape his arm over my shoulder. In fits and starts, I repeated the dream to him. I had no difficulty remembering its specifics. Unlike an ordinary dream, whose minutiae and emotional "pull" tailed off within moments of waking, every detail and nuance of the nightmare was like fresh paint slapped on my brain—slick, shiny, and sticky.

When I finished the telling, Zander got up, poured two mugs of coffee, and returned. He didn't say anything when he handed me my mug but was pensive as he processed what I'd recounted.

I sipped on my coffee, savoring its hot, biting familiarity. I leaned my head back against the sofa . . . and toppled down a rabbit hole in my own thoughts.

⌘

. . . ALL THE BOOKS SAY that the initial year of marriage is the honeymoon, that the real work of forging a lasting union normally takes place over the next ten years.

Normally? What's that? To suggest that Zander and I would experience a conventional "honeymoon" year would be an absurdity—and it was a sure bet that we would never share a predictable or typical "next ten years."

How could I have known that the possibility of an ordinary life went right out the window the first time I entered those tunnels in the old Manzano Weapons Storage Facility? I'd had no idea then how that single choice would alter every facet of my future—and now, my husband's future, too. Because of that one, fateful decision, anything and everything about "us" would forever fall outside the scope of common or ordinary.

Marriage has joined my life to Zander's and his to mine, but we are not in this alone. Trillions of intelligent nanomites have "rewired" the synapses of our brains, modified our bodies' base molecular structures, and enhanced our physiologies so that we can accommodate both their numbers and their needs.

The bottom line is that the nanomites—the two powerful swarms we call "nanoclouds"—are and will continue to be our companions in this journey through life. We share a symbiotic relationship with them as members of an alliance like none other.

Yes, the nanomites need us as "hosts" to carry them but, because of the changes they made in us, now we need them, too. The alterations to our cellular structures are irreversible. Should the nanomites ever decide to extricate themselves from us, our bodies would not survive. Put plainly, without the nanomites, we would die.

I guess what I'm getting at is that we've already struggled and worked through more difficulties and obstacles leading up to our whirlwind wedding than most couples face in a lifetime—making our relationship an outlier that defies categorization. We skew the curve so drastically that it's best not to compare our marriage to any "norm."

Our "partnership," our merger with the nanomites, has uniquely equipped us for the work ahead of us—the work we'd promised the President. In response to the President's plea for help in uncovering those involved in the plot to assassinate him and hijack his administration, the nanomites had secured a job for me with the NSA at Ft. Meade in Maryland.

Zander and I had married and, only days later, moved across the country to Columbia, Maryland. We spent the next fourteen days traipsing all over our new corner of the world, getting our Maryland driver's licenses, jogging miles around our neighborhood, sightseeing in D.C., visiting a prospective church, hiking the Allegheny mountains, finding fun places to eat out—in short, enjoying our honeymoon and forgetting the pain, struggles, and wounds of the last year and a half.

Three weeks. We'd been married a mere three weeks, and in that time, Zander's love had been the comforting balm I needed as I grieved my many losses.

My sister Genie gone. *Check.*

My childhood home gone. *Check.*

Jake—last tie to my beloved aunt—gone. *Check.*

Even my identity as Gemma Keyes gone. *Double check.*

Three weeks of married bliss, of no real responsibilities, of shutting out the world and its cares, of putting danger and intrigue far from our minds. Three weeks of the closest thing to "normalcy" Zander and I would know.

Three blessed weeks of, "Nano! Lights out!" more times than I'd believed possible . . .

But our idyllic honeymoon was ending. Come Monday—

⌘

"Jayda?"

"Huh? Oh. Sorry about that. Guess I wandered off."

"Yeah, I figured, but, um, while you were 'out there,' I was thinking about your whopper of a nightmare."

"Can't believe how tangible it was. Still is."

Zander probably intuited my tension, because he started rubbing my neck in gentle, soothing circles. "Is it okay if we talk about it?"

"I suppose."

He didn't jump right in, but eventually said, "Well, my first observation is that when you called on Jesus, the dream ended. I couldn't wake you up, and the nanomites couldn't wake you, but Jesus did. I think that is significant."

"I had tried to wake myself up, too, and hadn't been able to."

I thought for a long moment. "Zander, do you think this dream means something? I mean, you know, not real, but something spiritual?"

Zander smiled. "Are you saying spiritual things aren't real?"

My brow furrowed. "Real? Like, materially real?"

"By definition, spiritual things are not material or physical. Does that mean spiritual things are less real than material or physical things?"

Leave it to Zander to dig down into a thought-provoking theological issue. I pulled my feet up on the couch and turned sideways, sitting cross-legged so we could watch each other. "That's an interesting question. Jesus says in John 4, *God is spirit, and his worshipers must worship in the Spirit and in truth.* The Bible says God is spirit, and he is unquestionably real, so . . . I suppose spiritual things must be real."

"Sure they are. Just because we can't see or touch spiritual things doesn't make them any less real—or any less important—particularly in light of 2 Corinthians 4:18."

"Wait. I've got that one: *So we fix our eyes not on what is seen, but on what is unseen, since what is seen is temporary, but what is unseen is eternal.*"

"Yup. The seen, physical world is temporary. It will all pass away. The unseen, spiritual world, however, is eternal. Guess which one is *more* 'real'?"

I pondered Zander's assertions. Along with an accelerated metabolism, the nanomites had quickened my mental facilities, giving me the ability to read voraciously and retain what I'd learned. I had devoured and memorized the entire New Testament—in three translations—but memorizing Scripture and grasping its revelations and implications are two very different critters. As a new Christian, I had a lot to learn.

"Okay," I said, "let me rephrase my question: Do you think my dream has spiritual significance?"

Zander shrugged. "Some dreams are just the body's way of resting and recharging. Other dreams are the result of too much spicy barbecue or watching movies best left unwatched. But then there are dreams sent from God. The Bible is filled with accounts of important, meaningful dreams."

"Yes. After the President asked me to help him, I had a dream from God, remember? Within the dream, I found myself in a scene from the Book of Esther—*for such a time as this.*"

"That phrase wasn't the most important piece of that dream though, was it?"

I sobered. "No, it wasn't. The apex of the dream was when Jesus said, *Dare to trust me, Jayda,* and added, *Those who know me, dare to trust me.* His words gave me the courage to commit to the President that I would help him identify those who were helping Harmon overthrow his administration."

"Well, then, that raises a different question: What has changed?"

"What do you mean?"

"I mean, you said Jesus gave you the courage to accept the President's assignment, but now *you're afraid.*"

That stopped me cold—because he was right. I was scheduled to start my job at the NSA on Monday and, over the last week, I'd become increasingly troubled at the prospect. Whenever I thought about my first day on the job, the specter of Cushing-like adversaries loomed large in my imagination.

More running. More hiding. More danger. More loss and grief.

Zander watched these emotions flit across my face. "For a moment, let's table the fear factor, and focus on the dream itself. I think we should dissect the dream and identify its 'tells.'"

"Tells?"

"The symbols or indicators, if you will, that suggest the dream's meaning. For instance, what was pursuing you?"

I shuddered. "That snake."

The lines at the corners of Zander's beautiful gray eyes crinkled as he smiled. "*That* snake? Was it just any ol' snake?"

"No. *Categorically* no. The evil emanating from it was palpable. It was intelligent, too."

"Okay, so the granddaddy of all serpents. Um, ring a bell?"

"What? You mean Satan?" I almost scoffed—until I remembered Zander's question: *Are you saying spiritual things aren't real?*

My chin jerked up. "What? You think the snake was Satan?"

"No, I think the snake in your dream represented Satan."

"And so . . ."

"What other tells did the dream contain?"

"I don't understand."

"Seems to me that you should have been able to serve up a little Tempter Tempura or a rasher of Basilisk Bacon—easy peasy, right? But you couldn't. Why? What happened?"

"I was powerless. My ability to pull electricity and throw it was gone. The nanomites had abandoned me, leaving me to the snake's mercy!"

"And then the Lord spoke to you. Repeat what he said."

I frowned.

Weird.

Compared to everything else in the dream, what that Voice had told me seemed distant and hazy. Even though I had, minutes ago, quoted the message to Zander, I had to concentrate to recall the Voice's exact words.

"I think he said, *This is not a physical enemy, Jayda. You cannot combat a spiritual foe with material weapons, nor will your Help come from what you know or can do yourself.*"

"And I think that's it, Jayda. The point of your dream."

My frown deepened as I started to understand. "This assignment from the President. It . . . it isn't just about uncovering the plots against him?"

Zander didn't answer my question, at least not directly. "Dreams recounted in the Bible are prophetic in nature, foretelling what is ahead and often containing a warning. For example, years after Jacob's sons sold their younger brother Joseph into slavery in Egypt, Pharaoh, King of Egypt, dreamed of seven sleek, fat cows and seven ugly, gaunt ones. The seven gaunt cows ate the seven sleek, fat cows.

"The dream so disturbed Pharaoh that he woke up. Later, when he slept again, he dreamed a second time and saw seven healthy, good heads of grain and seven thin, scorched heads of grain that swallowed up the first seven."

"That's in Genesis 41," I offered. "The seven fat cows and plump heads of grain meant seven years of plenty. The seven gaunt cows and thin heads of grain meant that the seven years of plenty would be followed by seven years of famine."

"Yes. Note that Pharaoh's dreams were prophetic—foretelling the coming famine—but they also contained a warning—to prepare for those seven years of famine. Of course, Pharaoh was clueless about the meaning of the two dreams, but they distressed him—just as your dream bothered you."

"I think you mean 'terrified,'" I grumbled.

Zander laughed. "Okay. Just as your dream *terrified* you. Bothered or terrified. Same diff."

I shot Zander an evil glare that had zippo effect on him. He just grinned larger.

Drat.

"Why is it that I've read the Bible and can even quote it, but I don't have the depth of insight that you have?"

I was teasing—okay, I was whining, too—but Zander's response was anything but humorous.

"I'm not playing around when I repeat myself, Jayda: *Spiritual things are real.* Knowing a truth in your head or giving mental assent to it is not the same as perceiving and trusting in the deeper, *spiritual* implications— those *real* spiritual implications."

His response sobered me. "How does one go about understanding the spiritual, um, implications?"

"That is a great question, and it reminds me of a skiing lesson I took one year. The instructor hammered about ten things into our heads during that hour—keep your knees slightly bent, your weight over your boots, your skis beneath your knees; lean forward, into the mountain, not back; face downhill at all times; to turn, shift your weight onto the opposite ski—and do not rotate your shoulders to turn; keep them facing downhill.

"No matter how I tried, I couldn't, simultaneously, put into action every single thing he wanted us to do. I got frustrated and told him so. His answer has resonated with me ever since.

"What he said was that it takes *miles on the mountain* to bring everything together."

"Miles on the mountain?" I didn't follow.

"No matter what we want to master, only continuous application will get us there. Jesus said it this way, *If—***if**—*you hold to my teaching, you are really my disciples. **Then** you will know the truth, and the truth will set you free.*

"With God's word, what we know with our minds cannot bear fruit until we diligently and continuously apply it to our lives. 'Miles on the mountain' is a metaphor for 'application.' We study God's word, the Holy Spirit reveals the spiritual significance and implications of God's word to us, and we apply those spirit-breathed revelations to our lives."

"Oh!" *Miles on the mountain.* I caught his drift.

"The larger point I was making about Joseph and Pharaoh is that God used Pharaoh's dreams to warn and prepare Egypt to meet the coming famine."

Zander stared at me. "I think your dream is a warning to us."

"A warning?"

"Yeah, a caution. That the real enemy we will face as we take up the President's assignment is a spiritual one and the real battle will take place in the spiritual realm. I'm sure you're familiar with this verse: *For our struggle is not against flesh and blood, but against the rulers, against the authorities, against the powers of this dark world and against the spiritual forces of evil in the heavenly realms*—in other words, it's not people we're fighting."

"Ephesians 6:12."

The Bible reference was a reflexive response; I was focused on Zander's admonition. It was what he said next that shook me from my preoccupation.

"I believe a time is coming, Jayda, when what we have grown accustomed to leaning on—the nanomites, their invisibility, and the powerful abilities they've given us—all those things will be ineffective against our enemies. Victory will not turn on a physical battle but rather upon winning the spiritual war."

I shivered, and Zander drew me close to him. "Now let's tackle that fear, okay?"

"Yeah. Let's."

"Lord God, we commit our way to you. Where you lead, we will follow, and where you take us, we cling to your assurance that you will never leave us nor forsake us. Your love is faithful and perfect—and with your perfect love we cast out all fear. We may feel afraid, Lord, but by the grace of Jesus, our Savior, we will not draw back."

"Amen," I whispered.

⌘⌘⌘⌘

CHAPTER 2

SATURDAY EVENING

AXEL KENNEDY, head of President Jackson's personal security detail, addressed the Secret Service agent stationed at the elevator that led to the First Family's Residence.

"Meeting with *Stonewall*," he said, using President Jackson's Secret Service codename, which referred to another Jackson, Civil War General Thomas "Stonewall" Jackson.

The agent whispered into his comms, "Kennedy to the Residence," then stepped aside and opened the gate to the elevator for Kennedy to enter. Kennedy pushed the button to take the elevator up.

He found the President in the Residence dining room staring out one of the windows toward Lafayette Park.

"Mr. President."

"Thanks for coming, Axel."

Kennedy closed the dining room door, grateful—and not for the first time—that the Clintons had insisted that no Secret Service agents be stationed on the Residence floors during their time in the White House. The custom had remained after they left, although agents stood post on the lower floor at the elevator and at the staircase leading up to the Residence.

"Have a seat, Axel."

The President seated himself at the dining table, and Axel followed suit.

"What happened to Agent Bingham?"

Beth Bingham had spent two years on the White House detail and was a favorite with the President. She was regularly stationed at the elevator in the evenings—until today.

"I'm told she resigned from the Service due to a family situation. Quite sudden and unexpected."

"And the new guy on the elevator?"

"Agent Callister."

"He looks familiar."

"He should. He was on Harmon's detail."

The President sighed. "How many does that make?"

"Four in the past two months. Four reliable agents replaced by men I wouldn't trust to walk my dog."

The President and Kennedy were no longer confident of their privacy in the Oval Office and had taken to meeting in the Residence after they noticed the subtle but unmistakable shifting of personnel around them—agents from the late Vice President's personal detail being assigned to the

White House detail. They had no means of knowing which or how many of Harmon's detail had been privy to or part of his attempt to assassinate President Jackson and ascend to the Presidency. However, Kennedy and Jackson viewed each shift in the White House's protective complement as further evidence of an ongoing conspiracy, and they eyed the replacements with distrust, listing them on the adversary's side until proven otherwise.

"I thought you had some say in who is posted here?"

"On your personal detail, sir, but not on the White House detail. Mr. President, if I were to raise an objection against an agent from Harmon's former detail being posted inside the White House, it would signal that we were on to them."

"Them. The unknown *them*. Someone is rearranging the pieces on the board, Axel, and I confess, I'm beginning to feel outmaneuvered."

"I understand, Mr. President. The number of agents in the White House I would rely on to protect you in a make-or-break situation is shrinking."

"As a Washington outsider, I don't understand how this can be happening."

"It's the shadow government, Mr. President, the entrenched bureaucracy composed of political appointees and career government employees engaged in coordinated attempts to undermine your authority and legitimacy—*you*, sir, the democratically elected President of the United States! It's civil servants who are opposed to your political beliefs and agenda. They hide in the background, pulling strings to obstruct you through weaponized national intelligence actions, a complicit media, and the judicial overreach of like-minded allies in federal courts.

"You are the President for four or eight years, depending upon election results, but the Deep State, the bureaucrats working behind the curtains, will outlast you—making them the real power in Washington."

Jackson's long, dark fingers massaged his tired eyes. "It is one thing for the bureaucrats of a single department or agency to impede the executive branch. It is another thing altogether when allies with similar political objectives unite across government entities to overthrow the presidency. *That* is sedition and treason."

"It is, sir—particularly when unelected officials are able to thwart the will of the voters and effectively impose *their* values and objectives upon the American people. Harmon attempted a 'soft' coup to take over the executive branch. The only casualty would have been you."

"Only me? No, the American people who elected me would have been casualties with me. The problem remains, Axel, that Harmon could not have acted alone. We know he had a collaborator planted in the Army's Medical Research Institute of Infectious Diseases, the individual who provided him with the deadly cocktail he poured into my coffee. And based on recent personnel changes here in the White House, I'm guessing that the hierarchy of the Secret Service cannot be trusted either. And Harmon left a lengthy career at the NSA before he stood for one term in the Senate—before he so carefully courted me in order to reach the vice presidency. Who knows how many of his accomplices are embedded in the NSA? The Secret Service? FBI? Congress? The military? Or outside corporations and financial institutions, for that matter?"

Jackson rubbed his eyes a second time. "I had hopes that my man on the inside of the NSA would deliver some answers."

"You have my sympathies about Overman, sir. I know he was a trusted friend."

"We went to school together. Double-dated. His wife and Maddie were roommates. He was a true patriot, too. He must have gotten too close and given himself away for them to take him out."

The President's mood sank a little. "I hate for his wife to never know what happened to him. Do you think we'll ever find his body?"

"I doubt it, sir. As long as there's no body, no one can definitively say he was murdered."

Jackson's temper flashed. "And yet the media feels obliged to suggest that he ran off with a secret lover—with not a shred of evidence to support such a spurious claim!"

"Disinformation planted by our adversaries, sir. Nothing in Overman's background even hints at infidelity."

"I knew the man close to forty years. He'd never cheat on his wife. Not a chance. And I'm truly sorry I put him in harm's way by asking him to suss out Harmon's closest connections inside the NSA."

"You had to ask, sir. We had no other means of trying to find out if they will make another attempt."

"I am doing my best to govern this nation but waiting for the other shoe to drop is wearing on me." Jackson lowered his voice. "If we didn't have our little ace in the hole, my paranoia would be much higher. Is she in place yet?"

"Scheduled to start tomorrow, sir. I, um, realize you have a great deal of faith in this woman, sir, but to place all your confidence in her? If they found Overman out—with his seniority and the clearances he held—what chance does an entry-level contractor stand?"

"As I've said several times, you haven't seen her in action, Axel. I have. She's not defenseless by any means. Besides, the very fact that she's a low-level employee means she won't even show up on their radar. Trust me on this, please."

"Yes sir. If you say so."

Jackson had briefed Kennedy on the former Gemma Keyes, but without seeing with his own eyes what she could do, Kennedy remained skeptical.

"I'm concerned with how long it will take her to get any actionable intel, sir. Our enemies are systematically isolating you, surrounding you with potential assassins. We need additional allies. Have you . . . have you made a decision as to Harmon's replacement?"

Jackson shook his head. "I need to know beyond any doubt that the next Vice President isn't looking to stick a knife in my back."

"It's been six months, sir."

"The twenty-fifth amendment establishes no timeline for when the President must nominate a replacement. Lyndon Johnson went a year without a VP and Harry Truman governed for four years without one."

"Yes sir; however, I'm sure you understand my concern for your safety, your administration, and your . . . legacy. The Speaker of the House—"

"Speaker Friese is the overweening puppet of his party, a spineless, brainless shill whose only worth to them is his unquestioning obedience—and that man, that lapdog—is a single heartbeat away from the presidency!"

"Which is why moving quickly to select a Vice President—one we are confident is not in Harmon's corner—would, at the least, lessen the likelihood of another assassination attempt."

"Don't think that I don't know that, Axel. But whomever I appoint requires the confirmation of both houses of Congress, and that is proving to be a ticklish problem. The House and Senate are so evenly divided that getting my pick confirmed would be like asking America, 'Cats or dogs?'"

The President sighed. "You cannot imagine the pressure both parties are exerting on me, Axel. I've met with the majority and minority leaders from both houses and listened to them pitch their preferred candidates, each party vowing to vote against the other party's choice."

"As you said, a ticklish problem, sir."

Jackson tucked his chin to his chest as he pondered the dilemma before him. "I've listened politely to the maneuverings and machinations of both sides, all the while wondering: Which of these men and women colluded with Harmon, a man of my own party, to assassinate and replace me? Which of their nominees is the next Manchurian Candidate?"

Kennedy leaned toward the President. "Considering the seriousness of the situation, sir, I would feel better if we weren't relying *only* on your plant at the NSA. Would you be open to adding a second iron to the fire?"

"I take it you have a suggestion, Axel?"

"Yes, sir. While our mole is digging in at the NSA, I thought we could go at the problem from the other end."

"I'm listening."

"You remember Agent Janice Trujillo, sir? She was Cushing's *de facto* team leader, but she recognized that Cushing's actions were suspect, possibly treasonous. When the chips were down, she proved her loyalty to you, not to Cushing or her handlers. We can trust her, sir. And she already knows our mole and her handler."

"What do you have in mind?"

"I'd like to reach out to Agent Trujillo. Do you remember the first time we spoke to her? Cushing was MIA, and Trujillo said something about 'the absence of a visible chain of command.'"

"I seem to recall her saying that."

"She and her team are covert operators, sir. It's likely they received their assignment to General Cushing through untraceable channels— which is why, when Harmon died and Cushing went off-grid, Trujillo had no one else to report to."

"It's been six months since then, Axel. She can't have been sitting on her hands all this time."

"No, she has not. Even though she knew Cushing was dead, she had to pretend otherwise. She and her team waited for Cushing in New Mexico until DOD issued the bulletin stating that an Air Force transport had crashed in the Atlantic with Cushing aboard. Trujillo's default orders when an op ended were RTB—return to base—and await instructions. With her command officer officially dead, she disbanded her team and returned to her Virginia base of operations."

"How do you know this?"

"I asked Agent Gamble to keep tabs on her—unobtrusively. I asked him to convey a request for her to keep her head down and her nose to the grindstone. Since she left New Mexico, she's received several innocuous assignments, mostly busywork taking her out of the country and back. The thing is, I think Trujillo is the only other connection we have into Harmon's network. Harmon himself handled Cushing and her team, but he had to have kept others in the conspiracy knowledgeable of the operation."

"What are you suggesting?"

"I'm suggesting that whoever 'inherited' Trujillo as a resource is waiting, observing and testing her to see if she's been compromised, perhaps holding her in reserve. So far, I don't believe they have noted any taint in her loyalty to them.

"I think I see where this is going."

"Yes sir. I propose that we bring her under Gamble's oversight—carefully, of course—and keep her in readiness for when she receives an actual assignment."

"And becomes our double agent inside the enemy's camp."

"Yes, Mr. President. Initially, the enemy will work her 'blind,' without any face-to-face contact. However, when her handler does reveal himself to Trujillo, that 'someone' will be our 'in' to Harmon's network."

"I like it."

Axel frowned. "You've told me that our, er, 'ace' and her partner have extraordinary abilities. We would need them and their abilities at that point to surveil Trujillo's handler and infiltrate his or her chain of command."

"I know you doubt them, Axel, but I assure you: They can do the job. As regards Agent Trujillo? Set it up."

"Yes, Mr. President."

⌘⌘⌘⌘

CHAPTER 3

"JUST SO WE'RE CLEAR—and I can't emphasize this enough—your first duty, the most essential of your tasks, is to keep a low profile..." Gamble's warning trailed off mid-thought before he amended his admonition. "No, not a *low* profile, but *no* profile. Nada, zip, nil. We can't have either of you even registering a blip on our adversaries' radar. Do *nothing* to draw attention to yourselves."

I nodded and, out of the corner of my eye, saw Zander do the same.

Agent Gamble, Zander, and I were huddled in the darkened living room of a rental in a modest neighborhood outside of D.C. Not an FBI location or Secret Service safe house, but a house Gamble had leased himself using cash and a fake ID. Axel Kennedy, the head of the President's Secret Service detail, had passed a chunk of money to Gamble for such expenditures. Gamble had paid out more cash to have window bars and security doors installed, along with a state-of-the-art security system.

Zander and I had met Gamble in an alley two blocks away and, under the cover of the nanomites' optical invisibility, the three of us had made our way to our meeting place and entered through the back door. It was probably the slickest covert entrance on record—not that anyone was keeping records, since that would kind of defeat the whole concept of "covert," right?

Gamble cleared his throat. "We've poked and probed your cover, and it is very good, Gemma—"

"Jayda."

"Yeah, yeah. Jayda Locke."

"Jayda *Cruz*."

Gamble ran a hand over his face. "You're killing me. You know that, right?"

Zander and I laughed softly, but I fumbled for my husband's hand, glad to feel my fingers nestled within the warmth and strength of his. We had prayed over the nasty dream of two nights past, and its hold on me was fading. Now it was late Sunday evening, and I would start work at the NSA in the morning but still, as the saying goes, "It was about to get real," "it," in this case, being my infiltration into the most formidable intelligence service on the planet.

No biggie.

Uh-huh.

Gamble started over. "Your cover is very good, Jayda, better, in fact than what we could have provided, given such a small window of time. It is better—and it is totally outside our intelligence channels. That's a bonus."

"The nanomites."

"Thank the little guys for us."

"You just did."

Speaking of "the little guys," a stream of them had left me when we entered the house. They were checking it out to ensure that no one was bugging our meeting and to provide us with the safe house's exits and any incidental details.

"Right." Gamble wiped his face again. "Okay. Back on task, you two."

"You seem nervous, Agent Gamble," Zander observed.

"Yeah, well, it's not every day the President of the United States arranges my transfer to a post that requires practically nothing from me—a post that is, in reality, a cover for a covert op of the most delicate and sensitive nature—an operation predicated on treason at the highest levels of our government and, if botched, could trigger a Constitutional crisis and a political shakeup of unprecedented proportions. An op I am tasked to lead and that, furthermore, relies upon two untrained, unqualified, and untested assets."

I nudged Zander. "Huh. He might be talking about us."

"Ya think?"

"Well, I'm offended. Untrained, maybe, but unqualified and untested?"

We both grinned. Gamble did not.

"Not a laughing matter, you two. Despite your 'special abilities,' neither of you has any idea how vital your roles are to the preservation of this presidency—or how precarious is the situation."

Zander spoke up. "Question: Let's say, hypothetically speaking, that things were to go sideways. Breaking into the NSA has to be considered espionage—at the very least, right?"

"Espionage? On the face of it, yes, but so is weaponizing the nation's intelligence community to remove a sitting president. However, I can provide assurance regarding the legality of what Jayda will be doing. Executive Order 12333 delineates the goals, directions, duties, and responsibilities of the intelligence community, its purpose being to provide the President and the National Security Council with the information they need to govern.

"EO 12333, Item 1.4, reads, *The agencies within the Intelligence Community shall, in accordance with applicable United States law and with the other provisions of this Order, conduct intelligence activities necessary for the conduct of foreign relations and the protection of the national security of the United States.*

"Note the phrase, 'with the other provisions of this Order.' Line items 1.4 (a) through (e) spell out the specific authority and responsibilities of the intelligence community, but line item (f) adds, *Such other intelligence activities as the President may direct from time to time.*"

Gamble pointed to me and then to Zander. "Line item 1.4(f)? Such other activities? That's you guys."

Zander nodded. "Good to know."

"All right. Back to 'untrained.' Our White House contact has asked me to arrange for both of you to receive private, specialized instruction."

Zander perked up. "Spy training?"

"Call it a series of 'How to Stay Alive' workshops."

"Man, you know how to filch the fun out of everything."

I interrupted. "Where? And when? I start my job tomorrow."

"And I want you to be nothing more than a model low-level NSA contractor employee until we determine our first step forward."

"Gamble?"

"What?"

"You know that's not how it's going to go, right? It's not possible for you or anyone else to micromanage my infiltration. The moment I set foot inside NSA territory, the nanomites will start digging. Our initial goal will be to figure out what happened to the President's friend, Wayne Overman."

Gamble and I engaged in a staredown that he had zero chance of winning.

He broke off eye contact and frowned. "Jayda—"

"Don't worry about me, Gamble. The nanomites are undetectable. Things aren't going to 'go sideways.'"

"Yes, but you need to remember that everything at the NSA is bugged—phones, computers, work email accounts. They aren't messing around. If you thought security at Sandia was tight, you haven't seen anything—these are the world's spy masters, remember? It's likely that they have video cameras in every department, office, hallway, and broom closet. I wouldn't put it past them to have bugged the bathrooms, too."

"I'll be careful. I promise."

"Just . . . just don't count on your invisibility tricks going unnoticed, okay?" He sighed. "Guess I'm more nervous about you starting your assignment than you are."

I doubted that, but I put on a good front. "I hacked the White House, remember? Defeated its security measures and got to the President with no one being the wiser. You don't need to fret."

I managed to sound more confident than I felt.

Before Gamble could respond, I changed the subject. "Tell us more about this spy training."

"Call it Tradecraft 101. The basics of modern espionage: techniques, methods, and technologies. Your trainers are off-book contractors, all ex-military. These men are hardened, no-nonsense operators."

Zander asked, "How do you know we can trust them?"

"We served together. Seems like a hundred years ago now, but I'd stake my life on their loyalty to this nation and its President. Also, they won't know anything about you, and you won't know anything more about them than what I've told you."

He got all businesslike on us. "You are not to offer your names or any personally identifiable information. Pick a bogus first name for them to call you. Remove your wedding rings before you go. Not only are you not married, you are strangers, so act like it. Arrive at separate times from different directions. Total anonymity.

"A lot of what they'll begin with is terminology and head knowledge. When they move you on to tasks in the field, do what they ask of you without any nano-hocus-pocus. No invisibility or lightning bolts."

I stifled a snicker.

"You'll begin next week in your spare time."

"What spare time? Lowly administrative assistants put in forty-hour-plus weeks in addition to the commute."

"Nights and evenings. You told me you don't need as much sleep as regular people do, right?"

It was true. The nanomites had infused us with incredible stamina and resilience. Zander and I had energy to burn and required less sleep than most people did.

"You will report after dark this Wednesday for your first session. Your trainers will set additional sessions that accommodate your schedules."

I blinked. Zander and I called Emilio and Abe every Wednesday evening around nine, seven o'clock back in Albuquerque. We would have to call them earlier.

"Where?"

Gamble handed Zander a slip of paper. "Both of you memorize this address and the instructions; flush the water-soluble paper afterwards. Never speak the address aloud. Can't be too careful."

"Not a problem," I answered. The nanomites uploaded the information to their data repository while, with a single glance, Zander and I memorized the same.

"Just FYI, Agent Gamble. While Jayda is at work, I'll be looking for a job," Zander said. "Something in my wheelhouse. Can't let Jayda be the sole breadwinner. We need a second vehicle, and somebody has to make those car payments."

"Find something with flexible hours. We don't yet know how you will fit into the scheme of things, but when we require your help, we'll want you to be available."

Zander shifted. "Kinda narrows my options."

Zander and I had also discussed scenarios where I might need him to back me up once I'd made inroads at the NSA.

Gamble slid an envelope toward Zander. "I've been authorized to supply you with a weekly stipend. When this is all over, we'll arrange a more substantial payment to compensate both of you for your help cleaning out Harmon's collaborators."

Zander's pride bristled. "That's not necessary."

"It's not charity, Zander. It's compensation for the real work you'll be doing and the expenses you'll accrue."

Neither Zander nor I said any more. The move from Albuquerque had cost money, and I'd needed a car for work. We'd used up what remained of the cash I'd "appropriated" when I burned down the drug house in Albuquerque. The money Gamble offered would come in handy.

"We have a request," I announced.

"Oh?"

"We need some space to work out. Doesn't need to be fancy or big. Just an open, empty room."

Gamble didn't like not knowing the whole picture, and his expression said so.

"Stick fighting, Agent Gamble."

"What—for him?"

"For both of us. You have to admit, it will keep us in shape."

He eyed me and nodded. "You're the poster child for stick fighting, Jayda."

I suppose I was: Gus-Gus, my nanomite-created VR coach, had pushed, pummeled, and provoked me in the art of Filipino escrima fighting until my reflexes were beyond instinctual and every muscle in my body was honed and hard. My core was solid, too.

I grinned. "Consider our workouts another variety of 'how to stay alive' workshop." My grin widened. "My husband will benefit the most over the next few weeks."

"I'd pay to be a fly on the wall for that."

"*Whatever*," Zander tossed back.

The nanomites returned from exploring the safe house and reported their findings to me. I jumped topics again. "Huh. You installed a 3D printer in the basement?"

Gamble was surprised. "How did you know that?" Then he snorted. "Never mind. Yes, we had it installed last week, but not just any old 3D printer. Dr. Bickel provided the printer's very particular (and expensive) specs and a list of the materials the nanomites would require to print more of themselves."

"That can't have been an unremarkable work order for a residential house."

"You're right. We brought in Dr. Bickel's two technicians to retrofit the basement into a cleanroom and perform the install."

"Rick and Tony?" I had worked with Dr. Bickel's techs at Sandia, first as Gemma and later as Jayda, and I nurtured a fondness for them. However, Rick and Tony believed Gemma was dead—as did the rest of the world, with the exception of exactly seven individuals. And of those seven individuals, Axel Kennedy and Agent Trujillo knew only bits and pieces of my story and the extent of my (and now Zander's) abilities.

"Yes, Rick and Tony. They helped Dr. Bickel hide the nanomites from Cushing in his mountain laboratory and managed to convince Cushing that they knew nothing about Dr. Bickel's whereabouts. In my book, they have proven they can be trusted. Compartmentalization of this operation being as vital as it is, they were our best option to install the printer."

Gamble started to wrap things up. "The printer, of course, is so the nanomites can manufacture more of themselves, should the need arise."

The printer and materials are satisfactory to our needs, Jayda Cruz.

"Good to know, Nano."

"Use this house only for our weekly meetings and if you should require access to the printer," Gamble added. "If we need an emergency meetup, I liked how we communicated in Albuquerque."

He was referring to a Craigslist ad that read, "Wanted: Uncut Gemstones." The nanomites had inserted a line of code into the Craigslist webpage so that the words "uncut gemstones" triggered an alert that they received and passed on to me.

I pursed my lips. "And here I've been holding my breath, hoping to graduate to that big ol' Bat Signal in the night sky."

Gamble arched one brow. "That was my line, Jayda."

We all chuckled, and I was relieved to see Gamble unwind a little.

"We don't need to resort to covert communication methods," I told him. "We can use our regular cellphones. Our calls don't register with our carriers, and the nanomites scrub our phone logs. Our phones don't leave a trace of data."

Gamble looked uncertain. "You're sure?"

"Yes. The night the President called you? The nanomites evaded the Secret Service's monitoring of all cellphone signals coming into and out of the White House."

"All right then. Keep me apprised of your progress."

We left the rental the same way we'd arrived—invisibly—depositing Gamble at his car. Zander and I walked another mile to the restaurant parking lot where we picked up our vehicle and drove back to our apartment in Maryland.

⌘

WHEN GAMBLE ARRIVED at his apartment, he checked the burner phone he used exclusively for calls from Kennedy. He found a short voice mail.

"Call me."

A light summer shower had begun to patter the ground when Gamble grabbed the phone, walked back to his vehicle, and drove to a park a mile from his home. By the time he dialed the only number in the phone, rain was beating on his windshield, lending more privacy to the call.

Kennedy picked up. "Can you talk?"

"Yes."

"Okay. First, how are our transplants?"

"Ready to go and not nearly as nervous as I am."

"I understand. We have a lot . . . invested in this effort."

Every sentence they spoke was parsed in patently oblique terms. Kennedy paused a moment to marshal and construct his next thoughts. "I have further instructions for you."

"I'm listening."

"You are to contact a certain individual, *a mutual acquaintance,* although, on our end, we have only spoken with said mutual acquaintance over the phone. This individual is also known to our transplants."

Gamble ran through the possibilities. Only one fit the bill. "I believe I understand."

"Our transplants once considered this individual an enemy."

That clinched it. "Understood. Orders?"

"Bring into the fold. Wait for said individual to receive orders from on high. Goal? Identify and surveil up the chain of command."

"Roger that."

"Report in when you have something." Kennedy hung up.

Gamble thought through the call he was about to make. Her involvement would add a layer of complexity to the operation, but it also added her own mix of skills. She would be a great asset if things got dicey.

He had her number in his cell, but he didn't want to establish a link between them after six months of no communication. He also didn't want to call her on the same burner phone he used to call Kennedy. If the wrong person were to connect her to Kennedy through that phone, it would no doubt prove detrimental to the operation—and fatal for her.

Gamble mulled over his options. He knew a coffee shop that still had a pay phone. That would do for now.

He maneuvered his car through the now pouring rain and parked outside the coffee shop. It was late, going on 10:30, but the all-night shop had a decent number of customers. Gamble walked in, shook the wet off his jacket, and went to the counter.

"Tall Colombian latte, please."

While his coffee was being made, Gamble let his eyes sweep the shop. He sauntered to the phone and dialed.

"Hello?" Janice Trujillo's voice was cautious.

"Hi. Remember me?"

"Uh-huh."

"Are you busy? Up for a cup of coffee?"

"You buying?"

"Yup."

"Make mine decaf."

He gave her the coffee shop's address.

"Y'know, it'll take me forty-five minutes to get there."

"Pick a spot halfway between here and there."

She did, and Gamble found it on his smartphone. "See you in half an hour."

He grabbed his coffee and hit the road.

⌘

SHE WAS WAITING for him when he arrived at the all-night restaurant. The splash of gratification he felt when he saw her surprised him. She looked rested. Unstressed. Softer—and a lot prettier—than he'd remembered.

He slid into the booth across from her. "Good to see you, uh, Trujillo." He'd almost called her Janice but thought better of it at the last second.

A waitress wandered over. "Ready to order?"

"Just coffee."

"Decaf, please."

The waitress left, and Gamble commented, "Those were strange times, back in Albuquerque, no?

"Uh-huh."

His eyes casually swept the room before he added, "Which brings us to this evening."

She winced. "I thought as much."

"I'm sorry. Our . . . mutual friend called me. Uh, the friend who's from around here?"

Awareness came over her. On the table she scrawled 'WH' with her finger.

"Yeah. *That* mutual friend. He'd like me to . . . bring you on board."

She, too, glanced around the shop. "I don't know. I've had a few assignments out of country, but nothing lately. I figure they are still watching me, waiting to see if I've been turned or if I'm still useful."

"It's the 'they' above you that we're interested in. Are you in contact with anyone up the chain?"

The waitress delivered their coffee. Trujillo added half-and-half and stirred it in.

"No. Everything has been by courier."

"Would you be amenable to letting us know if and when a real person reaches out to you?"

She sipped on her coffee without answering. Finally, she gave a small, stiff nod.

"Yes. For . . . our mutual friend."

Gamble looked down. "Got it. Could we meet again in, say, two weeks?" He typed a date, a time, and the address of his rental into a text and turned his phone around so she could see it.

"Got it."

Gamble erased what he'd typed and closed his phone.

"Thanks for coming out in the rain to meet me."

She looked up. "I kind of wish it had been just for coffee."

He was surprised again. They stared at each other, assessing the other's reaction.

"Me, too, Trujillo. Maybe . . . sometime soon."

⌘⌘⌘⌘

CHAPTER 4

JAYDA CRUZ. IT IS TIME TO GET UP.

Jayda Cruz. It is time to get up.

Jayda Cruz. It is time to get up.

I'd gone to sleep praying and, although I'd slept deeply, when the nanomites awakened me at 5 a.m., I was still praying—but I can't say I'd slept all that well. Consequently, the nanomites' cheerful chirping grated on my nerves like fingernails on a chalkboard.

"Yeah, yeah. Pipe down."

Managing to sound aggrieved, the nanomites answered, "*If anyone loudly blesses their neighbor early in the morning, it will be taken as a curse.*"

"Proverbs 27:14," I answered. "Funny how God's word is eternally relevant."

Away in the distance, I heard them grumble, "*We are hard pressed on every side, but not crushed; perplexed, but not in despair; persecuted, but not abandoned; struck down, but not destroyed—*"

"Oh, give me a break. You are *not* persecuted."

I reached across the bed and jostled Zander. "Hey, you. Time to hit the pavement."

"Huh? Oh. Mmkay."

My feet hit the floor, and I whispered, "Lord, thank you for your peace, the peace that passes all understanding." I murmured over and over, "Thank you for directing my steps today and for shielding me from our enemies. I take refuge in the shadow of your wings."

Before the sun heated the air around us, we logged five miles at a dead run. We varied our route each morning to prevent monotony and, while we ran, we listened to upbeat worship music. Then we returned to our apartment to shower, dress, and (finally) have that first cup of coffee over our Bibles.

This morning was no different—except, of course, that it was my first day at the NSA.

I pulled out of our apartment complex and pointed my car toward the highway. Once I was in the flow of traffic, I began to repeat a passage I knew by heart. Yeah, I knew them all "by heart," but I wanted this one *in* my heart, particularly as I took my first step toward infiltrating the secure and daunting institution known as the National Security Administration. So, I began to recite the passage from Romans 8, repeating one verse, again and again.

What, then, shall we say
in response to these things?
If God is for us,
who can be against us?

I had recited the verse aloud nine times when the nanomites chipped in.

Have you forgotten the next verse, Jayda Cruz? "He who did not spare
his own Son, but gave him up for us all—how will he not also, along with
him, graciously give us all things?" That is the next verse.

"Yes, Nano, I know. I, uh, I'm meditating on this passage, a verse at a time."

And does repeating the words aloud somehow enhance your retention?

"Um, it's more that it enhances the meaning. Like Zander said, the deeper, spirit-breathed implications and how I apply those revelations to my life."

The nanomites went quiet on me. I figured they were chewing on what I'd said.

Remember me saying that when I became a Christian I began devouring the Bible? Well, after the nanomites' encounter with Jesus—after they had sworn their allegiance to him, to what they called "the one Tribe of Jesus"—they had listened in on the discussions Zander and I had regarding the importance of God's word, of studying it daily, of learning it.

Never to be outdone by us, the nanomites had uploaded the Bible to Alpha Tribe—and not just in English. No, the mites had taken it upon themselves to learn Hebrew, Aramaic, and Greek so they might study the Scriptures in their original languages.

Before long, the nanomites could parse, exegete, and distill Scripture with the authority of biblical scholars. They began to insert themselves—and various Scriptural admonitions—into Zander's and my conversations. They even added interesting historical and cultural commentary, having digested the works of the great theologians.

The result was . . . interesting.

What I mean is that the nanomites, as part of God's creation, recognized their Creator and, in their own way, worshipped him—you know, like how Psalm 96 says,

Let the fields be jubilant,
and everything in them;
let all the trees of the forest
sing for joy,

and how Nehemiah declares,

You made the heavens,
even the highest heavens,
and all their starry host,
the earth and all that is on it,
the seas and all that is in them.
You give life to everything,
and the multitudes of heaven
worship you.

God is the one who gives life to everything; he even gave life to the nanomites through Dr. Bickel's efforts—*but.* But, the nanomites are not the part of creation God has made in his own image and likeness: only people are. It is humankind, male and female, who bear the stamp of God Almighty in their body, soul, and spirit. It is men and women who, through Jesus, will inherit eternal life.

The nanomites viewed serving the Creator as the logical, factual choice, so, *yes,* the nanomites had mastered Scripture—but as knowledge, not as a matter of spiritual food. They regularly did not "get" the import of the passages they quoted; they didn't understand Scripture as living water vital to the inner man of soul and spirit.

They didn't understand because they possessed no "inner man."

I'm not saying that we will or won't have animals (or even nanomites) in heaven—I don't think we know that either way for certain. I'm just saying that Jesus came from heaven in human form to save humans from their sins.

In other words, being the product of mathematical programming, the nanomites had no personal appreciation of the redemptive power of God's word. What they *did* have was a penchant for moralizing from the wisdom books, often delivering their admonitions out of context or at the most inopportune junctures. Not that a Scripture-spouting nanocloud is a bad thing, but it did grate at times.

Like, have you ever tried to sleep with an incessantly chirping insect playing hide-and-seek in your bedroom? It was a *lot* like that—only stranger. More like having Jiminy Cricket stuck in your head.

On *steroids.*

With no on/off switch.

No volume control.

No fly swatter handy.

Ladies and gentlemen, I give you Exhibit A: In the two weeks after we settled into our apartment, my new husband and I had occasionally "slept in," and, um, we *may* have even indulged in a few "naps."

Ahem

Well, hello? It was, after all, our honeymoon. And, so what, if—*one time*—we ordered in and ate in bed? Like I said, *it was our honeymoon!*

But nooooo. The nanomites (who never sleep) apparently took exception to our laid-back pace and the frequency of our newlywed romantic interludes. One afternoon, when they were "indulging" us with their research on Maryland's Great Falls—a scenic hiking opportunity about fourteen miles up the Potomac from D.C.—Zander cut in on them with my favorite new phrase: "Uh, excuse me, Nano, but *lights out.*"

We grabbed hands and, laughing, ran for the bedroom.

The nanomites, managing to sound both disgruntled and disgusted, pontificated, *As a door turns on its hinges, so a sluggard turns on his bed. Proverbs 26:14.*

From the bedroom, Zander shouted back, "The wife God gives you is your reward for all your earthly toil. Ecclesiastes 9:9!"

I'm certain the nanomites (who were with us and *not* in the other room) heard Zander just fine. Pretty sure our neighbors heard him, too. Might explain why they weren't overly friendly.

The nanomites' contributions were sometimes so inane and (dare I say it?) downright hilarious that Zander and I had to choke back snorts and guffaws.

And we were not always successful.

I pulled myself back on task, going for Galatians 5:22 this time. "But the fruit of the Spirit is love, joy, peace, *patience*, kindness, goodness, faithfulness, gentleness and self-control."

Yup. Patience. O Lord, please give me patience—and I want it now. Right now.

Thirty minutes later, I left MD 32 West and took Exit 10A onto Canine Road. Over my right shoulder I caught my first glimpse of the sprawling NSA campus. As the road wound north and east, I passed by the imposing sign that read "U.S. Cyber Command," "National Security Agency," and "Central Security Service." Soon after, I merged with the lines of cars entering the security checkpoint.

I showed my Maryland driver's license to the guard, explained I was a new hire, and was routed into the Visitor Control parking lot from where, the guard explained, I should walk to the Visitor Control building and look for my contact.

When I stepped into the building, a Ms. Amali from HR—wearing something of a perplexed smile—extended her hand in greeting. "Jayda Cruz?"

"Yes. That's me. It's, um, nice to see you again."

She blinked several times and hemmed and hawed a moment before her confused expression cleared. "I apologize, Ms. Cruz. For the life of me, I couldn't remember interviewing you—and neither could the others on the interview panel—until just now."

"Not a problem," I murmured. "I guess I'm not very memorable."

Truth be told, Ms. Amali had never laid eyes on me. The nanomites had manipulated the hiring process, even fabricating my interview answers and scores and triggering a hiring recommendation. But as soon as I touched Ms. Amali's hand, a phalanx of nanomites had swarmed over to her, stimulating the chemical production of new synapses in her brain, implanting specific details of my "interview" into her memories.

She shook her head and whispered to herself, "How very odd."

I joined two other new hires in a side room where a security officer took us through the process of confirming our identities via our photo IDs and fingerprints before we received NSA badges (ID cards) and lanyards and established PIN numbers for our badges.

The first thing the security officer said was, "No personal cell phones or other wireless devices are allowed inside NSA buildings. The exceptions to the rule are NSA-issued cell phones for employees in management and supervisory capacities. If you have a cell phone or other wireless device on your person right now, please surrender it to me and retrieve it on your way out later today."

I had left my phone in my car just as I did at Sandia. The other new hires must have done the same because neither of them produced a phone.

The security officer continued. "You have received LIC badges—Limited Interim Clearance—indicating that you are awaiting completion of your security clearances to the full level your position requires. These badges—ID cards—will restrict your activities until the clearance process is complete and approved.

"Your badge contains an encrypted smart chip that conforms to the government's PIV—Personal Identity Verification—technical requirements and grants you access to federal facilities, buildings, information systems, and levels of security appropriate to your clearance and position.

"From today forward, you must have your badge to clear the campus security checkpoint. To enter most NSA facilities, your card must be inserted into an Access Control Terminal at a building or department entrance, and you must enter your PIN on the terminal keyboard.

"In the absence of an Access Control Terminal, or when passing an internal security checkpoint, the badge should be held up for viewing by a security police officer."

Ms. Amali took over. "Your badge must be displayed, front facing, at all times while within any NSA installation. Conversely, it must be removed or hidden from sight after leaving the base. Now, follow me, please."

We marched off behind Ms. Amali as she led the way to a conference room in a nearby building.

The remainder of the morning was spent in new-hire orientation. As a contractor employee hired out to the NSA, I had already completed my company's online benefit, time sheet, and employee policy courses, and had updated my profile in e-QIP, the government's security clearance database, so that my employer could request my new security clearance.

I had held a DOE Q clearance at Sandia. A Q clearance did not automatically translate to the DOD Top Secret clearance I needed for my job at the NSA, but it would make the security review process easier and faster. I already had a profile in e-QIP; all I needed to do was update my address, add my marriage and name change, and Zander's information and that of his family members.

My employer had also arranged for my digital fingerprints to be taken and submitted to the FBI—and not for the first time. My Sandia DOE Q clearance had required fingerprints, too. The nanomites had swarmed my fingertips, modifying them to match those on file for Jayda Cruz.

Once we three new employees were seated in the conference room, we sat through several briefings: orientation to the layout of the NSA campus, a concise history of the NSA and its mission, a thorough review of the NSA employee's security manual (loooong and tedious), and phone, email, and computer policies—along with our signatures on a series of forms that attested to our understanding of and agreement to comply with a myriad of regulations—with the very real threat of prosecution should we do otherwise.

I wore a neutral expression as I signed. I was already on the other side of that equation—by Presidential directive.

We broke at 12:30 for lunch with instructions to return to the conference room at 1:15.

"When we reconvene, I will escort you to IT, where they will set up your computer accounts and assign you your network authentication tokens."

After hours of brain-numbing briefings, my ears perked up.

"Nano. That will be our opportunity to explore this site's network structure."

Understood, Jayda Cruz.

Ms. Amali added, "Remember: While making the acquaintance of other NSA employees, speak only in generalities as to your position. Do not mention your department or what type of work you do. Inside and outside the NSA, this is the rule of thumb."

I didn't know about the other two new hires, but I didn't know yet where I would be working, only that I had been hired in an administrative position requiring project controls experience. Curiosity was eating me up.

We nodded our understanding to Ms. Amali and stepped into the hallway. The three of us looked at each other.

The guy in our new-hire group, a tall black man, held out his hand to me. "Seth Gillingham."

"Jayda Cruz."

Seth offered his hand to the third in our party, a woman who looked to have Indonesian or Filipino blood.

"Dalisay Jones. Just call me Dali."

I was right. Dalisay was a Filipino name.

She and I also shook hands before Seth suggested, "Shall we?"

We three strangers, acquainted only by our common experiences of the morning, set off together, but I already knew more about Seth and Dali than I should have. The nanomites had broken Seth and Dali's chip encryption (Ms. Amali's, too) and uploaded their PIV information to Alpha Tribe—including their identity certificates, electronic keys, credential number, PIN, and biometric data.

The nanomites were already constructing a database of appropriated PIV cards even as Gamble's warnings and admonitions ran like ticker tape through my thoughts: *I want you to be nothing more than a model low-level NSA contractor employee until we determine our first step forward.*

Nope. Doesn't work that way, Gamble.

After lunch, Ms. Amali escorted us to the IT Department. "Call the IT Help Desk for anything computer related." She pointed across the hallway. "And there's the Security Department. If you have checkpoint access issues, see them."

Huh. Convenient.

We sat in a row of chairs while Ms. Amali presented our paperwork to the IT Help Desk. IT personnel called us one at a time to issue us security key fobs or tokens—the second part in a two-factor network authentication process.

An IT guy instructed us to use our key fobs to log in to an IT terminal where we were prompted to type a fourteen-character complex password of our choosing. It took about half an hour for the three of us to complete the process—enough time for the nanomites to swarm IT servers and return to me.

49

I saw what the nanomites saw, but I set it aside for the time being.

"We are finished with today's orientation," Ms. Amali said. "We'll walk to the HR department so that you will know where our offices are located. There you will meet your department liaison, and he or she will escort you to your department and introduce you to your supervisor and coworkers."

Armed with our network authentication tokens, we followed Ms. Amali outside to yet another building, where she led us to the HR suite. Three individuals were waiting for us. Before Ms. Amali made introductions, she gave us these parting instructions.

"At the end of your day, please check in with me before you leave. If you have any questions or concerns, you may address them with me at that time."

Perfect.

A contingency of nanomites flew from me to her. I would pick them back up in a few hours. Until then, their task was to download every scrap of information in the HR files on Wayne Overman, the President's missing friend.

⌘

"JAYDA, THIS IS Macy Uumbana. She will escort you to your department."

I smiled and shook hands with the young woman whose gleaming smile shone from a face as black as a starless night. She was tall, drop-dead gorgeous, and *very* pregnant. Her belly jiggled all on its own, and my lips parted in amazement.

Macy laughed at my consternation. "Twins. They're sparring in there and, yes, I'm about ready to pop. In fact, this is my last week. That's why they hired you."

I couldn't think of a thing to say except, "Oh?"

She gestured, and we started down the hall. "Can't tell you how glad I am you're here. We can chat and get to know each other between here and our department, but nothing work-related. Got it?"

"Er, yes."

"So, you're from New Mexico? I've never been there."

"Yup." Taking her cue, I filled her in on Albuquerque and a few personal tidbits.

"You *just* got married?"

"Three weeks yesterday."

"Well, welcome to the East Coast. I imagine it's a lot different than what you're used to."

We left the main building via a short breezeway, entered another building, and stopped at a set of double doors with an access checkpoint.

Macy inserted her badge, keyed in a pin number, and walked through the turnstile. "Now you."

I did the same, relieved that my PIN number didn't trigger bells and alarms and a blaring voice shouting, "Intruder alert! Spy! Spy! Spy!" cuz that's exactly what I felt like.

The turnstile flipped over to the blessed absence of claxons, the lock on the double doors released, and we stepped inside.

"Welcome to the Repository, Jayda."

Like the newbie I was, I rubbernecked the wide room filled with cubicles, more excited than I could let on.

"Repository?"

"The Repository is the NSA's digital content management system, the database for indexing and cataloging the NSA's 'take'—all the information our stations gather."

She headed toward an office off to the right. "I'm going to introduce you to our department head, after which I'll take you to our team to meet your direct supervisor."

The department manager was on the phone but motioned us into his office as he finished his call. When he hung up, he stood and shook my hand. "Eugene Stephanopoulos."

His somewhat perturbed countenance mirrored the expression Ms. Amali had worn earlier in the day when she had first laid eyes on me.

"Hurry, Nano," I whispered.

On it, Jayda Cruz.

To the man I said, "Jayda Cruz. It's good to see you again."

"Right." He was amiable in a harried, rumpled kind of way, but he was also perplexed as he studied me . . . and then his puzzlement faded, and he blinked as though waking from a dream. "Right. *Jayda.* We met at your . . . interview."

"Yes. I'm delighted to join your department, Mr. Stephanopoulos. How is your little ballerina doing?"

Gene and his wife had a nine-year-old daughter who was showing promise in ballet. The nanomites planted the memory of Gene telling me about his daughter's recent recital at our interview. My reference solidified that "memory."

"Thanks for asking, Jayda. She's doing great. By the way, please call me Gene." He looked to Macy. "Macy will show you to your workstation, introduce you to your team, and help you get settled. Do you have any questions at this point?"

"A million, but I'm sure they will get answered in the course of time."

He smiled. "We'll knock out a few of them today at the least."

Macy led me through a maze of cubicles to a "room" of chest-height cubicle walls. Eight workstations lined the inside perimeter of the cubicle walls so that the backs of those seated at their workstations faced the center of the area.

"Everyone, this is Jayda Cruz, our new team member."

Seven sets of eyes fastened on me, including a middle-aged woman who stood and came toward us.

"Hello, Jayda. I'm Sherry Woods, the project controls team lead."

She introduced the other team members—Neville, Chantelle, Lynn, Neri, James, and Saul.

I said, "Pleased to meet you," six more times before Sherry turned me back over to Macy.

"Macy will talk to you about your role on the team; she will be training you all this week."

Macy showed me to the only unoccupied workstation. "This was, until last Friday, my workstation. It is now yours. I'm making do across the way," she pointed across the hallway to another cubicle-walled area, "until I leave at the end of the week. Why don't we sit over there where we won't disturb the team while I give you a broad rundown of what we do here?"

She showed me to a chair by her computer. "As Sherry said, we are the Repository's project controls team. I should explain first that you are taking Neville's place on the team because he has been promoted to my spot." She laughed. "That, of course, makes you low man on the team's totem pole, but it's not a bad place to be while you are learning the ropes."

Macy tipped her head over. "You have me for only a week, so I hope you are a quick study?"

"I think I can keep up."

"Good. Okay, I'm assuming you have some sort of background in intelligence? Cryptology? Signals? Analysis? Cybersecurity? Military security?"

"No, I'm afraid not."

Her lips parted like she wanted to say something. Finally, she murmured, "So, you're from Albuquerque where you worked at . . ."

"Sandia National Laboratories. Project Manager for the AMEMS lab. Before that, Lockheed Martin in Littleton, Colorado."

"AMEMS?"

"Advanced Microelectromechanical Systems."

"Uh . . ."

I laughed. "Tiny electrical-mechanical devices."

"Project management for tiny devices . . . but no intelligence background?"

"No. I assumed they hired me for my project controls skills."

"Uh-huh." But she seemed more confused.

"Something wrong?"

"No, well, it's just curious and . . . out of the norm for our contractors to put forward applicants with no military or intelligence experience, and more unusual for the NSA to hire someone without such a background."

Macy tapped a pen on the surface of her desk. "Also, while this position doesn't necessarily require intelligence experience, another contractor who already works in this department on another team had applied for this job and . . . well, I think we all got the impression that she was a shoe-in for it. She has all the skills and five years in Navy Intelligence . . ."

I could almost hear the unspoken, "whereas you have no intelligence training at all."

"Kiera—that's the woman who wanted the transfer to our team—applied for this position through your company, of course. However, as all the positions in the Repository report to federal oversight, a federal team that included Gene conducted the interviews. After the interviews ended, Gene mentioned that I would have little trouble training my replacement, so I guess we all thought . . ."

"You all thought Kiera had been selected." I cleared my throat, "Interesting."

And awkward!

Jayda Cruz, Kiera Colón was the applicant who scored highest in the interviews—before we inserted your application and interview results.

"You probably should have given me some kind of intelligence background, don't you think, Nano?"

We can add to your resumé, if you wish.

"Kind of late for that, seeing as how I just told Macy I *don't* have intelligence experience."

Macy lifted one slim shoulder. "Yes. It's interesting."

"Well, I, uh, I hope Kiera doesn't have hard feelings."

Macy slanted her eyes sideways and lowered her voice. "Maybe that's why I asked you about your background. Kiera is a lovely person, but she has kind of a sharp edge to her if you rub her the wrong way—you know what I mean? Her shifting temperament was, in my opinion, the only downside to her joining our team. She tends to take things personally."

"Well, um, I'll just try not to get on her bad side."

Macy gave me a look that might have meant, "That horse has already left the gate."

I fumbled to flip the conversation elsewhere. "How long will you be out on maternity leave, Macy? I was told that the contract I'm working under is for twelve months?"

That did the trick.

"Oh, I won't be coming back to work for a few years. My husband and I already have a three-year-old son, Daniel. We weren't planning on twins, of course, and the daycare expenses for three would eat us alive. I'll stay home with the kids at least until our boy is in kindergarten or first grade."

Macy then returned to business. "Since you don't have a background in intelligence, I'll begin with some basics about us here in the Repository. As you might imagine, intelligence gathering means nothing if analysts, theorists, and intelligence officers cannot retrieve information as they need it. Our department's job is to classify, catalog, and cross-index NSA information. When you consider how much data the NSA looks at daily—in the realm of 1.6 percent of all Internet traffic or around 30 petabytes—the task is Herculean in nature.

"The NSA monitors electronic signals and systems used by foreign targets, terrorist organizations, and suspected terrorist actors within the U.S. We catalog and index digital images, video and audio recordings, and the content of text messages, emails, websites, chat rooms, bulletin boards, and every form of social media. We also track FISA court proceedings—warrant requests to monitor suspected bad actors on U.S. soil."

"Do the actual files sit here in the Repository?" The idea of all that data nearby sent me into a giddy tailspin.

"Although this department is called the Repository because we manage the data, technically, the cataloged files themselves are the actual Repository and we are the Repository's managers. The files reside elsewhere in this building, in a secure server farm. No one who works in this department is allowed physical access to the server farm. And, although we rename files according to strict NSA conventions and organize files and folders electronically as they are cataloged and indexed, we cannot open data stored in the Repository."

What? Bummer!

"The NSA is the world leader in cryptology—the art and science of making and breaking codes—and all files are encrypted before they are sent to us. Anyone attempting to view the contents of a file would require both an encryption key to open it and the correct encryption software to decipher it.

"We have no means of loading software of any kind on our workstations, and IT scans our computers nightly to ensure that they have not been tampered with. Even should an insider threat attempt to copy or delete a file, it would be impossible. This entire building has no Internet access. Also, the Repository and its computers are air-gapped in that they, physically, have no connection to any other on-site network and have no data ports such as disk or USB drives. Basically, our workstations have access to the Repository catalog. Period."

"How are files, er, sent to the Repository team to be cataloged?"

"They come from NSA listening posts throughout the world through a one-way portal into a separate secure network where the files are scanned for malware or malicious code. The files are then downloaded to us nightly. That means that each morning our department has a substantial number of files to classify, catalog, index, and merge into the Repository. Every file contains unencrypted metadata, including code names, that helps us to determine where it belongs."

"This department has several teams. One team manages the Repository's taxonomy—the system's classification and nomenclature, the means by which content is indexed and retrieved—a structure of close to one million nodes. The taxonomy is plain text but highly classified. The taxonomy team maintains the catalog's structure and integrity, ensuring that its nodes are unique and inclusive, that is, comprehensive without duplication.

"Another team of analysts and security classifiers determines the security classification levels of the data and marks the files accordingly.

"A third team, working with the classification team, determines where data will reside within the catalog. Then they cross-index the files and place them in the catalog.

"Our team has two specific jobs. The first is to answer information requests by searching the catalog and providing encrypted files to the requestors. Our second task is to track incoming traffic to the department and our ongoing progress. We track our department's progress in project management software. We report our progress to Gene, who manages department resources accordingly.

"Neville, who moved up to my position, is now the primary project controls person on our team. You will be his partner. The other six members of the team answer information requests."

Macy logged into her workstation and showed me the department's workflow and network structure. The Repository's taxonomy was, as Macy had warned, huge, and the size of the database astronomical. Forget petabytes. The amount of data in the NSA Repository was far up in the xenottabytes.

As mind-boggling as was the number of "bytes" in a xenottabyte, I admit that I was practically salivating. I had landed next door to every bit and byte of data the NSA had. I would be sitting on the complete catalog of all NSA information.

I couldn't believe my luck.

No. Not luck, I amended. Christians don't "do" luck. I believe that the Lord directs my steps. Even the nanomites were part of God's plan for me to help the President, I reminded myself.

We might not have access to other networks on campus, but the entire Repository was open to the nanomites. Encryption keys? Encryption software? Child's play to the nanomites. While I learned the Repository's systems and managed my daily workload, they would search the Repository for clues to the conspiracy.

I would have to get creative to sneak them into other NSA networks.

In the meantime, Repository wire taps and phone logs would yield their data and, hopefully, provide us with important leads. FISA court warrants would open to the nanomites, too, and if those warrant applications provided grounds to surveil anyone in the President's administration, the nanomites would trace the applications back to those who had requested them.

As to the evidence we found pertinent to the conspiracy against the President? We didn't need the Internet or flash drives to download what we found.

We had Alpha Tribe.

⌘

WHEN THE DAY ENDED, I followed the crowd leaving the Repository to their parking area, making note of where to park and enter in the morning.

Then I hoofed it over to HR

I poked my head into Ms. Amali's open doorway. "Checking out as requested, Ms. Amali."

"Any questions or concerns?"

"No, ma'am. But thank you for asking."

"Then have a pleasant evening, Ms. Cruz."

"Same to you, ma'am."

The nanomites I'd left with Ms. Amali flowed back to me. I drove home with one eye on the road, the remainder of my attention on what the nanomites had found on our first day.

Wayne Overman's HR file gave me some insight into who he was as a person: husband and father—and an exemplary employee, if the commendations and promotions in his long work history were to be believed. And while we were at the IT helpdesk, I'd had the nanomites map the other networks on the campus and look into the NSA's badging software.

We could use the badging software to track Wayne Overman's campus movements in the weeks before he disappeared. It would take more time in the system to overlay that data with the schematics of the NSA campus and cross-check his movements against the badges of other as-yet-unidentified personnel.

I would need to return to the IT Department and send the nanomites on further explorations.

Jayda Cruz.

"Yes, Nano?"

We require time with the 3D printer.

"What? Has something happened? Has the nanocloud sustained an injury? Have your numbers decreased?"

No, Jayda Cruz. However, we require greater storage capacity. We wish to add capacity to Alpha Tribe's numbers.

An image of the Repository's taxonomy and network file structure popped into my head: *Xenottabytes of data.*

"It's not necessary for you to download the entire Repository, Nano! We are here to find out what happened to Wayne Overman and to identify those who are involved in the conspiracy to overturn the President's administration."

All knowledge is of interest to us, Jayda Cruz.

"Yeah, well, as the Apostle Paul said, "All things are lawful for me, but all things are not expedient.""

Strictly speaking, nothing we have done at the NSA is lawful, Jayda Cruz.

"We've been tasked by the President—directly—to uncover those involved in the assassination attempt, to investigate the possible murder of Mr. Overman, and find evidence of collusion to commit treason and sedition. You heard Gamble talk about Executive Order 12333. The President has directed us to infiltrate the NSA. His orders make our actions lawful—that is, those actions that help us figure out this conspiracy, not download all the data in the NSA Repository."

The nanomites didn't answer me, but I knew them well enough by now to recognize when they were sulking.

I sighed. "How much time would you need with the printer, Nano?"

At a minimum, forty-eight hours, Jayda Cruz.

"Well, I can't stay at the safe house forty-eight hours straight, Nano."

We see no reason why you cannot, Jayda Cruz.

It was my turn not to answer.

Why not, Nano? Because I don't want to spend my entire weekend twiddling my thumbs, cooped up in that less-than-comfy safe house.

I want to spend the weekend with my husband.

⌘⌘⌘⌘

CHAPTER 5

IT WAS TUESDAY EVENING. I answered the phone. "Hey, Gamble."

"I have that space you asked for, a friend of a friend's martial arts studio."

"What's the arrangement?"

"The arrangement is that if he notices anything out of place, he ignores it. He's being compensated—and the studio has no video security. The windows and doors are barred and alarmed, so he gave me the alarm code."

"Okay, cool."

He rattled off the info, but I ignored it.

We didn't need no stinking alarm code.

Besides, using the code logged an entry. If we cleaned up after ourselves, Gamble's "friend of a friend" would never know we'd been there. As far as he would ever know, he was being paid for nothing.

"This guy has lots of martial arts training equipment, including sticks."

"Great! Thanks for setting this up for us, Gamble."

"That's what I do."

⌘

"CALLISTER HERE."

The disembodied male voice on the other end of the call was matter-of-fact. "Sitrep."

"Sir, I have nothing definitive to report, only that the head of the President's detail is leery of recent personnel changes."

"Kennedy can't influence White House postings other than his own detail, and we've given the repositioned agents sufficient inducements not to talk should Kennedy contact them and attempt to probe their abrupt change of station or departure from the Service. Alterations to the President's schedule?"

"Kennedy appears to be meeting with the President in the privacy of the Residence more often than before. They may suspect that the Oval Office is tapped."

"It would be difficult for them to prove that since our assets within the Service do the daily sweeps. Can you bug the Residence?"

"It would be . . . tricky, Mr. M—"

"*Do not* use my name."

Callister swallowed. "It won't happen again, sir."

"Can you or can you not bug the Residence?"

"No, sir. I'm already on Kennedy's radar. He knows I was on Harmon's detail."

"Hmm. Leave it to me, then. I have . . . additional assets in place. What about VP candidates?"

"The President's discussions with his chief of staff and party leaders seem at an impasse. The candidates generating the most enthusiasm won't pass the vote in Congress to confirm them. The President and his staff have exhausted their short list and appear to be working up another list."

Silence stretched across the line as the caller pondered the information. When the caller replied, the response was terse. "I'll pass this information up the chain. Anything else to report?"

"No, sir."

Callister heard a click as the caller hung up.

⌘⌘⌘⌘

CHAPTER 6

WE SET THE PHONE on the table between us and put the call on speaker. Emilio answered on the first ring.

Zander greeted him first. "Hey, buddy. How's it going?"

"Hi, Zander!"

My heart melted as Emilio's bubbly excitement came across the line. How I missed that boy! We knew he missed us, too. Being away from him was the hardest part of our assignment.

I added my greeting. "Hey, you."

"Hi, Jayda! Hey, I have a new one. Betcha can't guess it."

A "new one" referred to the jokes and riddles we swapped during our calls each week. Emilio loved trying to stump us—which was impossible, what with both nanoclouds chiming in, trying to best each other. They seemed to take an odd, juvenile pleasure in our ritual and had accumulated possibly the world's largest storehouse of dumb gags, witticisms, brainteasers, and puns.

I played along with Emilio. "You just try us; we're ready for you!"

"Okay, here goes: What kind of exercises do lazy people do?"

"Um . . ."

We know, Jayda Cruz!

"Of course, you do, Nano."

We usually played along for a while, but Emilio had the patience of a gnat. "Give up? Huh?"

Zander offered a lame answer. "Girl pushups?"

I smacked him on the arm. "I can do as many pushups as you can, bub, and not girl pushups, either."

Emilio guffawed. "Nope that's not it. Give up?"

"Oh, all right. We give up. What kind of exercises do lazy people do?" Zander was grinning.

"Diddly squats!" Emilio shouted.

It was dumb but cute. We shook our heads and chuckled as Emilio hooted his triumph.

"That's a good one," Zander answered, "but now I have one for you. Ready?"

Zander seemed to draw from his own wealth of riddles—which made me question what kind of a kid he'd been at Emilio's age.

"Yeah, I'm ready," Emilio answered.

"Okay, here it is: What's green and red and goes a hundred miles an hour?"

We know, Jayda Cruz, we know! It's—

"Shhh. Let Emilio try, Nano." Sometimes I wondered if Emilio was more mature than the nanomites were.

Emilio fidgeted and sighed. Then we heard Emilio whispering, his hand obviously over the phone.

"Hey! No fair. You don't get to ask Abe."

"Shoot. Well, I guess I can't figure it out. What's green and red and goes a hundred miles an hour?"

Zander waggled an evil brow at me. "Frog in a blender."

My mouth dropped open. For a few seconds, Emilio, too, was silent. Then he "got it" and cracked up. While he howled with laughter, I shook my head and groaned.

"Zander, that's *terrible*," I whispered.

My husband wasn't the least bit repentant. "Naw, it's not terrible—it's *classic*. Emilio will repeat that one at school for weeks. He'll be the star of the playground."

I cupped my chin in my hand and waited for Emilio to laugh himself out. On the other end, we heard Abe say something.

Emilio popped back on the line. "Hey, Jayda?"

"Yeah?"

"Do you guys have plans for the Fourth of July?"

I flashed Zander a glance. Fourth of July? Was it almost that time?

Even though colorful, bunting-draped firework stands had popped up in strip malls and grocery parking lots, neither Zander nor I had paid much attention to them. We'd been oblivious to the changes around us, wrapped in our own concerns.

I looked at Zander. "Plans?"

"Yeah. For the first week in July." Emilio had stopped laughing, but he was simmering with excitement.

"Um, I have work and we have a few recurring commitments. Why?"

"Well, you get the Fourth off, don't you?"

I did? Oh, yeah. I did. And the Fourth was exactly two weeks from today.

"Yes, as a matter of fact, I do."

"Do they have good firework shows near you guys? Like, in D.C.?" Emilio sounded like he was going to burst.

"I . . . I suppose so."

Jayda Cruz, we can provide a list of multiple events to celebrate the holiday in or around Washington, D.C., including the National Independence Day Parade down Constitution Avenue, a concert on the west lawn in front of the Capitol building, followed by fireworks on the National Mall.

"I've been told we have lots of choices here, Emilio."

"And do you have a couch for Abe to sleep on?"

"What?" Zander and I exclaimed at the same time.

Emilio was bouncing around Abe's living room. "I can sleep on the floor, but Abe is old. He needs something softer. You got a couch or an air mattress?"

"What are you saying, Emilio?"

Apparently, Abe had listened without participation long enough. He wrested the phone from Emilio.

"Hello, Jayda. Zander. What my tactless boy is getting at—what he has bugged me about for a month straight—is that we'd like to come visit over the Fourth."

Now I was the one who was ready to explode. "You're coming? Here?"

"Well, I hope it's all right, because I've already bought our tickets."

In the background we heard Emilio holler, "We're gonna fly! In an airplane!"

"First time the boy will have been on an airplane," Abe added. "Now, if you don't have room for us in your apartment, we'll find a hotel and—"

"No, you will not! You're staying with us. Right, Zander?"

"Absolutely. We have a nice couch, Abe. It folds down, too. We wouldn't have you staying anywhere but with us."

Now I was the one jumping out of my skin. "When? When are you coming? And how long can you stay?"

"We'll fly into Baltimore at three in the afternoon on Monday and leave the following Saturday morning. Will you be able to pick us up?"

I was distraught that I wouldn't be able to go to the airport, but Zander answered, "I'll be there, Abe. We should get home about the same time Jayda gets off work."

We talked a little longer, but my heart was singing over their news: They were coming to visit. Abe and Emilio!

I tugged at the chain that hung around my neck and fumbled to find and hold the polished wooden cross dangling from it. At one time, Emilio and I had been enemies of sorts—he an angry, mistreated kid, stealing from the neighborhood (including me) just to eat; me his disgruntled, self-righteous neighbor, blind to Emilio's neglect.

Blind until I'd looked past my own nose and noticed how thin he was. Blind until I'd found him shivering and sobbing in the bushes, hiding from his uncle's drunken abuse. That evening I'd presented the kid with a peace offering of hot pizza.

Emilio had whittled the cross and rubbed it until its surface was smooth and glowing. He had left it on my front porch as a thank you.

I'd worn it ever since.

I held that cross and sighed. When I closed my eyes, I could feel our boy in my arms.

⌘

WHEN WE HAD HAMMERED out the details of their visit, we hung up and readied ourselves for the hours ahead of us. For, as Zander had put it, spy training.

I didn't like it; in fact, I hated it, but I stripped off my wedding ring anyway and left it at home. Zander did the same. Night had fallen. We parked a mile from our destination and took different routes into the seedy warehouse district where our classes were to be held.

An hour and a half after our phone call with Abe and Emilio ended, we reported to our first Wednesday evening "tradecraft" class. If I hadn't had the nanomites with me, I wouldn't have gone anywhere near the place. It was an ancient, three-story brick building surrounded by abandoned and falling down warehouses—many of them flophouses for the homeless and dope dens for the addicted. To get to our classroom, I had to waltz through a crime- and gang-infested neighborhood with dealers and prostitutes plying their trade on every corner. It was the hangout of pimps, alcoholics, two-bit criminals, and thugs—which is why we'd parked our car in a guarded lot where it stood half of a chance of being where we left it when we returned.

I wore dark, sloppy clothes and a dingy, oversized hoody pulled over my head and around my face, and I kept my head down as I pushed toward my destination. A reconnaissance wing of nanomites flew a few yards out in front of me, checking my blind spots, telling me which shadows to step into and which to avoid, changing my route twice to avoid trouble.

When some hulking dude in a watch cap cracked open a door I'd just passed and lunged at me, the nanomites zapped him so hard the impact tossed him back inside the hovel he'd emerged from. I shifted my gaze around to check if anyone had noticed and walked on.

"Um, don't do that again, Nano. I'm not supposed to use you tonight, remember?"

We have agreed to be inconspicuous during your class, Jayda Cruz, but how will the training benefit you if you are assaulted before you arrive?

Their reply did make me wonder why these guys were putting us— me, a woman, in particular—in danger. Not that I was in any real danger, but they didn't know that, right?

I sighed. Two blocks to go.

When I found the address, I pulled back into a moldy niche between two nasty warehouses and studied the place. The old brick-and-mortar structure stood alone, like an island in the crumbling urban decay. Its windows were blacked out and, as far as appearances went, it could have been any other unoccupied building. Must have been the look they were aiming for.

When the coast seemed clear, I went to a side door, as instructed, and knocked.

The door—heavy, reinforced steel that could have withstood a tank—swung open. An unseen figure whispered, "Follow me."

He led me down a dark, narrow corridor, through a set of doors into another hallway, this one illuminated in dull yellow, to yet another set of doors. These doors opened into our classroom at the center of the building. The room was spacious and well lit, but windowless. Zander was already there, looking anywhere but at me. So were four more guys who appeared to belong on the street hustling drugs.

"Sorry I'm a little late. The walk here wasn't exactly friendly."

The largest of the men stepped forward. "It wasn't meant to be. Welcome to Malware, Inc. This is our clubhouse, and this—" he gestured to the room, "is our training center. I'm your chief instructor, Malcolm; you can call me Mal."

He gestured to the other men and they fanned out. They were all fit and muscled with inscrutable expressions. A fifth guy, wearing a black watch cap, entered the room and joined the other men. As his eyes bored holes in me, he rubbed a spot on his chest.

"These are your instructors: Logan, Baltar, Deckard, Dredd, and McFly, who escorted you in. Obviously, these are not our real names. What should we call you?"

"Well, since we've got a cool sci-fi theme going on, how 'bout Ripley?" I jerked my chin toward Zander. "And who's that?"

"A classmate. He said to call him John-Boy."

I snickered. "What is this, a rerun of the Waltons?"

"Don't get personal, Ripley, or we'll start calling you Mary Ellen."

The steel-cage of my poker face snapped into place—to which I added a sharp, grating edge. "No, *Mal*. You won't."

I didn't have to sneak a peek at Zander to visualize his shock. He hadn't really known the old Gemma that well.

I jerked a thumb at the other instructors. "And I take it that you-all supplied some of the neighborhood's not-so-friendly 'local color'?"

"We did. We like to get a feel for the trainees before introductions."

"Fair enough." I met the searing gaze of the guy wearing the watch cap. "And did you 'get a feel' for me, Dredd?"

Silence.

Dead, cold, creepy silence—like I'd pushed the envelope waaaay too far.

Menacing silence . . . that gave way to snuffled guffaws and an undercurrent of chuckles.

Mal grinned and snarked. Three of our instructors pointed at Dredd and howled. Dredd, a little shamefaced, managed a half-grin.

"You've got chops, Ripley, I'll give you that," Mal said.

I shrugged. "I have a few moves." I flicked a glance at Zander.

His expression said he did not know me.

I don't think he was faking it.

After that, we got down to business. McFly delivered an hour lecture on "Mental State." "Mental state is the most overlooked but vital aspect of tradecraft—because sloppy mental behavior will get you killed. Lack of vigilance will get you killed. Overconfidence will get you killed. Carelessness will get you killed."

McFly's cold and implacable stare skewered us. "Don't want to die? Then stay frosty. Never take anything for granted."

He moved on. "Mission planning is a good example of the mental sharpness and attention to detail that is necessary. You must, I repeat, *you must* know the lay of the land and learn the mission venue inside and out— entry and exit points, all aspects of security, and who will be there.

"Even then, it is not enough for you to have formulated a good plan. Before you execute, you must think as the opposition thinks, see your plan from their perspective, identify the plan's vulnerabilities, and reformulate it to eliminate said vulnerabilities. That means you must know your opposition better than he knows you.

"When your plan is set, you aren't finished. You must plan for the unexpected and maintain your cool when the unexpected occurs. If the *bleep* hits the fan, your contingency plan will either save your life or end it—which is why contingency planning must be one hundred percent complete, ready, and waiting."

"Five-minute break," Mal called.

For an hour after that, Logan and Baltar talked about detecting and evading surveillance. "The first rule of tradecraft is 'don't give yourself away.' Unfortunately, the prospect of being outed—intentionally or unintentionally—grows exponentially according to the number of individuals other than yourself to whom your identity and mission are known.

"In any and every situation, to believe your identity is unknown and to act accordingly is potentially deadly. Again, your *mental state* must never presume that your identity is uncompromised, just as you must never assume your plan is foolproof. Surveillance detection, then, becomes the way you live—or the way you die."

Logan (*sans* the adamantium claws of his alter-ego, Wolverine) spoke at length on how to be observant, "Again, it's about mental discipline. You can learn how to watch and catalog faces, clothing, and vehicles, but learning and making it a lifestyle are two different things. As Ian Fleming wrote, 'Once is happenstance; twice is coincidence. Three times is enemy action.'"

He looked Zander and me in the eye. "Here at Malware, Inc., we skip the 'twice is coincidence' step and go straight to 'enemy action.' If you notice someone twice, it is time to act."

Then Baltar talked about proving you had a tail, then evading the tail. He spoke on "surveillance detection routes" (SDRs), and how to design an effective one.

Mal stepped in and handed both of us flash drives. "That's it for tonight. Here's a little 'light reading.' We'll meet again next week, same time and place, and put some feet to what you've learned. Good night. Dredd will take you back to your vehicles."

Dredd gestured to us, and we followed him to the clubhouse's first-floor garage. We climbed into a van that, like this neighborhood, appeared on the outside to be neglected and rundown but, on the inside was up-armored and in good working order.

"Where to?"

"Drop me anywhere I can grab a drink." It was the first thing I'd come up with to preserve the illusion that Zander and I hadn't arrived in the same vehicle. I also hoped my "grab a drink" reference reinforced my "tough girl" image.

Dredd pulled up to a curb. "This good for you?"

"Yeah. Thanks."

I got out. Fifteen minutes later, Zander called me. "Ready for me to pick you up, *Ripley*?"

I giggled. "Yes, please. I know we don't require a full night's sleep, but I'd sure like to log at least three hours."

"Me, too. I'm bushed."

⌘⌘⌘⌘

CHAPTER 7

MY SECOND AND THIRD day at the NSA had passed with little fanfare. Although I was itching to sic the nanomites on the trail of Wayne Overman, I'd decided to be discreet and spend my first week keeping my eyes and ears open while learning my job—not all that difficult given how quickly I absorbed information. I had determined not to make a move until I had a better sense of the place.

My resolve lasted until Thursday.

Jayda Cruz. It is time to get up.

Jayda Cruz. It is time to get up.

Jayda Cruz. It is time to get up. Proverbs 6:9: "How long will you lie there, you sluggard?"

"Yeah, yeah."

I roused Zander and stumbled from the bed to the bathroom. Five minutes later, we were out the door, into our morning run.

It was after our run when I changed my mind: I was ready to put the nanomites to work. While I showered, I thought hard about which tasks to assign to the nanomites first.

I wanted to track Wayne Overman's movements during his last weeks at the NSA, overlaid on the schematics of the NSA campus and cross-referenced against the movements of other NSA employees who came within Overman's vicinity during that timeframe. I figured Facilities would have the schematics. Safety and Security would have the badge-tracking software. Both departments should have dedicated drives on the main NSA network.

And, even though government regulations required that email accounts and phone logs of its institutions and agencies be preserved, I was worried that whomever was responsible for Wayne Overman's disappearance may have selectively expunged the last weeks of the man's digital footprint at the NSA.

I wanted the nanomites to download Overman's emails and phone traffic—from the time the President asked him to dig into Harmon's connections at the NSA until he disappeared. I hoped those documents would provide some clues as to what he'd discovered.

If Overman's email and phone logs hadn't been deleted, IT would have them.

"Nano, can you reach into the Facilities and Safety and Security drives from IT?"

Yes, Jayda Cruz.

With the exception of the Repository and any air gapped vaults or SCIFS in the facility, we can access all department drives from IT. We can, in fact, access all department drives from any computer on the main network.

"Good. That gives me some options."

The mites had touched on a big downside to working in the Repository. Because the Repository's network was physically separated from the rest of the NSA networks, the nanomites could not get to the main network from my workstation, nor could they leave our department on their own momentum. I needed to convey them to a point of network access.

It was still my first week on the job, but I'd seen how employees pretty much stuck to their own departments or areas—and every one of those had an access control point. I didn't know where, outside of the Repository, I could take the nanomites that my presence wouldn't arouse suspicion. HR? Maybe. IT? Also a maybe.

The problem was that both of those departments were at the other end of the campus from the Repository. I needed a plausible purpose for going to either place.

I toweled off and dressed. As soon as I pulled on the lightweight top I was wearing to work, I added the lanyard from which my badge and key fob dangled.

Key fob.

I fingered the little device, its regularly changing code necessary for me to log into my computer at work.

"Nano. I'd like you to disable this fob so that I can't log in this morning."

Done, Jayda Cruz.

I finished getting ready for work. Zander and I drank our first cup of coffee, then ate breakfast together while reading our Bibles. We prayed over the day, mentioning Zander's job search, Abe and our boy Emilio back in Albuquerque, and my efforts at work.

Zander laid a long, lingering kiss on me that left me breathless and silly as I headed out. Close to an hour later, I greeted Macy and my other team members, and tried to log in at my Repository workstation.

"Huh."

Macy scooted her chair closer to mine. "What's the problem, Jayda?"

"My fob isn't working."

"Here. Let me see."

She examined the tiny screen that should have displayed the six-figure code for me to enter. It was blank. Sure enough, my fob was dead.

"Weird. You must have gotten a lemon."

"Guess I need to return it to IT?"

"Yeah. Hey, Sherry? Jayda's fob isn't working. She needs to go back to IT."

Sherry agreed, so I wound my way out of the warren of cubicles, through the Repository doors, across the breezeway into the next building, and down the hall toward the distant IT Department.

"Nano, when we reach IT, please send in a search party to trace Overman's whereabouts for two weeks prior to his going missing. Overlay his movements on a detailed schematic of the NSA campus, and correlate his badge's movements with every other badge within his proximity. Upload the data to Alpha Tribe so that we can study it together this evening."

This task will take approximately 1.5 hours, Jayda Cruz.

"Huh? Why so long?"

This facility employs approximately thirty-seven thousand badge-wearing workers, Jayda Cruz, in addition to the influx of visitors from other NSA and intelligence sites.

The actual number was classified, but I figured the nanomites' estimate had to be close.

"Um, okay, then. I'll . . . I'll return at lunchtime to fetch the contingency we leave behind."

Hmm. I had a legitimate reason to visit IT this morning, but I'd need another excuse to visit the department a second time in one day. Ordinarily, I'd just walk through the doors in my invisible state, but . . .

"Nano, how many cameras are watching us right now?"

We have counted two live video feeds in every area we have been so far, Jayda Cruz.

"Uh, okay."

Gamble was right—not that the cameras themselves posed a big problem to the nanomites, but here, at the NSA, I was *supposed* to show up on video feed wherever I went, whereas I was *not* supposed to show up on White House cameras. Did the NSA have people eyeballing its video feeds 24/7? Would anyone notice if I disappeared from the feed for a few minutes? Could I risk it?

Maybe I'd get away with it, but "risking it" was exactly what Gamble had warned me *not* to do. The spy masters of the world worked here, so it didn't exactly calm my nerves that I had to pass the Safety and Security Department before I reached IT.

Rats. As Gamble had warned, the NSA was proving to be way more intimidating than the White House, throwing me off my game. Making me doubt my instincts.

Not to worry, I told myself as I approached my destination. *I'll figure it out. Something . . . something will come to me.*

I strolled into the IT Department and approached the help desk. "Hi."

The guy at the desk glanced up.

You know, I would bet my favorite donut that this kid was the poster boy for geek. In a lot of ways, he still looked like the president of his high school science club, when in actuality, he was probably my age.

Hmm. My age.

"Yeah? Can I help you?"

"Uh, sorry. Do you remember me? Jayda Cruz. I started work Monday, and you issued me this key fob."

"Oh. Yeah, sure. I remember you."

I'd told myself out in the hall that a solution would come to me, an excuse for returning to IT after lunch, and guess what? Something did— but not all schemes are created equal, right? At that exact moment a weird impulse popped into my head—an idea I acted on without additional consideration.

My left hand wandered up to my hair. My fingers twisted and curled a strand. I cracked a small, shy smile.

"It's Rob, right? I, um, I really hope you can help me."

Puh-thet-ic. I am the worst spy ever.

Okay, okay, I admit it. I do *need that Spy 101 training. Good grief. What did Gamble call it? A series of* "How to Stay Alive" *workshops?*

"What seems to be the problem?"

I exhaled. In for a penny, in for a pound.

Instead of handing him the fob, I leaned far over his workspace to place it on the desk in front of him, all the while smiling. A faint line of color edged its way out of Rob's buttoned-up polo.

Preempting a sniff of self-derision, I faked a helpless sigh. "Well, Rob, for some reason, the numbers on the little screen . . . thingy don't show up for me when I try to log in. But maybe I'm doing it wrong?"

I looked Rob full in the face, only twenty inches from him, and slowly blinked. Twice.

Rob's blush crawled up his neck.

Jayda Cruz. Your behavior is quite . . . uncharacteristic. We are confused.

I kept my eyes locked on Rob's. "Not now, Nano."

Rob wrenched his gaze away from mine to stare at the fob. "Uh, yup. Looks like it's dead."

"Oh! So, I wasn't doing it wrong?"

"Nope, I—" Rob made the mistake of looking back to me. "I-I . . ."

"You can fix it, can't you, Rob?" Yeah, I injected a touch, a mere soupçon of wheedle into my question.

Jayda Cruz. We can fix the device for you. You know this. However, we do not understand. First, you asked us to render it inoperable. Now—

"SHUT IT, Nano!"

I don't know. Maybe a microexpression crossed my face, a hint of my irritation with the nanomites?

Rob's eyes widened. He slowly pushed his chair away from his desk. Away from me. Looking anywhere but at me, he stuttered, "F-fix it? Um, no. We'll—that is *I*—will replace it. Give you a new one. Just . . . just take a seat at the terminal. . . over there, and I'll log this one out of use and assign another to you."

I beamed at him. "Thank you so much. You're awesome, Rob."

He couldn't help himself. His eyes flicked up to my adoring approval.

The pink creeping stain darkened and roared up his neck, jaws, cheeks, and forehead. If the roots of Rob's hair had spontaneously combusted, I would not have been amazed.

Amused, yes. Amazed? Not so much.

Five minutes later, after keying in my password and using my new fob to log in to the network, I left the IT Department.

I gave a happy little wave as I went. I might have been waving to the nanomites I'd left behind, but Rob definitely believed I was waving at him.

"Nano," I said as I hit the hallway, "Make sure you download the complete schematics to this place. I want to know the layout—every building, floor, department, office, and broom closet."

Yes, Jayda Cruz.

⌘

THE MORNING SPED BY, Macy demanding more of me as I showed her I could follow her guidance. I had to hold back, because to go any faster would have been, you know, *abnormal*. I cruised along at Macy's speed and didn't push it.

"Well, I'm impressed, Jayda, I really am," she said at one point. "You have an amazing grasp of new things. No wonder they picked you for the job."

"So, she's Wonder Girl, is she?"

I glanced up and saw a woman about my age. Her black eyes glittered, but her face seemed expressionless.

Macy's body language tensed up. "Hey, girl. How's it going?"

"Just came over to scope out the new kid on the block." She continued to study me with that tell-nothing stare.

"Um, Jayda, this is Kiera Colón. Kiera, Jayda Cruz."

"Cruz? Guess we're both Hispanic, huh?"

"I'm not, but my husband is. We just moved here from New Mexico."

"How nice." She turned to Macy. "You going to finish the week?"

"I suppose we'll find out. The doctor never thought I'd make it this far carrying twins, but here I am."

"You know I wish you well."

"Thanks, Kiera."

With another glance at me, the woman moved off.

"Geeze Louise," Macy breathed. "See what I mean about a sharp edge? Definitely lacking in social skills."

I sniffed. "Doesn't bother me."

⌘

WHEN LUNCH ROLLED AROUND, the employees in our department started leaving in twos and threes. As soon as I finished the task I was on, I would go, also. Then, after lunch, I intended to poke my head into IT, waggle my fingers at Rob, and add a simpering, "Thanks again, Rob! I was able to log in with my new fob!"

A few seconds. Enough time for the nanomites I'd left there to flow back to me.

The more I ran those lines around in my head, the more I wanted to gag. *Ick, ick, ick.* I despised girls who used their "charms" to manipulate guys.

Another thought hit me, one that carried a whopping dose of conviction: What was I thinking, flirting like I was *single*?

I glanced at my wedding ring. *Why, I'm a married woman.*

I almost laughed aloud. *I'm a married woman!* I loved the sound of those words, but I guess the magnitude of it hadn't yet sunk in: *I'm a married woman.*

Oh, wow. I'm really sorry, Lord; I wasn't seriously flirting. Doesn't matter, though, does it? It was wrong. I should have thought it out before I acted. Please forgive me. Won't happen again.

With my confession, the guilt I'd felt faded. Still, I had to laugh at my "discovery": *I'm a married woman!* I didn't think I'd ever get tired of saying it.

I locked my workstation and got my purse from one of my desk drawers.

"Lunch?" Macy asked. We'd had lunch together since I started.

"Yeah. I'm starved."

Don't know how I'm going to retrieve my nanomites, but sure. Lord? I need a Plan B.

Macy laughed. "You're always hungry, Jayda."

We walked (slowly, to accommodate Macy's rolling gait) to the campus cafeteria, a vast, bustling affair in the same building as IT but some distance from it.

"You know, we don't always eat here. The base has a lot of food options. Just depends on what you're hungry for."

"Good to know." *For sure.*

I hoped Macy wouldn't comment on how much food I loaded onto my tray. I'd devoured two power bars between breakfast and lunch, but I was still ravenous. And I had an apple in my drawer in case, before the day was over, my stomach started revving up like a *Grand Prix* engine clearing its throat for a big race.

After we'd gone through the line and paid for our food, we spied Saul, James, and Neville and sat down at their table. Before long, Chantelle, Lynn, and Neri joined us. As it had the last three days, conversation around the table was varied and ranged from sports and video games to the newest movies.

The topic that never came up was work.

When we finished our meals, although we had another fifteen minutes left, most of the group headed to our department. I hung back and said to Macy, "You go on ahead. I think I'll take a quick walk outside. Stretch my legs."

"In this heat? Girl, are you crazy?"

"Well, I don't recommend that you come with me," I laughed. "That twin juggling act you're lugging around might just fall out—and I am *not* prepared to handle that."

Macy cracked up. "Oh, my word! Jayda, I didn't think you had much of a sense of humor, but that is about the funniest thing anyone's ever said to me."

She was still giggling when she wobbled away.

"I can't believe I just resorted to a prego joke," I muttered to her back, "but I have got to retrieve the nanomites."

I turned the corner to the nearest restroom. The restroom didn't have a swinging door on its entrance but had, instead, a hairpin turn where you walk around a wall into the restroom proper. As I made the turn out of camera range, the nanomites dropped their invisibility on me. I spun around, jogged out of the restroom, to the IT Department, collected the nanomites I'd left there, and reversed the process to shed the nanomites' invisibility. The trip took me a whopping six minutes.

I grinned and patted myself on the back as I exited the restroom and returned to work.

"Pretty slick, if I do say so myself. Nothing to it. I can use these restroom entrances like Superman uses a phone booth."

I had to laugh. Who, born after the turn of the century, even knew what a phone booth was?

⌘

ZANDER PARKED HIS RENTAL car outside the offices of Columbia's Grace Chapel and stepped through the office doors. A welcome blast of AC struck him in the face.

"Ahhh . . ."

"I hear that more times than you would believe. The heat out there is just this side of Hades."

Zander laughed. "I'll bet you do, and it sure is." He stepped to the church secretary's window. "Hi. I'm Zander Cruz. I have an appointment with Pastor Lucklow."

"I'm Christine. Right this way, Mr. Cruz."

Zander followed the woman to the senior pastor's office.

"Pastor? Mr. Cruz to see you."

"Ah, yes. Thank you, Christine. Come in, Mr. Cruz, come in. How are you?"

"Well, thank you. And thank you for seeing me."

They sat at a small table in the corner of the pastor's office sipping the cold beverages Christine brought them.

"I'm glad to have the opportunity to get to know you better, Mr. Cruz."

"Please call me Zander. My wife and I have attended Sunday services at Grace three times now. We wanted to let you know that we are making Grace Chapel our home church."

"That's wonderful news. We welcome you both. Would you tell me something about yourselves?"

"Sure. Jayda, my bride—we're newlyweds—is a project manager. She started her new job on Monday. As for myself, until we left New Mexico for Jayda's new job, I was the assistant pastor at Downtown Community Church, Albuquerque, where I led the young adult and visitation programs."

"You don't say." Pastor Lucklow studied Zander. "If you don't mind me asking, I'd appreciate hearing your testimony and call to ministry."

"Of course, sir. Well, I'm grateful to the Lord for saving me out of a pretty rough life. For several years out of high school, I ran with a gang in my hometown of Las Cruces and, later, Phoenix. Drugs, alcohol, violence." Zander cleared his throat. "Sex. Pimping."

Zander swallowed again as Pastor Lucklow's eyes bored into his. "The name of this church is significant to me, Pastor: Grace Chapel. If not for the grace of God and the courage of a certain street preacher, I believe I would be dead right now."

Pastor Lucklow's expression did not change. "Tell me more."

"Yes, sir. As I said, a street preacher, a rugged and worn old guy, approached me one night. I was dealing, and I thought he was going to buy. Instead he told me that Jesus wanted to set me free from the trap I was in. Told me that Jesus loved me, that the Gospel was about transformation, a new life. Asked me, 'Do you like this life? Or do you want a new one?'

"For reasons I couldn't fathom at the time, I just up and left the corner I was working. Got into the old dude's car, and we drove away. I dumped the drugs I was holding out the window. He knew the gang would hunt me down if I stayed in Phoenix—they don't let you leave alive, you know—so he pointed the car toward Albuquerque.

"The whole time he drove, he shared Jesus with me, quoted entire passages of the Bible until my whole being was saturated with God's word. By the time we drove through Grants, I was ready."

Zander's throat tightened. "He pulled over to the side of the road and we prayed. He told me to call upon the Lord and beg Jesus to forgive me. I did. I bawled like a baby as my chains dropped away and the Lord washed me clean. Jesus saved me on I-40 at mile marker 86. That encounter with God is as vivid in my mind and heart today as it was seven years ago."

"Fascinating," Pastor Lucklow murmured. "What happened then?"

"Well, I followed that old man for months. He preached wherever the Lord led him, and we slept wherever we found ourselves. I learned a lot from him about sharing Jesus. Learned how to study the Scriptures, how to pray, how to confess my mistakes and failings daily and receive forgiveness. How to walk in the Spirit and follow his guidance.

"Then, one day, my old friend says, 'Kid, you need to go to Bible school.' Long story short, I spent two years working my way through Bible college. Before I graduated, I called my parents. They hadn't heard from me in close to three years. I asked them to come see me. We talked for a long time, and I apologized for all the grief I'd put them through. I told them about Jesus and how he'd saved me. The Lord blessed that time of reconciliation. My family forgave me, and my relationship with them has been restored.

"After a summer internship at DCC, the church hired me. I served there for two more years—until five weeks ago, when, as I said, we moved here because of the job offer Jayda received. Now I'm wondering what the Lord has for me. I'm looking for work, but I'd love if the Lord opened a door of ministry, too."

Pastor Lucklow leaned back in his chair and considered Zander. Zander endured the examination with calm patience.

I am, after all, a complete stranger to this man. Zander didn't know what God had in mind, but he felt something momentous at work.

That feeling only increased when, after a long moment of deliberation, Pastor Lucklow said, "Pastor Cruz, are you familiar with Celebrate Recovery?"

"Yes, I am, sir. I belonged to a CR group during Bible college."

"Oh? Interesting. In a curious turn of events, our Celebrate Recovery group has just lost its directors. Lovely married couple. They were called to a church in Ohio."

"I see."

"Our CR group is a thriving, growing arm of our church, a vital part of our ministry to the community. Your background . . ."

"Is in line with your group's needs?"

"Yes. Just so. At present, the CR assistant directors are leading the group but, in addition to having four children to care for, they have expressed that their desire is to support whomever God chooses to place in leadership rather than be the leaders."

Zander nodded, and Pastor Lucklow continued to study him.

"Pastor Cruz, our CR group meets every Thursday evening, 6:30-8:30, in the fellowship hall. What would you say to visiting a time or two? Check out what God is doing."

"I would be glad to, Pastor."

"Very well. I will be praying, asking the Lord for guidance."

"I will do the same."

Pastor Lucklow stood and ushered Zander to the hallway. "Would you please leave your contact information with Christine? And welcome to Grace Chapel. My wife and I already have lunch plans this Sunday, but we would be delighted to have lunch with you and your bride after service the following Sunday. We'd like to get to know you better."

"It would be our pleasure, Pastor."

Zander whistled a little tune on the way to his car.

Lord, thank you for this encouraging meeting. All your ways are wonderful.

⌘

"I'M HOME!" I CALLED.

"About time. I'm starving. Chinese buffet?"

That empty cavern within roared its approval.

We drove to what was already our favorite Chinese place, The Great Wall. After we'd each filled two plates and sat down with them, I leaned toward Zander.

"Had a good day," I mumbled around a mouthful of noodles.

"I take it we have homework this evening?"

I was occupied with stuffing my face, so I nodded.

"I had a good day, too."

"Uh-huh."

We smiled with contentment at each other and dug deeper into our food. I couldn't say more about my day until we returned to our apartment, but Zander could. When the rumbles from our stomachs started to die down, he elaborated.

"I met with Pastor Lucklow this morning."

"Did you tell him we're putting down roots at Grace Chapel?"

"Yup. By the way, he invited us to have lunch with him and his wife after church next Sunday."

"That's great."

"Our meeting was kind of fascinating. He asked me to share my testimony with him. You know, I learned something, watching *him* watch *me*."

"Oh?"

"The man knows how to listen. He gave me his full attention and interest. Really wanted to know how the Lord had worked in my life. And . . . he didn't flinch when I told him what I was like . . . before. In fact . . ."

I glanced up. "Yes?"

"He asked me if I was familiar with Celebrate Recovery."

"Celebrate Recovery?"

"It's a Christian program that uses biblical truths and principles to help people overcome drug and alcohol addiction and their underlying roots. Lots of wounded unbelievers find Jesus through CR. I belonged to a CR group when I was in Bible college, so I'm acquainted with the program. Pastor Lucklow invited me to sit in on the meetings."

Zander poured more tea for both of us. "He said that the leaders of the group were recently called to another church."

I arched my brows. "And?"

"And we agreed to pray and ask for the Lord's guidance. If I were to take on the group's leadership—and that's entirely up to the Lord—I'm sure Pastor would need to know me better, first. Could take a while."

"Pastor McFee will give you a good reference."

"I'm sure he will. He might even tell Pastor Lucklow that CR is a good fit for me."

Zander smiled. "It's up to the Lord. I'm happy to wait on his timing."

Our hunger pangs at abeyance, we drove home. On the way, I caught Zander up on my day.

"I dropped some nanomites at IT today, and they downloaded the schematics of the NSA complex. I've asked them to render a 3D model from the schematics, so we can explore the place and memorize the layout."

"Good idea. If you ever need me, I'll want to already know the ins and outs."

"Learning the layout is the first step in tracking Wayne Overman. I also asked the nanomites to download Overman's badging history. He disappeared about two months ago. I want to follow his last few weeks of movements."

"Okay. And what about . . . looking at the movements of others around him?"

"Yes. That's the next piece. If we see anything curious, particularly around the time of his disappearance, then we home in on those individuals."

Armed with a pot of decaf, Zander and I sat at our little dinette set and went together into the nanomites' "warehouse." They were ready for us with more than a 3D model of the NSA facilities. They had created a VR environment where we could travel through the NSA complex as though we were there.

"This way," I motioned to Zander.

I led him first toward the Repository, which, I was beginning to realize, sat far away from a lot of the other departments on campus. Waving at the cubicle farm in the large room, I said, "My team sits way over there. All the workstations in here have access to the NSA's intel taxonomy. The role of the Repository Department is to catalog and index the intel so it can be retrieved and then fulfill retrieval requests.

"One team here manages the catalog itself. Another team in the department is staffed with classification experts who determine the intel's classification levels and markings. Yet another team studies the metadata and decides where in the catalog the files go. Every file is named using code words for date, location, and content and is cross-indexed with related files."

"Quite an undertaking."

"It is. Can you imagine managing these files without computers?"

"Impossible."

"Yeah. Then there's our team. We answer the retrieval requests. A lot of data requests as well as new intelligence flow into the Repository every day. Our team also tracks the department's progress against the traffic we receive. That's my job. I enter tasks and resources in the project software.

"From our workstations, we can view the catalog and its files but cannot open the files. Every scrap of data requires both an encryption key and encryption software."

"That doesn't stop the nanomites, right?"

"Right. However, the amount of data in the Repository is hard to fathom. We're talking xenottabytes. It will take them a few days to sort it all."

I hesitated. "The nanomites have asked me to spend a couple of days at the safe house. With the printer. They want to upgrade the nanocloud's storage capacity."

"It would have to be a weekend, then."

"Well, I'm not looking forward to spending a weekend there and sleeping on a couch."

We left the Repository and crossed over to the adjoining building. I showed Zander the cafeteria, then the HR Department, Safety and Security, and IT. We walked back into the IT server farm and studied the racks and racks of blade server enclosures.

"Their hardware must be specially made for the NSA," I observed.

Jayda Cruz, we were able to reproduce the exact layout of this server farm and download a precise network configuration for your perusal.

"Good work, Nano. Zander and I will finish our tour and then we'll get back to you."

Would you care for us to guide your tour? We have studied the facility diagrams and can identify most areas in the complex.

"Most?"

A few rooms are unlabeled, Jayda Cruz. We may be able to deduce their use as we overlay the badging software on the complex layout.

"Zander?"

"Yeah. Go ahead, Nano. Lead on."

In response, the nanomites plotted a course before us using pale lights that led away from general employee access to a bank of elevators. Zander took my hand and, in our kitchen, at our dinette, he did the same. We entered the virtual elevator. I liked how my hand felt in his, how his fingers stroked mine. That warm, possessive sense felt good. Right. There was nothing controlling about Zander's touch. He was kind. Respectful.

I sighed with contentment. *I'm a married woman—*

"Earth to Jayda?"

"Hmm?"

"Time to get off."

The elevator had stopped and opened. Zander tugged gently at my hand, and we stepped into a foyer that spoke "power" with a capital "P."

U.S. and NSA flags bookended the seals of U.S. Cyber Command, the National Security Agency, and the Central Security Service. Large portraits of President Jackson and NSA Director Willem Bradshaw, both strong examples to the country's African American community, hung in prominent honor.

Jayda and Zander Cruz, this is the executive suite.

"I think we figured that out," Zander answered.

"How did you know to furnish this foyer in such detail, Nano?"

The network contains many photos, Jayda Cruz. This location is used to present awards and recognition.

"Got it." We wandered through the floor, noting the suites for the Director and Deputy Director, conference rooms, and so on—none of which were rendered in the complete detail the foyer had been.

We spent another hour walking NSA halls, entering offices and departments, noting the vaults and SCIFs, committing them to memory—particularly the exits and where they led. I knew the nanomites could direct me in a situation where (God forbid) I was being pursued, but the recollection of that dim place where the nanomites did not answer my frantic cries for help was never far from my thoughts. I needed to know the layout of the campus for myself.

Just in case.

"I think that's enough for tonight, Nano."

"I agree. I'm anxious to get to Overman's movements."

We are ready to project Mr. Overman's badge movements onto the 3D rendering, Zander Cruz. We will begin four weeks prior to his disappearance at your command.

"Uh, *make it so*, Nano."

The delight Zander felt in his Picard imitation was infectious, and I giggled my appreciation—only to choke on my half-uttered laugh when the rendering of the NSA complex . . . dropped out from under us.

Perhaps we rocketed UP, rather than the building plummeting DOWN. I couldn't tell which, but it didn't much matter, because the rapid, ongoing shift in perspective propelled my stomach to places it did not belong.

The complex zoomed OUT, then it zoomed IN.

Our view resolved to the main entrance of the multi-storied building. Ground floor.

"Whoa," Zander gasped, gripping my fingers like a lifeline.

"Oh, yeah. I need a warning for that."

"And I'll need a barf bag if you pull that stunt again, Nano," Zander growled.

Noted, Zander Cruz. Ordering barf bags now.

"No! Wait—*argh*. Never mind."

Shall we cancel the order, Zander Cruz?

"You know what, Nano? At times you are worse than clueless."

"Not something I've *ever* said," I snarked. My jibe earned me a dig in the ribs—where I'm most ticklish.

"Hey!"

"You earned that."

Recommencing program, Zander and Jayda Cruz.

Once the acute sensation of free fall had passed and I had swallowed down my stomach from where it had lodged in my throat, a trail of blue footsteps appeared, overlaid on the first-floor blueprints. A date and time stamp blinked off to the side of the rendering so that we could tell when Overman's movements took place.

The footprints entered the elevator—and the elevator shot up. The first floor dropped away, and the second floor rose in its place.

I was a bit more ready for the rollercoaster ride, but Zander moaned. This time I squeezed *his* fingers.

The blue footprints crossed the floor and stepped into what we knew was Overman's office—two levels below the Director's suite. Sometime soon, I wanted to visit Overman's office in person, but that foray would require forethought and planning. I doubted any helpful trace would remain in his office, but it was worth a try.

We soon recognized Overman's day-to-day routine—arrival at 7:00 sharp each morning, regular visits to conference rooms and other offices, hours spent in his own office, lunch at 12:30 each afternoon (frequently eating in the cafeteria, other times leaving the campus), and his daily departure time, around 5:00 or 5:30, once as late as 6:00.

"Long hours," Zander noted.

What we couldn't see were the activities Overman engaged in—phone calls, emails, meetings, conversations. The nanomites would scrub through those logs for us, and we would study them together another evening.

Day followed day of similar movements. Nothing appeared out of the ordinary—not until the evening Overman disappeared. He returned to his office from a meeting at 4:30. Five o'clock came and went, then 5:30 and 5:45 without his leaving for the day. At six o'clock Overman had still not left his office. The minutes ticked off until it was 6:15. 6:30. 6:45.

"Why is he still in his office?" I whispered.

With no warning, the blue footprints signifying Overman's badge left his office and walked to the elevator. Overman's badge descended the elevator. The elevator stopped on the first floor. Overman got out, proceeded to the front entrance as usual, then exited the building.

You have watched the current badge tracking to its end, Jayda Cruz. We recommend overlaying the movements of other badges within ten feet of Wayne Overman's badge.

"Play the last hour, overlaying the badges of other personnel who come within ten feet of Overman."

Rendering now, Jayda Cruz.

The nanomites played the footage on fast-forward. There was Overman, ostensibly sitting in his office. The timer off to the side showed an hour passing in five minutes. Again, we had no idea what was actually happening in his office. Was he on the phone? Reading or sending emails? Overman may as well have been Schrödinger's cat. We knew he was in there, but was he alive or dead?

At ten after six, two sets of footprints appeared in Overman's office.

"Wait. Back that up and pan out to the entire floor," Zander demanded.

The nanomites pulled back and reran the last few minutes at normal speed. Two sets of prints got off the elevator, walked directly to Overman's office, and entered.

"Pull back again, Nano," I asked. "Rerun from the time the two people get off the elevator. This time I want to see every badge on the floor."

The nanomites zoomed out and reran the simulation. No other badges showed up on the floor.

"He was alone." Zander and I spoke at the same time.

"Nano, can you tell us who those two people are?"

They are members of the security team, Jayda Cruz. Security police officers.

"What happens next?"

Zander and I watched as the officers' footprints moved away from Overman's office while he remained in it. The officers entered the elevator and descended to the first floor where they exited and returned to the Safety and Security Department.

Zander and I were silent for a minute. Finally, I said, "So, this tells us nothing other than Overman stayed late the night he disappeared and that two SPOs briefly visited him."

Yes. Nothing to suggest anything amiss. Although his normal departure from work occurs between 5:00 and 5:30, tracking records for the past year show Mr. Overman staying beyond six o'clock seven times. You have watched the current badge tracking to its end, Jayda Cruz.

"You said that already, Nano."

"Um, hold on," Zander interjected. "You said, 'the current badge tracking.' What do you mean by 'current'?"

We found that the tracking records have been altered, Zander Cruz.

I huffed in exasperation. "And you're just *now* telling us this?"

It was necessary for you to view the tracking footage released to base security and the police who investigated Mr. Overman's disappearance.

"And said tracking footage indicated nothing out of the ordinary."

Exactly, Jayda Cruz.

"Nano," Zander said, "Tell us more about the altered tracking records."

The alterations were quite sophisticated, Zander Cruz; however, we noticed that the logs were off by two milliseconds. A human would not have detected such a discrepancy.

"Two milliseconds?"

Yes. Two one-thousandths of a second. When the records were spliced, the resulting timeline of the events lost two milliseconds. It was, we are certain, an unintentional error, but an error nevertheless.

"Video footage," I whispered. "Show us the video footage of the elevator at the time Overman supposedly exited."

We can, Jayda Cruz, however the video is a repeat from August two years ago.

"A repeat?"

We scanned video footage of the elevator, beginning with the night of Overman's disappearance, going backward in time. We discovered that Wayne Overman wore the same suit, shirt, and tie on August 4, two years past, as he did when he arrived the morning he disappeared. Someone spliced footage of him leaving on that date two years ago into the feed from the night of his disappearance.

The police and base security have not discovered this manipulation of the video footage. They have not realized that the briefcase he carried that evening is not the same one he arrived with. Although the differences are subtle, we noted them. They are further proof that the video footage of his exit the night he disappeared was falsified.

I shivered. "Whatever happened, happened right there, at the NSA."

Yes, so we have discovered.

"You have more to show us?"

We recovered bits of the deleted badge tracking files, Jayda Cruz, and have recreated what we could. It provides a more accurate picture of the events that night.

Zander cleared his throat. "Show us, Nano."

The layout of Overman's floor reappeared, with Overman's badge in his office. The two security police officers entered his office. Moments later, they left his office. Overman's badge remained behind.

"What? Isn't this what we've already seen, Nano?"

Continue watching, Jayda Cruz.

The SPOs got into the elevator but, rather than going down, they went up two floors . . . to the executive suite. The officers' prints led to a large office where they joined three other sets of prints.

The five badges remained in the office for nearly fifteen minutes. After ten minutes had passed, I started fidgeting.

"What's going on, Nano?"

Patience, Jayda Cruz.

Another four minutes ticked by on the timeline before anything happened—before things started to become clear.

Four of the prints exited the office at the same time. They walked two abreast to the elevator. They entered the same way, two ranks of two badges.

"Curious," I murmured. "They look like they're marching or something."

"Not marching," Zander whispered. "Carrying."

I looked at him and back to the nanomites' rendering, not understanding.

The elevator with the four badges went down but did not stop at the ground level. It descended into the basement where the four badges, still maintaining their odd formation, walked to what the nanomites had labeled "loading dock."

After a minute, two badges disappeared from the screen. We watched the remaining two return to the elevator, go up, and step off at Overman's floor—where Overman's badge continued to blink inside his office.

The two SPOs entered Overman's office. Seconds later, Overman's badge blinked off.

"What just happened?"

"They broke or somehow shorted out his badge," Zander replied.

"But . . ."

"Didn't you get it?"

"No. I . . . I'm lost."

"Nano, the four badges leaving the executive floor. They were all SPOs?"

Yes, Zander Cruz.

"They carried Overman down the elevator, Jayda. Put him in a vehicle parked in the loading dock. Two SPOs drove off with him. Two returned to his office and deactivated his badge."

I stared at the layout again. "Nano. Zoom in on the executive suite."

The basement layout faded and gave way to the fourth floor.

"Zoom in on the office where the five badges were."

Two SPOs had removed Overman's badge from him and left it in his office. They had escorted him upstairs where he had either been killed or knocked unconscious. Four SPOs carried him to the basement and placed him in a vehicle. Two SPOs drove him away—and Overman was never seen again.

The office where Overman had met his fate was, like the rest of the NSA schematics, clearly labeled. My breath caught as I read the label: Deputy Director, National Security Agency. Senior civilian leader of the NSA. Responsible for guiding and directing the NSA's operations, studies, and policy.

The honorable Lawrence Danforth.

"Oh, Zander. We need to call Gamble. Right away. The President . . . he needs to know."

⌘

"HAVE YOU MET the Repository's new hire? Jayda Cruz?"

"You mean the gal who stole your job?" Rob snickered as he said it.

"Shut up, Rob. There's something off about her."

"Agree. She brought a dead key fob to the Help Desk this morning and played out some flirty little scene with me."

"Flirty? Doesn't sound like Cruz."

"Yeah? Well, she really laid it on thick. It was about all I could do not to laugh in her face. It was kind of fun, pretending to be taken in by it."

"Somehow, I doubt you did much pretending, Rob."

"You don't need to be so nasty. It wasn't my idea to dress and act the part of a geek."

"Rob, you *are* a geek. You were placed in IT to be our eyes inside the network—not to be cool."

"And you were tasked with getting access to Repository information requests, so I could trace those back to the requestors."

"Don't act smart, Rob. I was prepped for that job. You pulled the interviews and hiring recommendations yourself. I had the highest interview scores out of all the candidates . . . and then they hire this Jayda Cruz out of the blue and it turns out she's a nobody with zero intelligence background?"

"You did have the highest scores—until Cruz interviewed."

"How is that possible without any intelligence experience? Someone had to have manipulated the data."

"I've looked at the logs. Nothing. There's no evidence of tampering with the files."

"I don't know how they did it, but this Jayda Cruz is not what she appears to be. She's smart but, like I said, something's off. And if someone planted her here, that means there's another player in the game."

"I'll keep an eye on her."

"You do that. She didn't return from lunch today with her team. Macy mentioned she was going outside for a walk, but when she came back to our department she was fresh as a daisy. In this humidity? Not likely. She should have shown some signs of perspiration. I want to know where she really went."

"I'll track her badge movements when I get into work tomorrow and let you know what I find."

"Check the video feeds, too. I'll call you again tomorrow evening, same time."

⌘

OUR SESSION WITH THE NANOMITES—walking through their renderings of the NSA complex and reviewing Overman's badge tracking data—had taken hours. It was well after midnight before Zander and I spoke to Gamble. It took another hour to explain what the nanomites had uncovered to Gamble's satisfaction.

When he understood what the nanomites had found and could repeat it back to us, he said, "I'll pass this along ASAP."

⌘⌘⌘⌘

CHAPTER 8

I COULDN'T REALLY SLEEP the rest of the night, so when I arrived at work Friday morning, I was jumpy and on edge. It didn't help that the oppressive late-June heat seemed to dog me no matter where I was, even during my commute. I ran my car's air conditioner on high at seven in the morning and still perspired like I'd run a marathon at noon.

Macy noticed. "Hey. Everything okay?"

"Yup. This heat. Just didn't sleep well last night."

Macy's expressive brows jutted toward her hairline. "Huh. You. *You* didn't sleep well? Girl, you ever try sleeping with two kick boxers going ten rounds in your belly? Don't *tell* me you didn't sleep well."

I snort-laughed, slapped a hand over my mouth, and shook with stifled hilarity. When I could talk, it was only between gasps. "Oh, man . . . Oh, Macy. That . . . that's . . . I'm sorry, but that's . . . that's hysterical."

"Hysterical? Uh-huh. Really? Those boys' shenanigans have bruised my kidneys and permanently displaced ribs. They have stomped my bladder so flat it won't hold more than a teaspoon anymore—and every time I sneeze, it lets go."

"I-I-I—" It was all I could do to hold it together.

"Harrumph. Glad I could brighten your outlook, Jayda."

I grinned at Macy. She grinned back.

It was her last day at the NSA.

"I'm going to miss you, Macy."

"I'll miss you, too, Jayda. Wish we were going to work together longer."

"Will you let me know when the twins come? I'd like to bring you a hot meal and perhaps a few to put in your freezer for later. You know, for when, in those first weeks or months, everything gets to be too much, and cooking is the last thing on your mind?"

I could see that Macy was touched.

After Macy had assigned me a few tasks and returned to her desk, I slammed a protein drink and two power bars. Eventually, I felt a little energy seep into my bones. I even managed to yank my thoughts away from what the nanomites had shown us last night . . . I cringed every time I envisioned what had likely happened to Wayne Overman in Deputy Director Danforth's office—only two months ago.

I was updating the project plan's Gantt chart when I remembered Gamble's warnings before I started my job.

Your first duty, the most essential of your tasks, is to keep a low profile. No, not a low *profile, but* no *profile. Nada, zip, nil. We can't have either of you even registering a blip on our adversaries' radar. Do* nothing *to draw attention to yourselves.*

Nothing. *We tracked Overman's badge movements . . .*

I swallowed hard. *I should have left my badge in the restroom yesterday—hidden it in there. I shouldn't have worn it to IT after lunch.*

"Nano. We need . . . we need to go back and change my whereabouts yesterday in the badging software."

We agree, Jayda Cruz.

At lunchtime, Macy and I again walked together to the cafeteria. When we reached the restroom I'd used yesterday, I touched Macy's arm.

"I'll catch up with you."

"Sure, Jayda. I'll save you a seat."

I ducked into the restroom's entrance and zipped back out under the nanomites' cover. Ran all the way to IT. When I reached the doorway, I peered inside. Rob was seated at the help desk, typing furiously on his keyboard.

"Nano, I need you to amend my whereabouts yesterday and today in the badge tracking software. Make sure it doesn't show me coming here today or a second time yesterday."

When I crept inside the IT Department, a stream of nanomites left me for Rob's workstation, their "in" to the main network. I was close to the row of chairs where people waited in line, so I eased myself into one of them. Unfortunately, the chairs sat on linoleum.

And the stupid chair creaked.

Rob's fingers paused on his keyboard. His head came up. While I held my breath, he glanced around. Twice.

I sat as still as I could. "Nano. Find that creak and muffle it when I stand up."

It would be easier for us to plug the man's ears when the time comes, Jayda Cruz.

"Whatever works best."

I waited, fidgeting, figuring the nanomites would finish in under five minutes, but it was fifteen minutes before they streamed back to me and I tiptoed from the room.

I jogged back to the restroom, in and out in seconds. When I reappeared, I held my hand to my stomach—just in case anyone was to notice that I had spent going on twenty minutes in the bathroom. By the time I joined Macy and the rest of my team at our table, they were almost finished with their food.

"Jayda, what happened to you?" Macy asked.

I grimaced a little. "Dunno. My stomach is acting up. Been in the restroom all this time. Maybe I caught a bug somewhere?"

Macy held her palm toward me. "Do not share your grief with me, woman. I want some stomach bug like I want another month of hauling these two Sumo wrestlers around."

"Yeah. You're right."

I sat a few seats away and toyed with my food. The thing was, I *didn't* feel all that great. I was alternately okay, then overheated. It seemed to come in waves.

"Nano, what's going on? Am I sick?"

No answer.

I would press them on it later, but at the moment, I was content to sit quietly and worry over the fate of Wayne Overman. "Nano . . . can you come up with a way for us to find out what became of the President's friend?"

We have the identities of the four SPOs who carried him down to the loading dock, Jayda Cruz. However, to confront and question them would not be advisable at this juncture. It would alert others who are involved.

The nanomites were right. We could surveil the SPOs, even surveil Deputy Director Danforth, but we could make no overt move on any of them—not until the extent of the conspiracy was known and could be proved. Gamble would have to decide how to handle surveillance.

I sighed. How many NSA personnel had been involved in the conspiracy? Members of the in-house security force, yes. And an individual or individuals to doctor the video feeds and badge tracking data—and not just anyone. Someone very good at it.

How high in the NSA had the conspiracy gone? Deputy Director Danforth certainly. Who else? And where else? How could we identify all of the conspirators? How would we ever know if we'd gotten them all?

President Jackson has placed his hope and trust in me and in the nanomites to uncover what is hidden, but I am no spy. I have no training— and I have already made mistakes.

Suddenly, what he expected of me was overwhelming.

Eggshells. I was walking on eggshells, the fate of the president's safety and his administration resting on my shoulders. *My shoulders!*

If I were to make another mistake—give myself away and lose the tactical advantage of the nanomites—would the President and Mrs. Jackson suffer for my error?

O Lord, I am so out of my depth here.

I couldn't wait for this wretched day to end.

Rob sighed. "Okay, so I did what you asked, Kiera. First thing this morning after I got to my workstation, I checked out Jayda Cruz's movements yesterday."

"What did you find?"

He was quiet for a moment.

"Well?"

"Something kinda strange. I mean really strange. Like, *really* strange. And I, um, I am *not* nuts. I swear it."

"Yeah? I'm beginning to wonder, Rob."

"No, I'm serious. You said she was going outside to take a walk? Well, her badge never left the building. Instead, it looks like she came to IT from the cafeteria."

"She went back to IT after lunch?"

"Yeah, like, in and out of the restroom, then to IT. That's the first strange part. I took an early lunch and was back on the desk when the tracking software said she crossed our department threshold, except I never saw her. *She was not here.*"

"Are you sure?"

Rob snapped at her. "Give me a break. Like I could miss anyone walking in the door. My desk is practically *in the doorway.*"

"Sorry. Simmer down. Has to be a reasonable answer. Did you check the video feeds?"

"Well, of course I did, but . . ."

"But what?"

"That's the second strange thing. She walked into the restroom around the corner from the cafeteria."

"And?"

"And six minutes later, she came out."

"So?"

"*Listen.* Her badge says she went into the restroom, immediately *left* the restroom, came to IT, then *returned* to the restroom. But, the video feed didn't show her leaving the restroom for six minutes—not until after her badge went to IT and came back."

"Glitch in the video feed? In the badge software?"

"A glitch is when a camera goes down or a server crashes. Glitches don't explain two functioning systems contradicting each other."

"I assume you double-checked."

"Triple checked. Just to be sure, I rewound the video footage, took a screen cap of her entering the restroom and leaving the restroom and pasted the two images into a Word doc—then I checked the timestamps of the screen caps against her badge movements. Same result. Badge says one thing; video footage says something else."

He blew out a breath. "So, now we're getting to the creepy and strange part."

"What? What are you talking about?"

"Lunch time today. I was tracking this Cruz chick in real time. Actually, I set an alert on her badge to signal me when she was on the move. Same thing happens.

"She goes into the same restroom outside the cafeteria—and doesn't come out for nineteen minutes. *But*, her badge says she came to IT and was here, in the waiting area, for fifteen minutes."

"I think your fears have been realized, Rob. You *are* nuts."

"Nope. I screen capped the time-stamped video feed of her entering the restroom, screen capped her badge coming here to IT, and a second cap of the restroom entrance while her badge was in IT. I tell you, Kiera, I was tempted to send that file to my personal email account and then forward it to you."

Kiera answered, "No, don't do that. The firewall might flag it, and we can't chance blowing our covers."

"Said I was *tempted*, Kiera, not *stupid*. Anyway, that's not all of it."

"All of what?"

"All of the creepy-strange stuff."

The voice on the other end sighed. "What else?"

"Well, see, I'm glad I took those screen caps, because after her badge left IT? I went back to the video feed of the restroom. Sure enough, a minute or so later, she came out."

"No big eye-opener there," his caller retorted.

"Yeah, except . . . except, when I went back to the badge tracking software? It was all . . ."

"It was what?"

"Changed. It had changed. It no longer shows that she came to IT, today or yesterday afternoon."

"Rob . . ."

Rob's voice sank to a whisper. "I swear to you, Kiera, it *changed*. I can prove it, because I have the screen caps of both the tracking and the time-stamped video feed."

Before she could answer, he pushed on with dogged determination.

"There's definitely something off about this Cruz woman. Big time."

He didn't mention how he'd felt eyes watching him, how he'd heard the creak of a chair when no one else was in the room.

My credibility is in enough trouble as it is.

She cleared her throat. "Yeah, okay. Well, thanks, Rob. I'll think about what you've told me."

Not "what you've found" or "what the tracking software and video take *proved*." Just, "I'll think about what you've *told* me."

Rob hung up and closed his eyes. He thought about what he hadn't revealed to his caller. For a long time that day, he'd stared at the open document on his workstation, before he'd minimized it and chewed on the inside of his cheek. After considering his options, he'd chosen what he believed was the safest one.

He toggled back to the file, navigated to a junk folder on the IT network, and saved the doc with the innocuous file name of "misc-labels," then changed the document's file extension from .docx to ".exe." Should anyone notice the file, they would assume it was an executable file, not a Word doc.

He whispered to himself, "I know what I saw, Kiera. And I know there's something crazy weird about Jayda Cruz."

⌘

I FINISHED OUT MY first full week at the NSA and said goodbye to Macy.

"Don't forget," I said, writing out my number for her. "Call me when those bouncing baby boys make their landing."

"Bouncing? Don't encourage them to come out like that. I just hope the doctor has quick reflexes." Macy took my number and, surprising us both, I think, we hugged.

"Take care, Jay."

"You, too. I . . . I'll be praying for you."

"Thanks. I appreciate your good thoughts."

Jesus is more than good thoughts, Macy. I hope I can tell you how wonderful he is someday soon.

In a thoughtful mood, alternately praying for Macy and thinking about Wayne Overman, I drove home through the mad Friday commuter traffic. I was looking forward to the weekend—not particularly for R&R, but for time with Zander and for the opportunity to burn off the excess energy percolating through my body. Sitting behind a computer screen most of the day was difficult for me with my overcharged metabolism.

I could tell that Zander was feeling antsy, too.

How could I tell?

Here it was, Friday evening, the weekend stretching before us. We'd scarfed down a substantial dinner, and now Zander was pacing our apartment living room, his stalking back and forth a passable rendition of a caged tiger at the zoo.

Yes, he'd run five miles with me every morning, and he'd spent the week pounding the pavement searching for employment, but we were both overdue for a real workout—something challenging and, most definitely, *exhausting.*

And we hadn't heard back from Gamble regarding Lawrence Danforth. Had Gamble conveyed our findings to Axel Kennedy? I think the "not hearing back" was grating on both of us.

I interrupted his umpteenth journey between the front door and the kitchen. "Hey, how about we get out of here? We may have started Gamble's 'Spy 101' course, but I think it's time to get going on the *serious* training we talked about."

Zander halted. "Stick fighting?"

He was eager, and I grinned at his enthusiasm. Perhaps I grinned, too, because I knew what the nanomites' virtual reality trainer had in store for him.

It would be highly entertaining to observe.

"Yup. That dojo Gamble arranged for us is a few miles from here. He said the owner teaches stick fighting. That means he has escrima sticks. Want to check it out?"

"Let's go."

We parked in a packed theater parking lot two blocks from the dojo and, rendered invisible by the nanomites' mirrors, strolled down the alley behind the theater to the dojo's rear door. Since Zander had a lot to learn concerning the nanomites, I figured our outing could serve multiple purposes.

"Zander, ask the nanomites to unlock the door and disable the alarm."

"Right."

A moment later we were inside. A contingency of nanomites flew ahead of us to explore the interior. They returned with the dojo's simple floor plan and an inventory of its contents.

"Equipment this way," Zander said.

When we found the equipment lockers, I suggested that Zander choose two practice sticks—full-size padded rattan sticks about 24 inches long—and padded headgear. I appropriated a set of sticks for myself.

We went into the dojo and took off our shoes. Stood on the wood floor in the middle of the rectangular room.

"We'll need shoes for this eventually, but tonight we can practice barefoot," I said.

Zander looked from his sticks to mine. "What kind of sticks are those?"

"Regulation-weight escrima sticks. Made of seasoned hardwood."

Zander frowned. "You're going to come at me with those?"

I went all wide-eyed and innocent. "What? Oh dear, no. You and I are not going to spar. The nanomites have prepared a training program for you."

"They have a training program?"

"It's virtual reality, like how we walked through the 3D rendering of the NSA buildings. You close your eyes, go into the warehouse, and the nanomites will begin your training. And you won't need your practice sticks right away."

Eyeing me with a smidge of distrust, Zander set his sticks aside and closed his eyes.

I did, too. I wouldn't miss this for the world.

The nanomites' tank-sized VR instructor, Gus-Gus, appeared in front of Zander.

As I had observed in my first encounter with Gus-Gus, he was built like a boulder—a boulder with bulging tendons the size of lead pipes and muscles that resembled rocks popping out of his skin.

Zander freaked.

I opened my eyes in the dojo to find my husband halfway down the room. When he realized he was back in the dojo, he stopped running and spun around, his panicked eyes jittering back and forth. "What the devil was that?"

I couldn't answer.

"Are you . . . are you laughing at me?"

I was doubled over and couldn't breathe. My sides ached.

Zander's eyes narrowed. "You could have warned me."

Where's the fun in that?

I sat on the floor. Still could not draw air. I was laughing too hard.

I gasped, "S-s . . . sorry."

"No, you're not."

"Nooo," I agreed, another bout of glee stealing my breath away.

Zander shook his head. "Brat. What was that thing?"

I drew my knees up to my face and sucked air. "G-Gus-Gus."

"Gus-Gus?"

"VR . . . trainer."

Zander Cruz, your training program is running. Please reenter the warehouse and follow your trainer's instructions.

With a parting glare at me, Zander closed his eyes. I went with him into the warehouse's training environ and stood at a safe distance from Zander and Gus-Gus.

"I am your instructor, Zander Cruz. You will follow my directions."

I watched as Gus-Gus demonstrated the same simple three-part hand and foot movement drill he'd shown me in my first lesson.

Zander followed suit. Easily. Gus-Gus added steps and sped up the routines. Zander followed flawlessly what had taken me hours to master when I started my training. Yeah, me: Gus-Gus' uncoordinated, non-athletic, couldn't-even-throw-like-a-girl student. It had taken hours of repetition and perseverance just to come up to where Zander started.

I stopped laughing. "Dumb jock," I grumbled.

"Jayda Cruz."

My head jerked around at the unfamiliar voice. Behind me was a faceless, black-clad figure, more intimidating than Gus-Gus for his ominous lack of features.

"It has been months since you trained, Jayda Cruz. You have lost your edge and are no longer optimal in this art."

The figure drew his sticks. "I will soon have you back in fighting form."

Before I could react, he was on me.

"Owww!" I hopped away from my opponent, my left thigh stinging. I scrambled to locate my sticks. Before I got them in hand, my opponent had landed another blow.

Then my rusty training began to come back to me. I sidestepped, weaving my sticks in a fluid blur, and attacked. Over the next hour, I even managed a strike or two—my one to his five.

Yikes. I'm going to hurt tonight.

The nanomites would mitigate the bruising of my workout and even relieve much of the pain, but I would still suffer the stiff soreness of not having used my body this fully in weeks.

No, in months, I admitted. Not since the nanomites and I had rescued Dr. Bickel from the house on the White Sands Missile Range and Colonel Greaves had shot me with a Taser, killing most of the nanomites. Nearly killing me in the process.

Distracted by my thoughts, I miscalculated and fell into my trainer's trap. His slicing attack connected with my elbow, sending a shock wave clear up to my shoulder and into my neck.

"Yiiii!"

I opened my eyes, dropped my sticks, and limped to a bench alongside the dojo's wall. I leaned my head back and cradled my deadened arm.

"That was fun." Zander plopped down on the bench next to me.

"Um . . ." The nerves in my arm were waking up, screaming like an outraged troop of monkeys.

Jayda Cruz, we are sending aid to your injuries and inducing pain-alleviating neurotransmitters.

A long sigh of relief burbled in my throat.

Meanwhile Zander, ebullient and oblivious to my discomfort, raved on about Gus-Gus and what he had learned from his training program. "Best workout *ever*. Can't wait for our next session. How often do you think we can do this? I might have to find somewhere I can train in the daytime while you're at work. Say, let's order our own sticks and some shoes tonight."

I didn't answer him, and I didn't say what I was thinking just then.

Dumb jock.

⌘⌘⌘⌘

CHAPTER 9

OUR FRIDAY NIGHT WORKOUT was just what we'd both needed, but when I dragged myself out of bed Saturday morning, I was sticky and damp. For some reason, I'd heated up and sweated through my t-shirt during the night. Twice.

"Ugh." I started stripping the sheets from our bed.

Zander wandered into the bedroom, coffee in hand. "What's up?"

"Washing our sheets. I got all sweaty last night."

"With the air conditioning on?"

"Yeah. I know. Weird."

He helped me get the load in the washer and clean sheets on the bed, then handed me my coffee. Although we slept in an hour on Saturdays and enjoyed a first cup of coffee together on our little balcony, we basically followed the same routine after that: a five-mile jog, followed by Bible time.

By eight, we were out the door, pounding through our morning run.

Gamble called us later that morning, and we put him on speaker phone. Our conversation was brief and to the point. "I conveyed your findings up the chain and received a reply: The President wants to see you. Both of you."

Zander and I exchanged a look of consternation.

"Uh, when?" I asked.

"This evening. Five o'clock in the Residence dining room. Kennedy asked me to tell you that the President urges you to bring your appetites."

Even over the phone, I could "see" Gamble's bemused expression.

"Hmm. Well, then I guess maybe we should."

"Yeah. Message received," Zander added.

I glanced his way and snorted. My husband's normally healthy and tanned complexion had paled.

I'd been nervous when I'd met the President, too.

⌘

ZANDER AND I DROVE into D.C. and parked near Union Station. From the station, we took the Red Line Metro west three stops, got off, and hoofed it west toward the White House. Nearer our goal, the long outlines of late afternoon sun made it easy for us to walk into a patch of shadow and emerge under the nanomites' cover.

I could tell Zander was nervous, and I can't say I blamed him. By the time we reached Pennsylvania Avenue, he was a big bag of jitters.

"Hey," I whispered. "You know it's going to be okay, right?"

"A lot of firsts," Zander replied.

"I understand. First time meeting the President."

"I'm more concerned with 'first time breaking into the White House.'"

I smiled. Had it been six months since my "first time"? However, I'd had a wealth of other experiences with the nanomites under my belt that had bolstered my confidence, whereas Zander's relationship with them was new and, as yet, untried.

"We have an invitation, remember?"

"Not that the Secret Service knows of."

"And we're invisible."

"Riiight."

We strolled along Lafayette Park, observing the late evening tourists peering through the bars of the wrought iron fence and taking photographs of the West Wing and the White House's north-facing portico. We walked the length of the park and back—enough time, I hoped, for Zander to settle his nerves and prepare himself for our next move.

When we had walked back to the northeast gate, I pointed. A car was pulling into the drive, and the gate was still open.

"Here we go."

Up the shaded, curving drive we went, giving the guardhouse near the top a wide berth. I led Zander up the steps of the portico to the state entrance. The nanomites knew what to do. When I reached for the double doors, they were already unlocked, the sensors and other security measures temporarily defeated.

We slipped inside and let the door close behind us. We were both wearing new cloth-soled shoes, the kind that didn't squeak on tile or linoleum.

The Entrance Hall and Cross Hall of the State Entrance are pretty awe-inspiring, even the second time around and despite a Secret Service agent standing post nearby. I figured Zander was rubbernecking, but I was, too. After we'd gawked a few minutes, I touched his arm, and we moved toward the Grand Staircase on our left.

Zander and I crept up the stairs to the Residence level, the nanomites checking the way ahead of us. When we reached the Residence landing I felt more comfortable. I'd spent a whole night on this floor, briefing President Jackson on Harmon's plot and helping him plan his countermoves.

"Stay close," I whispered to Zander. I led the way from the landing to the West Sitting Hall. The door to the Residence Dining Room was open.

We stepped into the room, and the nanomites uncovered us. I even had the nanomites dissolve their disguise on my facial features.

The President and First Lady looked up. They were seated at the dining table, waiting for us—but before I could utter a word of greeting, the nanomites stopped me.

Jayda Cruz, we have detected a listening device in this room.

I placed my finger to my lips and shook my head.

"Nano, take care of the bugs, please." They were already flying from me before I finished my request.

My gesture had prevented our hosts from speaking, but it had not checked the look of fury that crossed the President's face when he realized what I meant. Mrs. Jackson, not quite on the same page yet, gripped her husband's hand, her eyes wide.

The four of us waited in silence until the nanomites returned to me.

We have permanently disabled the device, Jayda Cruz. It will appear that the apparatus shorted out.

"Thank you, Nano."

I addressed our hosts. "Good evening, Mr. President, Mrs. Jackson."

They both rose at my greeting, and Maddie Jackson responded first. She came toward us, smiling a welcome, taking my hand in hers. "Gemma. So good to see you again."

"Thank you, ma'am. It is good to see you, too."

The President held out his hand. "Miss Keyes, thank you for coming. I take it our dining room was bugged?" He was still furious, but not at me.

"It is an honor, sir. And, yes, the room was bugged. The nanomites have permanently disabled it; however, I should think whoever installed it will replace it as soon as they can."

I turned toward Zander. "May I introduce my husband, Zander Cruz?"

The President extended his hand. "Thank you for coming, Mr. Cruz."

As shell-shocked as he was, Zander managed the surreal situation. "A pleasure, sir."

Maddie Jackson glanced from Zander to me. "Our congratulations on your wedding—and our apologies for using the wrong names."

"Yes, ma'am. I'm Jayda Cruz now."

"It must have been difficult, my dear, to let go of your life as Gemma."

"In some respects, it was, ma'am. In others, it was quite freeing. No one is hunting Jayda Cruz."

"And we want to keep it that way," Robert Jackson said. "Come. Sit down with us. I hope you brought your appetites?"

"Always, sir," I laughed.

The table was set for seven and spread with enough food to feed a platoon.

Maddie Jackson took my arm and led me to the seat next to hers. "We invited our son and his crew to dinner with us this evening. His three boys are teens now, and they eat like NFL linebackers. Sadly, at the last moment—after the staff had laid the table and placed the food, in fact—my son and his family were . . . unavoidably detained."

She waggled her brows. "It's too bad, really. Our chef even baked his famous Coconut Dream cookies especially for our dinner guests. Robert and I would hate for them . . . to go to waste."

"Oh, me, too, ma'am."

Mrs. Jackson and I exchanged smiles of mutual appreciation.

The President gestured to Zander. "Please, Mr. Cruz, take this seat. Plenty of time to talk shop after we've enjoyed our dinner."

And enjoy it we did. While Zander and I plowed into the feast set before us, Robert Jackson cut into a lean steak with a side of steamed vegetables and Mrs. Jackson nibbled on a chicken salad. I caught Maddie staring at me as I put away a third helping of loaded mashed potatoes and reached for a slice of cake.

Shaking her head, she muttered, "It's not fair. Really, it's not."

I grinned around a forkful of red velvet cake with cream cheese frosting. "No, ma'am."

The President cast a woeful glance between my wedge of cake and his vegetables. "It sure isn't."

Laying aside his fork, he began to regale Zander with his and the First Lady's reaction to their initial encounter with me. "I thought I'd lost my mind, frankly," Jackson said. "Here was this earnest young woman who had somehow slipped through White House security, *standing in our living room.* 'Excuse me, Mr. President,' she says, *very* politely. 'May I have a few minutes of your time?'"

Jackson's mimicry was good enough to elicit chuckles around the table.

"Well, civility be hanged; I, of course, tried to yell for the Secret Service—only to discover that I could not open my mouth. Her nanomites had sealed it shut! I thought I had been dropped into an episode of the Twilight Zone."

"I'm very sorry, Mr. President. That had to be terrifying." I felt worse about it now than I had at the time.

"Terrifying? It was, but all in all, you handled yourself well that evening, Gem—er, Jayda."

Mrs. Jackson interjected a dry observation. "It wasn't long into their acquaintance, however, before they were shouting at each other."

Zander gaped at me. "You *shouted* at the President?"

I had the grace to blush. "I did—and I apologize again, Mr. President—but when I told him that his life was in danger, he . . ." I glanced at Robert Jackson, "you didn't believe me."

"I think you mean I accused *you* of being the danger."

"Yes, sir. That's when I lost my temper and, er, raised my voice."

Maddie Jackson took over the narration. "When their 'raised voices' awakened me, I barged into the living room, breathing smoke and fire, ready to raise a little dust myself. I found Robert and this unfamiliar young woman glaring at each other—and then, *poof.* The young woman disappeared."

She fixed Zander with a look. "It was, beyond all comparison, the strangest moment of my life."

"I can imagine, ma'am."

"I wager you can—but now you and, er, Jayda share this ability?"

Zander and I explained how the nanomites had doubled their numbers and why. We even talked a little of our unconventional courtship and wedding. President and Mrs. Jackson listened with genuine interest, asking questions and often shaking their heads in amazement.

When dinner was behind us—the remains of the feast bearing resemblance to the track of an F5 tornado—the President stood and ushered us into their private living room. A man I recognized stood as we entered.

Before anyone said anything, the President pointed to the ceiling and raised his brows in a silent question.

"Clean, sir," I reported after a brief pause.

"Thank the Lord. I hope it is all right with both of you that I have asked Axel Kennedy to join us for your briefing?"

"Of course, Mr. President. Good to see you again, Mr. Kennedy."

"I'd say, 'the feeling's mutual,' except I've never actually met you— or even seen you, Ms. Cruz."

I laughed in surprised realization. "I guess you're right. My presence last time was . . . covert."

President Jackson explained, "After we began working with Agent Trujillo to track down Cushing last December, I briefed Axel on what happened in the Oval Office when Harmon died. He'd seen and heard some confounding things that day, things he couldn't wrap his head around."

"As honored as I am for the President to take me into his confidences, I've had difficulty believing a lot of what he's said about you—and now there are two of you?"

"I'm afraid so. This is my husband, Zander Cruz."

"Pleased to meet you, Mr. Cruz." Kennedy glanced at the President, who nodded. "Would you mind . . . so I can lay my disbelief to rest?"

"You'd like a demonstration?"

Kennedy shifted in discomfort. "If you please."

I shrugged—and disappeared. Seconds later, I tapped Kennedy on his shoulder.

He spun toward me—and I reappeared.

He took a step back. "Unbelievable."

"Satisfied, Axel?" the President asked.

"Once more?

This time I disappeared and reappeared behind the President and Mrs. Jackson.

"Now, Axel?"

"Um, yes, sir."

"Then let's sit down and begin, shall we?"

The five of us found seats and the President spoke first.

"Well, Jayda, Agent Gamble conveyed your message regarding my friend Wayne to Axel, who passed it to me, but I confess that the details may have become a bit garbled in translation. I asked you here because I wanted to hear it from you directly."

"I understand, sir."

"I think it would help to hear everything you've done and found since beginning your assignment. Within this room and for the sake of this investigation, I give you permission to reveal and speak of classified information."

The President's words "your assignment" drove home the point that my "job" was only a cover, a front, a means to an end—and that end was to expose Harmon's fellow conspirators in his attempt to usurp the presidency. It hit me anew how important my role was, and how acutely unprepared I was to carry the weight of such a responsibility.

For the next hour I explained the department I'd been assigned to, my position in the Repository, and how I'd provided the nanomites with access to the NSA's main network. I detailed how the nanomites had downloaded the NSA's floor plans, badge tracking data, and video feed.

I segued into Wayne Overman's movements on his last day at the NSA. "The nanomites discovered that the badge tracking data had been edited to show that Mr. Overman left work as usual (although later than was his norm), thus drawing the investigation into his disappearance away from the NSA. Fortunately, the nanomites were able to recover enough of the deleted data to recreate his actual movements and the movements of those around him."

Jayda Cruz, perhaps it would be helpful if we projected a rendering of the data for the President's benefit while you provide necessary commentary.

"Great idea, Nano."

Before I could prepare my audience, the nanomites dimmed the lights in the room. A sparkling stream floated from me to the coffee table between our seats and resolved into a 3D image.

"Um, the nanomites are providing visuals for us. What you see here is the floor plan of Mr. Overman's floor and his office."

"Fascinating," the President murmured.

Out of habit and training, Kennedy had jumped to his feet and moved to the President's side when the lights dimmed. He stood guard there for a minute before resuming his seat.

I explained to my audience, "The nanomites have superimposed the recovered badge tracking data onto this floor plan. Please watch the footprints and keep one eye on the time stamp as it progresses."

As I walked them through the data, including Overman's escorted, after-hours trip to the Deputy Director's office and the four SPOs, in lockstep, carrying Overman down to the basement, the President's expression sank.

"When Axel reported your findings, I didn't want to believe them. Didn't want to admit that Wayne was gone. However, I see now how you came to your conclusions."

The projected schematic faded, and the lights came up.

"How do you intend to proceed, Ms. Cruz?"

"Sir, we have identified the four SPOs involved from their badge IDs, and we know the Deputy Director was more than complicit. He gave them their instructions."

"Yes, Danforth. He's a weasel, but at least he's a civilian—as was Harmon. The NSA Director, however, is Department of Defense. We know Harmon had a man inside the Army's infectious diseases unit, and I have been hoping that a single soldier is as far as the infection has spread into the DOD. If the NSA Director were to be implicated, it would suggest a much deeper vein of traitors in the military. I hope that you, Jayda, will be able to rule the Director in or out of the conspiracy."

Jackson looked at Kennedy. "Axel, the Residence dining room was bugged. Our friends here disabled the device, but they are right in saying our enemies will likely replace it at their first opportunity."

The President, with hunted eyes, studied Zander and me. "Our enemies appear to be embedded in all facets of government, and they are encroaching on us here in the White House, too—here where I am supposed to be safe and my conversations private. They have plants within the White House Secret Service detail.

"Since only my personal detail is allowed in the Residence and Kennedy trusts them, our enemies evidently have plants in the house's staff. Someone on the same staff that changes our linens and serves our food bugged our personal dining room, for heaven's sake!

"The Secret Service is supposed to sweep the house for listening devices daily, but if the Service is compromised, how can I have confidence that they haven't wiretapped the entire West Wing, even the Oval Office?"

He sighed. "My administration is under siege. I don't know how much longer we can pretend that we don't know about their infiltration of the White House."

"Sir," Axel spoke, "if you are to conduct the business of our nation, we must act—even if it reveals that we know we are under attack. I just don't know how we can prove who the bad actors are and provide justification for dismissing them. If we could ferret them out, catch them at it, we could have them dismissed."

I had been thinking hard and had come up with an idea. "I would help if I could, but I have my hands full at the NSA. What if . . ." I slanted a look at Zander. "What if Zander were to aid you? He and the nanomites could sweep the White House and deactivate any listening devices he finds. And he could turn the tables on the enemy's agents planted in the ranks of the White House detail. Zander can walk throughout the house without notice, listen in on those who listen in on you, identify those who have been planted here, and snoop through their phones looking for links to other conspirators."

Three people turned their speculative examination on Zander—who squirmed under their scrutiny.

"Suppose Zander did catch a plant red-handed. How would that provide the justification we needed to have them dismissed—or arrested?"

"Maybe . . . maybe we don't need to have them dismissed to get rid of them, Mr. President. I would like the opportunity to brainstorm other methods of removing them with the nanomites. In any event, even knowing for certain *who* your enemies are gives you certain advantages."

The President looked to Kennedy and back before he agreed. "All right. Zander, set a time to meet Axel tomorrow. And I freely confess that I'll feel a bit less outnumbered with you close by."

Mrs. Jackson excused herself from the room as the President, Axel Kennedy, and Zander discussed the logistics of how best to use Zander. I folded in on my own thoughts as they strategized.

When Maddie returned, the President stood—and we stood with him. "Thank you for lending us your husband, Ms. Cruz," Jackson said. "The next few days or weeks should be . . . interesting. As for you and the NSA? Carry on. I want the guilty held accountable."

"I'm sure you understand, Mr. President, that it would be inadvisable to move against the individuals we've identified within the NSA at this time. As you say, we want to root out in their entirety those who conspired with Harmon."

"What do you propose, Ms. Cruz?"

I had my ideas now, even if I didn't know how we'd pull it off. With Zander's assignment at the White House and mine at the NSA, we were going to be strapped for resources.

That didn't deter me from stating my intentions.

"Sir, we're going to follow the conspirators we've identified. We will invade every nook, crack, and cranny of their lives. Our scrutiny will be pervasive, relentless, and inescapable. We will not stop until one or more of them leads us to the next link in the chain."

I felt Zander's questioning gaze flick my way.

The President, however, signaled his approval. "Be careful, Jayda. And Godspeed."

"Thank you, Mr. President."

"Jayda." Mrs. Jackson held out a plastic container. "These are for you and Zander, dear. Know they come with our love and gratitude."

Humbled, I accepted the container of cookies. "Thank you, ma'am. We will enjoy them."

⌘

WE HAD SCARCELY QUIT the White House grounds before Zander pressed me. "We're going to 'invade every nook, crack, and cranny of their lives'? 'Our scrutiny will be pervasive, relentless, and inescapable'? You sounded like a secret agent from a B movie—a bad B movie at that. And don't we need warrants or something?"

"We're long past warrants, Zander. We're operating under the President's direct orders, utterly in the black."

"Does that make us any better than Cushing's team?"

I slowed to a stop and blew out a breath of frustration. "I don't know. I just don't know. I want to stay within the law, but . . ."

"But the President's enemies aren't affected by such scruples?"

"Yeah, I guess that's right."

"It's a slippery slope, babe."

"I know—and I don't like it. Whatever happens, when this threat is over, we cannot go on using the nanomites in this way."

"Agreed."

⌘

BLAKE MORNINGSIDE, U.S. Secret Service Deputy Assistant Director, entered his condo, locked the door behind him, and set the alarm. Seconds after, he heard the muffled ring of a phone. The man unlocked his desk and eyed the burner phone with disquiet. The caller ID showed no name, but he recognized the number.

Pull yourself together, he told himself.

He put the phone to his ear. "Yes?"

"I really would prefer that you reported to me with more regularity."

The breathy voice on the other end never failed to make his skin tingle. It was both seductive and intimidating at the same time. While he and the woman saw each other in public with some regularity, they never interacted; however, Morningside knew her quite well. He knew, too, that her requests were not to be ignored.

"I have nothing new to report. My agents tell me that the President hasn't made a vice presidential selection. He has an uncanny ability to see how the parties would react to each candidate. At this point, we surmise that he may have put the selection process on hold."

"You surmise? What do his conversations tell you?

"That he is considering waiting until the election to choose a running mate."

"That is entirely unsatisfactory."

Morningside scrambled for something further to report. "The President, uh, did mention the name of the governor of Utah in passing today. He thought she stood a chance at confirmation."

"A woman. You're saying the President cannot find a *male* candidate to satisfy our increasingly divided Congress?"

"I'm saying he mentioned her name."

"And why not a woman—as long as we control her? Control being the objective, of course."

She turned inward. "Hmm. A woman, indeed. Too many variables. Lest Jackson select a candidate we cannot easily manipulate, I believe I must take matters into my own hands."

⌘⌘⌘⌘

CHAPTER 10

ZANDER AND I ARRIVED LATE for the morning service at Grace Chapel. We were bleary-eyed from a long planning session with the nanomites that had lasted much of the night and from the three hours' sleep we'd snatched on the couch at Gamble's rental early this morning that were not entirely restful.

More on that later.

We'd raced home at nine this morning, showered and changed, grabbed breakfast at a drive-through, and beat it to church. The worship service was well underway when we pulled into the parking lot.

What we caught of it was wondrous. I might not have a great voice, but I loved singing praises to God. I sank into the worship and gave it all I had.

After service ended, we kept our lunch date with the pastor and his wife. We met them at the door of a local steak house where Zander and Pastor Lucklow managed the introductions.

"Thank you for inviting us to lunch, Pastor Lucklow. This is my wife, Jayda."

"Delighted to meet you, Jayda. And this is my wife, Karen."

We settled into a booth and were, within a few minutes, comfortable with Brian and Karen Lucklow.

"I allow myself a less-than-healthy lunch once a week," Pastor Lucklow confided, "and I can assure you that the ribeye here is first-rate."

"That sounds great." I was thinking, *I'll take two—and two loaded baked potatoes*, but Zander and I had agreed to keep our lunch portions within normal limits.

As I scanned the dessert list, I regretted our decision.

After we'd placed our orders, Pastor Lucklow and his wife focused their attention on me, asking me about myself, my work, my interests. For work I replied with the nonspecific "project manager for a government contractor" and the Lucklows, acquainted with others who worked in classified settings, did not press me further. We did live in the shadow of D.C., Ft. Meade, and the Pentagon, after all.

At one point in our conversation, Pastor Lucklow mentioned the church's Celebrate Recovery program.

Zander replied, "I apologize for missing the meeting Thursday, Pastor. Something came up that I had to attend to. We've been praying about the program and plan to attend this coming week."

"I'm pleased to hear that. I'll let the assistant leaders know you're coming."

We passed a delightful hour and a half with the Lucklows. We exchanged the many details people do when getting to know each other, and the Lucklows proved to be a happy, humorous couple with a wealth of experiences in the Lord. I hadn't spent a lot of time with truly mature Christians, but I loved our time with them and appreciated that Zander and I came away feeling replete in body and soul.

Well, replete in soul anyway.

We watched and waited as the Lucklows' car pulled out of the parking lot before we zipped back inside. After drooling with indecision over the restaurant's pie case, we came away with two selections: Zander picked the blueberry sour cream pie; mine was fresh strawberry.

As the hostess boxed up our pies we eyed each other's purchase.

Zander broke first. "Split and share?"

"Agreed."

On the way to our car, I said, "Y'know, I kind of feel like an addict sneaking off to meet my dealer."

Zander laughed. "I think the First Lady had it right. *It isn't fair* that we get to eat whatever we like, as much as we like—but it *is* the best part of life with the nanomites."

"When you sit to dine with a ruler, note well what is before you, and put a knife to your throat if you are given to gluttony, Zander Cruz."

"Out of context, Nano."

The nanomites made a one-syllable noncommittal noise that sounded like, *Pfffft*.

"Do not crave his delicacies, for that food is deceptive."

"Nano, I can't help but wonder if you're jealous because we said eating whatever we wanted was the best part of life with you."

Their reply was frosted with condescension: *Zander Cruz, we are given neither to pettiness nor the flawed human emotions of envy or jealousy.*

Zander and I roared. I laughed so hard I lost control of the pie boxes on my lap. Half the whipped cream on the strawberry pie ended up on the box's inside wall.

Later, as I stuffed the first bite of strawberries (with whipped cream scraped off the inside of the box) into my mouth, I was certain I heard low-level nano-grumbling.

"Mmmmmm," I moaned, smirking at Zander.

Zander bit into his creamy blueberry pie with exaggerated ecstasy. "Ohhhh, yeah. The *best*."

It was five minutes before we caught our breath and could take another bite. It was hours before the nanomites spoke to us again.

⌘

W<small>E MET</small> G<small>AMBLE AT HIS CAR</small> that evening and escorted him to the rental house for our weekly meeting. Catching him up on the newest developments took the better part of an hour.

The grilling afterward took longer.

"Let me get this straight. Zander, you're going to report to the White House tomorrow and start identifying Secret Service agents and White House staff members who have been planted there to spy on the President and his administration?"

"Uh-huh."

"And Jayda, you're going to somehow surveil four SPOs and one NSA Deputy Director 24/7—all while holding down a full-time job, attending weekly tradecraft training and Zander's Celebrate Recovery thing?"

"Uh-huh."

"You guys are killing me."

"You look healthy enough."

"Don't get smart with me, Ms. Cruz."

I giggled. "Listen, I won't have to physically be with the surveillance targets to keep tabs on them. We brainstormed with the nanomites late last evening how best to accomplish our purposes."

"And?"

"And then," Zander answered, "we spent the remainder of the night here. Gotta say, you could've bought a more comfortable couch."

"Well, excuse me."

Zander grinned at Gamble. "Not a problem, but if we're going to be spending more nights here, could you buy a bed for us?"

Gamble ignored Zander's request. "Why did you need to spend the night here in the first place?"

"Before we tell you, we need to talk about confidentiality."

"Confidentiality?"

"If we tell you how we're going to surveil our targets, you must first swear that you will never disclose to another soul what we've done. No one, under any circumstances. If you cannot agree to secrecy, we'll keep our means and methods to ourselves."

Gamble looked from me to Zander and back. He took a few minutes to consider our conditions. "Maybe it would be best if I didn't know."

"That's not a bad idea."

"But, then again, how can I provide proper oversight if I'm in the dark?" Shaking his head, Gamble muttered, "All right. I agree to your terms. Absolute secrecy."

"Okay, then. We spent the night here because the nanomites were making the 'bugs' we'll use to surveil our targets, and they needed the 3D printer to do it. They designed and printed a set of specialized nanomites that we will insert into the targets.

"I thought the nanomites didn't like to be apart from the rest of the, um, cloud or swarm or whatever it is."

"They don't. They hate it because it diminishes the nanocloud's effectiveness and what might be called their 'singular collectiveness.' They don't feel whole when they aren't 'whole,' as in together. Knowing that, the nanomites they constructed are different. They aren't part of the cloud. We call them 'nanobugs,' as in they're the 'bugs' we'll wiretap our enemies with."

"Nanobugs. Inferior nanomites? Second-class citizens?"

"When you put it like that, I suppose they aren't true nanomites. They are more like simple sub-nanometer microelectromechanical devices."

"Simple sub-whatever microthingamabobs. Right. *Simple.*"

"Okay, maybe not *simple*, but vastly simpler than the nanomites. The nanobugs lack the nanomites' extensive programming algorithms and storage capacity. They have limited and specialized skills and can only perform those few tasks they are encoded to do, which is to surveil their targets."

"Tell me more."

"Although the nanobugs' skills may be limited and specialized, that doesn't lessen their effectiveness with regard to our needs. Think of them as sophisticated spyware, undetectable 'listening posts'—a million freshly printed nanobugs to each array. All Zander and I need to do is come within close range of a target. The nanomites will do the rest."

"The rest?"

"They will insert the array into our surveillance target."

"Into them?"

"The nanobugs, like the nanomites, require a continual source of power, but since the array is quite small, their needs are low-level, not enough to drain the host. We could just stick the nanobugs under a lamp shade like one might leave an electronic bug, but we're surveilling a person, not a place. With an inserted array, our surveillance goes with the target wherever he or she goes.

"Each array (again, think of them as stripped-down, micro-mini-nanoclouds) will provide location accuracy on the subject, will collect audio from him and his conversations—including both sides of phone calls—and will scan nearby phones and hard drives and gather digital data such as texts, emails, images, and files. They can also send data on the target himself—heartrate, respiration, temperature, etc."

I didn't say it aloud, but I was thinking, *The array can send us data on the target, and they can perform other, specialized functions. You might say that we put the "fun" in "functional."*

I hid my mirth and continued. "The nanobugs' hardware and software programming enable them to connect wirelessly to any network or cellular signal within a one-hundred-foot range and continuously transmit data to the two nanoclouds. Our nanoclouds will monitor and save the data as it is streamed to them.

"As long as each array has a means to transmit data, it will remain in contact with our nanoclouds, providing real-time reporting. If an array is without a means to transmit data, it will store its collected surveillance and, when again able to transmit, upload data packets to the nanoclouds."

Gamble appeared thunderstruck. "But . . . it-it's like Big Brother on steroids. Can you imagine what would happen if our enemies were to acquire and duplicate such technology? *Can you imagine if our own intelligence community were to?* Privacy as we know it would be over. Finished. Kaput. And the ethical and legal implications . . ."

Zander and I nodded.

"When the nanomites revealed what they had come up with, we held in-depth conversations with them over those very concerns. The nanomites' stealth abilities are precisely why Cushing and her handlers wanted Dr. Bickel's research in the first place, why they hunted me, thinking they could extract the nanomites from me. Our enemies planned to use the nanomites to 'protect' the safety and security of America by ensuring that nothing was ever secret again—that is, secret from *them*. In essence, they wanted to protect freedom by destroying it."

"And yet here we are, about to do that very thing," Gamble objected.

"Yes. It is horrifying. When you think about it, Zander and I, in conjunction with the nanoclouds, already 'own' and control the most advanced tech on the face of the planet. If we were super villains, we truly could take over the world."

"We're not villains," Zander whispered, "but that doesn't mean that the age-old adage, 'total power corrupts totally' is any less plausible or possible. Jayda and I aren't infallible. We're not perfect by any stretch of the imagination. We, too, must heed the Bible's warning on the unreliability of the flawed human condition when it says, *If you think you are standing firm, be careful that you don't fall."*

I added, "Even Jesus wouldn't entrust himself to people, because he knew what was in their hearts. If no one can be trusted with such power, then we can't be trusted either—which is why we have made a pact with the nanomites."

"A pact?"

"Yeah. When this is over, when the President's administration is safe, the nanomites will send a self-destruct command to the nanobugs."

"That doesn't mean they won't print more bugs in the future."

"The nanoclouds have promised not to."

"Furthermore," Zander said, "only three of us will know about the nanobugs. We cannot disclose our surveillance methods to anyone, even the President. This, Agent Gamble, is what you agreed to."

Gamble ran a hand over his face. "Yeah, I get it." He blinked a few times, then nodded. "All right. I'll go along with you on this. But only because . . ."

"Because our government hangs by a thread?"

"Yeah. That."

⌘⌘⌘⌘

CHAPTER 11

THE FOLLOWING MORNING, Zander and I ran our five miles earlier than usual. Today I intended to plant nanobug arrays on the four NSA security police officers and, if possible, on the NSA Deputy Director. Meanwhile, Zander would stalk the West Wing and attempt to identify the traitors within the ranks of White House Secret Service detail and tag them with nanobug arrays.

Tag—you're "it."

Easy as pie, right?

Maybe.

We wanted—we needed—to spend more time in prayer before we left our apartment.

"Lord," Zander prayed over our clasped hands, "I need you. Jayda needs you. We cannot do this without your grace covering us the way the nanomites cover us. You warned us through Jayda's dream to depend upon you more than we depend on the nanomites or their abilities. So, Father God, we confess right now: We need you. We lean on you. Lead us, Lord, and we will follow. We pray in Jesus' name, amen."

"Amen," I echoed.

Ten minutes later, I was on the road to Ft. Meade, and Zander was headed for the Greenbelt D.C. Metro station. He would park there and ride the Metro into D.C.

⌘

ZANDER TRANSFERRED FROM the Green Line to the Red Line at Gallery Place and got off at Metro Center. He walked the rest of the way to 15th Street, cutting west on Hamilton Place. He used the visitor's entrance on East Executive Avenue to slip inside the White House through the East Wing. He was grateful for his soft-soled shoes as he, unnoticed, passed busy White House staff and Secret Service personnel.

At the prearranged time, he met up with Kennedy on the House's second floor in what was called the Map Room. Kennedy walked into the room and thought himself alone.

Zander appeared a few feet away. "I'm here."

Kennedy jerked and, instinctively, reached for his service weapon. "You about gave me a heart attack, Mr. Cruz."

"Please call me Zander—and this room is clean, by the way. No bugs."

"All right. *Zander*. Are you ready for this? Do you understand the weight of what you'll be doing, how much hinges on it?"

"I didn't sleep much last night if that's what you mean."

Kennedy took a deep breath. "Okay. I take it you've familiarized yourself with the White House's public floor plans? Of course, the public plans are generalized. We keep the detailed plans secret for the President's safety and security."

"The nanomites downloaded the actual plans when Jayda visited last December. I have them memorized."

"Memorized?"

"Yes. Everything. Right down to the Situation Room under the West Wing, the Presidential Emergency Operations Center under the East Wing, the tunnels connecting them, where your agents and snipers are located, and all your other security measures, including the frequency of your earwigs." (An earwig being the earpiece Secret Service agents use to communicate with each other.)

"Son of a sea biscuit." Kennedy's gaze seared Zander.

"I'm on your side, remember?"

Kennedy continued raking Zander with his suspicious, probing gaze until Zander shrugged.

"I'll be about my business, then."

"How do we contact you while you're here if we need you?"

Zander had the nanomites dispatch an array of nanobugs to Kennedy. "That's a good question, particularly since I haven't flushed out the unauthorized listening devices yet. Since we can't be sure of your privacy until I've swept the House and the West Wing, please don't say my name aloud. If you need me . . . tap the back of your cell phone three times."

Kennedy's eyes narrowed. "Tap my phone. Three times. Do you also need me to click my heels and chant, 'There's no place like home; There's no place like home'?"

"If it makes you happy." Zander watched Kennedy's mouth tighten. "Look, just tap the back of it. The nanomites will, er, detect it and report your location to me. I'll come find you."

"How the devil can the nanomites detect me tapping my phone if they're with you?"

"Does it matter? I'm here to do a job. The sooner I get to it, the sooner the President can breathe easier about his security and privacy."

Zander had the nanomites cover him. "I'll start in the West Wing."

"Mr. Cruz."

"Zander."

"Right. *Zander*. Well, *Zander*, if I find out that the President's confidence in you is misplaced—"

"You won't, and it isn't. He's my president. I will do whatever I can to preserve him and his administration."

Zander withdrew from the Map Room and made his way downstairs to the Palm Room. He eased out the door and across the West Colonnade that led to the West Wing. Inside, he followed a short hallway, turned left—and came to a standstill, daunted by the West Wing's tight quarters and level of activity. Fortunately, the nearest stairway leading to the level beneath the West Wing was straight ahead, but that was all that was fortunate about the proximity of those stairs.

He halted at the top of the flight of steps, studying the press of staff members coming and going—their expressions intent and purposeful, their pace hurried but quiet. Zander edged away as a man from the lower level took the steps two at a time to the top of the stairs then scurried away.

Zander stared down the narrow staircase, loath to put himself into the staircase's tight quarters, weighing the prospect of encountering someone rushing toward him if he did.

I wouldn't be able to dodge them if I tried.

After less than five minutes in the West Wing, Zander's nerves were jangling.

Probably should have arrived long before any of the staff did this morning. I could have swept the entire West Wing by now without all this cloak and dagger business—and without risking a heart attack.

He also admitted to newfound admiration for his wife. *Man, Jayda, I don't know how you do this with such ease. I'm half wrecked.*

Zander jumped back as a woman rounded the corner at a fast clip and started down the stairs.

Here goes nothing.

He moved in behind the woman and followed her down, taking a quick left at the bottom to reach the Secret Service Operations Center. When he arrived at their door, he was sweating.

I'm in the belly of the beast, Lord. Please help me remain undetected.

As he tried to calm himself, the door to the Operations Center swung open, and an agent exited. In the seconds the door was open, Zander caught a glimpse inside. He spied walls of monitors providing live feeds of both the interior and exterior of the House. Six agents manned computer workstations. Their eyes flicked from their workstation screens to the bank of monitors, roving over them, questing for anything out of the ordinary.

Zander placed his hand on the Operations Center's wall and sent the nanomites inside the wall where they located and followed the network cabling into the Service's network. They downloaded the President's schedule and the day's roster of agents.

Zander Cruz, four agents on today's roster were previously assigned to Vice President Harmon.

"Okay, Nano. Let's start with them. Show me their locations."

One of them is nearby, seated at a terminal inside the Secret Service Operations Center.

"Huh. And just how do you propose I get close enough for you to attach an array to him?"

A minute later, the agent who had exited the Operations Center returned and opened the door. Zander again glanced inside, but it was impossible for him to jump through the doorway behind the agent before he shut the door.

The thought of being trapped inside the Operations Center made his heart pump and his skin grow cold.

Zander Cruz, we detect an elevated heartrate. Do you wish us to administer calming endorphins?

"Uh, no. But thanks for the offer, Nano."

Any time, Zander Cruz. By the way, we have solved your dilemma and have inserted the array into our target. You may proceed to the next target's location.

"What? How did you get them to our target?"

He knew the answer before he finished asking: The nanomites had attached two nanobug arrays to the returning agent. The agent had, unknowingly, passed one of the arrays to the target and retained the other.

"Quick thinking, Nano—we may need the second array if we take out Harmon's agents."

Relieved to quit the confines of the West Wing, Zander went in search of the other three targets who were posted throughout the House. He walked the length of the West Colonnade, through the Palm Room, and into the House proper. One by one, as he located and crept close to the agents, the nanomites sent an array of nanobugs to them. Then he found his way back to the Palm Room and exited onto the West Colonnade.

Zander immediately felt moisture in the sweltering summer air and looked up. Thunderheads were building in the sky above him. "Nano. What's the weather forecast?"

Rain by noon, Zander Cruz.

"Thanks."

According to the day's schedule, the President was meeting with his cabinet.

"This is an opportune time to sweep the Oval Office, Nano."

Zander made the turn where the West Colonnade skirted the east side of the West Wing. He stole down the walkway, avoiding the two agents stationed on the walkway outside the Cabinet Room doors.

When he reached the Oval office, he peered through one of the windows and found it empty. Zander placed his palm on the glass and sent nanomites inside to investigate.

Zander Cruz, we found two listening devices in the President's office. We have permanently deactivated them.

Zander shook his head. "Okay, so the President's suspicions were justified. Let's walk around the exterior of the West Wing and sweep the offices and rooms on its perimeter, Nano, starting with the Cabinet Room, since that's where the President is now."

He retraced his steps to the Cabinet Room. With one eye on the agents standing post only feet away, he crept to the closest window and placed one finger on a window pane.

Zander Cruz, we have detected no listening devices in this room.

"Great. Guess we'll go the other way, then, and check what we can from the outside."

Zander headed back toward the Oval Office, intending to swing around the corner of the building toward the offices on the West Wing's south side. He had taken only a few steps when the nanomites interrupted him.

Zander Cruz, one of our arrays within the Operations Center is reporting activity.

Zander leaned against the outside of the Oval Office, closed his eyes, and went into the warehouse. He watched and listened as the feed from the nanobugs streamed into the warehouse. He picked up a few low voices from agents within the Operations Center, what sounded like soft commands spoken into wireless headsets. Nothing of note.

A screen appeared, evidently from the target's workstation.

"What am I watching, Nano?"

The target has opened a new window. This window has been configured not to register on the Secret Service network; however, we are watching it via the nanobugs. The target is transmitting audio collected from . . . a listening device within the Chief of Staff's office.

"We'll deactivate that device in a minute. Where's the audio going?"

We have the IP address, Zander Cruz. Attempting to trace it now.

"Okay. The agent has proven that he is on our adversary's team. You know what to do. Take him out."

Zander kept watching the live feed from the array of nanobugs, waiting for the command from the nanomites to the array to take effect. For several minutes nothing happened—until the agent closed down the window before the audio transfer was complete.

"Can you tell what's going on, Nano?"

The target's respiration has risen slightly. Skin temperature has cooled a degree; skin is clammy. He has remained seated at his station; however—

The live stream from the nanobugs erupted with the unmistakable sounds of retching and gagging, followed by the raised voices of other agents inside the Operations Center. Though the feed was garbled, the voices talking over each other, Zander made out several sentences.

"Oh, man, Carter! Couldn't you have used a wastebasket?"

"Boyd—get housekeeping on the line. Right now. And someone open the door. The stench is killing me."

"Crud. There he goes again. Carter! Use the *blank* waste can, man!"

Zander snickered under his breath. "One down. Three to go."

He opened his eyes. "Let's go clean up the Chief of Staff's office, Nano."

The south side of the West Wing was planted with shrubs and trees to shroud the Oval Office not so much from public view but from the view of a potential sniper. The trees also concealed a little patio with seating beneath the Chief of Staff's windows and a decorative concrete pond beneath the offices of the President's senior advisors. Zander threaded his way around shrubs and flower beds and stood on the pond's edge to reach the senior advisors' windows.

Zander Cruz, we detect no listening devices.

Zander moved on to the patio. The corner office belonged to the President's Chief of Staff. He placed his hand on one of the Chief of Staff's office windows.

Zander Cruz, we detect a listening device in this room. The device is active.

"Can you tell me what's going on inside?"

The Chief of Staff, Marcus Park, is engaged in a phone conversation. This is the audio our target was transmitting before he was interrupted.

"Can you tell who Park is talking to?"

He is speaking with the White House Press Secretary, Zander Cruz.

"Okay, well I guess what matters most is that he's being spied on— and we need to change that."

Minutes later, the nanomites reported, *Zander Cruz, we have deactivated the listening device.*

Zander turned the corner. The next office was assigned to the Vice President. Since the office was unoccupied, Zander wasn't surprised that it was clean. The National Security Advisor's office, however, was not. The nanomites made quick work of that listening device, too.

"These devices couldn't elude the Secret Service's daily sweeps unless the agents performing the sweeps know about them."

That is our deduction also, Zander Cruz.

"How do we find the names of the agents performing the daily sweeps?"

The nanomites did not immediately reply. When they did, they said, *Zander Cruz, our target in the Secret Service Operations Center has been sent home.*

"Excellent news."

The remaining array within the Operations Center, sent to one of the trustworthy agents, has provided us with the list of agents conducting daily sweeps over the past three weeks.

"And?"

And a pattern has emerged. Every sweep over that three-week period included one of the four agents formerly assigned to Vice President Harmon's detail.

"That validates the President and Agent Kennedy's concerns."

We agree, Zander Cruz.

Zander grinned. "Then take 'em out, Nano."

The order is given, Zander Cruz.

"You've been watching too much Trek, Nano."

Zander Cruz, we believe you have said, and we quote: 'Is there such a thing as too much Trek?' This antiquated projection of future space travel is quite entertaining.

Zander laughed under his breath. "Point taken. Let's go wait for the President so we can update him."

Zander retraced his steps, entered the Oval Office from its exterior doors, and waited for the cabinet meeting to adjourn. He wasn't quite as anxious as he'd been two hours ago, but it was still surreal to be walking around in the President's office, examining the tokens of history within its walls.

When he heard low voices approaching the office, he placed himself out of the way, adjacent to the far side of the President's desk. Kennedy entered first. He scanned the room for threats before he ushered President Jackson inside and closed the door.

Jackson's first words were, "I'd like to know how our friend is making out."

"I'll signal him." Kennedy drew his cell phone from his jacket pocket and carefully tapped the back of the case three times.

Zander cleared his throat. "Here I am, Mr. President."

"Good heavens. You gave me a start, Mr.—"

"Better not to use names just yet, begging your pardon, sir—although I can assure you that your office is clean. Now."

Kennedy stared from his phone to Zander. "How did you . . ."

"I'm tempted to let you believe that I instantly teleported here, summoned by your 'magic' phone, but I'm not going to yank your chain, Agent Kennedy. I was actually already here, hoping for an opportunity to report my progress."

Kennedy scowled, but the President was eager to hear from Zander. "So, you've already made progress?"

"Yes, sir."

"Take a seat, Mr., um . . . Never mind. Please sit down."

"Thank you, sir."

Zander sat on a couch and the President seated himself on a nearby chair with Kennedy hovering behind him.

"Tell us what you've found."

"Your suspicions were justified, sir. Our, ah, tiny friends found two devices here in your office and one each in your Chief of Staff and National Security Advisor's offices. Our friends have deactivated them."

The news brought the President no relief. He sat back and glanced up at Kennedy. "We were right. The conspiracy is still in play—they may try again to kill me."

"Not until they have a replacement for Harmon, sir—a vice presidential candidate of their choosing."

"And that's a whole other can of worms." Jackson returned his gaze to Zander. "What else do you have?"

"The four agents formerly on Vice President Harmon's detail. We caught one of them transmitting the audio of a phone call between the Chief of Staff and your press secretary. Then our . . . friends studied the list of Secret Service personnel who swept the West Wing daily over the past three weeks and uncovered an interesting fact. At least one of the four men was on that roster each time."

Kennedy swore under his breath. "Inserting bugs under the guise of sweeping for them. Making certain their taps weren't discovered. Traitors!"

"Yes, they are. I believe we've found and deactivated the more crucial bugs, but I intend to come in early tomorrow and sweep the entire house before any staff members arrive."

"Good idea. But now that we're certain of the four agents' treachery, we're back to the problem of ridding ourselves of these moles. How do you propose we do that?"

Zander couldn't prevent the grin tugging at the corner of his mouth. "I think you're going to hear of a particularly nasty strain of stomach flu making the rounds through the White House Secret Service ranks today. Four agents have already been sent home—or will be shortly. They will be quite, uh, indisposed."

The President leaned forward and whispered, "You made them sick to their stomachs?"

"Those men will worship at the porcelain throne so often and so vigorously, they'll wish for a quick death," Zander deadpanned. "And in a few days, when they recover and consider themselves fit enough to return to work? All four of them will suffer a regrettable relapse."

"Doesn't rid us of them permanently."

"No, but it gives us some time and relief, a week or thereabouts. It also doesn't tell their bosses that we're on to them. Not exactly, anyway. I didn't want to make it obvious to our enemies that only the four plants were targeted, so . . . unfortunately for a fifth and supposedly innocent agent, he will be unable to report to work tomorrow."

Kennedy's suspicion flared. "How did you do such a thing? What did you give them?"

"If you don't mind, I need to keep the details to myself."

"What if I do mind?"

"I'm sorry, but you'll have to trust me."

"You haven't touched the President's detail, have you?"

"No. Only the four suspected White House agents—and the innocent one as a deflection. I'll add a nonessential White House staffer to the sick list tomorrow, to further the ruse that stomach flu is going around."

Jackson turned to Kennedy. "Well? What do you think?"

Kennedy studied Zander with grudging admiration. "I think it's bloody brilliant, sir."

⌘

I SPENT MY DRIVE to Ft. Meade rehearsing how I would find and get close to the four SPOs to insert the nanobug arrays into them. I parked in my usual area and made my way to the Repository. It would be my first day without Macy's coaching, and I already missed her. Not the coaching so much, but her friendship.

Guess I needed to exert myself and get to know my team better.

"Morning, Sherry. Morning, everyone."

"Morning, Jayda. If you need any help today, please ask Neville."

Neville waved from his workstation. "Just give me a holler."

"Hey, Neville. Thanks. I will."

Not likely. I'd had the job locked from the second day; I just couldn't let Macy know it. Now that she wasn't looking over my shoulder, I could speed up, finish my tasks early, and "go" with the nanomites into the Repository to view their take.

The nanomites had "borrowed" an encryption key from one of the classifiers in the department, but it had taken them until last Thursday to break the encryption itself—encryption the NSA swore was unbreakable. I had been too preoccupied with tracking Wayne Overman's movements to give my attention to what they'd found, but today would be different . . . in several ways.

"Nano, dive into the Repository and begin looking for references to former Vice President Harmon, especially files designated for his eyes."

On it, Jayda Cruz.

I busied myself with my work—and finalizing my plans. Lunchtime couldn't arrive fast enough.

"Don't make the same mistakes today that you made last week, Jayda," I whispered.

When noon rolled around, Lynn and Chantelle invited me to lunch with them.

"We're hungry for sushi. There's a little sushi bar on the other side of the Parkway. Want to come?"

My stomach voted for sushi with a roar so loud that my teammates heard. When their laughter died down, I smiled and patted my belly.

"As you heard, my tummy would love to go with you guys. Sadly, I have an errand to run. I think I can just get there and back in an hour. Next time?"

"Sure, Jayda. Would you like us to pick something up for you? We have a menu."

"Yes; that's perfect!"

I chose a dragon roll and handed some cash to Chantelle.

"We'll see you later, then," Lynn said.

"Hey, I'll walk out with you guys."

We chatted down the long hall toward the exit to the parking lot. I even left the building with them. I waved and split off toward my car. Halfway there, I walked between two cars and "dropped" my keys. When I stooped over to pick them up, I had the nanomites cover me. I turned around and reentered the building.

It was nicely done. By "walking out" with Chantelle and Lynn, I'd avoided the rest of my team. No one would expect to see me for a solid hour. And I'd had the nanomites shut off my badge's tracking device when I turned around. As far as anyone watching my badge's movements would believe, I had left the building and had not yet returned.

In less than an hour, I needed to locate the four SPOs and tag them with nanobugs. If enough time remained, I would go in search of the Deputy Director, Lawrence Danforth.

Since it was lunchtime, the halls were busy with noisy, lunch-going employees, busy enough to mask my soft footfalls as I jogged toward the Safety and Security Department, zigging around the clusters of personnel headed out or toward the cafeteria. I made it to my destination in four minutes and tiptoed into the department.

It looked like the receptionist was at lunch, which made my job a snap. I placed my hand on her workstation.

Jayda Cruz, two of the officers of interest are on duty. The other two are scheduled at 3:30 p.m.

"The two who are on duty? Show me where they are."

Talk about Mission Impossible. One SPO was in a police car. He and another SPO were cruising the campus fence line and parking lots. The second SPO was posted on the fourth floor.

Same floor as Danforth's office.

"Huh. Nano. Is Deputy Director Danforth in the building?"

He is in his office, Jayda Cruz.

"Two for the price of one. Guess that settles it."

I didn't want to use the elevator, so I closed my eyes to recall where the building's stairwells were located and where the stairwell opened on the fourth floor. Moments later, I was sprinting through the hallways.

The door to the stairwell was alarmed and watched by a blinking video camera. The nanomites disabled the alarm and paused the camera while I pulled the door open and slid through. Then it was up four flights of empty, echo-filled stairs to the Executive Suite.

Adrenaline was shooting through my veins, so running those stairs felt good.

Zander and I need another trip to the dojo.

When I arrived at the fourth floor, the nanomites had the video camera skim the exit area for us before they paused it and disabled the door's alarm.

You may exit now, Jayda Cruz.

I slid noiselessly from the stairwell. My eyes cut across the floor, probing for danger. Most of the personnel were absent, probably at lunch like so much of the campus.

My first target, the SPO, stood his post adjacent to the bank of elevators. He looked bored. Danforth, I presumed, was behind the closed door to his office.

I crept toward his office first and placed my hand on the door.

Jayda Cruz, Deputy Director Danforth is on the phone.

"Can you insert the array from here?"

No, Jayda Cruz. We must be in closer proximity.

"Can you . . . can you cut off his phone call?"

Done, Jayda Cruz.

I heard muttering through the door, and, after more seconds, a receiver slammed onto its cradle and a chair scooted from a desk.

I stepped to the side before the door opened.

Deputy Director Danforth called to the SPO, "Johnson! Have the phones gone down?"

The SPO lifted his radio and spoke into it. When an answer came back, he replied, "No, sir."

Swearing, Danforth strode back into his office and lifted the receiver of his phone. "Huh. Working now."

Array inserted, Jayda Cruz.

"Excellent."

Johnson, the SPO, didn't sense me creeping toward him and never noticed a thing as the nanomites sent an array to him.

I checked the time as I reentered the stairwell. "Forty-five minutes still on the clock. Plenty of time to track down the other SPO, right?"

I raced down the stairs and back to the Safety and Security Department. Placed my hand on the receptionist's terminal. "Find the other SPO, Nano."

It took the nanomites a while to pinpoint the police car's exact location using the campus' external video feeds. It's hard to describe the expanse of the NSA's sprawling campus and the number of lots needed to serve more than thirty thousand employees. Acres of parking lots surround all sides of the campus and are scattered among the outlying buildings. Four security police vehicles patrol the lots continuously. I knew the nanomites could identify the right car; I just wasn't certain how long it would take them or if, when they did locate it, I would have enough time to reach it, plant the nanobugs, and return to work on time.

After five minutes of the nanomites scanning live video feed without a word on their progress, I grew impatient.

"Nano?"

It took the nanomites another three minutes to answer me. They popped up a layout of the entire campus in front of my eyes. Two lines, one red, one a squiggly blue, appeared on the layout.

Jayda Cruz, the vehicle containing the SPO in question is, at this moment, traversing the southeast fence line heading east. The vehicle's progress is marked by the solid red line; its projected path is indicated by the dotted red line.

We have determined that, should the vehicle continue at its present speed and if it turns north at the southeast corner of the complex as we anticipate it will, and if you leave now, running at 5.3 miles per hour, following the route we have computed—marked in blue—your path will intersect with the vehicle here.

The campus layout zoomed in with breathtaking speed and centered on an "x" three-quarters of the distance from the southeast to the northeast corner of the campus.

"That's a lot of 'ands' and 'ifs,' Nano."

You must leave now, Jayda Cruz. We will update the police vehicle's route and your projected intersect point in real time.

I flew down the halls and back out into the sultry air, the nanomites' route overlaid on the real world around me, a timer on the left counting down the time remaining before I was expected back at my desk. My projected route had me skirting parked cars, jumping short retaining walls, and dodging employee pedestrians returning from an early lunch—basically everything but leaping tall buildings in a single bound.

I was within fifty yards of the point of intersection when the "x" began to move. In fact, it jumped precipitously to the north, my route lagging far behind.

I was going to miss the intersect.

I poured on the speed. "Nano! What's going on?"

The patrol car has sped up, Jayda Cruz.

"You don't say. Tell me something I don't know!"

I saw it, racing ahead, and I did the only thing I could to ensure that I reached it in time. With a flick of my wrist, I sent a bolt of electricity toward the vehicle's left rear wheel.

The tire blew with a satisfying **BANG** leaving a trail of shredded steel-belted rubber.

Even more satisfying, the patrol car, its left rear wheel rim screeching on the asphalt, ground to a stop. Both officers bolted from the vehicle and crouched behind their respective car doors, sidearms drawn, scanning for danger.

Huh. Maybe they thought the tire had been shot out?

Even with the timer ticking down relentlessly, I hung back until the officers, not spotting a threat, holstered their sidearms, and emerged from behind their doors to study their car's missing tire.

Well, the tire wasn't missing, not *exactly*. It was strewn behind the vehicle for around twenty yards.

"What the *blank* happened?"

"Must have been a faulty tire. I'll call it in. You get out the spare."

The nanomites painted a big blue "x" on the SPO I was seeking. I breezed by him, dropped the nanobug array, and took off running. The nanomites routed me through several buildings I had no business being in, but they got me back to the parking lot before my lunch hour ended. I had the nanomites uncover me and activate my badge and (sweating like a pack mule) I walked inside.

With a minute to spare, I sat down at my desk. I was quivering from exertion and hunger and steaming like a baked potato fresh out of a microwave.

"Hey, Jayda. Here's your order and your change."

"Bless you guys. I'm starving." My hands shook as I pulled the container from the bag they handed me. Through the transparent plastic lid, the dragon roll winked and beckoned like the gold of El Dorado. I fumbled to pry open the container.

"My, don't you look all hot and bothered."

Kiera leaned against the cubical wall at the entrance to our team's area. Her expression was composed and noncommittal, but her eyes raked over me, missing nothing.

"Hey, Kiera. Yeah. I had some errands to run—and its sweltering out there."

"Must have been a marathon of a lunch hour.

I poked a whole piece of sushi into my mouth and talked around chews. "You have no idea."

I busied myself with eating, hoping the woman would leave, but she didn't.

"I'm sorry. Here I am stuffing my face while you're waiting on me. Did you need something?"

"No." She pushed off the wall. "Just wondered if you'd heard anything from Macy."

"Not yet. Want me to let you know when I do?"

"Sure. I'd appreciate that."

⌘

KIERA RETURNED TO HER AREA and sat down at her workstation. She fingered her key fob and made a show of trying to log in for a few minutes before turning to her supervisor.

"I'm having a problem logging in. Okay if I run down to IT?"

"Go ahead, Kiera."

She was deliberately going off script but reckoned she could pull it off this one time without arousing suspicions. When she walked into IT, Rob's eyes widened momentarily.

"I'm having trouble logging in," Kiera broadcast to whomever might be listening. "I was hoping you could help me."

"You're in luck. That's what we do here. Just give me a minute." He seated her at an IT computer with her back to the room's video camera and pulled a chair up next to her so that his body hid her computer screen from the camera.

"I take it there's nothing wrong with your login?"

"Of course not. Have you been keeping tabs on the Cruz woman?"

"Yup. And I'm glad you're here." He reached for the keyboard and accessed the camera system. "Watch this."

Chantelle, Lynn, and Jayda exited the building to the parking lot. Rob switched to another camera. There they were in the lot, Chantelle and Lynn moving in one direction, Jayda in another. He changed cameras again, this one more distant, but it showed Jayda walking between two cars. An object fell from her hand and she stooped over to pick it up, the camera losing her between the two vehicles.

The feed rolled on—without Jayda reappearing.

"Where is she?"

"Exactly. Where is she? With all the employees leaving for lunch, a casual look at the feed might not have picked up on it, but I watched this scene six times. She bent over between those cars and never reappeared."

"That's not possible. Where's her car? She ran errands during her lunch."

Rob smirked. "Want to know what's not possible? Running errands while your car sits in the parking lot."

"What do you mean?"

Rob tapped the keyboard and the video zoomed in. "See that car? That's Cruz' car." He tapped the keyboard again, zooming in on the plate. Then he toggled to another screen and pulled up the parking pass database. "See that pass? Jayda Cruz. Note the plate number."

"So, that's her car and?"

"And it hasn't moved since she arrived this morning, *but*—" Rob toggled back to the video feed and advanced it an hour. Same view of Jayda's car. A nearby vehicle had driven away and been replaced by another, but Jayda's car had not moved.

"Rob—"

"Wait for it."

The feed was stationary, unchanged. The next instant, there was Jayda, moving away from her car in full stride.

"What . . . did someone splice her in?"

"No. Note the time stamp." Rob reran the scene.

"But, it looks like a glitch—"

"Keep watching." Rob zoomed out and they saw Jayda moving toward the building entrance. Then he switched to the camera over the entrance and zoomed in.

"Notice anything?"

"She's red-faced and sweating. Like she'd been out in the heat for the whole hour. And she was still perspiring when I saw her a few minutes ago." Kiera lifted her eyes to Rob's "If she didn't get in her car, where was she during that hour?"

"I can't tell you, because her badge went 'out of range' the same moment she disappeared and came back into range when she reappeared."

"So, off the grid but . . . Did anything of note happen on campus during that hour?"

"A patrol car had a blowout. That's it."

"Not a flat but a blowout? At what—fifteen or twenty miles an hour?"

They stared at each other, frowning in concentration. Without a word passing between them, Rob pounded on the keyboard until he located a camera that had captured the patrol car the instant its tire blew.

Rob zoomed in. The video framed a spectacular blowout—as far as blowouts go. Shredded tire flew in all directions.

"Back it up, Rob. Before the tire blew."

Rob rewound the recording twenty seconds and set the feed in motion. An instant later, they both saw it—the streak of light that struck the tire before it exploded.

The video continued to roll while Kiera and Rob tried to understand what they'd seen.

"What the *blank* was that?"

"Wait. Stop the tape. Roll it back."

"You know it's not tape, right?" Rob griped. "It's digital."

"Shut up and wind it back—there. Did you see that?"

He rewound and played it again. "That flicker? Is that what you mean? That could be anything. Light bouncing off a car in the lot behind the camera."

"And was it 'light bouncing off a car' that zapped the patrol car and destroyed its tire? That was a *weapon*."

Rob was tired of her superior attitude. "Y'know, Kiera, you are a real pain in the *bleep* to work with. I tried to tell you last week that this Cruz chick was weird and up to something. You wouldn't listen. I *told* you how she went into the women's restroom and didn't come out for six minutes— but her badge had her running to IT and back."

Kiera studied him. "Okay, Rob, I'll bite. You said you took screen shots. Did you keep them?"

He opened a file directory and navigated to the folders where he'd saved the Word doc he'd pasted them in. With a click, the document opened, and Kiera paged through the images, noting their time stamps.

"According to the video feed she was in the bathroom . . . but according to her badge, she came here."

"Yeah. Like I said. Only *later*, the time stamps on the video feed and badge tracking changed."

"Rob?"

"Yeah."

"I want you to download video of everything we just looked at. Her disappearing and reappearing and the blowout. Especially the blowout and that . . . that bolt of lightning or whatever it was."

"It'll be tricky, covering my tracks. And what do I do with the files?"

"Use this." Kiera handed Rob a pen. They both knew it contained a hidden wireless flash drive—strictly *verboten*.

"Send me the files tonight."

"And if I'm caught?"

"If you get caught then you aren't as good as you keep telling everyone you are. Oh. And Rob? You'd better do it quick. Before someone tampers with the video."

⌘

LATER THAT AFTERNOON, long after I should have recovered from my run outside, uncomfortable heat surged up my neck into my face. I ignored it until the third instance left me gasping and fanning myself.

Chantelle looked over at me. "Are you okay, Jayda? Your face is all red."

"I don't know. Maybe I'll run to the restroom and wash my face with cool water."

I couldn't wait and bolted from my chair. I remembered some vending machines in the next building, tucked into an alcove off the main corridor. I quick-walked to the machines.

"Nano. Pull down a can of soda for me—and remind me to pay the machine back at the end of the day."

I grabbed the can as it came out and pressed it to my cheek. "Ahhhh."

All the way to the restroom, I rolled the can across my forehead, cheeks, and back of my neck. When I reached the restroom, I ran the cold-water tap and splashed water on my face until I felt halfway normal. Then I folded several paper towels together, soaked them in cold water and laid them across the back of my neck.

As I was finishing, I decided to use the opportunity to scrub the video feeds. I had the nanomites pop open the paper towel dispenser. I laid my badge on the stack of folded paper towels and closed the dispenser. Under the nanomites' cover, I raced to the Safety and Security Department, tiptoed to the receptionist's desk, sent the nanomites into the system to expunge any video oddities, and waited.

Done, Jayda Cruz.

I crept from the Safety and Security Department, ran to the restroom, grabbed my badge, and came back out. Minutes later I was at my desk.

"Better?" Chantelle asked.

"Yeah. Don't know what got into me."

⌘⌘⌘⌘

CHAPTER 12

A WHITE HOUSE STEWARD finished pouring two glasses of iced tea in the Oval Office. When he left, President Jackson and his Chief of Staff took their glasses in hand and sipped. Axel Kennedy stood apart from them, unobtrusive but vigilant.

"It's been a long day, Marcus."

"That it has been, Mr. President."

"What's my schedule like tomorrow?"

"National security briefing, 7 a.m. Breakfast with Secretary of Energy Mellyn at 8:15. Protocol officer at 9:30 to discuss Independence Day activities. Meeting with the party heads after lunch. Speaker Friese at 3:45. Oh, and I've penciled in Congresswoman Ballard at 2 p.m."

"She asked for a meeting?"

"Yes, sir. Fifteen minutes."

Jackson slid his eyes toward Kennedy while Park was referring to his day planner. Kennedy gave a slight nod, and the President returned his attention to Park.

"Fifteen minutes is enough time to angle for VP consideration, I would think."

"Mr. President, until you make a selection, I think we can count on all possible candidates putting themselves forward."

"It's a year and a half to the next election. I'm tempted to let the position ride until then."

"Do you dare keep the Speaker of the House, a member of the other party, next in line to the presidency?"

"I don't think his own party would be happy to see him in office."

Making it less likely they'll try to get rid of me, Jackson added to himself.

"Agreed, sir, still . . ."

"Let's leave it for now, Marcus. I'm due for dinner with the First Lady in a quarter of an hour. Tomorrow, then?"

"Yes, sir. Have a good evening, sir."

As Park departed, Jackson motioned to Kennedy to take his seat.

"Sounds like I have three candidates to sound out tomorrow, Axel."

"The most interesting fact, sir, is that all three are women."

Jackson stared at the ice floating in his glass. "A woman nominee could garner a few votes that might otherwise be cast along party lines."

"Yes, sir."

"The daunting aspect of this process is not knowing which candidate conceals my enemies' cat's-paw."

Kennedy nodded.

"Well, until tomorrow, then?"

⌘

WE WERE ON OUR WAY to the dojo. I didn't know how Zander felt, but I craved a challenging workout for relief from the stress of a long and difficult day. In spite of my run during lunch, I needed some demanding physical exertion.

"I'm not sure how you do it, Jay. A couple of times today at the White House, I thought I would hyperventilate, I was that nervous."

"I had my share of hairy moments early on, Zander. Over time, you get better at navigating the visible while invisible and better at working with the nanomites. After a while, your confidence grows, and it stops bothering you so much."

My phone rang. "It's Gamble."

I put him on speaker. "Hey, Gamble."

"Hey yourself. Just got off the phone with Agent Kennedy, the upshot being he pressed me for twenty minutes on how you, Zander, made those dirty agents sick to their stomachs. All I could tell him was that it had to be the nanomites—which only led to further questions such as how could the nanomites continue to make the agents sick for days afterward if they are with you and can't leave your bodies for extended periods. I ended up telling him to back off, that I couldn't help him because you guys keep aspects of the nanomites secret, even from me."

"Good answer, Gamble."

Zander chuckled. "Sending those traitors home with barf bags was the best part of my day."

Zander Cruz, your order of barf bags will be delivered Wednesday by USPS. Do you wish this order to be added to your monthly subscriptions?

Zander and I lost it. We dissolved into laughter so gut-clenching we couldn't catch our breath—which left Gamble grousing on the other end of the call.

"If you two clowns are done holding a laughfest at my expense, could you see your way to explaining just how you managed to make those guys sick? To satisfy my own curiosity."

"We weren't . . . we weren't . . . laughing . . . at you, Gamble."

"Y-y-yeah," Zander stutter-laughed. "N-n-not you."

"I'm so relieved—and *touched*. Now, how did you do it?"

I sobered before Zander did. "Turns out that two places in the brain—the 'bilateral vomition centers' in the medulla, to be exact—are what ultimately trigger vomiting. If you apply electric stimuli to those centers, you can elicit the desired reaction."

"Let me get this straight: You sent the nanobugs to the agents' brains to zing them and make them puke?"

"The nanomites gave the order to the array, and the nanobugs applied the stimuli."

"Over and over," Zander added with ill-disguised glee. He wiped tears from his eyes and blew his nose—and that set me off again.

"You two are . . . terrible!"

Zander and I tried hard to dredge up some shred of contrition, but it wasn't happening. Instead, we lapsed into soundless, shoulder-quivering mirth.

A long, quiet moment passed before we heard Gamble chuckle to himself. "But I gotta say, I love it."

⌘

"CAN'T WAIT TO GRADUATE to real sticks," Zander said about six times during our drive to the dojo. "When do you think Gus-Gus will let me?"

His enthusiasm for stick fighting had endured all week, and he'd insisted that we order training shoes and a variety of sticks.

"When you're ready for him to hit you with a 'real' stick," I grumbled.

Oh! How well I remembered!

"Huh. I hadn't thought about it that way."

I worked hard that evening to regain the speed and agility months without training had sapped from me, and I made slow but definite progress on that front. Zander, on the other hand, seemed born to exceed any skills I had labored so hard to cultivate.

I sat out a round and watched his sure, fluid movements and the incremental improvements Gus-Gus' instructions prompted. Of course, the nanomites were helping Zander with stamina and tempo, just as they helped me, but it was obvious that my guy was a natural and would easily outstrip me.

Sighing, I admitted, "He'll be able to beat me soon—probably by next week." Then I smiled. Zander's moves were so smooth and elegant, I couldn't help but admire him in motion.

How had I landed such a hunk?

And he was grinning with such delight when we left the dojo that I had to grin with him.

"Do you think we'll ever need to fight this way?" he asked. "I mean, the way we can draw current and throw it around, why would we need to stick fight?"

"I can't foresee when we'd need to, but you never know. Like the nanomites keep drilling into us, we must become and remain 'optimal.'"

⌘

EACH SUMMER, SIGHTSEERS brave the hot, sticky weather and flock to D.C. monuments, memorials, museums, and houses of government. Tour buses run from Union Station, across the front of the Capitol Building, down Independence Avenue to the Washington Monument, around the Tidal Basin and the Jefferson Memorial, past the Martin Luther King, Jr. and Lincoln Memorials, and up Constitution to the Ellipse, dropping passengers along the way, picking up others.

While the museums and other buildings lock their doors each evening, the National Mall—featuring most of the iconic, open-air monuments—is accessible twenty-four hours a day. This makes the Mall many a tourist's nighttime destination, a means of beating the heat and the daytime crowds at the same time. Fitness buffs, too, frequent the bicycle- and jogger-friendly trails winding around the Mall and the Tidal Basin.

Two solitary figures, a man and a woman, meandered the paths around the Korean War Veterans Memorial. They seemed no different than other visitors wandering the mall in the late evening. That they met on the tree-lined walkway at the far end of the Memorial where the shadows were deeper garnered no attention. The two "tourists" walked together for exactly five minutes.

"You asked for this meeting, Danforth. I assume it's of importance." The woman's voice, low and breathy, exuded an understated sensuality, a tool more than a dozen men had fallen prey to.

Danforth was not taken in by it. Back in their field days, he'd witnessed her in action, and a colder, more heartless agent he'd never known. Her tongue could whisper the sweetest of enticements one moment and flay the skin from a man's bones the next.

He had no desire to be on the receiving end of such a lashing.

"Some in our ranks are asking if there is any possibility that Jackson discovered Harmon's plan and, somehow, turned the tables on Harmon," he began.

"Oh? Are they questioning the autopsy results?"

"No. The autopsy proves that Harmon succumbed to an undiagnosed condition, but they are questioning the coincidence of his coronary event occurring on that particular morning. A fluke too convenient to be random."

She took his arm and leaned into him as a foursome of laughing, giggling teens approached. The couple lapsed into silence while the teens jostled by them. For a few moments, neither of them spoke.

When the teens were a safe distance away, the woman, retaining the man's arm, replied, "I admit to the too-neat convenience of it. However, I can conceive of no means by which Jackson or any of his staff could have discovered or been alerted to the specifics of our plans. Only one of the four of us could have given them away."

The man wished she would release his arm. Her cloying closeness made him sweat more than the heat of the night did.

Years ago, on a breathless evening such as this, the air redolent with the fragrant scent of flowering frangipani, he'd witnessed her rendezvous with a lover they'd discovered was a double agent. She had melted into the man's arms, her hands tugging up his shirttail and caressing and teasing his skin—before she'd slid a hiltless stiletto into his liver.

The blade had been so sharp and narrow that, as she'd pressed herself harder into her lover's embrace, he'd not felt its penetration until she pulled away. By then the knife was too deeply embedded for him to find it and yank it out. Even if he'd managed to grasp its end, he would not have been able to remove the knife—with its barbed blade—without shredding his blood-rich liver.

She'd watched him with curious disinterest as he vainly tried to extricate the instrument of his death. As he bled to death.

Danforth jerked his attention back to his whispered conversation with the woman.

"Could Harmon have given himself away? Robert Jackson is no fool."

"Harmon was the consummate politician. He could have lied to his mother and gotten away with it."

Danforth went at the concerns from another direction. "There is the question of the vial Harmon carried into his meeting with Jackson. Our people searched Harmon's clothing before he was transported to ensure he was carrying nothing that would arouse suspicions. When we realized it was missing, we immediately dispatched assets to his office and home. Same result. Where did it go?"

She sighed. "That is indeed perplexing, and I have given it much thought. Perhaps . . . perhaps there is a simple answer. Housekeeping could have picked it up in the Oval Office and thrown it away, thinking it left behind by the paramedics.

"I suppose, too, that Harmon could have aborted the plan and tossed the vial before he arrived at the White House. He was, we must admit, untested in such a close and personal action. Not," she smiled up into Danforth's face, "like you and I."

Danforth averted his eyes. "With respect, we see no evidence to support such a supposition. Harmon was committed to his role and there was no reason to abort the plan—which is why the vial's disappearance is most troubling. Its compound could be traced back to our man at USAMRIID. Worse still, if Jackson were to have found the vial and realized what it was, it would mean that he was aware of Harmon's intentions."

"Calm yourself. I agree that Harmon aborting the mission makes little sense. On the other hand, had Jackson and his people suspected Harmon, how could they have arranged his coronary incident? That, too, seems unlikely."

The woman thought for a moment. "Have our assets within the house noticed anything out of the norm? Has Jackson's behavior changed in any manner?"

"Nothing has been reported." He did not mention the flu bug running through the Secret Service ranks. She would have read some kind of nefarious action into it.

"Then we shall proceed on our alternate course. We will take the White House as planned—although our people may need years to worm their way into Bickel's lab and regain the ground we lost there. And I remain most disappointed in the loss of *that girl*. The nanotechnology she carried was imperative to our objectives. I am quite disappointed indeed."

The man, knowing the criticism was aimed at him, did not immediately answer. Harmon had been General Cushing's handler. After the Vice President's unexpected demise, the woman had pushed direct oversight of Cushing's operation up to him, but it had been too late: Cushing had vanished.

When he did respond to the woman, it was to deflect her jab.

"It seems clear, in hindsight, that Harmon had lost control of Cushing prior to his death. As I reported earlier, General Cushing, before she blew herself up—taking the girl with her—had gone rogue. Totally incommunicado. Even her team lead could not reach her."

The woman jerked her arm from his, giving vent to her anger. "Yes, yes, so you've *said*, and on more than one occasion. Does that replace the nanotechnology you lost? No! What Cushing destroyed is irreplaceable."

The woman withdrew several feet and worked to gather herself. The man breathed easier when she squared her shoulders and continued walking.

"Now, what about Harmon's replacement?"

Mercurial. The woman's temper could flash and dissolve in seconds.

Glad of the change of direction, the man answered, "As you well know, Jackson's greatest challenge is choosing a VP whom Congress will confirm. That narrows the field for him but works for us. As you directed, we are prepared to present the President with several candidates he should find amenable and whom we believe can be confirmed. They will, of course, be candidates we can control."

"Jackson *must* select a VP of our choosing, and I expect you to ensure the right outcome."

"Certainly." *As if I'd be fool enough to answer otherwise.*

They parted company then, strolling in different directions. The male made for his vehicle parked at a distance east of the mall. The woman turned toward the Lincoln Memorial, deep in thought.

No, I don't believe in coincidences, either, Mr. Danforth. If Harmon's death was *due to natural causes as the autopsy shows, then what became of the compound that should have been on his person? On the other hand, Harmon's death was far too convenient, the timing too neat for happenstance. If it was a deliberate act, that would explain the disappearance of the vial.*

Two irreconcilable sets of circumstances: One must be true and the other false.

Her snort of skepticism was followed by grudging acknowledgement.

So. Jackson had *to have known Harmon intended to poison him—and forewarned is forearmed. But, if Jackson knew, how did he uncover the plot? The exact details and timing of the operation were limited to the four of us—Harmon, Danforth, Morningside, and myself. If, by some means, Jackson did find out, how had he arranged a "natural" death for Harmon?*

Her thoughts returned to the galling loss of the nanotechnology and the last exchange she'd had with Harmon. It concerned a call between Harmon and Cushing on a secure line from within a SCIF—a call that resulted in Harmon unilaterally moving up the operation's timeline.

She slowed and stopped, dropping to a bench near the Vietnam Veterans Memorial, trying to solve the disturbing puzzle.

According to Harmon, halfway through his call with Cushing, the woman had "heard a noise" and become agitated. She had insisted that the Keyes woman was inside the SCIF, listening to their call.

A noise inside the SCIF? Had Cushing been delusional? How could the girl have gained access to a secure facility with no one knowing about it? And how could she have been in the SCIF and Cushing not seen her?

But Cushing had maintained that the girl was there, listening to her conversation with Harmon.

"Listening to Cushing's side of the call," Harmon had said, "not my side. Nothing to be gained by that."

Why had Harmon made the distinction? Unless . . . unless he had spoken of the plot to Cushing? And had failed to disclose his indiscretion to me?

"Oh, my dear John. Did you break operational security because of your history with that Cushing woman? Did your loose lips ruin our plans?" The more she thought on it, the more she seethed. "If you were not already dead, John, I would dispatch you myself."

And yet, how would the woman have overheard Harmon's side of the call unless . . . unless . . . No. Preposterous!

Hmm. Is it so unbelievable? Cushing reported that the girl had strange and powerful abilities, but we were focused only on capturing her for the nanomites. We put no credence into Cushing's wild assertions—and yet Cushing was convinced that the girl could do . . . unbelievable things.

Was Cushing right? Is it possible that the young woman overheard Harmon? Did she alert Jackson? Did she help him? If Cushing's testimony regarding the girl's abilities was true, could the girl have killed Harmon and made his death appear to be from natural causes?

The woman rose from the bench and paced. Thinking.

Implausible as it may seem, it is the only answer that satisfies all the facts.

She crossed Constitution Avenue and walked a block north. A car waited for her.

What a waste. If we could have turned the girl, by God, what a weapon she would have made! If. If we could have turned her. No doubt we could have. We had leverage on her in the boy and the old man.

She ground her teeth in frustration. *Her death set us back years.*

Her death?

A troubling question intruded. *What certain proof do we have of the girl's death? Could she . . . No. Doubtful. But still . . . we must be certain.*

The woman arrived at a decision. *I shall send a team to Albuquerque to reexamine the evidence. They will ferret out the truth surrounding Gemma Keyes' "death."*

⌘⌘⌘⌘

CHAPTER 13

AFTER CATCHING FOUR HOURS of sleep, Zander rose at 2 a.m. Tuesday morning and drove into D.C. He arrived at the White House near 4 a.m., making his unauthorized entry through the West Wing's staff entrance on the west side of the building.

The cleaning staff were hard at work that time of morning, but Zander moved around them with more ease and confidence than he would have yesterday. He sped through the West Wing's floors and offices while the nanomites checked for additional unauthorized listening devices. Finding no new devices in the West Wing, he then tackled the East Wing and the remainder of the White House proper.

He had cleared most of the East Wing before the earliest staff arrived and slowed his speed of progress. By 6:45, the nanomites had declared the East Wing free of threats and unauthorized listening devices—and by that time, the White House cleaning crew were clearing up their work. They switched off the vacuum cleaners, hauled them out of sight, and stowed their cleaning supplies. Then they, too, disappeared, and the daily life of the White House began.

Zander selected an aide in the White House communications department to transmit the "flu" to, a young woman who assisted in the daily press briefings. Minutes later, as he exited the West Wing to the West Colonnade, a member of the press corps left the White House Press Room on his way into the West Wing. The veteran journalist was not a fan of Robert Jackson and had devised more than one unprofessional "hit" piece on him since taking office.

Zander pressed himself against the West Colonnade wall as the journalist strode by.

I probably shouldn't do this, but . . .

Zander waited in the Rose Garden until the President's National Security Briefing was concluded. As the National Security Advisor left through the door leading to the West Wing's main corridor, Zander slipped inside. He did not make himself visible.

"Mr. President?"

Jackson turned toward the sound of Zander's voice. "Anything to report?"

"I came in early, swept the house and both wings, and found no devices, sir. For now, at least, the White House is clean."

"Thank you—I'm relieved." Jackson sat down at his desk, picked up a sheet of paper and—with unpresidential snarkiness—said, "Listen to this:

"'From the White House Medical Unit to all White House Personnel. Please be advised that five cases of suspected norovirus have been reported since yesterday. Norovirus presents with nausea, stomach and intestinal distress, low-grade fever, and muscle ache. We wish to remind White House personnel that norovirus is highly contagious. The most effective means of preventing the spread of norovirus is through regular washing of hands with an antibacterial soap. In addition, if you are sick, we urge you not to return to work until seventy-two hours following the cessation of all flu-like symptoms.'"

The President's chuckle grew into a full-on belly laugh. "Best news I've read in weeks. Thank you again."

"My pleasure, Mr. President. I've 'infected' another White House staffer to further the myth and . . . um, you may also hear of someone in the Press Pool coming down with the bug."

"Oh? Well, if you're going to infect a member of the press—only for the valid purpose of distracting our enemies, of course—I hope it's that pompous windbag from CNN."

Zander smiled to himself. "Of course, Mr. President. Now, if you have nothing further for me, I'll leave for the day. The nanomites are monitoring the 'sick' agents' communications. We'll let them recover just enough to report in to their handlers—and we'll be there to listen in."

⌘

"GOOD MORNING, NORA."

"Mr. President."

Jackson welcomed the Secretary of Energy, Nora Mellyn, with a light kiss on the cheek. "Maddie sends her love."

"Please tell her the same, Mr. President. It has been too long since we spent any time with the both of you."

"The genesis of my campaign seems an age ago. So does the precious time to spend with good friends."

"Speaking of precious time, thank you for seeing me."

"Breakfast awaits us. Shall we talk while we eat?"

They tucked into the scrambled eggs, toast, and fresh fruit. Jackson waited for his Secretary of Energy to bring up the reason for her visit. She had been superb on the campaign trail, a seasoned politician who left the other party to support Jackson. A friend whose loyalty to him had been proven over two grueling years as they inched toward the White House.

Those two grueling years had earned her the hatred of her former party when Jackson eked out a win over their candidate.

"Mr. President, may I ask a personal question?"

"Of course, Nora."

"Have you made your Vice-Presidential selection?"

"No, and I am very sorry it could not be you."

They locked eyes in frank respect.

"Because of the bad blood on the other side of the aisle over my defection?"

"Yes, although 'eternal malignant animus' might be a more apt description. You have earned yourself a spot on their wall of top public enemies."

She laughed softly. "It's not that I'm unhappy at Energy or ungrateful for the appointment. I truly think I could be the partner you want and need."

"I agree and think it's a shame, Nora, but it's not to be. At least for now."

Mellyn toyed with her fruit. "I understand, Mr. President."

⌘

A MEMBER OF THE PRESIDENT'S security detail opened the Oval Office door and allowed the President's party leaders to enter. Jackson greeted the Party Chairman, the Minority Leader and Minority Whip of the House, and the Minority Leader of the Senate.

"Please. Be seated. It's always a pleasure to meet with the party leaders."

"Thank you for making time to see us, Mr. President," said Party Chairman Stover. "We know your time is at a premium, so we'll get straight to the point: We're growing a little concerned over the time it is taking to replace Vice President Harmon. The longer Friese is the next in line, the more nervous the party grows, particularly our biggest donors."

The Senate Minority Leader stepped in. "Yes, Mr. President. We understand the candidate has to be confirmed by both houses of Congress. However, we have proposed several candidates whom we feel would be confirmed. You have not found any of them to your liking?"

"No, I have not."

"May we ask, sir, what you found objectionable?"

"I suppose I am looking for a partner who isn't in the pocket of all those 'biggest donors.'"

"Those donors supported your candidacy."

"I understand and am grateful, but I don't work for donors. I work for the American people. My vice-presidential pick needs to share my values."

Stover's mouth tightened. "Surely, the values of our donors and the American people are one and the same."

"In some respects, yes. In others, no. I won't sacrifice what is best for our nation because my party insists that I am beholden to special-interest lobbies or big-name donors."

"You *are* beholden to them, Mr. President. You would not be here without them—and the next Vice President will need our support to be confirmed."

"Mr. Stover, I would not be here without the vote and confidence of the American people. I would hope my party would support my choice— for the good of this nation and the advance of my agenda. The agenda you publicly approve."

As the air of tension in the Oval Office intensified, the Minority Whip quietly interjected, "Mr. President, since you have found our selections objectionable, can you at least tell us who you are favoring?"

"No one, at present. I have considered many candidates in the last six months, but I have yet to find the right fit for my administration."

Jackson stood, signaling the end of the meeting. "Now, gentlemen, I realize how busy you are and will let you get back to work."

The Minority Whip answered, "Thank you, Mr. President."

The others were silent as they filed out.

⌘

"CONGRESSWOMAN BALLARD, Mr. President."

"Thank you, Mrs. Blair. Welcome, Congresswoman. Coffee?"

Regina Ballard had a warm, genuine smile, one she turned on Jackson. "Thank you, Mr. President. I'll have a cup if you are."

The waiting steward poured two cups, set them on a tray, and placed the tray between them. Jackson nodded, and the steward withdrew.

"Mmm. Thank you, Mr. President. It's very good. A nice pick-me-up in the middle of a busy afternoon. Thank you, too, for squeezing me in today."

"I was glad I could. I'm sorry we've not had the opportunity for a one-on-one before this. Was there something in particular you wished to discuss with me?"

She put down her cup. "Yes, sir. I know you've been pressured by both parties and likely numerous factions within the government to select their candidate as your next Vice President."

"I have." Jackson kept his response even-toned.

"Well, sir, I am not here today to put myself forward. Rather, I am here on behalf of a colleague and, I wish to make it clear, without her knowledge."

"Oh?" Jackson was intrigued.

"She is the type of legislator who never puts herself forward, Mr. President, one of those rare politicians who puts her constituency above her political aspirations or even reputation."

"I'm all ears, Congresswoman."

"Kimi White Grass, Mr. President, a member of the Montana Blackfoot Tribe."

"A Native American." Jackson sat back and tried to recall what he knew about the congresswoman from Montana.

"Her father was Blackfoot; her mother was Hispanic. She would be the first Native or Hispanic to serve in such a high office. Congresswoman White Grass isn't well known, so I took the liberty of assembling a dossier for you, sir."

Jackson took the folder from Ballard. "Thank you. Your suggestion is much appreciated."

⌘

"I AM SO HUNGRY."

"I'm hungrier," Zander insisted.

"Well, I'm going to start gnawing the dashboard if we don't get to the restaurant soon."

Our second-favorite buffet was minutes away, and my stomach was bellowing like a love-sick wildebeest.

My phone chimed, and I glanced at the caller ID. "Oh! It's Macy." I put the call on speaker. "Macy?"

"Jayda, hi! We wanted to let you know that our boys are here, and they are perfect."

"Oh, my goodness, Macy. I'm thrilled for you both. Have you named them?"

"Yup. Denzel and Deshaun Uumbana—to go with my hubby Darius and our boy, Daniel."

"I like! They are all good, strong names. And you? How are you doing?"

"Relishing the ability to turn over without the assistance of a crane."

I laughed. "Well, when will you be home from the hospital and when would be a good time to bring some meals for the family?"

"I go home tomorrow. My mom is here until Friday. How about Sunday afternoon?"

I glanced at Zander, and he nodded.

"Perfect. Any likes/dislikes? Food allergies?"

"I only ask that you avoid spicy foods since I'm nursing the babies. Darius and Daniel will eat whatever you put in front of them. You just have to jerk their plates away before they start chewing on them."

"Oh, I totally feel you. My husband is the same way. See you Sunday, Macy—and congratulations again. I'm so happy for you guys."

I hung up just as we pulled into the restaurant parking lot. "Boy, I'm so glad we're here. You know, we should ask restaurant management about frequent flier miles. A punch card? Bonus points? Something."

"Right. And, please, be sure to jerk my empty plate away before I sink my teeth into it—because I'm the one who was threatening to gnaw on the dashboard five minutes ago."

Laughing and holding hands, we ran to the restaurant doors.

⌘⌘⌘⌘

CHAPTER 14

"MR. PRESIDENT, THEY are ready for you."

"Thank you, Marcus."

Jackson entered the Oval Office. The eight men and women waiting for him, senior members of the Congressional Black Caucus, stood at his entrance.

"Good morning, everyone."

"Good morning, Mr. President."

When Jackson had taken his seat and his visitors had done likewise, he nodded to the most senior member of the group. "Congressman, this is your show. What can I do for you today?"

"Thank you, sir, and thank you for seeing us. Of course, the entire nation is waiting with interest for your vice-presidential selection."

Jackson inclined his head, signaling the man to continue.

"As our caucus members discussed this issue, we all agreed that the Vice President's unfortunate passing presented us with an unprecedented opportunity."

"Us?"

"Why, yes, sir. You and us as African Americans. It would be a truly historic turn of events for a sitting black President to choose another African American to serve as Vice President. An even greater statement of social equality and progress would be for that Vice President to be an African American woman."

Jackson kept his face impassive. "Have you such a candidate to put forward?"

"Delia Whitney-Butler, Mr. President. She has an impeccable reputation, having served fifteen years at Treasury, four of those as Deputy Secretary of the Treasury. We've polled, and found she has broad support on both the East and West Coasts."

At least she isn't that mad hatter from Florida, Jackson thought.

"I do not know Ms. Whitney-Butler personally, but she has, as you said, an impeccable reputation." He left it there and waited for his visitors to move the ball forward.

The congressman glanced at his companions and then the President. "Can we take it then that you are amenable to our suggestion?"

Jackson folded his hands. "Yes, of course, and I thank you for bringing your recommendation to me. It would be a proud day, indeed, for America to have its first woman VP as well as its first African American VP."

"But?"

"But I'm discovering that selecting a vice president who can be confirmed by both houses of Congress is more difficult than choosing a running mate for a general election. I wonder . . . have your polls looked at how your fellow lawmakers would vote for an African American VP given the country already has a black President?"

"You would have the vote of every member of our Caucus, Mr. President." This came from one of two women in the room, an outspoken black representative from California. "Perhaps it is the optimal time in history to put our candidate forward and dare the whites in Congress to decline her nomination."

She ended her delivery on a strident ring that caused a few members of her caucus to shift with discomfort.

"We could undoubtedly do that. However, you must remember, Congresswoman, that I govern an entire nation—not just the fourteen percent who are African American—and I must work with the whole Congress if I hope to enact any of my agenda while in office."

He hesitated, knowing the reaction he was about to elicit. "If we were to strong-arm Congress on this one issue, would we not risk leaving a bitter taste in the mouths of the other eighty-six percent of Americans, including the seventeen percent Hispanic population? Hispanics and Latinos, as you are no doubt aware, make up a significant voting bloc in your own state. I would hate to kiss my reelection chances goodbye based on this one choice."

The woman stared at Jackson with unveiled disdain. "I told the caucus that's what you would say."

Jackson stared back. "I am the President of the United States, Congresswoman, the President of all Americans, not just African Americans. I am working to unite us as fellow citizens and sojourners on the journey toward a more just and equal society. I still prefer to think of America as a melting pot—where character, accomplishment, contribution, and cooperation lift all of us up—rather than a nation divided by race or ethnicity."

"So you say," she sneered.

Jackson ignored her and turned his attention to the group's spokesperson. "Thank you for coming to visit me today. I like Delia Whitney-Butler's record and, if I win a second term, will consider appointing her to a cabinet position. We need more capable women in top roles in our government."

The Congressman dipped his head. "Thank you for seeing us, Mr. President."

Jackson cleared the discord of his meeting with the Black Caucus from his head and summoned his Chief of Staff. "Have you read Congresswoman White Grass' file?"

"Yes, sir. I have two aides vetting her now. They are adding to Congresswoman Ballard's report as we speak. In a nutshell, White Grass spent three terms in the Montana House before she ran for federal office. She's a loyal party member but has bucked the leadership on issues her constituency are clearly against."

"Any negatives? What about her personal life?"

"We're digging into that now, Mr. President. By the way, sir, Senator Delancey has asked for some time this afternoon."

"Really? A sane and reasonable visitor? Bring him on."

⌘

"MR. PRESIDENT, THANK YOU for squeezing me into your always-busy schedule."

The President nodded to Axel Kennedy, who stepped out of the Oval Office and closed the door behind him.

"Not at all, Senator Delancey. I've been looking forward to your visit. Coffee?"

"No caffeine for me this late in the day, I'm afraid. I would take a glass of water though."

The aging senator from Alabama hobbled to a sofa and eased himself down. Jackson handed the senator a glass of water and took the seat opposite him so that they were facing each other—on the same sofas President Jackson and Vice President Harmon had occupied the morning Harmon tried to poison the President. Harmon, himself, had died instead.

President Jackson glanced at the coffee table, recalling the moment when Harmon had pitched forward, his shoulder striking the corner of the table before he rolled onto the floor and expired, a pink-tinged froth on his lips. Jackson shuddered at the memory.

"Mr. President?"

Robert Jackson returned to himself. "I apologize, Senator. It is hard to sit here without remembering the Vice President's death."

The old man's expression softened in sympathy. "A horrid business. Horrid. Even though . . ." and the Senator turned a candid eye on Jackson, "even though I was no fan of Harmon's, his death was a shock nonetheless."

"It was. And finding his replacement is proving to be a devilish challenge."

"No doubt. No doubt. However, I can't imagine you relish that dolt Speaker of the House—even if he is from my party—being next in the line of Presidential succession any longer than necessary. You must be quite keen to fill the VP slot."

Jackson observed the venerable politician. Although near the end of his career, the man was known as a shrewd but fair dealmaker and an arbiter of peace on both sides of the aisle. Had he requested this meeting to offer up a candidate?

"Keen? That I am. However, given the nation's contentious political scene, selecting a suitable man or woman whom our divided Congress will confirm is well-nigh impossible."

Delancey cradled the tumbler of water against his vest. He chose his next words with care. "Mr. President, I intend to retire at the end of my term. That tidbit, of course, is still a closely held secret. Let the cat out of the bag too early and there'll be such a pileup at my door for endorsement that I'll never get anything done in my last two years.

"Ah! Two years and then I'll devote what's left of the rest of my life to my sweetheart. Winnie eschews the limelight, you know; she has always preferred to live a private life. When I retire, we will quietly immerse ourselves in the work of our foundation"

Jackson nodded. The Delancey Family Foundation was world-renowned, a charitable organization dedicated to educating third-world children.

Delancey sipped on his glass before adding, "Mr. President, I've seen just about everything in this city in my forty-plus years in office. I would hate to leave public service without the assurance that our executive branch is in good, stable condition. Is there anything I can do to help you with your VP selection process?"

"Can you magically change Section 2 of the Twenty-Fifth Amendment?" The President spread his hands. "I'm open to suggestions, Senator, if you have someone in mind who could fill the bill *and* pass confirmation hearings and a majority vote in both houses."

Jackson's Chief of Staff, Marcus Park, stepped into the Oval Office. "Mr. President? I apologize, but your 3:45 is here."

"Who is it again?"

Park's eyes flicked toward Delancey. "Speaker of the House, Mr. President."

Jackson's mouth thinned. "Tell him I'm running ten minutes behind."

"Yes, Mr. President."

"Speak of the devil," Jackson murmured. "For months this office has seen a steady stream of lawmakers, career politicians, military and intelligence advisors driven by special interest groups, all with their own *perfect* VP candidate, every one of them with strings and wires leading to a hidden control bar."

He sighed. "Don't get me wrong, Senator; I'm open to suggestions, but most of the proffered candidates are either more interested in their own political futures or are the sponsored shill of some big-money corporation. I am, however, as I said before we were interrupted, interested in your recommendations."

"That is very generous of you, Mr. President, and I confess that I did come to throw a few names into the hat. Have you considered Governor Mendoza of Utah? The Hispanic voters like her."

"I do, too, but your party leaders find her too conservative."

"I suppose I should have known that. What about Representative Peters?"

"Defined by his outspoken immigration stance. He wouldn't even make it through committee."

"You've probably vetted Senator Choi, too?"

"Doesn't want the job, I'm afraid—not that I blame him."

Delancey offered a weak smile of apology. "I'd like to be of help to you, Mr. President, but I admit you have quite the dilemma before you. If you consent, I could poll my counterparts on both sides and see if an acceptable dark horse emerges?"

"A most kind offer, Senator. Please feel free to do so. Discreetly."

The rheumy eyes of the veteran politician twinkled. "Is there any other way?" He set his glass on the coffee table and struggled to his feet. "I know you prefer for guests to exit through a different door when another visitor is waiting. But if you have no objections, I would like the Speaker to see me. Might twist his tail a little if he imagined I was filling your ears with anything other than the party line."

Jackson chuckled. "Please be my guest, Senator. Twist away."

The Oval Office has four doors—one to the President's private study, one to the West Wing's main corridor, one to the President's secretary that then leads to the West Wing's hall, and one exiting to the Rose Garden. Jackson saw the Senator to the door to the main corridor. Marcus Park was waiting with Speaker of the House Friese, a youthful, somewhat hyperactive individual of forty-five years who had diligently worked his way up the party ladder by kowtowing to his party's powerful leaders.

"Afternoon, Speaker Friese." Delancey delivered his greeting in his most charming Southern manner. "I suppose you've come to offer up our party's vice-presidential requirements?"

"Yes. I have the good of the party in mind."

The inference was that Delancey did not.

Delancey waggled his eyebrows. "Ah. That's the difference between us, I suppose. I prefer to work for the good of all Americans."

Before Friese could react, Delancey smiled and clapped Friese on the back. "Good luck in there, junior. You're gonna need it."

Friese flushed with indignation, but Delancey had already turned his back and was ambling away.

"Mr. Speaker?" Jackson distracted Friese by welcoming him into the Oval Office. Then he resigned himself to thirty minutes of politely listening to the Speaker's conditions for approving Jackson's vice-presidential selection.

⌘

"WE'RE TAKING SURVEILLANCE detection out onto the streets tonight," Mal announced.

I tried not to let my enthusiasm show. "Okay."

Mal and McFly were the only instructors present. McFly drew our attention to an on-screen map. He held a laser pointer.

"We're here. We're going to drop you two in separate locations, approximately two miles from here. We have two tails prepositioned in both locations. Your task is simple: Identify and lose your tails and make it back here without being tagged.

"Mal and I will run overwatch from our van. You'll have an hour to complete the drill."

Mal took over. "We're going to run two SDR drills tonight. Both times we'll do an AAR—an after-action review—to critique your performance and capture the lessons to be learned."

"Got it."

Zander, AKA John-Boy, nodded.

We didn't need to exchange covert glances, because we'd already decided that Gamble's injunction against our use of "nano-hocus-pocus" should apply only when we were under direct observation. For Zander and me to benefit the most from our training, the SDR drills needed to be realistic—and the nanomites *were* our reality.

Tonight's class fit the bill perfectly . . . and I was looking forward to a little fun and games.

Mal and McFly loaded us into their van. They had darkened the van windows so we couldn't see out of them as they drove from their garage and away from their neighborhood. A quarter of an hour later, after driving a circuitous route—probably to disorient us but not the least bit effective—the van stopped.

"You're up, Ripley."

Since I was first out, I wouldn't get to see where they dropped Zander. No matter. I jumped from the van door and scanned my surroundings. I started toward a coffee shop on the corner.

Jayda Cruz, you are approximately two miles northwest of your starting point.

"Thanks, Nano."

I walked into the coffee shop, went straight to the back where I figured I'd find the restrooms and a back door. Just as I reached the rear exit, I paused, changed my mind, reversed course, and hit the women's restroom.

I waited there for ten minutes, thinking. Mal's team had probably designed an "easy" first exercise, with the coffee shop as the obvious place to lose a tail. That meant they would be watching for me at both the rear and the front. Well, they were in for a surprise.

When I left the restroom, I was invisible. I stood by the front door until a young couple got up and, hand in hand, opened the door and left. I breezed through with them and started south.

I spotted Dredd across the street, kitty-corner from the coffee shop. His eyes shifted every few seconds. I even saw him whispering into his sleeve.

Laughing, I moved on. Three blocks up the street, I turned a corner, stepped into some shadows, and reappeared. Then I sauntered east until I reached a busy intersection. I hailed a cab and gave him directions.

"Nasty part of town," he offered.

"Don't you know it."

He tipped his head and drove on.

A block from the intersection I'd given him, I said, "This is good; pull over here."

"Suit yourself, lady."

I paid the cabby in cash and jumped out. I was two blocks east of Mal's clubhouse, near the alleyway that ran behind it. I slipped into the alley and made my way to the rear of the building. The only way into the clubhouse from the alley was through a high, barred window, latched and locked on the inside.

"Nano."

They jetted from me and sprang the lock. The barred grill swung out. I backed off and took a run at the window, planting one foot several feet up the wall, using the impetus to reach the window ledge. I pulled myself up and tried the window itself. It wouldn't budge. Years of paint and warping had sealed it shut.

I hung from the window ledge for a minute, thinking, scanning around. When I looked up, I saw the fire escape above my head.

"Okay. Plan B."

I dropped to the ground, backed away again, and ran at the wall. This time I planted my foot higher and pushed harder, leaping for the bottom rung of the fire escape's ladder.

The ladder was locked in place and didn't move, but that was okay. I had started to climb up, hand over hand, when I remembered the window grill hanging open below me.

"Nano."

The grill swung shut and locked.

My feet touched the bottom rung of the ladder, and I climbed up the fire escape, up and over the edge of the roofline. I'd already done my homework. I found the hatch right where, from the warehouse, I'd spotted it on Google Earth.

As hatches go, it was a little odd. It had looked simple enough from above, but it took the nanomites several minutes to worm their way through and release it. When I hauled on the hatch, I saw why it had taken them so long. The hatch was made of two-inch steel lugged down by four heavy-duty hydraulic cylinder latches.

Nobody was getting into the clubhouse from the roof—except me, of course.

I peered into the hatch and was surprised a second time. The hatch opened to a ladder and vertical, chimney-like space guarded by a second, identical hatch.

"Defense in layers. Guess they really don't want anyone coming in from the roof. Going out, yes, but getting in? Nope."

The nanomites were already working on the second hatch, so I looked around from my vantage point. It was more obvious from here that Malware, Inc.'s clubhouse truly was an island in a decaying urban setting.

When the second hatch gave, I dropped down a second ladder and found myself in the third floor proper. From there, I made my way down to the training center.

I heard Zander sneak in the side door ten minutes later.

"Hey, John-Boy."

Zander's grin was large. "Most fun I've had in months, Ripley. Almost as fun as the dojo."

When the team reassembled in the clubhouse at the end of the hour allotted, we were finishing our fourth hand of rummy. We'd helped ourselves to their coffee and discovered a deck of cards at the same time. I had yet to teach Zander Samba. Maybe after our crazy life settled down.

"Hey, guys." Zander shuffled the cards and had me cut them. "Want me to deal you in?"

All he received were narrowed eyes and muttered growls in response.

⌘

MAL AND HIS CREW made us run two more SDRs, not one. By the time the lengthy class ended, we'd beat the SDR drills 3-0. The AARs were short and a teensy bit tense. Zander and I high-fived, and the Malware, Inc. instructors seethed. They said nary a word as we left, but if looks could have killed . . .

"I think the guys are peeved with us."

"Impressive deduction," Zander drawled.

When we trudged into our apartment, I wanted exactly two things: sleep and a walk-in freezer. I settled for opening the refrigerator and standing as close as I could to its interior without actually climbing inside—'cause if I could have climbed inside, I would have.

"What's going on, Jayda?"

"Hot, really hot. Comes in waves."

"This isn't the first time you've felt like this?"

I shook my head.

"Nano, what's wrong with Jayda?"

Both nanoclouds were conspicuously silent, so he pressed them. "Nano, what's going on with Jayda? We need to know. Is she sick?"

No, Zander Cruz.

They offered no further explanations. When more time had elapsed (and when Zander's fuse was about to reach his powder keg) they answered, *Jayda and Zander Cruz, if you will take a seat, we will explain.*

Take a seat? Zander caught my eye and frowned. Neither of us liked the ominous intro.

"Come on, Jay." Zander tugged me away from the fridge, and we sat down on the sofa together, me fanning myself.

Zander commanded, "All right, Nano. What gives?"

Jayda Cruz, do you remember when we spoke of your endocrine system? How our joining with your body sped up your metabolism, enabling you to become an optimal fighter?

"Yeah. I remember." And I remembered that those changes had rendered me infertile.

With the depletion of your supply of ovum, your ovaries no longer produce sufficient quantities of estrogen and progesterone. The symptoms you are experiencing are known as hot flashes. They signal the onset of menopause.

Stunned, I could not think straight. Menopause? That was for older women.

"I-I . . . but I'm not even thirty!"

Your body is still producing hormones, but in irregular amounts, and we, insomuch as we are able, have been stimulating the production of the necessary hormones. Since we are unable to attenuate your discomfort, we recommend that you ingest a measure of hormones. A sufficient addition of hormones will alleviate these and other symptoms.

Zander got his head around the nanomites' news before I could. "What other symptoms?"

Depression. Anxiety. Irritability. Muscle ache and headache. Fatigue. Night sweats. Sleep disorder—

"Okay, that's enough, Nano. Where would we get the hormones?"

Typically, a physician would diagnose premature menopause and prescribe hormone replacement therapy in pill or cream form. However, we do not recommend that Jayda see a physician.

"Why not?"

It is likely that her blood workup would show . . . unusual readings prompting concern. The physician would call for further tests. Further tests would not lend themselves to keeping Jayda's physical transformation—or us—a secret.

"You mean, they'd think I was a freak of nature and turn me into a lab rat."

Obviously, not of nature, Jayda Cruz.

"So, a freak *not* of nature. That's comforting," I retorted.

"Hey, calm down, Jay. It's going to be okay. We just need to get a prescription for hormones through a different avenue, right, Nano? Without a doctor's exam. Then these, er, hot flashes will subside?"

Yes, Zander Cruz. Almost immediately.

"Okay, I'm sure you can figure out how to swing the meds, but why didn't you tell Jayda what was going on sooner?"

Again, the nanomites did not answer right away.

"Nano?"

We were . . . concerned that Jayda would be angry.

I stared at my shoes and the carpet under them. I *was* angry, but I was going to have to get over it. Somehow. The nanomites had already asked my forgiveness for making irreversible changes to my body without my knowledge or permission, and I had given it. I had given my forgiveness to them because Jesus had given his forgiveness to me.

It was just that the ongoing repercussions of those changes meant I had to deal with the emotions that went along with those repercussions. Like the layers of an onion, these further ramifications of the nanomites' actions also needed my forgiveness.

Yes, I needed to forgive, but I also needed to be real.

"You're right, Nano. I can't pretend that I'm not angry. I . . . I didn't anticipate this outcome, but I guess it makes sense."

We are sorry, Jayda Cruz.

"I know you are, Nano, and I realize you were . . . afraid to tell me."

I expected them to say, *We do not experience the human emotion of fear, Jayda Cruz*, but they didn't.

Maybe they didn't experience the feeling of fear as we do, but the nanomites had an intense dislike, an aversion that bordered on paranoia, of being separated from each other, from fellow tribes and the collective.

"You were afraid I would withdraw from you, Nano. Shut you out."

They didn't answer, but Zander nodded. He knew, like I knew, how much our unions with the nanoclouds mattered to them.

"Nano, although I am angry at this moment, I am, nonetheless, in charge of my choices. I choose to forgive you. I will get over my anger. I will . . . I will adjust to these . . . circumstances. Somehow."

I had a picture in my mind of the nanocloud as I'd first seen it—sparkling blue and silver. Bright and alive. At this moment, I could only visualize it as dull, gray, and dejected.

"Don't worry, Nano. It will be all right. You'll see." I might not have sounded all that convincing, but I meant what I said.

Zander cleared his throat. "Uh, Nano? Could you help us out here with the medication Jayda needs?"

We will, Zander Cruz.

"All right, then. Jay, let's try to get some sleep, shall we?"

We crawled into bed and, instinctively, Zander pulled me into his arms and held me close. I tried not to cry, but I couldn't do it. I buried my face in the crook of his neck and wept like there was no tomorrow.

⌘⌘⌘⌘

CHAPTER 15

"HEY, JAYDA, HOW ARE YOU feeling today?"

"I'm fine," I grumped as I plopped a battery-driven fan onto my desk and pointed its little gust of air at my face.

"Okaaaay." Stung, Chantelle flounced back to her workstation.

We both knew I was lying, and we both knew why: I didn't want to talk about how I felt.

Work that morning went pretty much as usual. I didn't have the ambition to do more than the bare minimum the job required. Still, I needed to tag the other two SPOs with nanobugs, so I dragged myself off to the restroom at lunch, ditched my badge in a paper towel dispenser, and ran over to Safety and Security to look at their shift schedule. One of the SPOs I was seeking was out on patrol; the other was detailed to a SCIF.

There was no way I was going to chase after another patrol car in this heat. Although the SCIF was two buildings away, it was the lesser of two evils.

Jayda Cruz.

"Yes, Nano?"

We have detected something of concern.

"Oh?"

An IT employee has accessed your video and badge tracking data. He has been monitoring and reviewing your movements.

"You fixed the files though, right? They don't show anything out of the norm?"

We did alter the files, Jayda Cruz. However, this employee viewed the data both before and after we adjusted the files. We believe he downloaded video footage of your activities before the film was corrected.

"Downloaded? Downloaded to where?"

We deduce it was a cleverly disguised flash drive, quite contrary to NSA policy, and no longer on the NSA premises.

I jogged down the hall to the nearest exit on the way to the SCIF. Out the door, around the next building, off to the right toward my objective.

"Which employee, Nano?"

He goes by the name of Rob Tellerman.

I felt like I'd been punched in the gut. "Rob! Goes by? What does that mean?"

It is not his real identity, Jayda Cruz. It is a good cover, but not as good as yours.

I stopped where I was: Someone was monitoring my movements. Someone planted at the NSA. Planted to watch me?

Our tradecraft training rang in my ears: *In any and every situation, to believe your identity is unknown and to act accordingly is potentially deadly. Again, your mental state must never presume that your identity is uncompromised, just as you must never assume your plan is foolproof. Surveillance detection, then, becomes the way you live—or the way you die.*

I picked up my pace and reached my destination. The SPO stood at an access control point. Only individuals with the proper clearances and who had been preapproved to use the SCIF would get by him. I eased up behind the guy, sent the nanobug array to him with a wave of my fingers, and crept to the nearest exit.

I hot-footed it back to my building and to the restroom to fetch my badge, pondering the nanomites' revelations, trying to decide what to do about them. I rounded the restroom's hairpin curve entrance, becoming visible as I did so.

"Hello, Jayda."

I swung around at Kiera's greeting, schooling my face to act surprised but not guilty. "Oh. Hey, Kiera. How are you?"

She cozied up to me wearing a smug, shrewd smile. "Oh, I'm fine, but I think we need to talk, Jayda, don't you?"

"Uh, what do you mean?"

"We've been watching you. You're very good, but you've made mistakes. Now I want to know who you really are."

"Huh?"

"Say, where's your badge, Jayda? Did you . . . lose it?"

I looked down. "Oh, crud. I must have left it—"

"Oh, look! I found it." She held up a lanyard and let my badge dangle from it. "You left it in that paper towel dispenser over there."

I shook my head. "In the what?"

Nanomites launched themselves at my command.

"Why would I—Kiera, that's sounds crazy." I leaned toward her. "Say, are you okay?"

She scoffed. "Don't play games. It's you—" She blinked twice in slow motion, then her eyes rolled back in her head and she collapsed in my arms. I dragged her to a wall and sat her down against it.

"Nano, you know what to do. Take out about twenty minutes' worth."

They went to work removing the last twenty minutes of synapses in Kiera's brain. Someone would find her unconscious in the restroom and call for help. I wanted to be far away when that happened.

More tradecraft admonitions pounded in my head. "Your contingency plan will either save your life or end it—which is why contingency planning must be one hundred percent complete, ready, and waiting."

I left the restroom under the nanomites' cover. When Kiera woke up, she wouldn't remember a thing about lurking in the restroom to ambush me, but her partner would. I didn't have much time to fix that.

I struck out for IT. It was lunchtime and the IT department was empty—except for Rob. As I crossed the threshold, I sent the nanomites. They flew across the room and Rob jerked, quivered, then fell forward; I caught his head before it bounced off his keyboard. I helped him to lean back against his seat while the nanomites got to work shredding synapses.

We can in no way mitigate for his preceding memories, Jayda Cruz. He will remember prior instances of monitoring your movements.

"I know, Nano. That's why we need to figure out who these two people really are as soon as possible."

When they had finished with Rob, I asked them to wake him up. As soon as his eyes began to flicker, I dashed off toward Safety and Security. It took the nanomites fifteen long minutes to alter the badge tracking data to show I'd spent my lunch in the cafeteria and amending video to back my badge's movements. They used old video to show me walking into the cafeteria, inserting me behind a crowd of other employees. They had to fabricate a tiny clip of me sitting behind a post that blocked the camera's angle, and a similar bit to show me walking out. Under the nanomites' direction, I left Safety and Security, ran to the cafeteria, and exited at exactly the time the fabricated clip showed me doing so.

When I returned to my desk in the Repository, I was fatigued, famished, and stressed beyond belief. I'd blown the primary axiom of spy craft: *Don't give yourself away.*

And now my mission at the NSA was in jeopardy.

⌘

I EXITED THE BASE at the end of my workday and sent my car onto the highway on autopilot. My mind was preoccupied with what I would say to Gamble—and how he would react.

A buzz announced the arrival of a text. "Nano. Read the text, please."

Jayda Cruz, the text reads, 'Your prescription is ready for pickup at CVS Pharmacy, 8640 Guilford Road, Columbia, MD 21046. Our pharmacy hours are Monday through Friday, 9 a.m.–9 p.m., Satur—'

"Okay. Got it. Thanks." I'd think about how the nanomites managed to get the prescription later.

"Nano, dial Gamble, please."

Gamble picked up the second ring. "Yes?"

"I blew it, Gamble."

I poured out what had happened and what info I had on Kiera Colón and Rob Tellerman—which wasn't much other than the addresses HR had on file. "The nanomites told me that Rob's ID is phony, so I imagine that Kiera's is, too."

Gamble was upset, but he didn't berate me. Instead, he said, "You have enough on your plate. Let me handle this from my end."

I was happy to let him.

⌘

I WENT THROUGH THE CVS drive-through and picked up a 90-day supply of hormones (the prescription written by a Dr. Sommers) and went home to Zander. I wanted to stay in and mull over the situation at work, but he reminded me that the Celebrate Recovery meeting was that evening.

"Let's get something to eat. We'll talk, then head over there," he suggested.

"Yeah. Okay. Let me take one of these pills first."

We called in an order for two large, deep-dish pizzas and two salads from a local pizzeria. They were ready when we got there, which left us some time to sit and talk while we scarfed down our dinner.

I told Zander what had happened, blow by blow. He marveled at how quickly I'd responded but, unlike Gamble, he was upset and worried.

"Who do you think these people are?"

"I have no idea yet. I hope Gamble can figure it out."

We left the pizza joint and arrived at the church just as the assistant leaders were unlocking the fellowship hall where the group met.

"Hi. You must be Zander and Jayda. I'm Tom Peters; this is my wife, Becky."

After chatting for a few minutes, we went inside with them and helped set up chairs. I followed Becky into the kitchen. While she made coffee and lemonade, I arranged cookies on a plate.

"I've never been to a Celebrate Recovery meeting before. Zander has, but it's all new to me."

"Well, Celebrate Recovery is something like AA, only it is specifically Bible-based and is for every kind of addiction. It is also for the family members of addicts."

The meeting was eye-opening for me. Tom called everyone together and we sang a couple of worship songs. When we were done singing, Tom led us in a Bible study. I appreciated the study. I had thought it would be about some aspect of addiction; instead, it focused on deepening our relationship with the Lord.

Then we broke into two groups, pulling our chairs into tight circles in opposite corners of the fellowship hall—guys in one circle, gals in the other. The women's circle had only five participants—Becky, myself, and three others. The men's circle, on the other hand, had fifteen or so participants.

"This time is for sharing our victories, our struggles, and our prayer requests," Becky explained. "We break into separate groups because sharing can be daunting enough without compounding it with members of the opposite gender."

She glanced at me. "By the way, we always remind everyone that what is said in Celebrate Recovery stays here. This is a place of trust and confidentiality. We don't repeat what is shared, even with our spouses."

I nodded my understanding.

Over the next hour, I listened to the women talk about their issues, their walk with the Lord, their families, and their needs. We shared Bible passages and prayed for each other.

I was mostly quiet and observant until Becky asked me, "Do you have any prayer requests, Jayda?"

To myself I answered, *Boy, do I.*

If I'd told them what was really burdening my heart, I might have blurted, "Well, shucks. You see, I'm on assignment for the President of the United States. I'm supposed to uncover the remains of this conspiracy to end his life and steal the presidency. No biggie—but, golly gee, today I totally blew my cover, and I don't know what's going to happen next."

I had to settle for "You know, I would appreciate prayer for my work. I've started a new job and am finding it . . . tricky."

Without comment, they began to pray for me. I was first amazed and touched—then the discouragement and self-flagellation fell from me like flakes of rust. I was strengthened; my heart was encouraged.

The two groups came together at 8:30, and the meeting ended with a time of visiting over punch and cookies.

I enjoyed it all.

I needed this, this friendship and care, Lord. Thank you.

⌘

GAMBLE ENTERED THE OFFICE where he spent most of his days and logged into the FBI's database. He hoped to identify the crack Jayda suggested he'd find in Rob Tellerman's ID. It took him all of two minutes to run Tellerman's name and come up against a security flag: Rob Tellerman's profile was classified and locked.

"Huh." He ran Kiera Colón's name. Same result.

He glanced at the addresses he'd scribbled down during his call with Jayda. Then he grabbed his keys and headed out.

⌘

KIERA AND ROB SAT at the table in Rob's apartment, poring over the printed screenshots and watching the video clips that defied the screen captures. Kiera was nursing a headache and was in a foul state.

Rob was reluctant to aggravate Kiera in her present state of mind—except . . . except nothing about the afternoon made sense anymore, and he couldn't let it go.

"I called you," Rob mumbled, "and told you that her badge had been in the women's restroom off the cafeteria for more than fifteen minutes."

"And I let my supervisor know I wasn't feeling well and went to the restroom to wait for her."

"Well, so what happened then?"

"I already told you. I made it to the restroom and was ready to ambush her . . . and then I don't recall anything until I woke up with paramedics standing over me."

She rubbed the spot on her forehead that seemed to ache from deep within. "I've never passed out like that before—and now you say the video feeds and badge tracking data have all changed. *Again.* If I didn't have a vague remembrance of finding her badge in one of the paper towel dispensers before I blacked out, I would accuse you of making the whole thing up."

Rob cleared his throat. "I need to tell you something."

"What?"

"Something similar happened to me."

Kiera cracked one eye in his direction. "What do you mean?"

"I was monitoring your badge and hers. Just like you said, both of your badges were in the restroom."

"And then?"

"And then I woke up and Cruz's files had been altered."

"Except for these screen captures." Kiera touched one of the printouts. "If it weren't for them . . . You were smart to do this, Rob."

It was the first, albeit reluctant, compliment she'd paid him. He didn't know how to respond.

"Let's recap," Kiera went on. "This Jayda Cruz somehow evades video detection and runs around campus unseen. While she's out doing whatever she's doing, she either turns off her badge or leaves it hidden in the restroom so what she's up to can't be tracked. Afterward, she hacks into the system and changes all the data?"

"See, that's super puzzling, Kiera. Nobody could hack the video and badge systems and change their data as quickly and completely as she does in mere minutes. *I* couldn't do it that fast. It's . . . spooky."

"You know what's really spooky, Rob? Waking up missing minutes of your life. That. *That* is what's spooky. And speaking of 'spooky,' that has to be what we're dealing with: A world-class spook—but for whom?"

Rob shivered. "Are we in over our heads, Kiera? Do we need to ask for help?"

Kiera didn't answer; Rob figured she was running the situation in her mind—including just how nuts their chain of command would label them if they reported what they'd seen and experienced.

A knock sounded on Rob's apartment door. Rob jerked, but Kiera slowly reached into her purse and pulled out her Glock 21.

She tipped her head at Rob and crept to one side of the door. Rob stood to the other side. When Kiera nodded, he asked, "Yeah? Who is it?"

"Special Agent Ross Gamble. FBI. I'd like to speak with you, Mr. Tellerman."

Kiera frowned. When she jutted her chin, Rob demanded, "Put your credentials to the peephole."

Rob, then Kiera, studied them. Kiera gave Rob another nod. He stood behind the door and she moved behind him. Rob opened the door partway but blocked the entrance.

"Thank you, Mr. Tellerman."

"What can I do for you, Agent Gamble?"

"May I come inside?"

"I don't see why you can't ask me what you want from there."

Gamble smiled. "That depends. Do you want your neighbors to hear me ask who you really are, Mr. Tellerman?"

Kiera signaled Rob with a tap on the shoulder. He opened the door. As soon as Gamble stepped inside, Rob closed it. Kiera, not altogether convinced of Gamble's identity, moved out from behind Rob and leveled her gun at Gamble.

Gamble nodded amiably. "Oh, good. You're both here." He looked around. "Nice place, Rob. May I sit down?"

Rob cut his eyes at Kiera, who nodded.

"I guess."

"Great." Gamble settled himself in a side chair. "Well, you're probably wondering why I've come calling." He glanced at Kiera. "Would you mind putting that away? I'm sure you know how to handle a firearm, but I'd feel better if it were pointed elsewhere."

"How about I just keep it handy?" Kiera lowered the gun to her side and moved across the room, about ten feet away. "Now, what do you want?"

"What? No polite conversation? No 'getting to know you'? Just cut to the chase?"

She nodded.

"All right, then. A funny thing happened to me today. Oh, wait. I guess funny things happened to you guys today, too. Am I right?"

Rob and Kiera did not move.

"Okay. As I was saying, a funny thing happened to me today. You see, I ran your names in the FBI database and, *shazam!* Both your files came up classified—which is significant in two respects, don't you think? No opinion? Aren't you curious? No?

"Well, here it is. One, I knew before I searched the database that your IDs were fake and, two, the fact that your fake IDs were classified tells me why: Both of you are FBI, working undercover. And I'll bet," Gamble looked from Rob to Kiera, "I'll bet that your assignment is to look into the disappearance of Wayne Overman. He vanished without a trace, and the disappearance of such a high-level NSA executive—one privy to so much classified information—raises national security concerns. How am I doing so far?"

"Haven't a clue what you're babbling about."

"Why, sure you have. The thing is, I have a similar assignment . . . only my assignment comes from higher up the chain of command—a lot higher up."

Kiera scowled. "I'm a lowly clerical worker. A government contractor employee. Haven't the foggiest idea what you're talking about, Agent Gamble."

Gamble stood, causing Kiera to put both hands on her sidearm and lift it.

"I'm a nice guy, so let me spell it out for you two—in the *nicest* of ways, of course: I'm warning you to lay off a certain mutual acquaintance, one of your coworkers." Gamble dropped his good-natured façade. "You either stop monitoring her movements, or the next 'request' you receive will be more, shall we say, *strongly worded.*"

This time Kiera looked uncertain.

Gamble pointed at Rob. "Your purview, Mr. Tellerman, is the IT help desk at the NSA—IT, not Safety and Security. Safety and Security functions do not fall into your network permissions, and they frown upon unauthorized intrusions.

"Just so you know, should you venture into NSA video surveillance or the badge tracking system again, your management at the NSA will be apprised of your activities—including how you downloaded files to a contraband device. I think you'll lose more than your job and clearance, don't you?"

He flicked a brow at Kiera. "This is your first and only warning: *Back off.*"

On his drive home, he called Jayda and left voice mail. "I've handled the situation. Your friends at work shouldn't be a problem from here on out. I'll fill you in when we meet next."

⌘⌘⌘⌘

CHAPTER 16

IT WAS FRIDAY, the end of my second week at the NSA. All things considered, we had made considerable progress toward completing our assignment for the President—but I couldn't believe how full Zander's and my life had become in that little time. Sundays were church in the morning and meetings with Gamble at night. Twice a week Zander and I trained at the dojo. Wednesdays were our tradecraft classes, Thursdays were Celebrate Recovery—and in between we were scanning and filtering data the nanomites uploaded to Alpha Tribe.

A lot of data.

No wonder they wanted to upgrade their storage capacity!

While I was at work, the nanomites spent much of their time decoding and searching Repository files, looking for connections between Harmon and others that might lead us to hard evidence against those who had colluded with him. According to them, they found lots of "interesting information," but nothing that helped our investigation.

Maybe being hired to work in the Repository wasn't the great positioning we first thought it to be. At least Kiera hadn't come by my cubby today to dig her suspicious eyes into me.

Thanks, Gamble.

As far as gathering intel from my job, our best leads to date came not from the Repository but from the nanobug arrays. The nanomites monitored the four SPOs I'd tagged as well as the Secret Service agents from the White House detail. Most of what we heard was innocuous, but certain patterns did begin to emerge.

The SPOs' work routines were consistent and predictable. Nothing unusual there—except for occasional calls from a certain burner phone. It took the nanomites only one such call to identify Lawrence Danforth's voice coming from the burner. Before long, we had an idea how many NSA SPOs Danforth controlled directly—how many and which ones.

It was daunting that Danforth had corrupted more than a dozen of the NSA's police force.

And once the nanomites had identified Danforth's burner cell, they went to work mining that phone for Danforth's other calls. One number stood out as being Danforth's most frequent connection: Since he spoke weekly with that number's owner, we were anxious to discover the identity of the party on the other end.

If we hadn't tagged the White House Secret Service plants, it may have taken us longer to figure out who Danforth called most often. The "sick" agents were the key to that connection.

During the first three days they were out sick, the agents spoke to no one. I chuckled every time I visualized them sprawled on their bathroom floors, weak from heaving up their toenails. On the fourth day, the nanomites had the nanobugs ease up a little to simulate recovery from the dread "norovirus." We were anxious to discover who they would report to.

By the afternoon of the fourth day, each of the sick agents had called two numbers, one a desk phone, the other an unregistered cell phone—the same cell phone Danforth spoke with weekly. During the agents' calls, the nanomites pinpointed the location of the desk phone—the corner of H and 10th in D.C.: Headquarters of the U.S. Secret Service.

No bombshell in that, right? The agents' boss worked at Headquarters. Uniformly, the agents reported to the White House detail chief that their health was improving and that they hoped to return to work the following day. Of course, we didn't want them returning to the White House just yet, so . . . each of the agents would suffer a regrettable "relapse" over the following twenty-four hours.

Tsk tsk.

But the agents also called a second number, a cell phone, and that call, too, the nanomites discovered, terminated within Secret Service Headquarters. The agents' conversations with the man on the other end were similar to those they'd had with the chief of their detail: "I'm recovering and will return to work soon."

The man's response? "You had better. All our listening posts are off-line."

The nanomites pulled and cataloged the audio greeting from every desk phone at the Service's headquarters until they matched the voice at the end of the cell phone. It belonged to Secret Service Deputy Assistant Director Blake Morningside.

Morningside was too high up the food chain for rank-and-file agents to call, even agents on the White House protection detail—and yet they had. Better still, once we had put Morningside's name to the number, we then knew who the NSA Deputy Director spoke to on a weekly basis.

Bingo. Danforth had engineered Wayne Overman's death and disappearance; Morningside ran the dirty Secret Service agents within the White House. Danforth and Morningside spoke weekly. Secret Service Deputy Assistant Director Morningside and NSA Deputy Director Danforth were major players in Harmon's plan to usurp the presidency.

Zander and I joined the nanomites in the warehouse to study the diagram they were constructing—the identified participants in the collusion, how they were connected, and where they were placed in the government. Harmon's plot to assassinate the President was beginning to take on a recognizable shape.

It bothered me that we hadn't yet identified Harmon's man on the inside of the Army's Institute for Infectious Diseases, the man who had provided Harmon with the biotoxin to kill President Jackson. But getting someone inside USAMRIID to unmask Harmon's man would be problematic and take time we didn't have. We were more likely to uncover him through his connections with the accomplices we'd already identified.

As we studied the nanomites' diagram, Zander zeroed in on the call log from Danforth's burner. "Huh. See all these one-off incoming calls to Danforth's burner?"

"What of them?"

"Nano. Eliminate all the callers we've identified from Danforth's call log over the past, say, nine or ten months."

Thirty-three unknown callers remained.

"Interesting. He received calls from these thirty-three numbers once and only once; they are never repeated. Nano, show us these calls on a timeline."

The nanomites displayed a line that stretched from last fall to within recent weeks.

"See how they are spaced out over the last year? Never less than a week apart; not more than four a month. And notice the call length? Really short. Three minutes tops."

"They could be marketing calls. You know how persistent and annoying they are."

"Do you spend three minutes on the line with a telemarketer?"

I saw his point. "No. I hang up immediately. Hmm. What are you thinking, Zander?"

"Well . . . what if it's the same caller using a different phone each time? What if this guy bought a whole bunch of single-use, disposable phones? What would that tell us?"

I nodded my comprehension. "That he was—is—being very careful."

"And who do you think would exercise that much caution?"

"Someone nearer the top of the heap?"

Zander Cruz, you have made an astute observation. We have now collected and cataloged the metadata from these phones. Although we have little to go on, we will attempt to uncover where and how these phones were purchased.

It hit me.

"Suppose . . . suppose the phones were bought in bulk—like a case lot or at the same time from the same place?"

"I guess it's possible. But I doubt someone as careful as this caller appears to be would make that kind of mistake."

I pondered the diagram. "So, thirty-three disposable phones over the past ten months. Maybe that's how we track this caller. If this is Danforth's boss in the conspiracy and they talk regularly, shouldn't we expect another call soon? Shouldn't we be ready when the next one comes in?"

"You're right. Tracing the phones isn't necessary—we just need the nanomites to listen for the next call and trace it in real time."

Zander Cruz, it will be difficult to trace a call in under three minutes. We can, however, catalog the voice and attempt to identify it.

"Do your best, Nano. Unmasking Danforth's superior is our new objective."

⌘

OUR NEXT STINT IN THE DOJO took an unexpected turn.

Zander Cruz, Jayda Cruz, we have altered your training regimen.

"Oh?"

You raised a valid concern after our last session. You will not always have your sticks with you. It is also possible that you would encounter a situation where we are unable to draw sufficient electrical current to power your integrated weapons.

"Integrated weapons?"

The weapons you possess as a result of our integration into your physiology.

"Oh. Yeah. Integrated weapons." I lifted one shoulder. "Uh, okay. So, what's the new drill?"

Your updated training program will focus on using materials at hand, forming effective weapons from ordinary objects. You will be required to innovate, to think on your feet. Scenarios will evolve from general to specific, from elementary to complex.

"Thrilled, I'm sure."

My experience with Gus-Gus and Ninja-Noid being what it was, I figured our updated training program would "evolve" from "general" pain to "specific" agony, from "elementary" trauma to "here's a taste of the hurt locker."

Our one solace was that the simulations had the two of us training and fighting together.

We started the first scenarios in possession of our escrima sticks. Six opponents attacked at once. Zander and I intuitively fought back-to-back and did pretty well. If it had been real combat, we would have prevailed.

After a short break, we reentered the simulation. The "room" was the same size, but now it was furnished—meaning we had all kinds of obstacles to work around. Or trip over. I didn't much like it, but who can say what a battleground might consist of?

The same six opponents swarmed into the room. Zander and I could no longer hold a strict back-to-back defense. Too many things got in the way, although I didn't see any of the sims stumbling or tripping, just us.

Grrr!

"Maneuver into that corner, Jay! We'll use the walls to keep them from overwhelming us."

Normally, I wouldn't think a corner a good thing, but he was right; we were able to fight side-by-side without being flanked. We'd taken out three of the sims when they began to push us further into the corner where we wouldn't be able to swing our sticks effectively. On top of that, the corner contained two chairs and a small, elbow-high table.

"Hold the line, Zander! Don't let them back us up!"

"Easy for you to say."

And then one of my sticks broke in two. One half went flying; the other piece was too short to be of any use.

If I'd had false teeth, they would have fallen out of my mouth.

"Improvise, Jayda!"

"Easy for you to say!"

The sims were encroaching, pushing us back, and I was down to a single stick. I felt the edge of the table brush against my waist. I grabbed the table edge and swung it like an oversized Frisbee at the sim battering me. He fell back a pace. I reached for a chair and crashed it over his head.

I was left holding half the chair's frame. I beat him with that and it broke down further.

"Good move, Jay."

Huh?

I looked at my hands. One held an escrima stick; the other a sturdy chair leg about the right length.

"Hey. Not bad."

With two sims left, we gathered momentum and fought for more room. Then we attacked.

Three minutes later, we won, and the simulation ended.

My breath came in ragged gulps. "Not . . . gonna have . . . chairs next time."

Zander's chest was heaving, too. "The nanomites . . . have been hiding their sadistic streak, haven't they, Jay? Am I . . . right? All our jokes . . . at their expense? They've been patiently storing them up until now, waiting . . . for the right situation for payback?"

"Duh. If they weren't before, they will be now."

"Oh. Yeah. Ooops."

⌘⌘⌘⌘

CHAPTER 17

I SPENT MOST OF SATURDAY cooking. Back when I was "Gemma Unemployed" and had to economize to make ends meet, I'd cooked from scratch and eaten out infrequently. Now, with what Zander and I packed away on a daily basis, dining out at all-you-can-eat buffets was cheaper than shopping and cooking for two bottomless pits.

However, I'd promised Macy a hot meal tomorrow and several for the freezer—so here I was in the kitchen, humming happily and cooking up a storm.

After I'd put away two pans of enchiladas (easy on the red chile for Macy and the babies' sake) and a deep-dish gourmet mac and cheese that would feed the family twice, I went to work on the meal I'd deliver hot and ready tomorrow afternoon.

I put all the ingredients and spices for spaghetti sauce in a pot to simmer before I started cutting up salad greens. I made the equivalent of two salads for a family of four—one for Macy and her family, one for us. After I put the salads in the fridge, I sliced fresh French bread, mixed up some savory herb butter—without garlic, for Macy's sake—and slathered the butter on the bread slices.

Zander wandered into the kitchen and sniffed. "Smells great."

"I'm making enough for us, too."

"Yum."

"Tomorrow after church, when we come home to change our clothes, I'll cook the pasta and heat up the sauce and bread."

⌘

SUNDAY MORNING SERVICE was awesome. We were settling into our new church, and we loved it. When they announced that the church would hold a baptism after next Sunday's service, Zander looked at me.

"You haven't been baptized, have you, Jayda?"

My mouth made a tiny "o" shape. "No, I haven't."

"Want to get in on the action next week?"

I nodded. "I do."

We approached Pastor Lucklow after the service.

Zander asked him, "Pastor, is it too late to sign up for the baptism next week? Jayda has been a Christian for about eight months, but she hasn't been baptized yet."

Pastor Lucklow smiled. "The class is this afternoon. Will you have time to attend?"

"I'll make time, Pastor," I answered.

"Then I look forward to baptizing you next week." He glanced around. "Do you also have a moment for a brief word?"

"Of course."

He took us aside where the noise was less and asked, "I believe you visited Celebrate Recovery Thursday evening, Zander? What did you think of the group and its ministry?"

Zander squeezed my hand. "I think the Lord wants me to help with this ministry, Pastor."

"I have spoken to Tom and Becky, and they tell me that those they've talked to in the group agree, brother. How would you propose that we work you into the leadership of the program?"

I recognized the joy that flashed across Zander's face. I had seen it when he preached in the park to the homeless; I had seen it when he preached at DCC back in Albuquerque. It was the joyful passion of sharing Jesus with others.

"Easing me into the role over a couple of weeks would be best, Pastor. I can attend, participate, and get to know the members better before we make it official."

"That's very wise, young man. I appreciate your approach. The program leadership is a part-time staff position. What do you say to us starting your salary in two weeks?"

"I accept, Pastor."

We both sighed. An answered prayer!

We had lunch after church with Tom and Becky to celebrate Zander's appointment and get to know them better. It was fun feeling like we'd made our first "couple" friends—although observing them rope, "rassle," and corral four active kids (ages five through eleven) in the restaurant was a bit like watching Olympic-class cat wranglers.

When the food arrived, silence descended on the table and Tom prayed a blessing. The kids tucked into their lunches, and I marveled. "Wow. You guys have mad skills."

"Comes with the territory," Becky said. "Every day you either win or lose—and you can't afford to lose, not even once."

She favored me with a friendly wink. "You'll find out."

I smiled, nodded, and toyed with my fried chicken. With the addition of hormones to my daily routine, the aggravating hot flashes were beginning to subside, but each morning's pill was a reminder that my body's reproductive system was at the end of its life. Nevertheless, I was determined not to indulge in any self-pity. It was a luxury that sported a hefty spiritual price tag.

I was beginning to understand that every day came with its own spiritual battles and, like Becky said, I could not afford to lose, not even once.

Maybe I wasn't ever going to "find out" as Becky had suggested, but I had made my peace with not having children of my own. My life was replete—and complicated enough—as it was.

⌘

AFTER LUNCH WITH TOM, Becky, and their brood, we went home and changed into shorts and t-shirts. We gathered the meals I'd prepared, drove to the Uumbanas' home and, arms laden with plastic containers and a wrapped baby gift, rang their doorbell.

Macy and her husband lived in a modest home not far from Ft. Meade. We heard squeals and laughter as heavy footsteps trod to the other side of the door. A tall man with a little boy riding high on his shoulders threw open the door. The man looked like he'd slept in his clothes and had just gotten up.

"Hi. You must be Zander and Jayda. I'm Darius and this—" he swung the giggling boy down and plopped him onto his feet "—this is Daniel. Say 'hello,' Danny."

Instead, the boy buried his face in his dad's pant legs.

"C'mon, Danny. Say 'hello.'"

"No!"

Zander and I laughed.

"Well, come on in," Darius said. "Macy is in the bedroom, but she'll be out shortly."

"We came bearing gifts—mostly the edible kind," I said. "One hot meal for this evening and three frozen meals. You might want to put the frozen food back into the freezer if you have room."

Darius seemed touched and a little overwhelmed. "That's really kind of you folks. I-I don't know what to say."

"You could say, 'What's for dinner?'" Zander joked, relieving the pressure.

"Whatever it is, it smells delicious. Um, follow me. I'll show you the kitchen."

The kitchen was a wreck. Dirty dishes and fast food containers were stacked haphazardly everywhere.

"I'm sorry the place is a mess. I work nights and sleep during the day. Well, I'm *supposed* to sleep during the day. Things are a little chaotic right now what with trying to get two newborns to sleep at the same time."

"Why don't you guys get to know each other? I'll put the food away."

Darius, with Daniel on his shoulders again, led Zander out onto their little patio. I set to work on the kitchen. I had put the food away, cleared up the trash, and had most of the dishes in hot soapy water when Macy found me.

She had one swaddled bundle on her shoulder, and she seemed happy but weary. Circles hung under her dark eyes. "Look at you, Jayda! Are you an angel of mercy?"

"Hardly," I laughed. "Just a friend."

I thought Macy was going to cry.

I reached for her and we hugged. "Hey," I said softly. "This is what friends do."

"The minute my mom left, everything went to the dogs. Darius started working extra hours to make up for the time he missed when the babies were born and I . . . haven't kept up."

She sniffed. "The babies are wonderful, but I'm still figuring out how to feed them both at the same time, so they will sleep at the same time—which translates to little sleep for me. Between them and Danny, I'm practically comatose."

"Don't worry. You'll get it figured out." I tried to lift her spirits. "Do you guys like spaghetti? That's the sauce in that pan on the stove. The pasta is in that microwavable dish; it's already cooked and just needs to be heated up along with the bread. And there's fresh salad in the fridge."

"I'm sorry I asked if you were an angel, Jayda. You obviously are."

I laughed. "Naw, girl! Now, tell me about those babies."

"Would you rather see?"

"Would I!"

She slid the bundle from her shoulder into the crook of her arm. "This is Deshaun."

I stared in awe at the perfect—albeit squishy—little face. Deshaun's head was topped with a mass of black, spiraling hair. One arm wriggled free and stretched up over his head. My gaze was drawn to his tiny fingers and miniscule fingernails.

"Oh, Macy. He's so beautiful."

"I have another just like him in the bedroom."

We giggled. Deshaun stretched and arched his back and cracked one eye. It didn't last long. He went limp in blissful sleep.

"I guess I should try to put him down while I can."

"I'll finish up here while you do."

I had finished the dishes, swept the floor, and made a pitcher of lemonade from a can of powdered mix when Macy returned.

"Lemonade?" I offered.

"Would you consider moving in with us?" she joked.

We laughed again and took glasses out to the men.

Later, after we'd enjoyed a fun and relaxing few hours with Macy and Darius, Daniel tugged at Macy's shirt.

"Mama. Babies woke-ded up. They's hungry."

Little Daniel's manner was so serious and concerned that Zander and I hooted. Daniel didn't like that and launched a scowl in our direction to let us know.

"You hear them crying, honey?" Macy asked.

"Yas. They's hungry."

"I'll bet they are. Well, let's go get them, shall we?"

He nodded vigorously, then pointed at me. "You come." I was surprised—and it was more of a command than a request.

"You want me to come, too?"

"Yas. You come."

He grabbed my hand and led me into the house, down a hall, to a bedroom. The high, unmistakable cries of two newborns rattled the closed door.

"Ay-yi-yi," Macy muttered. "Little vampires!"

We crept inside. The two babies were in the same bassinet, one at the head, the other at the foot. Both were wailing, and the bassinet shook with their energy.

"Why don't you pick up Deshaun while I get Denzel?"

I didn't know much about holding babies. Macy laughed when she saw me holding my little bundle straight out in front of me like a hot casserole dish.

"Hoo, girl! You are a newbie, aren'tcha?"

"Help. I haven't a clue."

She put Denzel in the crook of her arm. "Like this. They fit just so."

While she fed a hungry Denzel, I managed to get Deshaun into a reasonable imitation of Macy's example. It must have been okay, because the tiny boy settled and drifted into sleep.

He was so perfect, so beautiful, he took my breath away. I marveled at his clear, bronze skin and the long eyelashes that laid like feathers on his cheeks.

I spent half an hour staring at Denzel's contented face before Zander and Darius came inside. Daniel was hanging over his dad's arm, zonked out. At Zander's nod, I remembered we had the baptism meeting shortly and our regular meeting with Gamble after that. "Oh, wow. It's later than I thought. We should get going. You guys probably need to nap when the kids do!"

Zander cleared his throat. "I was telling Darius about Celebrate Recovery and, of course, that led to me telling him I'm a pastor. Macy, Darius, before we go, would you mind if Jayda and I prayed a blessing over your family?"

Macy's brows lifted. "Um . . . what do you think, Dare?"

Darius looked uncomfortable, but he answered, "Yeah. I'd like that."

I placed my free hand on Macy's shoulder; Darius drew near his wife, and Zander put his hand on his shoulder.

"Lord God," Zander prayed, "You see this beautiful couple, and you love that they have set their hearts to raise these children well. We ask, Lord, that you would give them wisdom—your infallible wisdom—and give them the understanding and patience they need to continue as they have begun. Lord, we ask you to bless this family and draw them to you, in Jesus' name. Amen."

"Amen," I whispered.

Darius and Macy were quiet, but when they looked at each other, something good and precious passed between them, and I smiled.

"We're glad you came, Jayda and Zander," Macy said. "We'd love for you to come again."

⌘

TRUJILLO KNOCKED SOFTLY on the rear door of Gamble's rented house. He opened without a word and closed the door behind her before speaking.

"Thanks for coming, Trujillo."

"Not much has changed since we last met."

He snorted a laugh. "On your end, maybe."

"Oh? Now you've made me curious."

"I think you'll be more than curious before the evening is over. First, I want to assure you that we've swept this house. It's clean. Tonight is the first time since I rented it that anyone could have seen me come in."

She eyed him. "That's an oddly worded statement."

"Yeah. I know. You'll understand in a bit. I also wanted you to know that I've spoken to our mutual acquaintance. He has authorized me to bring you in on our operation."

Trujillo lowered her voice. "Just checking: You're saying *the President* has authorized you to bring me in?"

Gamble nodded.

Then she held up a hand. "Wait. You're conducting *an op* for the President?"

"Let's sit down and I'll explain."

Gamble outlined Harmon's plan to assassinate the President. He didn't get into the weeds explaining how Harmon's plan was thwarted—not immediately.

"The President—and rightly so—has a low level of trust at the moment. Furthermore, the circle that knows about our other friends must remain small and tight."

"Other friends?"

"We have a lot of ground to cover this evening, Trujillo."

⌘

GAMBLE HAD ASKED US to meet him at the house this evening rather than at his car. It wasn't a strange request, just a departure from our established routine. When we let ourselves in the rear door, we saw why: He wasn't alone.

"Uh, Gamble?"

"Come in. Jayda, Zander, you remember Agent Trujillo?"

We did, of course, but she did not recognize Jayda. Her eyes slid from me to Zander and back. She was unable to hide her disbelief and suspicion.

"This woman is Gemma Keyes? I don't think so, Gamble."

Gamble spoke to us. "The President has asked me to bring Agent Trujillo in on our operation. He has two purposes in mind by involving her. One, we're short on resources we can trust. Trujillo here already knows most of your back story, and she stuck her neck out for you when things came to a head in Albuquerque. In the President's mind, she's proved her loyalty."

He pointed at me. "Jayda, would you mind doing that thing, so Agent Trujillo can see Gemma?"

The nanomites dissolved their disguise; Trujillo gasped and fell back a step.

"H-how . . . how did you do that?"

"We'll get to that in a moment. Like I said, we have a lot of ground to cover. Jayda and Zander, although Trujillo's chain of command has been conspicuously silent since Cushing died, the President believes her new handler will eventually initiate personal contact with her. That's his second purpose for bringing her aboard: When Trujillo's handler contacts her, we'll use you two to backtrace that individual up the chain and, hopefully, snag a bigger fish."

Gamble gestured to the living room furniture. "Let's all take a seat and bring Trujillo up to speed. Jayda? Why don't you start."

When the nanomites restored Jayda's features, I began the necessary overture. "Agent Trujillo, the last time we met—the night Cushing blew up my house—you said that you didn't know everything about me or why Cushing was so desperate to capture me. You also said you'd seen things that didn't make sense. I think your exact words were, 'things that boggle the mind.'"

"That's right." She looked to Gamble. "Are you going to explain all that to me now?"

Gamble pointed at me. "She will."

I chuckled under my breath. "This is going to take a while."

It took two hours, what with all the questions and various demonstrations.

Trujillo was a seasoned operator. In the field she'd witnessed the stuff of nightmares and had probably participated in her share of them. None of her experiences had prepared her to suspend disbelief at what could only be construed as supernatural powers at first blush.

"This is the last time you'll see Gemma Keyes," I warned her. "She died last December."

The nanomites reassembled Jayda's features, and Trujillo blinked multiple times, trying to process everything we'd revealed to her. She was silent as she studied my altered features.

"My name is Jayda now, and Zander and I are married. Our task is to flush out the remains of Harmon's conspiracy against the President. Gamble is right: We're shorthanded and could really use another set of eyes and ears. If the President says you can be trusted, we'll trust you."

"I-I, of course, whatever the President asks of me. I'm in."

With that, Gamble took over the meeting. Zander and I reported our findings from the week and answered a bazillion questions.

We didn't get to bed until after three in the morning.

⌘⌘⌘⌘

CHAPTER 18

MONDAY, THE START OF ANOTHER WEEK—the day Abe and Emilio would arrive. Zander left the apartment early to again check the White House for bugs. Later, he would pick up Abe and Emilio from the Baltimore airport. I would have to wait until my workday was over to see them.

My thoughts were on Abe and Emilio's visit, and my usual attention to my work was "off." Too off to do any lunchtime sleuthing, so I went to the cafeteria with Chantelle and Lynn. While we ate, I filled them in on our visit with Macy and her family.

"She's doing okay, but she looked tired. Juggling the three-year-old and the twins means she isn't getting a lot of sleep."

"You took them some meals?"

"Yes."

Chantelle looked at Lynn. "We could do that, too. Put a few more meals in their freezer."

"I'm game if you are. Let's do it."

"Do you and your husband have plans for the Fourth, Jayda?" Chantelle asked.

"Yes. We have family arriving from New Mexico this afternoon—well, they are as close to family as I have, since I don't have any relations."

I had to explain about Abe and Emilio—but from Jayda's perspective, not Gemma's.

"When I met Zander, he was the associate pastor at Abe's church. Abe and Zander were good friends. When Zander and I started dating, Abe took me on, too. He became something of a grandfather figure to me.

"Emilio, who is eleven going on forty-five, lived with his uncle, Abe's next-door neighbor. Unfortunately, Emilio's home life wasn't very good. His uncle was involved in criminal activities. Drugs. Gangs. That sort of thing."

Chantelle and Lynn's eyes widened.

I shrugged. "It happens. Then Emilio's uncle up and disappeared, leaving Emilio alone."

"Disappeared?"

"Yes. We still don't know what became of him." *Not the specifics, anyway.*

Smiling, I added, "Abe took Emilio in and is now fostering him. Zander and I consider Emilio ours, too. Kind of a group project. That's how I came to regard Abe and Emilio as family."

"That's amazing," Lynn said.

"Yup. We're pretty jazzed that they are coming to visit. Zander will take them around D.C. tomorrow. On Wednesday, we're planning to do the Independence Day parade and watch the fireworks on the Mall that night."

"Sounds like fun, but it's also going to be crazy crowded. Like, *insane* crowded. You'll take the Metro and get there early, right?"

"Yes. I know it will be a madhouse with a gazillion other people doing the same thing, but Emilio's never been to D.C. I want him to have the experience."

⌘

"THANK YOU FOR COMING in to sweep the White House again. Have you anything to report?"

Zander stood before the President and Axel Kennedy in the Oval office. "No, sir. The nanomites have detected no unauthorized listening devices. The House and the Oval Office are clean."

"Thank God," Jackson breathed.

"May I ask a question, sir?"

"Of course."

"It's been a week today since the dirty agents on the White House detail came down with the flu. They began feeling better on Friday; however, yesterday they experienced a regrettable 'relapse.'"

Jackson chuckled. "Thank you for that—and I have to say that whenever I need a moment of stress relief, all I have to do is recall their, er, *state of indisposition*. But you said you had a question?"

"Yes, sir. I imagine whoever is running these agents is chomping at the bit for them to return to work. Have you given any thought to a more permanent solution?"

Jackson looked to Kennedy and back. "Unfortunately, the bureaucracy prevents us from influencing those decisions."

"Jayda and I had an idea to buy us more time, sir."

"Please. We're open to suggestions."

"Direct the White House medical officer to issue an order that any White House staff infected with 'norovirus' are not to return to work until they have been symptom free for two weeks—to prevent a recurrence of the outbreak. It's overkill, sir, but perhaps the doctor would be amenable to your suggestion?"

Kennedy nodded to the President. "I believe we could get away with that, sir."

"Be circumspect, Axel. We don't want word getting out that the order was at my behest."

"Yes, sir."

The President stood. "I hope you will excuse me, Zander, but I have a meeting with my chief of staff."

"You are a busy man, sir."

Robert Jackson held out his hand, and Zander took it.

"I don't know how all this is going to play out, Zander, but I want to thank you again for your service to us. To me."

"It is my honor, Mr. President. Please call me back if I can be of assistance."

Zander blinked when he felt a familiar warmth cross from himself to the President's hand.

Moments later, as he left the White House, he asked, "Nano, why did you do that? We can't be listening in on the President of the United States!"

If you wish to respect the President's privacy, Zander Cruz, we will restrict you from the array's feed.

"It's more than that, Nano. Remember all the legal and ethical concerns Jayda and I discussed with you? And I fail to see the need."

We felt it prudent to position an array near the President. His security is our ultimate objective, is it not? However, if you insist, we will send the array a self-destruct order.

Zander grumbled a little longer before answering. "As long as you keep the feed to yourself, I suppose the idea has merit. But remember: When we finish our assignment, the arrays—all of them—are toast."

Toast, Zander Cruz? Ah, we see. A humorous euphemism. Very clever. "There is a time for everything, and a season for every activity under the heavens." Even a time to laugh. Ecclesiastes 3.

"Yeah, yeah."

⌘

ROBERT JACKSON PACED the Oval Office, his vexation evident. "I tell you, Marcus, if the Speaker of the House weren't such a dolt—that was Senator Delancey's appellation for Friese, not mine, by the way—I would struggle on without a VP until the next election cycle. Truman managed without a Vice President for four years. Surely I could do the same."

"Unfortunately, sir, the Speaker . . ."

"Yes, he *is* a dolt. I cannot, in good conscience, risk keeping him next in the line of succession. The man's nothing more than a tool of his party, utterly unqualified to be Commander-in-Chief in his own right."

Jackson placed his chin on his hand and stared down at his desk's blotter. "If I put up a man or woman my party wants, the other party will never allow a vote—and my preferred candidate is actually the choice most hated by the other party."

He snorted a wry laugh. "The doves think me too much of a hawk, and the hawks think me too much of a dove."

"The hawks believe you are weak only because you've not yet been tested."

"Regardless, if I select a candidate considered middle-of-the-road, both sides will buck me every inch of the way."

He sighed. "That's the problem these days. Instead of allowing an up-or-down vote, both parties block the process. At least Senator Delancey said that he would use his considerable influence to bring a vote to the floor—even if he couldn't support my pick. They sure don't make 'em like Delancey anymore. Why, he—"

Park interrupted. "Sir!"

"What is it, Marcus?"

"Sir, you've hit on it."

"I don't follow."

"Delancey, sir. He's your pick for VP."

Jackson started to object, but Park, in a rare display of discourtesy, spoke over the President. "Please consider him for a moment, sir. Yes, he's up there in age, but you said it yourself, sir, it's only until the next term, until you pick a new running mate and win the election.

"Think of the positives: The man is a legend—a war hero, a POW, seven times a U.S. Senator, a patriot and peacemaker respected on both sides of the aisle, although he has slowed down a bit over the last few years."

"Delancey's a member of the other party, Marcus."

"It's not unprecedented, Mr. President. And the beauty of it? The other party can't refuse to confirm him without poking themselves in the eye. As for our side? Delancey's politics run closer to our party's platform than his own party's. He has voted our way against his party leadership many times."

"The idea . . . has merit." Jackson tried to find a hole in his Chief of Staff's logic but found himself agreeing instead. "He did tell me that he intends to retire from the Senate at the general election anyway."

"Going out as VP would be the crowning achievement of Delancey's career, sir, and his personal and political clout would be a huge help in pushing through your agenda."

Jackson tapped a pen on his desk. "The governor of his state is a member of our party. He would appoint one of ours to finish out Delancey's term."

"Win-win." Park smiled. "It will be hailed as an inspired move, sir. And again, it would be only until the next general election."

Jackson slowly nodded. "By all that's good and holy, I believe you may be right, Park."

"Thank you, sir. And if I may be so bold?"

"Say on, Marcus."

"Our party, their party, the media. All of them. Hit them before they have a clue it's coming."

Jackson blew out a breath and made his decision. He pressed the intercom button on his desk phone. "Get Senator Delancey on the line, please, Mrs. Blair—and keep the call under wraps, please."

"Yes, sir."

"Marcus, if I can get Delancey to agree to serve until the election is over, I'd like to make the announcement Wednesday during the White House Independence Day Reception—like you said. No one will have an inkling it is coming. It will be a done deal before they can pick it apart."

"An auspicious occasion, sir."

"Finally. Finally, the way ahead is clear."

Jackson lapsed into silent thought.

Delancey is an honorable man, and he is too old to want the presidency. I need not fear that he will drop a bioweapon into my coffee.

Jackson exhaled on his relief, letting go of the months of stress. The intercom raised him from his reverie.

"Mr. President? I have Senator Delancey on the line."

Jackson picked up the phone. "Senator? Might I prevail upon you to drop what you're doing and have dinner with me? Yes. Shall we say, six? And, Senator? Would you be so kind as to keep our dinner engagement to yourself? You will? Thank you, Senator."

He set the phone down. "He's coming, Marcus."

⌘

ZANDER HAD PICKED UP Abe and Emilio from the airport and taken them to our apartment. Emilio must have been watching for my car from our living room window, because the second I pulled into my parking slot in front of our unit, he burst from the door and ran down the stairs to me.

There he was—*my boy*.

I watched him come, a lump stuck in the back of my throat. He had a fresh haircut, but not the awful shaved-head look Mateo had given him. More than that, with three healthy meals a day, Emilio had filled out. He was no longer a starving, neglected boy, scared but defiant, hiding far back in the bushes to avoid Mateo's drunken fists.

"Jayda!"

As he threw his arms around me, all I could think was, *What in the world?* When we left Albuquerque less than two months ago, the top of Emilio's head hadn't reached my shoulder.

Now I hardly had to look down to stare him square in the eye.

"You're growing up too fast," I protested.

He just laughed and hugged me harder.

⌘

THE WOMAN'S OUTRAGE was palpable. "You've had boots on the ground in Albuquerque for five days—more than enough time to find what I sent you to unearth. What is taking so long?"

The lead operative on the other end of the call shifted uneasily. "We had to arrange to interview the members of the FBI pathology team here. That took a few days, but the interviews got us nowhere. We sensed that they were hiding something—their stories were too closely aligned—but as soon as we pressed them harder, one of the doctors complained to the SAC. He started asking his own questions, like who did we report to. When he didn't get the answers he wanted, he shut us out entirely."

"You mean you bungled your mission."

"No, ma'am. I'm working another angle, something requiring incentive."

"Money?"

"Yes. I've baited the hook and dangled it in front of my target. It is only a matter of time before he caves."

"I provided you with plenty of cash; time is something I have less of—and patience in even smaller supply."

"I understand, ma'am." He paused. "If the target cannot be incentivized, do you authorize . . . other inducements?"

She thought a minute before answering. "The disappearance of a federal officer, even a pathologist, would focus more attention on your visit than scrutiny would bear. Sweeten the pot. If that doesn't produce a more positive outcome, you are authorized to threaten him with the loss of something—*someone*—more dear than money."

"Understood."

⌘⌘⌘⌘

CHAPTER 19

Independence Day

BECAUSE OF THE HOLIDAY, I had the day off, and Malware canceled our regular Wednesday evening class. That meant Zander and I had the entire day—and the evening—to spend with Abe and Emilio. I was *so* ready for the fun ahead of us!

The four of us grabbed an early breakfast at a pancake joint and made it to the nearest Metro station by eight. Like Chantelle had warned us, the Metro was jammed with tourists and vacationers bent on celebrating Independence Day in D.C. At each subsequent stop, a new crowd boarded—or tried to. At some point, the train was too full to handle all the onboarding passengers, forcing them to wait for the next D.C.-bound train.

Emilio insisted on sitting next to me—which I didn't mind a bit—but his attention was elsewhere. Everywhere. He was soaking it all up, and I was soaking him up.

Across from us, Zander grinned. I grinned back.

Perfect moment. Perfect day.

We exited the Metro at the Federal Triangle Station and hiked down 12th to Constitution Avenue. Traffic had been blocked off Constitution from east of the Capitol Building to west of the Ellipse. Loads of other people had gotten to the parade route before us, but we eventually planted ourselves on a waist-high brick wall where, if the crush of parade watchers in front of us sat down, we'd be able to see into the street. If they stood, so would we.

The parade was awesome. Zander bought little American flags on sticks for the four of us from a vendor. Our flags were but grains of sand compared to the numerous and huge Stars and Stripes in the parade. We waved our little flags anyway—at every marching band, float, and military unit that marched by. We waved at contingencies of Marines, Air Force, Navy, Army, Coast Guard, and various state National Guards. When the Revolutionary War marchers came through, I thought Emilio was going to lose his mind.

He pointed and shouted in my ear, "Jayda! Look! Look! They's from the Civil War!"

When my ear stopped reverberating, I shouted back, "I think you mean the War of Independence."

"Is that a different war?"

Good grief, what were they teaching kids in school?

"Yes. Eighty-some years apart."

"Oh." He didn't care. He was having a grand time.

⌘

PRESIDENT JACKSON, Maddie Jackson, Senator Delancey, and his wife Winnie observed the festivities through the thick glass of the Oval Office out onto the White House's south lawn. The crowd of White House staffers and their families were enjoying the food and games of the White House Independence Day Reception. A select group of media representatives mingled among the guests, shooting video and still photos, doing short stand-up pieces with the gathering in the background.

"I love seeing children playing on the White House lawn," Maddie murmured to Mrs. Delancey.

Winnie Delancey was a diminutive woman compared to her husband, and at least ten years younger than him. She nodded her agreement with Maddie's comment, then glanced up and smiled into her husband's face.

The four of them saw when the event organizers informed the guests that the President was about to speak. The crowd began to move toward the small platform and podium outside the West Wing's gardens.

Jackson's Chief of Staff asked, "Are you ready, Mr. President?"

Jackson nodded to Kennedy and Marcus Park. He and the First Lady strode from the Oval Office to the podium. Senator and Mrs. Delancey, moving a little slower, followed behind them.

A cheer rose from the reception guests as the First Couple mounted the platform. The Jacksons waved and smiled to ongoing applause until the President stepped to the microphone.

"Thank you. Thank you all. Ladies, gentlemen, children, and members of the media, today we celebrate the birthday of our nation. Maddie and I count ourselves blessed to have you and your precious families as our guests on this Independence Day. We are even more honored at the service you render our nation and this administration on a daily basis."

Shouts, whistles, and more applause interrupted Jackson. He smiled and saluted the kids who were waving furiously at him. Then he motioned again for silence.

"I felt that today was the perfect day to make an important announcement. Senator Delancey? Will you join me on the platform?"

Delancey assisted Maddie Jackson to step down from the platform before he climbed up and stood beside the President.

"Senator Delancey stands here with me. He needs no introduction, but I will elaborate on his patriotism and service to our country: Devoted husband; Viet Nam War veteran who, as a downed fighter pilot, spent nearly three years as a prisoner of war; respected attorney and lawmaker in the capital of his home state of Alabama, now close to completing seven terms representing his state in the U.S. Senate—and the devoted husband of Winnie.

"Honored guests, I wished for you to be the first to know: Today I officially nominate Simon Delancey to serve as my Vice President. Senator Delancey, I hope to welcome you soon to the West Wing."

Jackson and Delancey smiled and shook hands, while around them a frenzy of applause and photography erupted at the announcement.

⌘

WHEN THE PARADE ENDED, we made our way toward the National Mall. Zander, Abe, and Emilio had spent most of Tuesday at the Smithsonian National Air and Space Museum—Zander and I actually had spent eight hours wandering through that place on a particularly rainy day—but I was eager to show Emilio all of the large D.C. landmarks—the Lincoln, Jefferson, and Dr. Martin Luther King, Jr. Memorials; the Washington Monument; the war memorials; and the White House.

The White House. As much as I wanted to tell him we'd been in the White House as guests of the President, I kept that bit of information to myself.

Jayda Cruz, we are picking up a breaking news story you will find of interest.

"Oh? What is it?"

President Jackson has announced his vice-presidential nominee, Senator Delancey of Alabama.

"Wow! That's great. I'm sure glad he found someone he could trust."

Senator Delancey has a distinguished record.

"You've looked into him?"

Yes, Jayda Cruz.

"Good to know."

The four of us climbed the steps to the Lincoln Memorial and sat down for a while, just enjoying the awareness of history surrounding us and the view down the reflecting pool. Emilio sat between Zander and me. He grabbed Zander's hand and laid his head on my arm.

"This is a cool place, Jayda."

"I think so, too."

Other tourists sat on the steps or wandered up and down. Kids shouted and ran around, jumping from step to step, chasing each other. The Fourth was one of the busiest days in D.C., and it felt to me like we were part of something wonderful, something the other visitors knew and appreciated in the same way we did.

My husband—my wonderful, gorgeous man—smiled at me over our boy's head.

His face seemed to reflect what I was thinking: *What a perfect day! What a treasure, Lord. I'm so content in this moment, so—*

"Death to America! Death to this city, the Seat of Satan!"

I couldn't see what was happening through the streams of tourists, but within microseconds, the crowd parted—and the running, screaming, stumbling, and trampling began.

We were only yards from the hole opening in the crowd.

Not far enough away to avoid what was coming.

I scrambled to my feet and sprinted toward the sound of that voice, against the flow of people lurching and running to escape death and dismemberment.

"Jayda! No!"

I shoved flailing bodies out of my way and pressed ahead until I glimpsed him only feet away—a small man, bearded, wild-eyed—willing and ready to immolate himself and others—but in my mind, it was Cushing. Cushing and Genie and Jake all over again.

"No!" I screamed. I threw my hands up and pushed all the current I could marshal at him. *Into him.* The man staggered and dropped his hands to the steps to keep his balance.

"Nano! Now!"

Two bolts as narrow as my wrist whooshed from my palms, converged, and blasted into the man's legs. The blast flipped him high in the air, threw him in a complete somersault, and slammed him onto his back. The man's head smacked the granite with a sick kind of thump.

He did not move.

I stood only feet from him, chest heaving. I surrounded the prostrate form with a bubble that would protect myself and others nearby—except the man himself—should the explosive vest detonate. However, the nanomites inside the bubble were busy lasering through the wires on the man's vest.

People were still running and shrieking. They didn't know the danger was past.

Park rangers and Capitol Police rushed up the steps to the supine figure. They paid me no mind, and I suddenly realized I was invisible—and had been invisible since I charged the terrorist. If I couldn't be seen, I wondered how the tourists would report what had taken place.

Jayda Cruz, Zander is asking you to return to him.

"Is everything under control, Nano?"

Yes, Jayda Cruz. The subject is unconscious, and we have defused the bomb.

Numb. I was numb and shaking. I looked around for Zander. For Emilio. For Abe. I couldn't see; my eyes weren't working right. I was weeping. I had been terrified out of my mind that someone would hurt those I love. I stumbled blindly away from the terrorist. The nanomites steered me to Zander.

When I touched Zander, he put his arm around me and pulled me farther from the commotion. "C'mon, Jayda. You did it; you saved us and all these people. I'll yell at you later for risking your life."

I must still have been invisible, because no one paid Zander any mind. All eyes were focused on the scene on the steps. He drew me down the stairs and off to the left of the memorial, where we found Abe, his usually glossy complexion a pasty gray, and a wide-eyed Emilio.

He crashed into me, his arms like steel bands around my waist.

Guess I was visible again.

"Jayda! I thought you was gonna die!" Now that he could see me again, see that I was okay, he sobbed into my shirt.

"I couldn't let that man hurt you, Emilio."

Zander urged us to keep moving. "Lots of people had their phones out when that guy started shouting. Someone had to have caught you in action."

"The nanomites made me invisible."

"Yeah, but your *actions* weren't invisible." He complained further in Spanish, occasionally throwing in an English word, like "electricity," "bubble," and "lightning bolts."

I was more concerned with leading headlines such as, "Terrorist Flies into Air and Flips a 360." A hysterical giggle burst from my chest. I couldn't stop it.

Zander Cruz, we deleted images and footage from as many cell phones as we could reach.

We both heard the nanomites. "Even one or two will create a stir, Nano," Zander replied.

The mites didn't answer.

When we reached the trees on the back side of the Vietnam Veterans Memorial, I refused to go any farther. I collapsed onto a bench, and Emilio sat with me.

Zander, his hands on his hips, stared into the distance. He was upset, but I knew he would come around.

Abe tipped his head at me. "That was a brave thing you did, Jayda. Your fast acting saved our lives and saved a lot of families a world of grief."

I nodded. Maybe I did save other families, but *my* family had been my only concern when I acted. I suppose that was understandable.

We rested there for a while, keeping tabs on the busy scene over at the Lincoln Memorial. Emilio recovered his equilibrium first.

"I smell hot dogs."

Jayda Cruz, we detect no restaurants nearby.

I laughed under my breath. "Nano, I think Emilio can smell food a mile away."

I got up. "Come on. Let's head down the mall. I think there are food trucks on the other side."

We found a truck that had hot dogs and bought seven—one for Abe and two each for the rest of us.

As the sun started to go down, we (and everyone else) headed toward the Reflecting Pool, looking for a plot of grass to claim as our own for the fireworks.

It was a beautiful display, but I didn't enjoy it as much as I might have before the attempted terrorist attack. I sat between Zander's legs and Emilio sat between mine. Emilio leaned back on me, and I held him close.

Lord, please help us finish this assignment. I want to go home.

⌘⌘⌘⌘

CHAPTER 20

"NORMALLY I WOULD LOVE to come with you to Celebrate Recovery," I told Zander the next evening, "but I should stay home with Emilio."

Abe had already expressed interest in attending the meeting with Zander. With them leaving Saturday morning, I wanted to have Emilio to myself for a few hours.

After Zander and Abe left, I introduced Emilio to a new board game: Catan. He caught on quickly and we laughed and groaned our way through several spirited rounds. I won the first two games; Emilio shouted his victory when he defeated me in the third match.

"This is a fun game," he said as we packed the game into its box. "I wish . . ." He let his words trail off.

I didn't have to guess what he was wishing for, but I figured we needed to talk about it. I put the boxed game away, sat down on the couch, and patted the seat next to me.

He came and sat by my side. Stiff. Miserable.

I stroked his arm once. "What is it you wish, Emilio? Can you tell me?"

When he hung his head and a shudder ran through him, I pulled him into my arms. He didn't resist. In fact, he clung to me.

His answer was garbled between gulps and sobs, but I managed to make out the words, "Jayda, I miss you. Why can't you and Zander come home? Why can't you work there? Why you gotta live here?"

I squeezed my eyes tight and savored holding Emilio close to me. He likely didn't know how much I loved him and wouldn't understand how I longed to comfort him, to be near him all the time.

All I could answer him was, "This won't be forever, my sweet boy. We . . . Zander and I have a job to do here, but . . . when it is done, we'll come home. I promise."

He lifted his face to study me. "How long, Jayda?"

I heaved a sigh heavier than the Washington Monument. "I don't know, *mijo*. I can only say that we must stay until the job is done, until our assignment finished."

Those dark brows of his pulled together in concentration. "Your assignment?"

Emilio frowned, and then his brows shot up. "Are you . . . are you an' Zander . . ." his voice dropped to a conspiratorial whisper, "Are you guys, you know . . . secret agents?"

I'd never considered Emilio dull-witted. Quite the contrary; he was street savvy, perceptive, and extraordinarily bright—too bright, obviously, since he'd caught me off-guard.

He also had something of a "super-hero" fixation when it came to me. Still, how in the world had he cobbled "secret agent" out of the few phrases I'd uttered?

"Uh . . ."

"You can't tell me, right? 'Cause it's secret. 'Cause you're hunting down bad guys?"

"Um, no . . . of course not."

Those brows drew down a second time, and he glowered at me. "You lyin', Jayda?"

I slapped on my poker face and pulled the "adult" card. "Don't be disrespectful, Emilio, and don't ask questions I cannot answer."

He continued to study me without blinking. When he responded, he sounded too grown up for my liking. "It's okay, Jayda. I understand."

Then he hugged me, and I cherished every second of it.

⌘

ZANDER AND TOM CO-LED the Celebrate Recovery meeting that night, and during the circle time, Zander helped Tom facilitate sharing. It was a natural and effective way to ease Zander into the group's leadership role.

Abe, too, seemed pleased by the meeting and asked for prayer for himself and Emilio. "I'm an old man set in my ways, and he's a youngster with more energy in one day than I have all month. We're getting along fine, but he needs some healthy outlets for all that energy."

"That used to be my job," Zander told the group. "I played ball with him and ran him ragged—until we moved away."

When the circles broke up for fellowship time, Zander and Tom agreed it had been a good meeting.

"Um, Pastor Cruz, may I have a word with you?"

Zander turned. It was Jack. According to Tom, Jack had been attending CR for several weeks. "Sure, Jack. What can I do for you?"

The man's discomfort was evident. "I . . . I've made a lot of mistakes, Pastor. I've screwed up my life pretty thoroughly and I . . . I've hurt a lot of people. Drugs and drinking are the main reasons I ruined my life. I admit that."

Zander nodded and said nothing. He let Jack talk.

"Well, in all the dumb stuff I've done with my life, I somehow managed one really good thing, my daughter, Kaylee. She's four now. Cutest little thing you've ever seen—big brown eyes, curly hair, a kind heart."

Jack looked at his shoes. "I'm not allowed near her. Last time she saw me, 'bout six months ago, I was drunk. Made a fool out of myself. So . . . I don't get to see her again until I can prove I've been clean and sober for a while."

Zander nodded again and gave Jack's arm a quick squeeze. "You've made a good start, Jack."

"Yeah. A start. Long road ahead. I see that."

"We're here for you, Jack."

"Thanks. I-I appreciate that."

He had something more to say, so Zander just waited.

"The thing is, the thing I wanted to ask you . . . my sister Rachel sees Kaylee pretty regularly. She and my ex are still friends. Rachel called me today and said Kaylee is in the hospital."

Zander realized how hard Jack was struggling not to break down, and his face creased in concern. "Is Kaylee all right?"

"Rachel said they're doing a bunch of tests on Kaylee, that she has . . . a really high white cell count. That she probably has leukemia."

Jack's tortured eyes met Zander's. "The courts say I can't go to the hospital to see her. Can't be within 100 feet of her at any time, but I'm dyin', Pastor."

"Would you like me to visit Kaylee and her mother for you?"

Unshed tears of relief shimmered in the young man's eyes. "Would you, please? Tell my ex—her name's Donna—tell her I'm trying to stay sober, that I'm sorry for the hell I've put her through. And . . . ask her, would it be okay if you prayed for Kaylee for me?"

Zander again gripped Jack's arm. "I will. Please write down the info I need—hospital, Donna and Kaylee's last names. I'll go tomorrow. And give me your number so I can call you afterward."

"I don't have a phone, Zander. I live at a shelter right now. They let residents use their phone to look for work and such. If you give me your number, I'll call you."

Jack wrote the information Zander needed, and Zander slipped the paper into his pocket. About fifteen minutes later, he and his co-leaders finished cleaning up the meeting room. Tom showed Zander how to lock up the church and set the alarm.

"One more thing, Zander."

"Yes?"

"Pastor Lucklow asked me to give you these."

Tom handed Zander a small cardboard box. Zander opened the box and pulled out a business card. The card read,

Zander Cruz
Celebrate Recovery Ministry Leader

He found the church name, address, and Thursday evening meeting times on the other side of the card. His cell number was listed last.

"I don't know what to say. Pastor Lucklow has put so much trust in me, and he hardly knows me yet . . .

"I think he and your former boss in Albuquerque had an extended conversation. Pastor McFee had nothing but the highest praise for you, your walk with God, and for your ministry work. As for these cards? We've found that we need them whenever we share with someone about the program. It's an easy way to put meeting info into the hands of a person ready for change."

"Well, I . . . I'm honored."

During the drive home, Zander began to pray for Jack. For Donna. For Kaylee. "Lord, more than ever, I understand how drinking and drugs destroy not just the user but entire families—for generations. O God, I ask you to have mercy upon this broken family. Pour your conviction upon Jack and fill him with godly sorrow that leads to a true and deep repentance—and to everlasting life in you."

⌘

ZANDER WALKED OUT of the bedroom the following morning. He had showered and put on a freshly pressed shirt and tie.

"Yum! You look great today." I leered at my handsome husband, and he planted a lingering kiss on me—to Emilio's vocal disgust.

"That's gross, man! You gonna make me lose my breakfast."

"You won't always feel that way," Zander promised, laughing.

Emilio shook his head. "Naw, man. You crazy."

"Why *are* you dressing up this morning?" I was curious.

"I need to make a hospital visit this morning. Visit a sick child."

Abe joined the conversation. "Emilio and I thought we'd take the bus into Baltimore and visit the National Aquarium. Can you meet us at the aquarium after you finish?"

"Uh-huh. My call shouldn't take me too long, but you will probably be glad to get there early. Where will you catch the bus?"

"I'm hoping Jayda will drop us at the mall to make our connection."

"Well, shoot," I groused. "Now I want to go, too."

"You can call work, tell 'em you sick," Emilio suggested.

"And that would be a lie, wouldn't it?"

Emilio heaved a longsuffering sigh, then put his nose in the air. "Well, we gonna have fun 'thout you."

I ran my hand over his short hair. "I hope you do. I'm so glad you guys are here—even if I have to work and can't run around with you that much during the day."

Zander pulled his Bible toward him. "Speaking of work, we'd better start our Bible time before it's time for you to leave."

⌘

SOON AFTER ABE AND EMILIO left with Jayda, Zander got in his rental car and followed his phone's directions to the hospital where Jack's daughter was a patient. Zander parked in the visitors' lot, went through the hospital's main entrance, and found his way to Kaylee's room without too much difficulty.

The difficulties began when he introduced himself to Jack's ex-wife.

He knocked lightly on the door and put his head in. "Good morning. Are you Donna?"

A twenty-something-year-old woman, frowzled and bleary-eyed with fatigue and worry, glared at him. "Who wants to know?"

Zander stepped into the room and pulled one of his cards from his shirt pocket. "My name is Zander Cruz. I'm a ministry leader at Grace Chapel in Columbia."

She ignored the offered card. "Not interested."

He glanced at the small, still figure on the bed. "May I have a moment of your time? Perhaps in the hall?"

Stifling an oath, Donna hauled herself up. "You better not be wasting my time." She pushed him ahead of herself into the hall, closed the door behind them, and put her hands on her hips. "Well? Whatever you're selling, I'm not buying."

Zander projected what he hoped was a warm, disarming demeanor. "Donna, I assure you, I'm not selling anything. I facilitate a program at my church called Celebrate Recovery. Do you know what Celebrate Recovery is? Have you heard of it?"

"Nope."

The warmth of Zander's smile collided with Donna's frosty glower and dropped twenty degrees. Froze in place. He switched to a more matter-of-fact approach. "Uh, well, Celebrate Recovery is a program for individuals who struggle with addictions."

"I've got the perfect candidate for you—that *bleeping* no-good, *blank-blank* ex-husband of mine."

"You mean Jack."

She eyed him with more suspicion. "How do you know Jack?"

"He has begun attending our meetings."

"Good for him," she sneered. "Does that mean he'll actually get a job and start supporting his daughter?"

"I—"

"Do you know how hard it is being a single mom, Mr. *I'm-a-ministry-leader-at-some-*bleeping*-church*? Do you know how hard it is to raise a child with a deadbeat dad? *Do you?*"

Zander said nothing for a moment, but he heard, beneath the rage, a cry for help. "Donna, you are carrying a heavy load. What can I do to lighten it, to help? Do you need groceries? Rent money? A car?"

He didn't know why he'd said, "a car." Maybe looking through umpteen car lots in the last two weeks had predisposed him to say the word *Lord, we can barely afford a second car ourselves. Did I just stuff my foot into my big mouth?*

But the look that crossed her face was incredulous. "Y-you would get me a car? But . . . how did you know . . ."

Zander blinked. "I'm not a wealthy person, Donna, but my Father is. A car? Would a car help you? Is that what you need most?"

"Y-yes. We . . . Kaylee is so sick. When they let her out of the hospital, she'll need ongoing tests and treatments. We have to ride the bus everywhere. It takes us an hour—sometimes longer—to get to her appointments. If we had a car . . . if Jack paid child support . . ."

Filled with sudden boldness, Zander said, "Donna. It may take a little time, but we're going to find a car for you."

Donna's hardness cracked a little. Behind the façade, Zander saw hope warring with despair and doubt. He tipped his head toward the door to Kaylee's room.

"Jack told me last evening that Kaylee is ill. He is very concerned for her."

A little of the anger that had gone out of Donna resurfaced. "He's *concerned?* How touching!"

Zander took Donna's hand and sandwiched it between his. She tried to pull it away, but he held on and squeezed it gently to get her attention. "Donna, I want to say something to you. Something important. Is that all right?"

She looked down at her hand in his. When she looked back up, he saw tears in her eyes.

"Donna? Is it all right for me to tell you something important?"

She gave a nearly imperceptible nod.

"Thank you. What I want to say is this: Jack knows how badly he's messed up. He admits to how badly he's let you and Kaylee down. He wants to do better, and he's trying to break the hold addiction has on him. It's not going to be easy or fast, but if he continues the way he's begun, he will, eventually, be able to hold down a job and support Kaylee as he should. He told me himself that he wants to do right by you and Kaylee."

Zander again gestured toward Kaylee's room. "Jack is heartbroken that Kaylee is ill. Although he wants to be here to support you through this difficult time, he acknowledges that the restraining order is his fault, that he deserves it.

"So, he asked me to come visit you and Kaylee in his place. That's why I'm here. To offer you assurances that Jack intends to do better soon. Jack also asked if I would pray for you and Kaylee. Would you allow me to do that? Would you allow me to pray for you and pray for Kaylee?"

Donna's face crumpled into deep lines of stress. "Does . . . does Jack know Kaylee has leukemia?"

"Yes, and he is grieving—just as you are. Despite his many hurtful choices, Jack loves Kaylee. Will you allow me to pray for her? For you?"

Donna slowly nodded. "Yeah. All right."

Still holding Donna by the hand—and Donna clinging to his—Zander led her into Kaylee's room. He approached the bed and studied the little figure under the blankets.

Beneath her brown, curly hair, Kaylee's face was abnormally pale. Translucent. One arm lay outside the covers. Zander noted the IV catheter in her arm and the deep bruising around it and elsewhere on her arm. A nasal cannula delivered oxygen to the child as she slept.

"The doctors call it acute lymphoblastic leukemia," Donna whispered. "Her bone marrow makes defective white blood cells. Those are the leukemia cells. Her bone marrow has made so many leukemia cells that they are crowding out all the healthy blood cells and platelets."

Zander squeezed Donna's hand. "God knows how to help Kaylee. Let's pray, shall we?"

"I . . . I haven't prayed in a really long time."

"That's okay. Why don't you agree with me as I pray?"

"Yeah. All right."

Zander took Donna's hand and laid it on Kaylee's forehead. He placed his own hand on hers. "Lord God," he prayed, "we come to you in the mighty name of Jesus, asking that you heal Kaylee's body. You know where the problem is; you know what is causing these abnormal cells to multiply. We ask that you fix this problem, that you stop the production of leukemia cells."

He added, "I thank you for strengthening Kaylee's immune system and increasing the number of good blood cells in her system. Lord, I also ask you to draw near to Donna and encourage her heart."

Then, he prayed, "Father, Donna needs a car. Nothing is too difficult for you, Lord, so right now, we ask, in the name of Jesus, that you provide the car Donna needs. Thank you, Lord, for hearing us and for answering. When you answer, we will give you all the glory. Amen."

"Amen," Donna breathed.

Outside Kaylee's room, Zander prepared to say goodbye. "I'll go right to work to find you a car, Donna." He took out his phone. "May I have your number? If it's all right, I'd like to check in with you in a few days."

She gave him her number. "Um, Zander? You wanted to give me your card. May I still have one?"

He grinned and plucked one from his shirt pocket. "Of course."

"Thank you. Thank you for coming, and . . . tell Jack thank you, too."

"I will."

As Zander left the hospital and headed for the National Aquarium to meet Abe and Emilio, he murmured, "Well, Lord? Looks like we're gonna need two cars. Good thing you own the cattle on a thousand hills."

⌘⌘⌘⌘

PART 2:
THE HEAD
OF THE SNAKE

CHAPTER 21

THE HEAT OF SUMMER took a break on Saturday when we woke to a pounding rain.

Jayda Cruz, the rain will abate midmorning. Flights out of BWI will not be affected.

"Okay. Thanks, Nano."

Rats. On one hand, we needed Abe and Emilio safely away from us and the work we were doing. On the other hand, I hated that they were leaving so soon.

Although it was early, Abe was already up when I came out of our bedroom. He was standing at the window watching the torrents running from the roofline. Emilio, however, was bedded down on the living room floor; he was snuggled down into his blankets, oblivious to the world.

I knelt over Emilio's slumbering form and whispered, "Up and at 'em, Tiger."

He grumbled, of course, and I tousled his hair and planted a kiss on his cheek. Then I set to work assembling breakfast: waffles, eggs, sausages, OJ.

We left our apartment just after eight and delivered our precious cargo to their departure gate half an hour later. It was not an easy goodbye. Emilio held himself with stoic indifference, but I couldn't.

"We'll see you soon," I blubbered.

"When? When is soon?"

"I don't know, Emilio. Will you pray for Zander and me? Pray that we do our job well and get it done?"

Emilio sniveled a little but fixed his eyes somewhere over my shoulder. "Then you'll come home?"

"Yes. Then we'll come home."

"Okay. I'll pray."

Abe hugged me, too. "Be strong, Jayda. Remember Joshua 1:9: *The Lord your God will be with you wherever—wherever—you go.*"

"Yes. Thank you."

Abe and Emilio rolled their suitcases toward the nearest airport entrance, and I stared after them, bereft.

Please, Lord. Please help us to finish our assignment. Help us to identify those who helped Harmon. I want to go home to our boy.

When the doors slid closed, I lost sight of them and turned away, but as Zander and I left the airport, the Scripture Abe had partially quoted rang in my heart.

Have I not commanded you?
Be strong and courageous.
Do not be afraid; do not be discouraged,
for the Lord your God will be with you
wherever you go.

Thank you, Lord, I prayed silently. *I will not*—I cannot—*allow myself to be afraid or discouraged. Thank you for reminding me.*

We were almost home from the airport when Zander's phone rang. "Get that for me, Jay?"

"Sure." I answered and put the phone on speaker.

"Zander? It's Jack."

"Hey, Jack. How are you doing?"

I could tell that Zander couldn't wait to share about his hospital visit to meet Donna and pray for Kaylee. Jack's news stopped him in his tracks.

"Well, I'm not sure, man. The strangest things have happened since the CR meeting Thursday evening."

"Oh?" Zander glanced at me, then back to the road.

"See, I went for a job interview yesterday at this landscaping place. I told the guy, the owner, I told him straight up that I was clean but recently so. He said he was sorry, but he couldn't afford to hire someone to work on a landscaping crew he couldn't rely on, who might lose him customers if he didn't show up at the job."

"Um, I guess I can see his point, Jack. Can you?"

"Well, sure. The thing is, though, he walked me through their nursery—it's huge, by the way—and on the way to their parking lot, he showed me all their plants and shrubs and stuff."

"Uh-huh."

"He mentioned they had a weird bug infestation going on, weird because the insects were behaving strangely. Not to bore you or anything, but my dad was an arborist, and I grew up hearing about plant disease and such.

"Anyway, I suggested that the infestation could be a parasitic fungus that grows inside insects and causes erratic behavior—the most damaging being that the fungus causes the insects to climb to the tops of trees and bushes, so that the fungus can maximize the spread of its spores."

"Interesting." Zander again glanced at me and made a face. *Interesting and kinda gross.*

Jack laughed. "You're kidding me, right? It's as interesting as dirt. Well, this guy starts asking me all kinds of questions about how to care for plants, shrubs, and trees, and we spent like half an hour just talking—and then *he hires me.*"

"What? Really?"

"Really. Not to work on a crew, but to work in the nursery. It's not a great paying job, but it's a job. The state will take child support out of my checks and give it to Donna and, after I save a little, I'll be able to move out of the shelter, get a place of my own."

"Praise God, Jack! What wonderful news."

"Want more?"

"Um, more good news?"

"Yeah, and this is where it gets really strange. I was leaving the nursery, see, when the owner says to me, 'Jack, do you by chance need a car?'"

Zander's jaw went slack. "He what?"

"Yeah, man. He asked if I needed a car! He has an old VW bug that runs great, but he just bought an SUV and doesn't need the bug. I told him thanks, but there's no place at the shelter for me to park it. I couldn't afford to license it or buy insurance, either."

"Um, Jack?"

"Yeah?"

"How'd you like to be Donna's hero?"

"You kidding? I'd give my right arm."

"Actually, all you need do is give her that car."

Zander filled Jack in on his visit to the hospital. Jack was, of course, more concerned about Kaylee's condition than about the 'coincidence' of the car, but he listened as Zander explained.

"Jack, you would love for God to eventually repair your broken marriage and family, wouldn't you?"

"Absolutely, Zander."

"Well, the Lord has his ways of fixing things, sometimes via the most roundabout and unlikely circumstances. Donna's greatest need right now is for a car. Kaylee is going to require a lot of medical treatment and getting her to and from appointments will be difficult, not to mention exhausting, if Donna has to rely on public transportation. I told her we would help her get a car. Do you see God's hand at work now?"

"Zander, this blows me away. I-I'll call my new boss and tell him I've changed my mind."

"Don't be afraid to tell him what the car is for, Jack. I have a feeling it will bless your boss to know his gift is going to help your sick daughter."

⌘

GAMBLE VISITED A CORNER drug store and used their pay phone to dial Trujillo's number.

"How's it going?"

"Can't complain."

"Uh . . ." Gamble's voice stuck in his throat. "Are you hungry? I thought we could catch some dinner."

"If I have to catch my food first, I'll die of starvation before it's on the table."

Gamble chuckled. "Let me rephrase that. Could I buy you dinner?"

"I think so."

They met at an Indian restaurant and ordered chai lattes before studying the menu. "Albuquerque only had a few Indian restaurants," Gamble said by way of cracking the awkward silence between them. "I've eaten at this place five times since I moved here. It's great."

"I love just about anything in a sweet coconut curry sauce."

"Hey, me, too. And if you give me garlic naan to sop it up, I'll make a meal out of it."

Trujillo's eyes came to life, and she grinned. "I wondered if you'd ever call me. You know, for this."

Gamble laughed in relief. "If I'm honest, I wanted to in Albuquerque, but . . ."

"But things were about as complicated as they could get."

"Yeah, A certain crazed general . . ."

This time it was Trujillo who breathed a sigh of relief. "Those were . . . strange times, and that was the assignment from Hades."

Gamble reached across the table and covered her hand with his. "I'm glad you came out of it all right, Trujillo."

"Thank you. Me, too."

She twiddled with her spoon. "So, how exactly did you meet our little 'jewel'?"

Gamble laughed. "That's quite the story."

"Am I cleared to hear it?"

"Yes, by Presidential Order."

She looked around the restaurant then back to linger on their joined hands. "Think you could call me Janice?"

"I'd like that."

Amused but cautious, she studied him. "It's Ross, right?"

He nodded. "Guess we got used to calling each other by our surnames."

"Well, I'm glad we can change that."

⌘⌘⌘⌘

CHAPTER 22

SUNDAY MORNING, at the end of the service, I lined up with eleven other candidates for baptism. I'd seen a few baptisms as a kid and had been underwhelmed. But today? Today I was excited and nervous at the same time, because each person was to profess their faith in Jesus before the pastors "dunked" them.

I was fifth in line. A teen by the name of Josh was first, and I had thought he was a shy kid. However, before he stepped into the water, he straightened his shoulders and spoke clearly, loud enough to carry across the sanctuary, even without a microphone.

"I want to confess to all of you today that without Jesus, I would be dead. I tried to kill myself four times. Each time, the Lord performed a miracle and brought me back. I know he intervened because my parents and my sister were praying for me. I was trapped in a lot of nasty stuff of my own choosing, but they loved me anyway and they never gave up on me.

"The last time I tried to kill myself, I went up to our cabin where no one would find me in time. I took a bottle of pills that should have put down a horse. Instead, I woke up two days later in a pool of my own dried vomit. I woke up . . . and God spoke to me."

Josh's voice gave out momentarily, and he had to clear his throat. "I woke up, and God said, 'Josh, this is a picture of your life without me: You are lying in your own vomit. I sent Jesus to rescue you from your despair, but this is your last chance. You know the truth; now you must act on it.'"

The kid couldn't have been more than seventeen, but he seemed much older when he said, "I knew then that I could try any means to end my life—any means at all—and this time, it would work. Suddenly, I was terrified. If I died, I knew I would spend eternity in hell. I-I cried out to Jesus and begged him to save me, begged him to forgive me."

Josh's parents and sister, sitting in the third row from us, were weeping.

Josh looked away, into a distance we couldn't see. "Jesus came to me. I felt a fire inside, burning, cleansing, washing me clean. I got up, took a shower, cleaned up the cabin, and went home. All the way, during the drive, the presence of God was on me. That was two weeks ago. I'm here today to publicly confess my salvation, to profess my faith in Jesus Christ. I don't deserve what he's done for me, but I am so grateful."

I was so caught up in the power of Josh's testimony that I never heard the other professions of faith. When it was my turn, all my nervousness was gone. I said the congregation, "Hello. My name is Jayda Cruz. A year ago, I would never have dreamed I'd be a Christian, let alone be getting baptized.

"You see, I'd been raised in church and wounded in church, so I had erected a wall as hard as concrete between me and God. In fact, I despised Christians. You wouldn't believe me if I told you how the Lord managed to break through that wall."

I smiled at Zander, and he chuckled. No, *that* part of my story truly was unbelievable.

"It is enough here and now to say that Jesus brought me to a place of surrender. Surrender is an essential part of being a believer in Christ. I had to surrender my unforgiveness, my bitterness, my will, my way of doing things. I had to surrender everything to the Lordship of Christ. Since he is my Savior and Lord, I am acting in obedience to his word and asking to be baptized."

I went down into the water and came up to shouts, applause, and the nanomites quoting Acts 2:38 in my ear: *"Repent and be baptized, every one of you, in the name of Jesus Christ for the forgiveness of your sins. And you will receive the gift of the Holy Spirit."*

My heart was full.

⌘⌘⌘⌘

CHAPTER 23

"GOOD MONDAY MORNING to you all. This is Jillian Framer, reporting live from Capitol Hill, where both the Senate and the House Rules and Administration Committees are set to take up hearings on the President's nominee for the vacant office of Vice President. The last time the country experienced a Vice Presidential vacancy was in 1973 during the administration of Richard Nixon, when Nixon's first Vice President, Spiro Agnew, was forced to resign over a charge of federal income tax evasion."

"Jillian, what can you tell our viewers about the tone within Congress over the nomination of Senator Simon Delancey?"

"Tom, Congress' first reaction could have been described as 'perfect astonishment.' Not much goes on in Washington these days that takes the city by surprise, but the President's announcement, made on the south lawn of the White House during his Independence Day Reception, stunned lawmakers—first for its unexpectedness and, second, for Jackson's nominee himself, who is *not* a member of the President's party.

"However, now that the initial shock of surprise has passed, the President's move is being hailed by members of Delancey's party as "out-of-the-box," and "a brilliant stroke of bipartisanship." While the President's party is somewhat less enthusiastic, they have yet to publicly criticize President Jackson's selection."

"Jillian, how does the congressional reaction bode for Delancey's confirmation?"

"Frankly, Tom, Delancey may be the *least* controversial administration nomination for any office in decades. Senator Delancey is well known to the American people and respected by the majority of Congress. If Gerald Ford's hearings and approval were conducted in six weeks, we may be looking at less than that for Senator Delancey.

"Reporting live from Capitol Hill, this is Jillian Framer, WJLA News."

⌘

ZANDER WAS ANXIOUS to get out of the house and revisit Donna at the hospital. He'd called yesterday to make sure she'd be at Kaylee's side this morning. She'd sounded despondent when he'd spoken to her.

"They are going to start chemo tomorrow, so I need to be there around 8 a.m. The doctors said the drugs will make Kaylee sick to her stomach . . . and they said she'll lose all her beautiful hair," Donna whispered.

"I'm so sorry, Donna. Try to remember that Kaylee's hair will grow back when the chemo is over. Listen, I have a few errands to run first thing tomorrow, but I'll see you after, okay? Hang in there."

Lord, chemo is so rough on kids. I hope the news about the car will cheer Donna up a bit—it truly is an answer to prayer!

Zander put on slacks and a new shirt and tie, left the apartment, and drove to Jack's job site, a prosperous-looking landscaping concern. Jack introduced Zander to his boss.

"Pastor Cruz, this is my boss, Leonard Hammond."

"Nobody calls me Leonard, Pastor Cruz. Please call me Lenny."

"Nobody calls me Pastor Cruz; please call me Zander."

They shared a mutual chuckle, then Lenny said, "Okay, *Zander.* What's this Jack tells me about the car I offered him?"

Zander grinned larger. "It's one of those times when you know God has had his hand at orchestrating things, Lenny. You see, I was at the hospital Friday with Jack's ex-wife and their little girl, Kaylee. We were praying for a car for Donna about the same time Jack was here, applying for work."

Lenny looked from Zander to Jack, then back. "Seriously? The same day?"

"That's what I understand. He applied here Friday, right? I met Donna the same day. Jack didn't call and tell me that you'd offered him your old Vee-Dub bug until Saturday, and he didn't know I'd prayed with Donna for a car until we talked."

"And your little girl? Why is she in the hospital, Jack—if you don't mind me asking?"

Jack chewed the inside of his mouth. Zander could see how hard it was for him to frame the horrific words. "The doctors say she has . . . leukemia."

Lenny was silent for several moments. "I'm really sorry, Jack. Of course, Donna can have the car."

Zander nodded. "Thank you for your generosity, Lenny. Without a car, Donna would have to use public transportation to take her sick child to her appointments. You can imagine all the germs and bugs that would subject Kaylee to."

Lenny shuddered. "I'm glad she won't have to do that."

"Lenny, if it's okay with you, I wanted to get the make, model, and VIN so I can buy some auto insurance before I bring Donna by to pick up the car."

"Not a problem. In fact . . ." Here Lenny fidgeted as though wrestling with a decision. "Ah, what the *blank.* Will you let me pay for the first six months of insurance? The title change will cost something, too. I'd like to give you some cash to cover that."

Thunderstruck, Jack rasped, "Boss . . ."

"Don't start with me, Jack. You just get rid of that fungus crap that's killing my shrubs; I'll handle the details with Zander here."

Jack didn't budge. "Th-thank you, Lenny."

"Yeah, yeah." He jerked his head at Zander. "Follow me. You," he pointed at Jack, "get to work."

He strode away. Zander grinned at Jack, slapped him on the shoulder, and ran to catch up with Lenny.

⌘

ZANDER MADE IT TO THE HOSPITAL after eleven—later than he'd wanted, but still in the morning. He couldn't wait to take Donna to fetch the car.

But as he approached Kaylee's room, he hesitated. About a dozen people milled about in the hall or stood in Kaylee's doorway.

Zander's heart plummeted. *Lord? Please! Please help Kaylee and her mom—*

"That's him! That's the guy!"

The crowd rushed Zander. Before he could react, hands grasped at him and voices shouted for his attention. They pulled him in different directions, the crowd's insistence growing.

Five or six doctors and nurses, hearing the commotion, spilled from Kaylee's room. Donna came out with them. She stared at Zander with wide eyes.

"Is that the man?" A tiny but senior-looking female doctor pointed at Zander.

"Yes. That's him. Zander Cruz."

The doctor motioned to the other medical staff. "Get those people off him and bring him to me."

The staff members were ineffective in calming the crowd; the hands pawing Zander were desperate. He felt one of his shirt buttons pop and fly into the air. Next, his breast pocket tore. He was certain his sleeves would give way next.

Topmost in his thoughts was, *Oh, man! This was my new shirt!*

"Hey! *Hey!* STOP THIS, I SAY!" The doctor's authority cut through the pandemonium.

Brought to their senses, most of the dozen sets of hands released Zander. One woman clung to his arm.

"Mrs. Wong, release that man or I will have security remove you from the hospital."

"No! I need him to come pray for my son. He *must* come!"

Zander glanced down at the woman and saw how desperate she was. "Is that what you want from me? You want me to pray for your son?"

"Yes. He is dying from cancer—like Kaylee."

The crowd's clamor jumped up. "Please! Please pray for my boy!" "No, please come lay your hands on our daughter!" "We'll give you money—anything you want—just come, please, and pray for our baby!"

"But—"

"*I said, SILENCE!*"

The crowd hushed again, but belligerence distorted their expressions.

Zander felt like he had been jerked into an alternate dimension.

Lord, what is happening?

The sensation intensified when a curly-headed rocket burst from Kaylee's hospital room and jetted down the hallway away from the crowd. Donna ran after, shouting, "Kaylee! Kaylee, come back!"

Zander's mouth fell open—and two-dozen hands again engaged in a none-too-gentle tug-o-war over possession of his body.

The doctor who'd shouted for quiet strode up to Zander and grasped his arm. She slapped away the hands claiming it. When she'd extricated him, she commanded, "You. In there. Now."

Zander allowed the woman to drag him into Kaylee's hospital room; he was, in fact, grateful to be rescued from the wild rabble in the hallway. The rest of the medical staff in the hallway followed them into the room and closed the door.

"Those people out there are nuts!" Zander exclaimed. "They about tore me in pieces. What in the world is going on?" He glanced at the doctor's credentials. "Dr. Gupta."

Dr. Gupta folded her arms and frowned. "That, Mr. Cruz, is what I intend to find out."

Zander nodded. "Okay."

"Did you visit Kaylee Grober Friday morning?"

"Yes. Sure. I'm a licensed minister." He frowned. "But wasn't that Kaylee who ran down the hall just now? She seems a lot better."

"A lot better? *A lot better?*" The woman, the top of whose head barely reached Zander's arm pit, waved her finger under his nose. "*Mister* Cruz, we want to know what you did to Kaylee."

"What I did . . ."

A frisson of foreboding crept up Zander's back—along with the story Jayda had told him of the nanomites eradicating a man's brain tumor. He'd even had his own experience with the nanomites mending him after Emilio's uncle had beat the ever-living snot out of him. And Abe! Abe had suffered so much brain trauma that he would not have made it if it hadn't been for the nanomites.

Zander licked his lips and asked silently, "Nano . . . Nano, did you—"

Zander Cruz, we did nothing.

"You didn't, um, fool with Kaylee's bone marrow? Kill the leukemia cells? Perform some kind of nano-surgery?"

No, Zander Cruz. We understood that we were not to draw attention to ourselves. We did nothing . . . although we most certainly could have.

They uttered those last words with acerbic disdain.

"But if you didn't, then . . ." Zander's query tapered off and he wiped his face with a hand.

Only one possibility remained; he had just one answer for Kaylee's doctor.

"Dr. Gupta, I am a follower of Jesus. When I was here Friday, I prayed for Kaylee. I asked Jesus to heal her. That is what I did—and that is all I did."

Dr. Gupta's hand fell to her side. She took a step backward, so she could better stare up into Zander's face. The two nurses and three doctors observing their conversation went still.

"May I go now?" Zander asked. He was anxious to see Donna and Kaylee.

One of the attending physicians asked, "Aren't you interested in Kaylee's condition?"

"Well, sure. Of course, I am."

"Dr. Pradesh." Dr. Gupta shook her head. "We cannot share Kaylee's medical information with Mr. Cruz."

"Oh. Right. I apologize. I got caught up . . ."

Zander, sliding his eyes from one doctor to another, edged toward the door. Then he remembered the small mob waiting for him.

"Those people out there. Who are they?"

"Parents. Parents of other pediatric oncology patients."

"And they all want me to pray for their kids?"

"I assume so," Dr. Gupta sniffed.

Zander, shaking his head, backed through the door. On the other side, the parents waited.

This time they were silent.

Deferential.

Organized.

A spokesperson emerged from their ranks. "Pastor Cruz? My name is Kyle Oxbow. We know you prayed for Kaylee and healed her. Respectfully, would you please pray for our children?"

Zander took a breath, but Kyle didn't let him speak.

"And we want to apologize for mobbing you, for pulling on your clothes."

Someone handed Kyle something that he took and held out to Zander. "Here's, ah, the button we tore off. We apologize, and we, uh, would like to buy you a new shirt."

Zander took the button. "That's not necessary. And I'd be happy to pray for your children. It would be my privilege."

Far down the hall, he saw Donna coming his way, a dejected Kaylee in tow.

"Okay, let's figure this out. If you will go to your child's room and wait for me, I'll be along shortly. How many . . . ?"

"There are eight on this floor."

"Eight children."

"Yes. Not all the parents are here this morning, but we've kind of gotten to be friends, you know? Since we share the same, um, problems."

He could have said, "the same heartache" or "the same anguish."

"I understand. I'll visit each child; I won't leave until I've prayed for all of them. I'll start as soon as I have a word with Donna."

With their eyes glued on Zander as if they were convinced he would bolt and make a run for it, the group of parents slowly disbanded and went to their kids' rooms. He noticed that several stood in the room's doorway. Waiting. Watching. Ready to give chase, if needed.

Zander breathed slowly. "O Jesus! What wonders have you done?"

Donna drew near while Kaylee alternated hopping up and down and dropping to the floor, trying to break the hold her mother had on her hand.

"She wants to run," Donna said. Unchecked tears slid from her face and soaked the front of her blouse. "She hasn't had this much energy in months. She wants to run and run and run. Instead of starting chemo, the doctors drew blood all day yesterday and this morning. They performed every test they could think of. They can't find any leukocytes. Her cell count is normal. Even the bruising is gone."

Zander stared at Kaylee's left arm. Where it had been pale and mottled with blue and purple on Friday, he saw only clear, pink skin.

Kaylee's brown eyes beamed up at Zander, and she raised her free hand to him. Zander bent over, Donna let go, and the girl came to him. She hugged him and breathed into his ear.

"Jeees."

"What?" Zander whispered back.

She dimpled. "Jeees."

"Jeees?"

Then he understood. "Jesus?"

She wagged her head with vigor and pointed up. "Jeees."

⌘

ZANDER GOT HOME that evening after I did. The slump of his shoulders told me how beat he was; the fire in his sweet gray eyes hinted at how elated.

"Zander, what's going on? Where have you been?" Then I looked closer. "Hey! How did you trash your new shirt?"

"First things first. I spent the last two hours with Pastor Lucklow. That's why I'm late."

"Doing what?"

Zander laughed. "Kind of a debrief or an AAR—according to Malware, Inc."

"You've lost me."

He rubbed his chin. "Yeah, that was my line for most of the day."

"Want to tell me over dinner?"

"Definitely. I'm starved. Skipped lunch."

"You skipped lunch? Now I'm really intrigued."

He wouldn't say another word until we were tucked into a private corner in our favorite Chinese restaurant. Then Zander started with his meeting Jack's boss, Lenny, and how Lenny had paid for Donna's auto registration and insurance.

"That was so kind of him! And did you take Donna to pick up her car?"

"I'll get to that; you really need to hear my day in sequence. So, after we paid for the insurance and printed out temp proof of insurance cards for Donna, I went to the hospital."

Because of the vivid way in which Zander described his encounter with the mob of parents and the doctors, I could almost feel the hands grabbing and fighting over him. "Is that why your shirt is torn? But, why? What did they want?"

"They wanted me to pray for their children, Jayda, the way I prayed for Kaylee."

"But . . ."

"There's no 'but' this time. Just as I was about to be torn apart like a Thanksgiving wishbone, Kaylee flew out of her hospital room at speeds close to Mach One. She jetted down the hall with her mom trailing behind. Donna had a devil of a time catching Kaylee."

"Are you kidding?"

As hungry as I knew Zander had to be, he couldn't eat much. He was too full of news and excitement. "Donna told me that Kaylee was supposed to start chemo Sunday morning. Instead, the doctors drew blood and ran tests on her all day."

Zander tapped his chopsticks on his plate with nervous joy. "Kaylee's blood was *normal*, Jay. No cancer cells anywhere. She's healthy and full of get-up-and-go."

I put my hand over my mouth. "Oh, no! The nanomites—"

"Nope."

"What? No?"

NO, Jayda Cruz. We did NOT heal Kaylee's body.

Zander leaned forward and mock-whispered, "Careful. Touchy subject."

I stared into Zander's face, finally understanding his jubilation. "Jesus did it? Jesus healed Kaylee?"

"Yes, he did. And every parent in the pediatric oncology wing, after witnessing the staff's uproar and Kaylee streaking up and down the hallway like a twin-turbocharged entry in the Indy 500, wanted me to pray for their child. So, I did. And I shared Jesus with them, too. I told each child how much the Lord loves them, that Jesus was *God's* child, that Jesus volunteered to suffer and die in our place.

"A few of those kids were old enough to truly relate to the sacrifice God the Father made. I prayed with children and I prayed with moms and dads to receive Jesus as their Lord and, in one case, an entire family surrendered to Christ."

Stunned, I sat back. Now it was my dinner that grew cold.

"This is . . . this is miraculous. And wonderful. And marvelous!"

Zander's face crumpled. He squeezed his eyes closed, and tears leaked from under his eyelids. "I've been overwhelmed all day."

"Oh, my sweet husband . . . God is so good, and we are so blessed!"

He cleared his throat. "When I was finally able to get away from the other parents and back to Donna, Kaylee had been discharged—discharged with strict instructions to have blood drawn every-other day for a month.

"I took Donna to the landscaping company and introduced her to Lenny. It was a little difficult explaining to Lenny why Kaylee—who was bouncing around like a kangaroo on crack—didn't look the least bit sick. So, I just told him the truth, that the doctors were stupefied. I told him we knew it was a miracle, that Jesus had healed Kaylee."

"And Jack? Did he see Kaylee?"

"Yes. Jack was watching us from across the nursery floor. When Kaylee spotted him, she was off like a shot."

Zander wept again, covering his eyes with his fingers. "There's no way to describe that moment: Jack dropped to his knees and Kaylee jumped into his arms. They hugged like forever. It was such a beautiful moment. We were all crying—Me, Donna, and Lenny."

"Donna didn't get upset? She won't report Jack for breaking the restraining order?"

"I don't think so, or at least I don't see Donna reporting him—and technically, *he* didn't break the restraining order. Anyway, Donna just looked at me and said, 'Please tell Jack thank you. For everything.'

"Then Lenny gave her the title and the keys to the car. Jack sent Kaylee back to her mom, and they drove off home."

My husband smiled. "I went over to Grace Chapel and unloaded on Pastor Lucklow. Like I said, an AAR. We made so much noise rejoicing, that Christine, Pastor's secretary, came to see what the fuss was about—so then, I had to repeat it all."

He sighed, grinned, and picked up his chopsticks. "And that, my dear, is why I was late getting home."

⌘⌘⌘⌘

CHAPTER 24

JAYDA CRUZ. IT IS TIME TO GET UP.

Jayda Cruz. It is time to get up.

Jayda Cruz. It is time to get up. "*A little sleep, a little slumber, a little folding of the hands to rest—and poverty will come on you like a thief and scarcity like an armed man." Proverbs 24:33 and 34.*

"Whatever! I'm up already." I dragged myself from the bed and stumbled to the shower. Despite yesterday's wonderful events, I hadn't slept well. As the hot water hit me and my mind began to wake up, that stupid, horrid dream of several weeks past reared its ugly head.

Again.

Although Zander and I had prayed over the nightmare and although the abject terror of it had faded, the dream was never far from my thoughts. Over and over it played. For almost four weeks at this point! We'd dissected the dream from every angle, but my disquiet persisted, as if an element of the dream remained locked, an aspect I hadn't yet grasped.

Whatever "it" was, it nagged and troubled me. Last night, it kept me from restful sleep.

What is it?

I leaned against the shower's tile and let the steaming spray pound me while I rewound the dream to the place where I'd first spotted the serpent's winding form beneath the mist.

Although the head of the snake was severed, the President has uncovered evidence . . .

"Yeah, yeah. Enough already." If I never heard Gamble's voice repeat those words, it would be too soon.

Where did I leave off? Oh, yeah.

Through the soupy fog I followed the broad, pointed snout leading the undulating body closer, ever closer in my direction. Then I caught the quick glimpse of one golden eye.

Although the head of the snake was severed, the President—

"Shut up! I'm trying to think here!"

The serpent's head rose from the mist and fixed its malignant eyes on me.

"The head." I shivered despite the hot, stinging needles of the shower. "But Harmon died, so what can it mean?"

The snake's eyes held me in their thrall, and I felt myself falling deeper into them. "In the name of Jesus, *stop*. Just STOP IT!"

I pulled my gaze away from the snake's—then jerked it back. Something had changed. The alteration was subtle but marked. No longer entranced by the serpent's gaze, I focused on what was different.

The eyes . . . they were darker, more of an amber, and something about their shape bothered me. They had a slight slant to them, and—

What had teased and eluded me burst on my consciousness.

As if the spray pummeling my skin had turned to ice water, the force of the revelation dropped me to my knees in the shower stall. The air whooshed from my lungs.

Instead of being concealed or obscure, the truth had been *too* obvious.

"Harmon *wasn't* the head," I whispered. "Someone else is."

I scrambled to my feet, wrenched the faucets off, and grabbed a towel. "Zander!"

No answer.

I dried off and dressed as quickly as I could. "Zander? Zander!"

"Yeah?" He appeared in our bedroom door, hair disheveled but coffee in hand.

"The dream! I've figured it out. The dream—the part . . . the other piece of it." I was flustered and incoherent.

Zander saluted me with his mug. "Hon, you need coffee."

Yes, I did. Minutes later we were seated at our little dinette, a mug grasped between my hands.

"Okay, now what about the dream?" Zander asked.

"It was too simple," I replied. "What Gamble said, *Although the head of the snake was severed?*"

"Yeah? Head severed. Harmon dead. Got it."

"*No*. That's the point. It wasn't Harmon. We thought he was the head, but he *wasn't*."

Zander went still. I saw when the gears engaged.

"But, if Harmon wasn't the head . . ."

I nodded. "All of us—the President, Kennedy, Gamble, you and I—we've been operating under the presumption that Harmon was the leader of the conspiracy, that *he* was directing the other players. My infiltration of the NSA was to flush out the remnants of the plot. We assumed that with Harmon's death, the plan to unseat the presidency was largely over."

"But . . . if we are wrong?"

"Then the conspiracy is alive and intact—like the serpent concealed in the mist, hidden, but still stalking its prey."

"The President."

"Yes. We need to tell Gamble. Now."

I grabbed my phone and keyed in Gamble's number.

He answered on the second ring. "Yeah?"

"Gamble. I need to tell you something, something important."

⌘

WE HIT THE DOJO THAT NIGHT basically to work off our frustration. Well, my frustration.

Okay. I was the one frustrated. Seriously so.

Zander and I viewed the final revelation from my nightmare as a momentous and vital piece of information. But, when we'd called Gamble that morning, let's just say that he had been less than enthused.

"Let me get this straight. You, Jayda, had a bad dream. I had a bad dream once. Right after I ate Thai food. Turns out I'm allergic to MSG— and it was loaded with it. Gave me hives. Made me itch."

"It wasn't that kind of dream, Gamble. When I woke up, I remembered every tiny detail of it and was able to repeat it to Zander."

"But you had this dream, what, a month ago now? And just this morning it made sense?"

"It always made sense, Gamble, but one piece of the meaning sort of eluded me. I've been trying to puzzle it out since then, and I finally got it."

"Jayda, I don't mean to imply that you guys are strange or anything, but not everyone believes that dreams have real meaning."

"Some dreams do, Gamble. Not all, but some."

"And you can tell which ones do and which ones don't . . . how?"

Grrr!

I knew then that we weren't going to convince him. Nevertheless, I had persisted. "The upshot, the reason I called, is this, Gamble: We've been working from the supposition (to quote you) that Harmon was 'the head of the snake.' But if Harmon wasn't 'the head,' and if he wasn't the leader, then someone else is. And that means that the conspiracy is still active. We should be looking for the real head, the hidden leader."

He grunted, not convinced. "Okay. I'll pass your thoughts on to Kennedy, but I doubt he'll put any more credence in the source than I can."

Then he hung up.

"He doesn't believe me, Zander."

"I don't think it's about believing you, Jay."

Jayda Cruz, perhaps this scripture applies to Agent Gamble: "The person without the Spirit does not accept the things that come from the Spirit of God but considers them foolishness and cannot understand them because they are discerned only through the Spirit."

"The nanomites are right, Jayda. Gamble doesn't believe in God-given dreams because he doesn't believe in God, because he hasn't surrendered to Jesus. That makes him blind to the realm of the Spirit."

The nanomites chimed in, adding, *"The mind governed by the flesh is hostile to God; it does not submit to God's law, nor can it do so."*

"You shouldn't encourage them, Zander."

"Even when they get it right for a change? It's simple, really: Gamble doesn't know God, so he can't perceive the things of God."

I'd gone off to work in a huff, but I'd kept to myself and had nursed my worry and aggravation most of the day. That evening, when I got home, I was still frustrated and more than a little down.

Zander and I ate dinner and headed straight to the dojo. It took two hours of non-stop sparring as though my life depended on how I fought, but Gus-Gus and Ninja-Noid managed to beat most of the vexation out of me.

I was no longer frustrated. Just depressed.

Ugh.

On the way home, Zander's hand snuck out and snagged mine.

"Hey. Will ice cream make it all better?"

"I dunno," I sighed. However, after a moment of reflection, I asked, "Ice cream with sprinkles?"

"But, of course."

"And crunched-up Oreos?"

"Yup."

"And gummy bears?"

"You can have anything you want, sweetie. So, ice cream?"

"Yes, please."

I sniffed to myself, *Ha-ha, Mr. Special-Agent-Man Ross Gamble. I'm having ice cream and you're not—and I'm not sharing with you.*

Ya big dummy.

Somehow that made me feel better, too.

⌘⌘⌘⌘

CHAPTER 25

Wednesday, July 11

"JOHN-BOY. RIPLEY. Welcome to your third tradecraft class."

Mal was still a little peeved with us. "It's obvious from last week's SDRs that it wasn't your first rodeo, and we've decided—so as not to waste your time or ours—we've decided to take inventory of your skills and focus on what you need."

He handed each of us a sheet of paper. I pursed my lips, rubbed my nose, and kept my eyes down. I was *not* going to smirk.

"Fill this out, and we'll go from there."

Some of the lingo on the sheet was unfamiliar, but the nanomites supplied meaning and context for what I didn't understand. I answered the ten questions and handed my sheet to McFly, who was hovering around our seats.

He and Mal looked over our questionnaires.

Mal cleared his throat. "Neither of you are proficient with a handgun?"

We both shook our heads.

"Well, then, looks like firearms are your weakest area, and we should focus there. You've never fired a gun?"

That question was directed at me. "No. Never."

"But you have, John-Boy?"

"Yes. I've handled 9mm and .45cal semiautos. Can't say I'm any good, but I've loaded and shot them."

"Okay. We'll cover the basics here then take you to an indoor range for practice."

"An indoor range this time of night?"

"We have an understanding with an owner."

With that, Baltar drilled firearms safety into our heads and had us handle blue guns—polyurethane hand gun replicas designed for training law enforcement and military.

"The first rule of gun safety is: *All guns are always loaded.* Doesn't matter if you think a gun isn't loaded. Doesn't matter if you *know* a gun isn't loaded. Doesn't matter if the gun is a trainer. You always treat a gun as if it were loaded. Always. Got it?"

Zander and I nodded our understanding and stared at the "LE-blue" semiautos and magazines on the table in front of us.

"The second rule of gun safety is: *Never cover anything you are not willing to destroy.* That means you never point the muzzle of a gun at anything or anyone unless you are willing to kill it.

"When you are handling a firearm, always point the muzzle in a safe direction, usually down. Do not sweep the muzzle across someone's body. Ever. Got it?"

"Yes."

Logan stepped to our table, a blue gun in his hand. He stood sideways and held the gun at about a thirty-degree angle. It was still pointing toward the floor, but we could see it. He held his index finger outside the trigger guard, along the barrel.

"The third rule of firearms safety: *Keep your finger off the trigger until your gun sights are on your target and you have made the decision to shoot.*"

Logan moved to the side of the table next to Zander. "Now, stand up."

Zander and I stood. Deckard stood behind Zander, and Dredd hovered behind me.

"You will lift your gun with your dominant hand and hold it at the angle I am holding mine. Your dominant hand goes on the grip first with your trigger finger in the 'index point' position as mine is. Bring your other hand to the grip and wrap its fingers over the fingers of your dominant hand, then align your thumbs side by side."

I was scared spitless, but I picked up the gun in front of me and did as instructed.

Dredd murmured, "Snug your firing hand into the grip, Ripley. You want a firm hold, high on the grip, with the web of your palm pressed into the grip."

I adjusted.

"Better."

"Fourth rule: *Be sure of your target and what is behind it.* A round can penetrate doors and walls. You can easily kill someone you cannot see."

The next hour was spent handling the guns. We loaded and unloaded training magazines with training rounds, inserted the magazines into the training guns, chambered a round, released the magazine, and expelled the chambered round. Again and again.

"A chambered round can kill. Always check that the gun is empty. Lock the slide back and slip a finger into the chamber to ensure that no round remains. Even then—"

"All guns are always loaded," Zander and I recited together.

The guys grinned their approval, and we moved on to stripping, cleaning, and reassembling the guns.

"You are only as proficient with a firearm as you are familiar with all of its needs and functions. Handling a weapon over and over in a safe manner makes you less likely to negligently discharge it."

The guys then demonstrated the isosceles stance, where the shooter squarely faces the target, feet set apart at shoulder width, upper body leaning forward at the waist, knees slightly bent, arms extended toward the target, forming an isosceles triangle.

"This stance is comfortable for most shooters and helps you to balance your weight side to side. It is a stable shooting position—but it is not always the right position. When you've become proficient with this stance, we'll also teach you the Weaver and fighting stances."

"Shooting a handgun is a perishable skill," Mal said, "meaning that continual practice is necessary to earn and retain your skills—so let's get some practice in."

We got into Malware's van and drove for half an hour. When we got out, we were parked in front of an indoor range that looked like it was made of preformed concrete walls. Mal had a key and was familiar with the location of the lobby lights.

"Ears and eyes," McFly intoned. He handed us shooting earmuffs and safety glasses.

We donned muffs and glasses and entered the range itself through two sets of doors that kept most of the noise confined to the fifteen shooting lanes inside.

Dredd hung paper targets on clips in lanes five and ten and, with the push of a button, ran them out to three yards. Baltar pointed me to lane five and stood behind me while McFly stood behind Zander on lane ten.

"Three yards. Nine feet. This is close quarters for handguns. When you've demonstrated that you can put three consecutive rounds inside the target ring, we'll move you out to seven yards."

The guys then drilled us on about a hundred different things to remember while shooting: weight forward, elbows slightly bent; sight down the barrel—line up the two rear and single front sights; squeeze the trigger—don't pull or jerk it; hold the gun steady; don't allow the recoil to pop the muzzle up.

Zander and I loaded and shot three magazines each, then reloaded and shot again. Baltar's commands over my shoulder started to sound a little like Gus-Gus counting off steps and demanding that I go faster.

After twenty minutes of nonstop load-and-shoot, we were done. Baltar supervised me stripping, cleaning, and oiling my weapon, then reassembling it. Even though we'd worn ear protection, my head was muzzy from the echoes of enclosed shooting.

Back in the van, I glanced at Zander. He was buoyant, pleased with our training activities.

Me, I was okay, but I was pretty sure Baltar's voice would haunt my dreams tonight.

Zander leaned toward me. "Miles on the mountain, Ripley," he whispered. "Miles on the mountain."

⌘

Thursday

ZANDER DROVE ALONE to the weekly Celebrate Recovery meeting because Jayda had stayed late at work for a required class. He found the parking lot fuller than usual. Busier. He stepped from his car and spied a small crowd waiting at the door. Getting out his keys to the fellowship hall, he walked toward the door.

"Pastor Cruz!" Zander recognized the man and his wife from his second visit to the hospital where Kaylee was a patient.

"Hi. It's Josh and Emily, right?"

"Yes. Pastor, thank you for praying for our son. We wanted to let you know that he's responding to the treatments—so much better than the doctors told us he would."

"I . . . I'm so glad."

"You gave us your card and it had the Celebrate Recovery meeting times on it. We brought my brother and his wife, too."

Another couple asked, "Do you remember us from the hospital, Pastor Cruz? You prayed for our boy, too, and he has gone into remission. We wanted to thank you in person . . . and we wanted to hear more about Jesus."

"Welcome. I'm delighted you've come."

Actually, I'm stunned, Zander thought.

Tom and Becky drove into the parking lot. Zander caught Tom ogling the crowd of newcomers.

It's gonna be a great night, Zander realized.

"Come on in, everyone. We'll be serving coffee and cookies in a few minutes."

⌘

Saturday

WHEN HER PHONE CHIRPED an incoming call, the woman was in her car, speeding away from D.C. toward her home in Virginia. She raised the soundproof glass between herself and her driver and answered.

"Yes?" She had been expecting the call; the team she'd dispatched to New Mexico had better have the answers she sent them to unearth.

"As you requested, we have reinvestigated the incident in Albuquerque."

"Get on with it."

"We have three salient points to convey, ma'am. Point one, we have confirmed that the explosion was caused by a sophisticated but homemade device. This is consistent with the assertion that Cushing wore an explosive vest of her own construction into the house.

"Point two, the FBI forensic team that collected and inventoried body parts reported that only two individuals perished in the explosion: the twin sisters. We had extrapolated from other sources that Cushing's remains— what little could be gathered—were identified via DNA samples and disposed of. Her name was inserted weeks later in the passenger manifest of the Air Force transport plane that went down in the Atlantic."

"Yes, yes. I know this. What about the sisters?"

"We interviewed the FBI pathologists. Consistent with their report, they asserted that DNA tests positively identified remains belonging to Gemma Keyes and her sister, Genie Keyes. However, being identical twins, the sisters shared the same DNA profile, so it was not possible to separate body parts based on DNA. The team's federal oversight told them that two women had been positively placed in the house at the time of the explosion. Consequently, they were instructed to separate body parts into two caskets for burial."

"Cut to the bottom line."

The man knew not to feed her irrelevant details. "Yes, ma'am. With adequate financial and *personal* inducements, one of the pathologists cracked. He admitted that of the body parts collected, none were actually duplicated. That is, he saw no physical evidence that *two* young women perished."

"Ah."

"Yes, ma'am. It now seems likely that only one of the twins died that day, that federal agents manipulated the incident reports to establish that both sisters perished."

The woman was silent as she processed what she'd been told. The caller knew not to interrupt until spoken to.

When she broke her silence, she asked, "You had a third point, I believe?"

"Yes, ma'am. According to eye witness accounts, two federal agents coordinated the cleanup. One of them was local FBI, which was to be expected. The other, however, was a woman, one Janice Trujillo."

"She acted as Cushing's team lead."

"She did. We reached out—circumspectly—to the other members of Cushing's team. Turns out, Trujillo was the only member of the team to participate in the incident mop-up. The other members had been dispatched into the field."

"For what purpose?"

"Cushing had been off the grid for days. Supposedly, the agents were sent out to follow up on leads in their search for Cushing."

"Supposedly?"

"Two team members described their assignments as make-work, tasks designed to keep them occupied. They had the feeling Trujillo was shunting them away from Albuquerque. It was apparent from our questioning that they did not know Cushing had died anywhere but in the plane crash."

"Very telling, indeed. Where is this agent Trujillo at present and what has she been up to the past six months?"

He had anticipated her follow-on questions. "She and her team remained in Albuquerque for a month awaiting orders. When the Air Force announced Cushing's death, they returned to D.C. and disbanded. Since then, Trujillo has received three short assignments overseas."

"Her handler?"

"Cushing's operation was deep black, ma'am. Above my clearance."

Yes, exactly. Danforth did well to limit this woman's recent assignments, to watch her closely and test her loyalty—but the fool missed the crucial factor from the get-go.

"Your orders, ma'am?"

"Stay put until I'm certain I won't need you further where you are."

Satisfied that her agent was ignorant of the connection between Cushing and Harmon—and, therefore, Harmon's connection with Danforth, the woman hung up.

Removing a throwaway phone from her handbag, she dialed Danforth's cell.

"Pick up Janice Trujillo. Take her somewhere . . . remote and question her. I want the truth about Gemma Keyes."

"And afterward?"

"We will keep her only until we've exhausted her usefulness."

⌘⌘⌘⌘

CHAPTER 26

WE MET GAMBLE AT HIS CAR for our regular Sunday night meeting, intending to walk to the house without anyone seeing us. We said hello, but Gamble seemed fussier than usual.

"Have either of you heard from Trujillo?"

We shook our heads. "No. Not since last Sunday," I answered. "Was she supposed to meet us here or at the house?"

His response was curt. "Here. Ten minutes ago. And she's not picking up my call."

"Well, she's probably on her way."

"You're probably right. She does live about an hour from here."

Fifteen minutes ticked by, Gamble fidgeting as we waited. When Trujillo still hadn't shown, Zander and I grew concerned, too.

Gamble called Trujillo again. It rang and rang before going to voice mail.

"You know where she lives?" Zander asked Gamble.

"Yeah. Let's go."

We piled into his car. He dropped us not far from our vehicle. We got in our car and followed him.

Janice Trujillo had a tiny house (what we in New Mexico called a casita) behind a much larger home. The driveway belonging to the large house wended around a three-car garage, and dead-ended at the far back of the acreage where Trujillo's place was sheltered under some old maple trees.

Trouble. We knew it right away. Her front door hung open on one hinge.

Gamble was out of his car, sidearm drawn, before Zander came to a stop behind him. I think Gamble sensed that the house was empty, because he waited for us at the demolished door.

Inside, we found the debris of a struggle. Maybe "a fight" better described what we found.

Trujillo had hurled whatever came to hand at her attackers: a lamp, a planter, a heavy framed picture. I sniffed the air and trailed my finger along a table before we followed the swath of potting soil and broken pottery into the kitchen where she'd retreated before her attackers.

There she'd thrown pans and dishes and knives. The floor was cluttered with stainless steel cookware, broken plates, and knives. Three of them. A small streak of dried, brown blood in the shape of a skid mark on the tile gave us hope that she'd hit her target at least once.

I stooped down and touched the dried blood. As I bent over, I spied a syringe that had rolled under the jutting cabinets.

I picked up the hypo and showed it to Gamble and Zander.

Jayda Cruz, we have analyzed the scene.

I saw their analysis as soon as it was complete.

"Here's what the nanomites say happened," I said. "Two attackers, at least one a woman, kicked in the door. If they had guns, they did not use them. Agent Trujillo must not have had her service weapon handy, either. No expended rounds or traces of gunshot residue."

"One was a woman?"

"The blood on the floor tested positive for female hormones—but it isn't Trujillo's blood type. I'd say Trujillo got a few licks in before they overpowered her. The trace drug in the syringe is a fast-acting tranquilizer."

Gamble nodded, distracted. "To render her docile. They came to take her, not to kill her."

"We have to ask ourselves why she was taken," Zander said. "Why her? Why now?"

"I need to make some calls." Gamble bolted outside. We followed him but kept our distance.

He spoke at length with someone, then hung up. The look on his face wasn't encouraging.

"Just got off the phone with the FBI forensics team in Albuquerque. Last week two men with federal credentials interviewed the forensics team members about the explosion that took down Gemma Keye's house and killed Genie . . . and Gemma."

"Someone's digging," I whispered.

"Yes. And I think they found part of what they were digging for— enough to figure out who would know more."

"Trujillo. They knew she was there, in Albuquerque."

"You mean *her handlers* knew she was there. She had to have written and transmitted after-action reports. Standard operating procedure."

I looked at Gamble. "You're saying they've taken Trujillo to find out more about me—but before last week, she wouldn't have known me in my new identity. Wouldn't have known what I—what *we*—can do. Wouldn't have known our assignment. Now? Now she knows everything."

"Do we . . . can the nanomites tell how long ago she was taken?"

"From the condition of the blood, the nanomites deduce the attack happened this afternoon. Maybe two o'clock."

Trujillo had been in our enemies' hands for close to eight hours.

Gamble—big, tough FBI Special Agent Ross Gamble—shuddered. I'd never seen him as shaken as he was now.

Zander took the initiative. "Nano, we need you to hack into the feed of all overhead satellites and nearby traffic cams. Find the vehicle that took Agent Trujillo and track it."

We cannot work fast enough without increased bandwidth, Zander Cruz.

"The nanomites say they need faster Internet than what our phones can provide."

"It's about the nanomites' computing power outstripping our phones' network speed," I explained. "The bandwidth of the connection limits how many satellite feeds they can access concurrently."

"Well, then we need to get the nanomites within range of a high-speed cable junction box," Zander said.

Gamble snapped out of his funk. "At the top of the drive. I saw a box there."

Zander gunned our car to the top of the drive; he angled the vehicle so that the passenger window was alongside the cable box. Gamble pulled in behind us.

Nanomites spooled away from me into the box, and their search speed jumped exponentially. For a moment, I imagined every user in the neighborhood losing their Wi-Fi signal—and the bedlam that would ensue.

Too bad.

Gamble climbed into our back seat. "What can you see?"

"Everything they can see," Zander replied.

I closed my eyes and went into the warehouse where the many feeds the nanomites were scanning seemed larger and closer. I sensed Zander near me, but I kept my attention on the flashing, changing panorama.

As fast as the images flipped by, I kept up. And then the feed froze . . . and gave way to a single "window." The window zoomed in at dizzying speed and paused. When I caught my breath, I recognized the neighborhood, the large house, the drive. It was satellite video, but nothing was happening.

"Speed it up, Nano."

They fast-forwarded until a vehicle—a dark SUV—turned into the drive. The nanomites followed the SUV down the drive. Before it made the turn toward Trujillo's house, it stopped. Two figures emerged.

"Zoom in close, Nano."

A man and a woman, as we had deduced.

"Give me a close-up of the man, Nano."

The man's features blurred and then came into focus.

"I know him. He's an NSA SPO."

"Tagged?"

"No."

He was not one of the four SPOs I'd tagged with a nanobug array. He and the woman were "new" members of the conspiracy, and the numbers were growing.

"Nano, fast forward."

We watched the fast-forward video of an unconscious Trujillo being dragged to her abductors' SUV and the vehicle retreating up the drive. When the SUV reached the top of the drive where we were presently parked, it turned right.

Jayda Cruz, we have fast-forwarded the satellite feed to the vehicle's destination and have recorded their route. We can now provide explicit directions to where the vehicle is parked without an Internet connection.

"Good job, Nano."

I turned to Gamble. "We don't need to watch anymore; the nanomites know where Trujillo is and will direct us. With us or follow us?"

"I'll follow. We may need both cars."

Our two vehicles sped away, relying upon the nanomites to guide us. I knew Zander and I could rescue Trujillo from her captors—but could we reach her before she gave us up? Or worse, before they killed her and dumped her body where we'd never find it?

It boiled down to a question of time and Trujillo's will. Her captors had already had her for eight long hours.

Lord, I prayed. *Agent Trujillo is one of the good guys. Please help her to hold on.*

We drove on into the night, moving steadily south and east.

Toward the coast.

⌘

AN HOUR AND A HALF LATER, our route wound through dirt tracks and one-lane plank bridges between coastal islands. I checked my phone.

"No service out here."

It was impossible to tell exactly where we were for the meandering road and the water that surrounded us. We saw no houses. I doubted that the marshy area was inhabitable, subject as it had to be to tide and the vagaries of storm surge.

Eventually, we arrived at a fenced area, but the fencing was old and rusted. Sections of the chain link leaned precariously or had collapsed. Faded signs wired to the fence read, "Property of the U.S. Government. Trespassers Will Be Prosecuted" but, from all appearances, the place was abandoned.

The nanomites directed us through an open gate. We drove further and arrived at what I could only describe as a ship graveyard—acre upon acre of decaying docks glinting under the moonlight, their pilings standing in water as grossly putrid and dead as the rusting hulks moored to them.

Some of the lifeless skeletons had keeled over and come to rest on their hulls in shallow water; a few ships were anchored farther out in a wide inlet, their structures sinking by inches as the years passed, some so low in the water that lazy waves washed across their decks.

The docks formed a damp, tangled maze overgrown with seaweed and algae. Many timbers had rotted through, making them impassable. Who knew which docks were safe or unsafe to drive on?

In addition to the treacherous conditions, we were driving through the night with a moon only days into its first lunar phase. Worse, the nanomites had advised us to turn off our headlights to avoid detection. Once our eyes adjusted to the dark, we had barely enough starlight and moonglow to navigate by—just enough to reveal how disgusting, dangerous, and vermin-ridden the graveyard was. Rats scuttled before us, their eyes blinking red when they stopped to stare at us.

And the stink? *Nasty.* I could only guess at the stench of decomposition during the heat of the day.

"Dead flies in perfume make it stink, and a little foolishness decomposes much wisdom," Jayda Cruz.

I swallowed down my gorge. "My nose tells me there's more decomposing here than dead flies, Nano."

If the satellite video had not enabled the nanomites to track the SUV that had carried Trujillo here and record its route, we would have become lost in the labyrinth. We inched ahead, under the nanomites' sure guidance rather than our own vision: Where the SUV had safely gone, we could also.

Jayda Cruz, the vehicle is parked just ahead. We advise you to leave your vehicle here. However, you will not be able to proceed far on foot.

The nanomites replayed grainy overhead video for us of the SUV coming to a halt. Zander and I watched Trujillo's attackers yank her from the back seat. She must have regained some consciousness, because they forced her to stagger between them—to a small, open boat tied up between the barnacle-encrusted skeletons of two ships.

The man stepped into the boat and reached for Trujillo. As he did, she came to life and kicked out at him while trying to shake the grip the woman had on her.

Her escape attempt was short-lived: The man grasped her foot and jerked it out from under her. Trujillo dropped on her back on the slimy dock.

When the woman kicked Trujillo's side, Trujillo curled into a ball, her face etched with agony. It was awful to watch. I was glad Gamble couldn't see it.

Moments later, the boat motored away, toward a rusted ship anchored in the inlet.

"Nano, why are they taking her out there?"

Jayda Cruz, the boat is a clandestine NSA facility hidden in plain sight.

"How do you know this?"

We found a number of NSA facilities listed in the Repository.

"Hmm." Seems the Repository was not entirely without value to us after all.

We have found many interesting and perhaps useful documents in the Repository.

"Later, Nano. Trujillo is out there on the water, and we're stuck here. How do we get to her?"

We have located a small, usable craft at the end of this pier.

"That's great! Let's go."

Zander and I got out and motioned to Gamble. "This way. And remember that sound carries farther over water."

Gamble whispered, "God bless my doctor. He's been bugging me to re-up my tetanus vaccination. If we get out of here alive, I'm stopping at a 24-hour pharmacy on my way home to get my injection." He shuddered. "This place is a vile, revolting petri dish."

We crept past the SUV; its engine was cool to the touch. We pushed on down the dock.

We have arrived at the craft, Jayda Cruz.

I stared around in the dark. "Where, Nano?" All I saw was an upside-down aluminum boat with a gash the size of my foot in its side.

The craft is in front of you, Jayda Cruz. As Jesus said, "Launch out into the deep and let down your nets for a catch."

"What? In *that?*"

I pointed as I protested. Zander and Gamble saw what I was pointing at. They both shook their heads. Emphatically.

"Nano, this thing has a hole in it. It won't even float. And we'll need paddles."

Have Zander and Gamble turn it over and place it in the water.

Zander heard the nanomites, too. "Put *that* thing in the water? Sure, pal."

You of little faith, why are you so afraid?

He snorted. "Why, indeed? Well, this oughtta be quick."

He gestured to Gamble. "Give me a hand. The nanomites want us to put this in the water."

"Nope. Uh-uh. That thing will sink like a rock if we get in it—and have you noticed the charming bacterial stew floating around these pilings?"

"The nanomites must have a plan, Gamble, or they wouldn't have told us to use this piece of junk."

Gamble glanced from the mortally wounded boat to the ship out in the inlet—the ship where Trujillo was undoubtedly suffering for her silence.

He cracked his neck. "Right. Let's do this."

He and Zander lifted the lightweight boat and flipped it over. From under it, a nest of disturbed rats squealed and scurried in every direction.

I about lost it right there. When a particularly gross specimen ran across my foot—its little claw-like feet scrabbling and scratching my shoe—I had to stuff my fist into my mouth to keep from shrieking.

Zander kicked a few of the slower rats off the dock and shifted his end of the boat toward the water.

"Keep it together, Jay."

I was too busy chewing on my knuckles to answer.

"Hey! Watch your step, Cruz."

Zander looked down and found his foot halfway over a hole in a dock plank. "Thanks, man."

"So, we're dropping this thing in the water, right? Are you sure?"

"Yup."

The tide was out so the water line was several feet below the dock. Zander and Gamble got on their knees on the dock's mucky surface and grasped their ends of the aluminum boat.

"I'm burning these trousers when we're done," Gamble declared.

"If you don't, I'm siccing the EPA on you."

They lowered the boat toward the water and let it fall the last foot—where it bobbed complacently.

Gamble was stunned. "How's that possible?"

Zander understood. "The nanomites are filling the hole. Come on, we need to get in—I don't know how long they can maintain the plug."

"You don't know how long they can maintain the plug? But 'Come on, we need to get in'? No freaking way."

Zander ignored Gamble and, placing his hands on the slimy dock edge, dropped into the boat. "Ready, Jay?"

"Yeah." I grasped Zander's shoulders and let him pull me to him. The boat began to drift away from the dock.

"Come on, Gamble."

He shook his head. "Nope. Besides this being totally impossible, how do you plan to get us out to the ship? No motor. No paddles."

"Watch." I held my palm to the water on the far side of the boat, away from the dock and toward the inlet. A spurt of electricity struck the water and it churned. In response, the boat edged closer to the dock.

"See?"

Gamble started to rub his face with his hand but stopped himself in time. "*Gah!*"

Without further protest, he climbed down into the boat and wiped his palms on his doomed trousers. Zander pushed us off, and he and I crouched in the stern, our palms toward the water behind us. The thick, murky water boiled, and our little craft moved toward our destination, riding lightly over the swells, leaving little wake.

It wasn't a large ship from a distance. Up close it was considerably more daunting. No lights appeared as we approached, but we saw our adversaries' motorboat tied up to a ladder. We nudged their boat aside and tied on, so we could reach the ladder.

Zander climbed up first and disappeared over the side. A moment later, his head appeared above us. He motioned to us.

When the three of us were standing on the ship's deck, the nanomites instructed us further.

Jayda Cruz, proceed with caution amidships on the port side. You'll find a closed bulkhead door. The satellite video shows our targets entering the ship there.

We found the door—a corroded slab of metal with a wheel for a handle. As far as we and the nanomites knew, the man and woman who had snatched Trujillo—and Trujillo herself—were the only people on board.

"I'll lead the way," I whispered."

"What? No, either Gamble or I should go first," Zander protested.

Gamble shook his head. "Nope, don't look at me. Honestly? I don't want to be between those guys downstairs and you two—what with you-all shooting bolts of electricity. I'm happy to take the rear and watch our six."

"Look, Zander, I have more experience with . . . this kind of stuff." I touched his hand. "I need you close behind me in case I miss something."

It was mildly manipulative, appealing to another facet of his protective instincts, but it was also true. I did have more experience with the nanomites in "combat" situations—and I did want him checking for what I might miss.

"Fine," he growled, "but I'm sticking to you like glue."

He placed his hands on the door's wheel. The door was as rust- and crud-rimed as the rest of the ship; Zander's first crank on the wheel produced a scree of protest. Our efforts to approach undetected were about to end.

Zander Cruz, let us open the door.

"Yeah. Be my guest, Nano."

It took the nanomites several minutes to noiselessly ease the door open. Gamble secured the open door to the bulkhead, so it wouldn't swing closed on us—leaving us lost in the ship's utterly black interior.

I hesitated.

The Lord is my light and my salvation, Jayda Cruz. Whom shall I fear?

"Uh, right, Nano." I stepped over the doorsill into the unlit passageway. Turns out, I need not have feared the darkness: A glow near my shins lit the way a foot or so ahead—and the memory of another dark night—lost and stumbling my way down the flanks of a mountain—washed over me. Shaking myself, I pushed into the passageway, Zander and Gamble close behind.

I soon came to a ladder leading down into the hold. We could continue ahead or go down. I gritted my teeth and touched a rail on the ladder. The nanomites would be able to detect skin cells on the rails and tell me if human hands had recently touched it.

"Which way did they take her, Nano?" I was really hoping they'd say "ahead" and not "down."

They took the ladder, Jayda Cruz.

"Well, of course they did."

"*I will praise you, Lord my God . . . you have delivered me from the depths, from the realm of the dead.*""Nice word play, Nano. Comforting, too." More sarcasm.

Clenching my jaw, I grasped the goobery rails and descended into the bowels of the ship—vowing to scrub myself raw with a gallon of antibacterial soap after we got out of here.

When the three of us were assembled at the bottom of the ladder, the way forward became clearer: From far down the passageway, faint light and the echo of voices reached out to us.

A minute later, we saw another bulkhead door hanging partially open. I stuck my finger around its frame; Zander and I saw what the nanomites "saw" in that brief glimpse.

The compartment had been the ship's mess. A steel table and two benches that had once been riveted to the cabin's deck were shoved against the bulkhead to make room for the compartment's present use: Agent Trujillo dangled from the overhead by her wrists. Her unconscious body sagged forward. Her face was a bruised, bloody mess; her shirt hung in tatters.

Trujillo's two interrogators were the cabin's only other occupants. I was happy to note their fatigue and exasperation. Trujillo had not been as easy to break as they had figured she would be. Maybe we'd arrived in time after all.

"What next?" Zander whispered in my ear."

"This."

I held my palms toward each other. A spark ignited; my hands trembled and shook as fire arced between them and grew. Then blue current snapped and crackled around us, building, rising, turning the passageway from the depths of night to brightest day.

From within the cabin, the man shouted, "What the *bleep* is *that?*"

Zander grabbed the door and threw it all the way open and, surrounded by a shield of nanomites, I stepped over the sill. The man fired his gun three times, but the nanomites deflected the rounds. A bolus of electricity shot from my hand to the man. The force of the bolt launched him across the compartment where he crumpled against the bulkhead. With a similar move, I dispatched the woman.

As I began to power down, Zander and Gamble reached Trujillo. They lifted her bound wrists from the hook in the overhead and laid her on the deck.

"She's alive." Gamble's relief warred with his fury. "We need to get her to a hospital right away."

Jayda Cruz. You are being watched.

We hadn't noticed the tablet positioned on a bench—a tablet in video chat mode. Someone had been witnessing Trujillo's interrogation.

That same someone had seen us enter and dispatch her captors!

I grabbed the tablet. On its video screen, I glimpsed part of a face—and then a hand grabbed the device on the other end. A second later, the video feed ended in static.

"They pulled the network connection. Nano! Can you trace the location of this call?"

Negative, Jayda Cruz. There is no cellular service out here. The tablet had to have been using a satellite feed to stream the interrogation.

"Can you piggyback onto the tablet's satellite feed?"

No. The feed was terminated at its source. We will back-check the tablet's call logs and attempt to identify the device on the other end when we are again within cellular data range.

"Come on," Gamble growled. "We got what we came for. We need to get Trujillo away from here."

Zander gestured to our unconscious prisoners. "What do we do with these two?"

"We'll take their boat and let ours sink. They won't be able to leave. I'll send someone for them later—hopefully, they'll have information we can use."

Zander wanted to help Gamble with Trujillo's limp form, but Gamble was having none of that. He slung Trujillo over his shoulder like a sack of flour—then noticed me watching him.

I had to be wearing a bemused expression.

"What?"

"I was just remembering . . . you hauling me up the mountain and into the tunnels when I was nearly dead. Don't know if I ever thanked you properly."

"My lot in life, I guess." He jerked his chin at Zander. "Head up the ladder. I'll hand her up to you."

Zander ran into the passageway to follow Gamble's orders.

Before I left the cabin to follow them, I confiscated the tablet and pointed to Trujillo's former captors. "Nano, take care of them."

The nanomites would expunge our prisoners' most recent synapses; Trujillo's interrogators would remember nothing of my attack—but those who had been watching via the video call? There was nothing we could do about them.

Up on the main deck, we had to figure out how to get Trujillo safely down into her captors' boat. It took some maneuvering, but we got it handled. Gamble laid Trujillo on the bottom of the boat and squatted next to her. I positioned myself in the bow, above Trujillo's head. Before Zander sat in the stern, he untied the aluminum craft. Then he started our new boat's electric motor and pointed the bow toward the docks.

As we pulled away from the rusting ship, the nanomites released their "patch" on the aluminum boat, and I watched it sink into the dark water.

Gamble, no longer sensible to the slime around us, unbuttoned his dress shirt and took it off. I lifted Trujillo's shoulders. Together, we managed to get his shirt under her bloody shoulders. She groaned once and then was silent.

"Jayda, can the nanomites do anything to help Janice?" Gamble asked.

"I think so." I turned inward. "Nano, how is Agent Trujillo? What can you do for her before we get her to a hospital?"

In addition to cuts and bruising over her back, Agent Trujillo has sustained multiple broken fingers and facial bones and facial contusions of a serious nature. She will require surgery. We are monitoring her vital signs and cauterizing bleeds as quickly as we can.

"They're stopping the bleeds, Gamble, but she needs surgery."

I was focused on Trujillo until a soft choking noise made me glance up at Gamble. I hadn't seen him like this before—and I don't mean disheveled and clad in a t-shirt. The way his eyes were fixed on Trujillo, how he'd called her "Janice," and the strangled sound in his throat told me more than he probably realized.

When we reached the docks, Gamble insisted we put Trujillo on the back seat of his car, and he asked me to drive. I wasn't surprised when he sat in the back with Trujillo's head cradled on his lap. As we slowly wound our way out of the ship graveyard, the nanomites located the nearest trauma center. We sped from the marshy coast, the mites providing turn-by-turn directions down a back road that would eventually intersect with a state highway. Zander, driving our car, followed close behind us.

⌘

"WE'VE LOST TRUJILLO."

Danforth and his companion had followed Trujillo's interrogation from a specially equipped and shielded room within a farmhouse that sat on a wooded lot in the Virginia countryside, some thirty miles west of D.C. When the unfamiliar young woman had exploded into the ship's mess hall and, with what appeared like lightning bolts shooting from her hands, had dispatched Trujillo's captors, Danforth had nearly lost control of his bladder.

His companion, however, had not so much as flinched. She had leaned toward the screen, fascinated. Even when two men had followed the woman into the ship's mess and proceeded to take down Trujillo's unconscious body and ease her to the deck, Danforth's companion had not moved or displayed emotion other than rapt attention.

Moments later, when Trujillo's rescuers noticed the tablet that was live streaming the interrogation, Danforth's companion had calmly yanked the network cable from their laptop, terminating the feed. She had acted quickly, exhibiting the cool response for which she had once been legend in the field.

Then she had proceeded to pace the room they were shut up in, to close herself off from her surroundings and think—another behavior for which she was known.

He repeated, "We've lost Trujillo and our link to this Keyes woman."

Roused from her contemplation, she paused to level a jeer of disdain in his direction. "Have we, indeed?"

Danforth had the annoying habit of stating the obvious.

The woman's amber eyes smoldered. "Actually, I do not consider the intervention to be a loss. Rather, what we witnessed tells us more than Trujillo ever would have. We've seen for ourselves that Cushing's preposterous claims about the nanomites were true—*and more*."

She folded her hands together. "Since we know that Gemma Keyes escaped the explosion Cushing caused and *is* alive, the woman we saw on the video call must be her, must be Gemma Keyes in a clever and convincing disguise. Who else could it be? So! We have definitive proof: Keyes is alive, she has the nanomites, and the nanomites have given her powers we have only dreamed of."

Her mouth curved with cunning satisfaction. "And while I did not know this mystery woman with the amazing abilities, did you, perhaps, recognize either of her companions?"

"No, I don't think so. Only caught a glimpse of them at the end."

"Ah, then let me enlighten you, Lawrence: One of the men was Zander Cruz—*Gemma Keyes' former boyfriend*. My people in Albuquerque tell me he is now married to one *Jayda Cruz*. Ergo, we may presume that we have now "met" Jayda Cruz and that she and Gemma Keyes are one and the same."

She strode up and down the room again, then pivoted on her heel. "I wish you to sterilize the black site, Lawrence, and then locate and capture Jayda Cruz and her companions."

"They could be anywhere."

Her contempt turned his stomach to gelatin. "How many vehicles do you think left the black site this evening, Lawrence? They can't have gone far, and they will be seeking medical attention for Agent Trujillo. You are second in command of the most powerful intelligence organization in the world—*use it*."

He ground his teeth. "I risk exposing myself by tasking NSA resources for unsanctioned operations."

"Then you must be discreet. Lawrence. Use only vetted personnel we can trust, *but get it done*. This woman is key to our achieving our long-term objectives."

⌘⌘⌘⌘

CHAPTER 27

WE BROKE FREE OF the graveyard's twisting labyrinth, back into the dark, winding dirt tracks of the coastal islands. Even with the nanomites' sure directions, it took us a while to reach a state road not much better than what we'd left—except that it had, at one time, been paved. When my tires hit the pitted and crumbling asphalt, I punched the gas. No bueno. The rough road forced me to slow down.

Gamble's voice came from the back seat. "Gemma?"

I didn't have the heart to correct him. "Yeah?"

"They saw you in action. The people watching on the tablet."

"I know."

"And I doubt that they can afford to let Trujillo go free after what they did to her. I had you drive because they may be setting up roadblocks . . . or sending aircraft to find us. To waylay us. I'm counting on you . . . you and Zander."

"We'll keep you and Trujillo safe, Gamble."

Yeah, things might work out tonight, but it wouldn't be as easy going forward. Had the unknown viewers gleaned any identifying information on Zander or myself from the video call? The smallest detail had the potential—the strong probability—of blowing our covers to oblivion.

Goodbye Jayda and Zander Cruz.

We must have left the cellular dead zone, because I heard Gamble dial his phone. "Mal? I'm in deep water, brother, and need your help."

Mal? Of course—old military buddies. Loyal to a fault. I didn't hear what Mal had to say, but it was short. After that, Gamble issued curt, precise instructions.

"I'm sending you the location of a mothballed ship. It's out in the water a couple hundred yards from the nearest dock. Dispatch a small team. You'll need an inflatable to reach the ship. You'll find two targets, male and female, below deck. We've disarmed them, but it'll be a race to beat their handlers to them."

Gamble listened. "Yeah, we want them for what they know, so have your people hide them well. Right now, we're on our way to the nearest trauma center, and I need the rest of your team for security there. Yes. Thanks, man. Hold on for the location of the ship and directions to the hospital."

Gamble muted the phone. "Gem—sorry, *Jayda*—can you have the nanoguys send directions to Mal through my phone?"

"Yup. One sec." A moment later, I said, "Done."

Gamble unmuted his phone. "Mal? Did you get the directions? Good. Have your people follow the route to the ship exactly, because once you get near the inlet, the way in is treacherous. Yeah. See you at the hospital."

He hung up. "Thanks, Jayda."

"No problem."

Like Gamble said, we needed Trujillo's interrogators, but I wondered if Mal's team would beat our enemies' rescuers to the ship. The man and woman we'd left behind in our haste to get Trujillo medical attention had information our enemies would be loath for us to acquire.

Perhaps thirty minutes had elapsed since we released Trujillo. Although we'd been on the road less than half that time, our circuitous route away from the ship graveyard hadn't taken us all that far from it— not far as the crow flies, anyway. I had punched our speed up another notch when a different and chilling possibility occurred to me.

"Hey, Gamble? What if . . . what if instead of rescuing Trujillo's captors, their handlers decide to 'clean' the scene instead? Mal's team could be walking into—"

Jayda Cruz, we are picking up rotor vibration. Pull to the side of the road NOW.

I swerved toward the shoulder and stomped on the brakes. Zander screeched to a stop near our rear bumper. As we scrambled out of our seats, we heard choppers approaching.

I shouted to him, "Cover the cars!"

Zander and I stood back-to-back between the two vehicles and extended our arms, mine over Gamble's car, Zander over ours.

The nanomites flowed from us like a dense fog with their mirrors deployed. Two large vehicles were a lot of area to ask them to cover, but they only needed to shield what the helos could see of us from the air—in particular, the heat plumes from our engines.

Two choppers came in fast and low, one close behind the other, following the winding road, their wash kicking up dust and debris. The nanomites' shields canted toward the helos, keeping our vehicles masked from downward-looking scopes.

The choppers blew by us without slowing. We stayed as we were for a minute.

Jayda Cruz, you may proceed now.

"Thanks for the warning, Nano."

I leaned into the car. "Gamble, Mal and his team aren't going to reach Trujillo's captors in time."

He pulled his phone out and dialed. When Mal answered, Gamble said, "Cancel the pickup, Mal. We just avoided two inbound choppers—"

I flinched as the sky behind us ignited. Out of reflex, I looked back—only to shield my eyes against the intensity of the flames shooting above the tree line . . . from the direction of the ship graveyard. Not long after, the concussion boom reached us.

Gamble ended his call with, "Mal? Yeah, the tangos we left in the ship are toast. Make all speed for the trauma center."

I was listening to Gamble's call when the nanomites broke in.

Jayda Cruz, we are receiving information from Lawrence Danforth's nanobug array.

"What about Danforth?"

Zander, who was hovering nearby, tuned in on our conversation.

We have ascertained that NSA Deputy Director Danforth was one of the two individuals watching Agent Trujillo's interrogation via video call.

I had to tamp down the anger that surged in me. *Lord, please help me to remain calm and objective. I cannot allow my feelings to dictate what I choose to do.*

To the nanomites I said, "Who was the other person with Danforth?"

Unknown at this time, Jayda Cruz—and it is not of first importance. Danforth and his companion observed the means by which you took down Agent Trujillo's captors. Soon after, Danforth called for the helos to locate your vehicle as it fled the shipyard, and he ordered the helo strike to sanitize the NSA black site.

"But you hid us from the helos, right, Nano?"

Yes, Jayda Cruz. However, we are not in continuous communication with Danforth's array. The nanobugs were able to report only while he was giving orders over a phone, and we were able to receive their communication only when we reentered cellular range.

"I understand not being able to receive from the arrays while we are without cell service, but why not continuous communication when we do have service?"

We postulate that Danforth is operating from within a shielded facility such as a SCIF. When he used the facility's secure phone, the array utilized that connection. However, because we were out of cellular range, they were unable to reach us directly. They, instead, sent an information packet to a predetermined network location. We picked up the packet when we reacquired cellular service.

Jayda Cruz, this is what is of first importance: Danforth's associate recognized Zander Cruz from the tablet's video feed and has deduced that Jayda Cruz is Gemma Keyes.

The blood drained from my face, and I turned to look at Zander. His face reflected the dismay I felt.

We will keep you abreast of further information as we receive it.

"Thanks, Nano."

Half numb, I got back into Gamble's car and drove on. Eventually, we merged onto a state highway and, ten minutes after that, I stopped the car in front of a hospital emergency entrance. The ER team raced out and took Trujillo from us. We followed them inside, but even though Gamble showed his cred pack, when the ER team reached the double doors to the treatment area, they shut us out.

"We'll park," I said to him, "and meet you in the waiting room."

Zander and I parked our vehicles, and we joined Gamble in the half-filled lounge. He was already fretting.

"I can't protect her if I can't keep track of where they've taken her."

"We know where she is, Gamble. Before they took Trujillo from your car, I sent a nanobug array to her. The nanomites will keep tabs on her condition and exact location. Right now, she's still behind those doors," I pointed to the double doors we'd been prevented from entering. "The doctors are assessing her injuries, but her vitals are good."

Gamble's gratitude showed on his face. "Thank you."

I smiled. "Not a problem. She's one of ours now."

"I guess you've figured out . . ."

"That you're sweet on her? Kind of hard to miss."

I knew, too, that it had been a long time for Gamble. Not since a woman named Graciella, who had been an undercover DEA agent working with Mexican *Federales*. The coordinated drug bust had gone bad, and Arnaldo Soto had captured, tortured, and killed Graciella. The ghost of that failure was partly why Gamble was so agitated. He would never again let a woman he cared for suffer if he could prevent it.

He would die first.

Zander blinked his surprise. "Oh."

I chuckled and tipped my head toward my wonderful but sometimes clueless guy. "Not always the sharpest stick in the stack."

Zander bristled. "Hey!" Then he grinned and slapped Gamble on the back. "Glad to hear it, man."

It was the friendly banter Gamble needed to loosen up a little.

"How about I get us some coffee?" I asked. "We're going to be here a while."

Forty minutes and several cups of coffee later, Mal and his crew rolled into the hospital's ER. His men were way overdressed considering the warm humid night, but t-shirts and shorts didn't provide the best concealment for the kind and amount of weaponry they carried.

An anxious security guard spied Mal and his team at the same time Mal spotted our little group. Sending his guys to mount a guard outside the ER entrance, Mal walked up to the guard and had a word with him. Several words, in fact.

The guard finally capitulated, but he kept an anxious eye on Mal as he sauntered over to us.

He nodded to Gamble and arched one brow at Zander and me. "John-Boy. Ripley. Guess I shouldn't be all that surprised to see you two here." To Gamble he said, "Heard reports on the radio of an unannounced military test lighting up the sky."

"Our adversaries have some serious connections. They had those helos in the air in no time. It was apparent that they were looking for us—and the two tangos we left behind. The problem is, we don't have many resources we can trust."

"I see." Mal gestured toward the ER doors. "Who's in there?"

"An invaluable black-ops ghost."

"And you need us to keep him and you three off-grid?"

"Her. And, yes."

"How long?"

"Unknown."

"I can send John-Boy and Ripley away with Deckard and McFly; the rest of us can stay with you."

"Until we see how this plays out, I want to keep John-Boy and Ripley close for the, uh, added fire power."

"Added fire power? Them? They don't know one end of a gun from the other."

When Gamble didn't reply, Mal's eyes narrowed. "These two are not the nubes you led us to believe they were, are they." It was a statement, not a question.

I frowned. "Uh, guys? We're right here."

Gamble ignored me. "Not exactly, Mal, but it's . . . complicated."

"Complicated? Between us?"

"Need-to-know, Mal."

I turned inward as the nanomites spoke. *Jayda Cruz, when the helos failed to locate you and Zander Cruz as we fled the shipyard, Danforth tasked NSA resources to search local hospitals for agent Trujillo. As we speak, Danforth is assembling a tactical strike team. Their objective is to capture you. All others are expendable. They are coming.*

I scanned the waiting room, seeing innocent civilians whose lives Danforth considered worthless. Mere collateral damage. "Nano, expunge Agent Trujillo's records from this medical facility. Hurry!"

They answered softly, *We tried but were too late, Jayda Cruz. Danforth had already accessed her chart. He has tasked satellite surveillance over this facility and dispatched the assault team. Estimated time of arrival is ten minutes.*

I interrupted Gamble and Mal. "They know where we are. We have ten minutes before an assault team arrives. They have orders to take me alive—but everyone else is expendable."

Gamble cursed. "Assault a hospital? Are they crazy? This is the absolute worst place for close-quarters battle! All these civilians—it would be a blood bath. We need to grab Trujillo and get out of here, lead them away from here."

"No," I whispered. "They aren't focused on Trujillo at this moment. Just us, Zander and me. They have satellite coverage? Fine; we'll let them see us leaving. They'll follow us and leave this place alone."

"That's suicide," Mal said evenly.

"Maybe not."

"Where to, then?"

"What do you mean?"

"My team and I will go with you. Do you have a plan? A defensible position to fall back to? If not, we can lead them back to the clubhouse."

I looked at Zander; he replied to Mal, "Their goal is to capture us, not kill us, but they will view you as fair game."

Mal grinned. "I have twenty-five years of acting the role of 'fair game,' much to my adversaries' dismay. Listen, if they intend to take you, then we don't need to worry about another helo strike, right? The clubhouse is fortified and armed. Trust me when I say that we're prepared for any contingency."

His generosity and courage choked me up. "But this . . . this isn't your fight, Mal."

"The *blank* it isn't. This is America, and what they're doing is patently illegal. Any unwarranted attack on a fellow American is an attack on all of us. So, come on, Ripley. We're wasting precious time."

Zander and I looked at each other. Nodded.

"Thank you, Mal."

"Thank me later. Gamble, I'm leaving Logan with you for backup. The rest of us will escort Ripley and John-Boy back to the clubhouse."

Gamble stared at me. "I wish you good luck, Jayda."

Zander had my arm and was dragging me toward the exit. I smiled a little. "I trust in someone bigger than luck, my friend. I'll be praying for you and Trujillo."

⌘

ZANDER AND I STOOD next to our car in the parking lot for several seconds. We turned our faces up to the sky, giving Danforth a good look. I even waved.

See me, Danforth? Come and get me yourself, if you dare, you coward.

Seconds later we peeled out of the parking lot with Mal's team riding our bumper. The nanomites had the assault team's vehicle location; they guided our little convoy away from them and set us on the most direct route to Malware, Inc.'s clubhouse.

Zander and I held our breath, waiting for the nanomites to tell us that whoever was watching the satellite feed had seen us leave the hospital and had conveyed our present location to our pursuers. The strike team was less than four minutes from the hospital when they slowed, turned, and darted forward on a different bearing.

Jayda Cruz, Zander Cruz, the assault team has changed direction. They are receiving real-time guidance from an NSA post watching the satellite feed and are on an intercept course to our projected location.

Zander was driving our car, and I saw his jaw tighten.

"Zander, why don't we have the nanomites freeze the satellite feed? The NSA won't have eyes on us anymore. It will give us time to hide."

"If they lose us, won't they go back to the hospital to take Gamble and Trujillo? You know Gamble won't let them have Trujillo. He and Logan have guns and will fight. All those people . . ."

"Yeah. You're right."

Intercept within three minutes.

"Nano, can you spoof the feed, have them turn the wrong way a few times, throw them off our route long enough for us to get ahead of them?"

Consider it done, Jayda Cruz.

A moment later, they said, *Jayda Cruz, we have bought you some time. Turn left ahead.*

We were breaking the speed limit in every zone we rolled through, but we did not slow. The nanomites spoofed the satellite feed twice more, recouping time for us to reach the clubhouse ahead of the assault team.

I never dreamed I'd be so glad to see the dregs of Baltimore, but those abandoned warehouses may as well have been sided in sheets of solid gold, so relieved was I for their rundown silhouettes to come into view. Then we turned a corner and the clubhouse was dead ahead—that three-story brick island in the middle of what already resembled a war zone.

Zander pulled aside for Mal's SUV. The clubhouse's garage door swung open, and we drove inside after the SUV.

It was all business after that. Baltar and McFly raced into the clubhouse. Deckard and Dredd yanked down a second garage door over the first and locked it in place—the second door also constructed of reinforced steel panels.

Mal gestured for us to follow them. "That was some circuit you led us on, John-Boy."

"The strike team almost cut us off three times. Had to reroute."

"Huh. And how do you know that?"

Zander shrugged. "Let's just say I had overwatch assistance of my own."

"Yeah? Well, when this is done? We're gonna have a nice, long chat, you two and me."

"We'll see," I answered.

"Fair enough. Let's get busy. We don't know how much time we have before they get here."

Jayda Cruz, the assault team is two minutes out.

"We've got exactly two minutes."

Mal slid his eyes over to me. "Then we need to hop to it."

He led us into what can only be described as their operations center. It was down a short hallway from the training center, also located in the interior, the hub of the building. Baltar sat at the controls, watching multiple exterior views on a wall of monitors.

"Holy guacamole. You guys have a better setup than the White House." Zander whispered.

When three sets of eyes swiveled his way, he cleared his throat. "Please tell me I did not say that out loud."

Then the strike team, in two assault vehicles, rolled around the corner, and we were occupied with their approach.

"Lenco BearCats," Baltar expounded. "Customized jobs. Each one accommodates ten armed personnel. Looks to me like these rigs carry the Mk 19, 40mm belt-fed grenade launcher."

I squirmed inside. Malware's clubhouse suddenly felt like tons of brick rubble looking for a place to fall down.

Mal answered my disquiet, "We spent two years reconstructing this place, Ripley. The exterior walls are three feet thick, concrete reinforced with high-grade steel overlaid with recycled brick. If, after a few hours, their guns were to breach the perimeter, they'd meet similar obstacles in the interior walls surrounding us and the training center."

He tapped a monitor. "But not to worry. Watch there."

I squinted and located a dark form emerging from the third-floor hatch—the one I'd accessed during our first SDR drill. It was McFly. He aimed something at a warehouse across from the clubhouse. A line snaked over and went taut. Moments later, McFly zipped across the way and disappeared into a window.

The camera view switched to the warehouse where McFly had disappeared. He reappeared two floors up. Again, a line shot across the street—this time directly over the assault vehicles to the warehouse opposite him.

"We own both those buildings. Certain aspects of them have been, uh, modified, for our needs. We let the 'neighborhood' use parts of these properties to keep up the pretense that they are abandoned, but we keep the locals locked out of our tactical spaces."

Movement caught my attention. Men in black gear poured from the two vehicles and spun away in two stacked lines, one to the left, one to the right. They melted into the shadows of the warehouses.

As soon as they cleared the vehicles, the BearCat gun turrets took aim at the clubhouse.

"Watch now."

McFly sailed across the street, over the assault vehicles. The short gun slung from his shoulder burped twice. Whatever he fired floated toward the first vehicle's turret and touched down like a feather. The same with the second vehicle. McFly coasted across to the opposite warehouse window, but not before streaks of semiauto rounds tried to tag him.

The armed attackers had noticed him too late, though.

As McFly zipped into the warehouse window, the top of one of the assault vehicles blew. Then the other. A soldier crawled out the back of one burning vehicle, coughing and hacking. I didn't see a similar form crawl out of the second.

Mal winced. "$300k+ taxpayer money per vehicle. Molten slag."

"I know they're trying to kill us and all, but won't you have to answer for destroying expensive government property?"

"Two things, Ripley. First, you're assuming they'll win and take us into custody. They won't—they just lost their control comms and heavy artillery. Second, you're assuming they'll get around to prosecuting us afterward. They won't do that, either. This operation is completely off-book, illegal as all get out. See any insignias on the attackers' uniforms? No? Take it from me: Whoever is behind this, they don't want the public—chiefly their Congressional funding oversight—to know a blessed thing about this op."

"Hey, Gamble must have called in the cavalry," Baltar said, pointing. "Look there."

A vehicle similar to the two assault vehicles (both of which were now burning like bonfires) turned the corner. The new vehicle was dark blue with bright white lettering that read "FBI."

Baltar indicated another monitor. The black-clad attackers were fleeing. Keeping to the shadows of the warehouses across from the clubhouse, they raced to the end of the block and evaporated into the night.

"Is that it?" I asked, my throat tight.

"I doubt it," Mal answered. "They'll stay away as long as the FBI is here, but you can be sure we haven't seen the last of them. They seem to want you pretty bad, Ripley."

He jerked his chin at Zander, then me. "You two. Time to have that talk."

We followed along after him, but I'd left nanobugs on Baltar. I wanted to keep tabs on the FBI presence.

Mal showed us to his office. "Have a seat."

We sat. He sat.

"Well?" I asked.

"Well, for starts, you and John-Boy here know each other."

"You introduced us at our first tradecraft class a couple weeks back."

"Nope. You guys 'know' each other."

"Know each other how?" Zander asked.

"Come on, guys; I don't care if you're together." He pointed at my hand. "Look. Neither of you wore a wedding ring in class. Kind of a giveaway."

We didn't respond.

Mal sat back and considered us through lazy, speculative eyes. "It'd be too bad if they were to take you, Ripley, because you're a fine-looking woman, and I thought maybe we'd shared a moment back there. I was even thinking of asking you out. You know. Dinner, drinks, dancing . . . a long night of getting to know each other . . . intimately?"

He raked his eyes over me and smiled. "Or should I consider you off limits?"

I'd seen Zander's anger only a few times, like when Mateo Martinez had provoked him. I'd seen him angry, and I'd seen him deadly serious. As he answered Mal through stiff lips, though, he was neither angry nor serious—just the deadly part.

"Yeah. You should."

Mal chuckled softly. "You're way too easy to provoke, John-Boy. You should work on that."

"And you should move on."

Mal cleared his throat. "I was just proving my point. 'Nuff said." He jumped back to business.

"Everything else notwithstanding, we're wondering what the deal is with you guys. Too many things don't add up. You aren't ex-military. You don't know guns. You aren't spooks. You aren't analysts. We can't tell *what* you guys are—but you managed to lose my guys during our SDR exercises *and* break into the clubhouse. And you—" he jabbed a finger in my direction, "you knocked Dredd on his can. So . . . what gives?"

Zander shrugged; he was still letting off steam. I gave Mal my wide-eyed "who, me?" routine. Neither Zander nor I spoke.

Mal sighed. "Okay. I get it. Whatever it is, it's above my pay grade. Meeting over."

"Uh, do you mind if John-Boy and I hang out here a while, Mal?"

"What do you mean?"

I slanted a look at Zander. It hadn't dawned on him that our covers were "blown," but I knew they were—and using our real identities to work the President's assignment now seemed like the most colossal mistake ever.

"I think we need to stay with you guys until we hear from Gamble." *Meaning the President.*

"Of course. I already told you we haven't seen the last of the assaulters, but not to worry. You're safe here. Feel free to hang out in the training center as long as you need."

Turns out, it's a good thing we did.

⌘⌘⌘⌘

CHAPTER 28

I SLEPT CURLED UP on a sofa in the training center. Zander sprawled in a chair, his long legs stuck out in front of him. We logged maybe three hours before Gamble called early in the morning.

I swiped sleep from my eyes and yawned. "Morning. How's Trujillo?"

"She had surgery to set her fingers and repair the broken bones in her face, and she's doped to the gills. Doctors need to keep an eye on her for a couple of days minimum." He added, "I hear the FBI showed up at the clubhouse and scared away the bad guys."

"Not before McFly McFlitted down a zip line over the assault vehicles and blew their turrets off."

"Yeah, my source told me one of the drivers didn't make it out. His body was badly burned, and they haven't yet identified him."

"The rest of the attackers bugged out when the FBI showed up. Thanks for sending them, Gamble."

"Hey, I'm always up for exposing unlawful military actions, but you can also thank the President. I conveyed everything that happened to Kennedy, and he put the President on the line with us. It was the President's decision that I report an unauthorized paramilitary action to the FBI. He knew they would respond with an FBI strike force."

"Well, it was a smart move."

"Have the nanomites heard anything further from Danforth's array?"

"I just woke up. Zan—I mean John-Boy—is still out, but no. The nanomites tell me they are not in ongoing contact with Danforth's nanobugs. Confirms our suspicion that Danforth is in a shielded facility. Hey, Gamble?"

"Yes?"

"The nanobugs sent out a data packet while Danforth was ordering the helo strike. Danforth may be in a shielded facility with a 'secure' landline, but the nanobugs were able to send data through that line when it was in use.

"Here's the zinger: The array reported that Danforth's companion recognized Zander and has decided that Jayda is Gemma in disguise. Bottom line? We're blown, Gamble. We can't go back to our apartment, and I sure can't go back to work."

"Uh, yeah. That might be awkward."

"Awkward? *Ha-ha-ha.* You're cute, Gamble."

"Me? Cute? You must be sleep deprived."

"Not as much as you. Listen, we're going to stay at Malware's clubhouse until we know what to do next. Seems like the safest place for us."

"Okay. And you know where to find me. Logan and I are swapping shifts keeping an eye on Trujillo."

"Roger that."

Gamble chuckled. "Take care, Jayda."

I left Zander sleeping and went in search of coffee. I checked Mal's office, but it was empty. I struck pay dirt in the operations center.

Baltar the Bleary cracked a smile when I stuck my head in. I guessed Baltar to be the oldest of Mal's crew; his five o'clock shadow (plus twelve hours) had that gray/grizzled tint of the over-forty crowd.

"Hey, Rip. Sleep?"

"A couple hours. Not you, huh?"

"No, but soon. Too much activity going on last night."

"The FBI?"

"They had firetrucks and a big crime scene unit down here. Closed off the street. Mal went out and talked to them, mostly to stonewall them. After all, we just live here. We didn't invite the intruders. Never seen them before. Nothing more to tell."

"Uh, hello? McFly dropped incendiary shells on them?"

"Like Mal told them, we never fired a shot. We aren't responsible for crazy paramilitary people blowing themselves up in the street. By the way, the feds hauled off the charred BearCat remains an hour ago. What a waste."

Something he said niggled at me. "Wait. You guys live here?"

"Yeah. We have our own apartments on the second and third floors. We have a few part-time employees, too, meaning they have homes and families. We treat them like firefighters: They spend a couple shifts here each week. After the attackers ran off, Mal called in four part-timers to beef up our numbers—Fiona, Mulder, Banner, and Neo. You'll probably meet them today."

"I thought you guys only did training."

"No, that's a small slice of our repertoire. We do high-profile security work and government contracting in addition to training."

"Interesting."

I sniffed the pot near Baltar. "Mind if I have a cup?"

"Help yourself, Ripley."

⌘

"Satellite imagery shows them driving into that building's garage. They are still holed up there."

She nodded. "Have the FBI departed?"

"Yes, and the remains of the assault vehicles have been hauled away."

"Good. Are your people regrouped and prepared as I directed? Do they understand that it is imperative to take the woman alive and undamaged?"

Danforth nodded.

"Hit them again. Now."

"In broad daylight? The FBI . . ."

"Deploy the strike teams as I've instructed. I need to keep Jayda and Zander Cruz busy while I solve the challenge of how to trap them."

"I'd prefer for the operation to be discreet."

"The time for discretion is over, Lawrence. The clock is running, and the plan goes forward this week. Give your people the green light."

Danforth submitted. He picked up the secure landline and issued the orders.

⌘

STEAMING CUP IN HAND, I wandered back to the training center and sat down on the arm of Zander's chair. "Morning, babe."

Zander yawned, stretched, sniffed—sat up, and took notice. "Is that coffee? Smells divine. Want to share?"

"Hmm." I indulged in another blissful slurp before, feigning reluctance, I shook my head. "Honey, I love you—but love has its limits."

He stroked my arm and looked up from under his thick, dark lashes.

"All right. Listen. I didn't want to have to do this, but you leave me no choice."

He pursed his lips and canted a Flynn Rider brow in my direction. "Here comes the smolder."

Preen

Locking my unimpressed gaze on him, I blinked once and took a looong, slooooow pull on my mug. Smacked my lips in appreciation.

"Dunno. This is really good."

His mouth widened in a toothy smile. "How about now?"

"Uhhhh, nope."

"Okay, this is kind of an off day for me. This doesn't normally hap—"

I drained my cup. "Ooops. All gone."

"Hey. You broke my smolder."

I leaned toward him, feigning a bit of my own smolder. "What if I told you of a place, a magical place, where coffee runs free in pure, rich mountain streams—and one has but to ask to receive all one desires?"

"Shrew. You know where the pot is."

I giggled. "Yeah. C'mon, sweetie. I'll show you to the burbling fountain of life."

"You'd better. I just gave my best performance—ever."

I led him to the operations center and pointed at the coffee pot. "Behold!"

Baltar cracked another grin. "Morning, John-Boy."

"A good day to be alive, Baltar."

Those were the last words I heard Zander speak before—

Jayda Cruz—Danforth has given orders to attack the clubhouse a second time!

Every nerve in my body jangled at their warning. "Nano, when?"

The strike teams were prepositioned; they are coming NOW.

"Baltar! We're under attack!"

Baltar hesitated only a microsecond before he hit a switch. A low alarm sounded throughout the clubhouse. We heard the rush of feet as Mal, Dredd, McFly, Deckard, and the Malware personnel we hadn't yet met grabbed their weapons and deployed.

My eyes were locked on the screens in front of Baltar. "There!"

Malware, Inc. had cameras mounted on the warehouses surrounding the clubhouse. One camera was angled toward the clubhouse's roof.

A Black Hawk helo swooped over the roof. Two heavy lines dropped from its doors. As we watched, attackers fast-roped down to the roof.

"They're setting a charge on the hatch!"

Baltar spoke into his headset. "Mal, we have company on the roof. At least a dozen."

"Copy. Dredd? Get your team upstairs to greet our visitors."

"Roger that."

"Baltar—" I pointed at other monitors. Two teams of twelve were on the ground, one team at the garage, the other at the side entrance. The assault was designed and coordinated to hit the clubhouse at three different points simultaneously.

"I see them." Baltar spoke into his mic again. "Mal, we have two squads of tangos on the ground attempting to breach the side entrance and the garage."

"Copy that. All available personnel to the main floor."

Zander asked, "What do you want us to do, Baltar?"

"You and Ripley stick with me. We're in the core of the clubhouse. If, by chance, we're breached, get to the panic room and lock it down." Without taking his eyes off the screens, he pointed through the operations center door, across the training center, to another door. "It's the safest place here, and it has a bug-out hatch."

"But we can help you fend off the attackers," I said.

Baltar was too busy to outright laugh at me. "Sure you can. Just stay put."

Zander and I watched the battle play out on the monitors while Baltar fed updated information to Malware team leaders. The problem, as I saw it, was in the sheer numbers. I counted thirty-six assaulters to Mal's nine defenders—ten, counting Baltar.

Twelve, counting us.

More than sufficient if we counted the nanomites.

The attacking team on the roof blasted through the hatch, only to find the second one. That did not deter them. While they set their second charges, Dredd and his crew positioned themselves to pick off the attackers when they broke through and dropped into the third floor.

Instead, we saw the attackers on the roof toss several somethings down the chimney. They lay flat on the roof to protect themselves from the intense light and noise that followed. Even over the monitors, the ongoing mini-explosions were deafening.

Baltar cursed. "Freaking nine bangers!"

Deafened and disoriented, Dredd pulled his team back to safety. Immediately, the attackers dropped into the third floor and spewed an unrelenting barrage of rounds.

Baltar reported the news. "Mal, third floor is breached. Repeat. Tangos inside."

"Copy that but cannot assist—"

The Black Hawk had not flown away; it had waited, hovering high above, out of camera range. Now it descended, straight down to street level, its rotor wash pummeling the clubhouse, the three barrels of a GAU-19 .50cal Gatling gun taking aim at the garage doors. As the combatants on the ground raced away from the clubhouse, I realized that their presence had served to lure Mal and his team to defensive positions just inside the two entrances . . . where the Black Hawk's belt-fed BMG rounds would shred them to bits.

Baltar screamed, "Incoming .50cal! Pull back! Pull back!"

The rattling roar of the Gatling gun reached us in the operations center as it decimated the garage doors, punching through two layers of armored steel like so much tissue paper. Its work done, the Black Hawk rose and lifted away, and the two dozen assailants charged into the clubhouse.

Mal's voice came over the speakers. "All units! Fall back to defensive position Bravo. Repeat, fall back to defensive position Bravo!"

Baltar pressed a few buttons. "Bravo open for business."

When he received no response, Zander and I ran to the training center. Moments later, Malware's personnel, dirtied and bloodied, rushed into the room. A man we didn't know secured the training center's blast doors behind the last of them.

Mal counted his people: Dredd, Deckard, and the man on the door; McFly and three others, one a woman.

Mal asked Dredd, "Mulder?"

"Sorry, Mal. He took out two of theirs, but . . . he didn't make it."

Mal shook his head and strode to operations. "What's our status?"

"Thirty-four bad guys inside perimeter Alpha."

"Are we locked down?"

"Yes. But look."

We assembled around Baltar's station, and he pointed to three monitors. The attacking teams were stacked far back in the passageways and around the corners. Waiting. Waiting on their demolition experts to finish laying charges—not against the blast door, but against the reinforced concrete walls in two separate locations.

"They'll be inside in five minutes, give or take a few ounces of C4."

Mal turned to Zander and me. "Time for you two to go."

He pointed at the woman we didn't know: She was big, broad, and hardened. "Fiona will escort you through the bug-out passage."

Fiona growled at Mal. "You're sending me away?"

"You have a kid at home, Fiona, so yes—and it's not open for debate."

He turned to us. "John-Boy? Ripley? When you come out the other end, you'll be on your own. We wish you well."

"But—"

Mal jerked his chin at Zander. "John-Boy? Get her out of here."

With Fiona leading the way, Zander pulled me from the ops center, kicking and screaming. "Zander, we need to help them!"

"We need to let them do their jobs."

"Their *jobs*? You mean dying to protect *us*? We need to protect *them*, Zander!"

He slowed to a stop, conflict twisting his mouth.

"Zander, we cannot run away and have their blood on our conscience. We have to stay here and fight. You know what we can do."

Fiona yelled to us. "Come on!"

"No, Zander. No. We can prevent the deaths of our friends. We can even prevent the deaths of those coming to kill them."

He was struggling, I could see that. His instincts—and all that Hispanic *machismo*—told him to protect his wife; I prayed the Holy Spirit would convict him of his duty to protect more than me. Maybe the Holy Spirit was using the nanomites, because they picked that moment to chime in.

Zander Cruz, "Whoever breaks through a wall may be bitten by a snake." Ecclesiastes 10:8.

"The nanomites are right. These attackers won't be expecting us when they break through those walls. You and I really can 'float like a butterfly, sting like a bee,' but our sting will take them out of the game without killing them."

Finally, he nodded. "Okay. Like you said, I'm newer and less experienced using the nanomites to fight, but yeah, you're right. We can end this with less bloodshed."

He pulled me closer to him, until his face was in mine and his breath was hot on my face. "But if you go and get yourself killed, Jayda Cruz, I'm never taking your advice again. You hear me?"

He planted one on me, a kiss both harsh and passionate—and then the wall beside the blast doors imploded.

I had my hands up even as we staggered under the overpressure. The nanomites flew from me in a dense stream, widening as the distance grew until a pulsing shield surrounded the two of us, deflecting flying debris.

"Zander! Widen the shield!"

He mimicked my stance; his nanocloud burst from his fingertips, and our shields joined, grew, and intensified. I had expected a bombardment of rounds to strike the shield, but the soldiers threading through the breach in the wall took one look at us and veered away, some toward Fiona on our left, most toward to our right where Mal and his team were firing from the ops center.

"Fiona!" I jogged toward her, throwing out a phalanx of nanomites to shield her at the same time, momentarily shifting the shielding.

Something punched me in the gut, low in my right side. The nanomites had taken some of the impact, but still . . . the pain knifed through me and bent me almost double.

"Jayda?" Zander extended more shielding over me. Multiple rounds pinged off the current the nanomites had projected to protect Fiona.

"Get Fiona," I gasped.

Zander sent a rope of nanomites to her. The rope grabbed hold of her and jerked her to us, pulling her under the shield. When she, in response to her training, lifted the muzzle of her rifle to return fire, Zander pushed it down, "Don't! The bullets will bounce back."

Consternation crossed her face, but she seemed to realize how counterproductive—how dangerous—firing it within our shield would be.

"Jay, are you all right?" Zander asked me.

The nanomites answered for me. *Zander Cruz, do not worry. The wound is through and through. We are mitigating the damage.*

I felt both heat and pain in my groin and clenched my teeth, so I wouldn't moan.

"Don't worry about me," I ground out. "We need to save our friends."

He nodded. "Can you walk?"

"I think so."

"Let's move toward Mal to cover them."

Zander and I, towing a blinking, bewildered Fiona in our slipstream, edged toward the ops center. The nanomites shifted the shield to deflect enemy rounds as we moved. Our shield soon took most of the fire intended for our friends, the shells bouncing or ricocheting away without penetrating.

It also seemed that, the closer we got to Mal *et. al.*, the less the attackers fired on them. Or maybe they were loath to fire on us?

"Get behind us!" Zander shouted to our crouching friends.

They were too amazed (and possibly terrified) to respond.

"Come on!" Fiona urged. "We are safe behind them. Hurry!"

"Go, go, go!" Mal ordered. He and his men rushed to us. Once they were near enough, the nanomites narrowed and closed the shield, forming an impenetrable dome over us.

"Don't fire," Fiona explained to Mal and his men. "Just . . . watch."

Another explosion shook the training center, and a second hole opened up, this one behind us. A line of attackers rushed in. A few opened fire, but their rounds accomplished nothing. With all of Mal's team within the dome, the rounds pinged off the wall of electricity, most harmlessly. A few bounced back to wound the shooters.

The attackers began to realize that their firepower was useless. Disbelieving of what their eyes told them, they slowly lowered their weapons to stare at the sight of the sizzling wall of fire around us.

"Nano, how many attackers are within range?"

All but three, Jayda Cruz. Three remain in the corridors outside the training center.

"We'll have to get them afterward. Zander?"

"Yeah?"

"Time to take them out."

I closed my eyes and drew down on all the current available to me. Zander, taking his cue from me, did the same. A hum crackled across the training center. It intensified by the moment. The lights in the clubhouse flickered and dimmed, and tongues of fire licked at our protective dome. The dome quaked and shook and, within the trembling, vibrating dome, Mal and his team felt the current building—and they cowered under it.

Then, slowly, the clubhouse floor dropped away, and Zander and I rose. Electricity snapped around and through us and darted to our fingertips. We gathered it into our hands, grew it into pulsing orbs, and took aim.

We hurled bolus after bolus of energy into the attackers' ranks. Guided by the nanomites, the bolts connected and "punched out" the soldiers, one and two at a time.

As the other attackers saw their compatriots falling like dead men to the floor, they panicked. Some tried to run back through the holes blasted in the training center walls, but we caught them before they could escape. The last half dozen men, at the sight of bodies stacked up amid the rubble of the breaches, gave up. Befuddled and confused, they dropped their weapons and tried to surrender.

"Aw, we're not gonna hurt you," I said to myself. "Not much, anyway. Just give you a nap—which is better than you deserve."

We dissolved the shield, dropped to the floor, and advanced on the remnant, flinging fire from our fingertips, knocking them out.

"Three more out there," Zander said, pointing through a hole in the wall. "Can you make it?"

"Yeah, but let's use the doors." My gut felt like an active volcano, and I didn't fancy a climb over the stacks of unconscious bodies.

Zander held his palms facing outward, toward the training center entrance. The fortified, hydraulically sealed steel doors thrummed and trembled. They shook, shook harder, then burst open.

Zander and I, the nanomites guiding us, hunted down the three remaining attackers. We found the last one hiding in a corner, weeping.

"Please don't kill me! Please!"

I said softly. "We're not going to kill you, and we haven't killed any of your friends. You'll be all right."

Sobbing in relief, he never saw the pulse that knocked him out.

"What next, Jayda? So many witnesses . . ."

"They won't remember—and neither can anyone from Malware."

"Oh. You mean the old 'destroy the newest synapses' trick?"

"Yup." I spoke aloud to the nanomites. "Nano? How long did the assault last?"

Twenty-seven minutes from the first roof breach, Jayda Cruz.

"And how far back did Zander and I first expose our 'powers'?"

Nine minutes, fourteen seconds, Jayda Cruz.

"Mark that point and delete all memories back to that moment, please? From everyone here except us."

I had an idea and glanced at Zander. "What if we asked the nanomites to . . ." I explained my idea.

"I like it, Jay. I like it a lot."

"Cool." I gave the nanomites instructions, and a spurt jumped from us to the man at our feet. Half a minute later, the nanomites returned.

We are done with this man, Jayda Cruz.

We went back to the training center. Dust from blasted concrete and smoke from expended rounds hung heavy in the air. We found Mal and his crew bunched together where we had left them. They were arguing among themselves. At our return, they lapsed into watchful silence, wary and uncertain.

"Nano, start working on the attackers, please. I'd like to talk to Mal's people first."

I took another step and gasped. "Ow."

Zander put an arm around me and helped me toward them.

"I suppose our secrets are out," I murmured, "although I'm certain you have lots of questions." I shrugged. "Normally, we avoid public displays of our abilities, but we just couldn't allow more people to die today."

Mal coughed and cleared his throat, but had trouble forming words. "You . . . and him . . ."

"It's okay, Mal. We know how bizarre it is. We'll explain more in a minute."

I swept my hand to indicate the thirty-some bodies. "To clarify, these guys aren't dead, just unconscious. When they wake up, they will remember breaching the training center, but nothing about us. They will have a vague recollection of breaching a room filled with knockout gas, and—poof—lights out."

Mal found his voice. "Uh, Ripley, there's no such thing as a safe KO gas. That's the wishful fantasy of spy movies. Use of a KO gas can stop breathing altogether—meaning casualties."

"Yeah? Well, I guess they'll think you've created a new and safe gas, won't they? In any event, they won't remember what we did to them, and that's the important thing."

"Whoever sent them watched the battle live via these guys' helmet cams."

"We can't mitigate for that. We'll have to deal with them another way."

McFly spoke up. "These guys are gonna be very unpopular with whoever sent them. Triple our numbers and they couldn't bag you two?"

"Yes, but they'll be alive. Sadly, they will be worthless to their handlers."

"What do you mean?"

"They will experience a mystifying reluctance to practice the art of war . . . ever again."

Mal put his hands on his hips. "You can do that?"

"I think so."

He looked around at his team. Baltar was shaking his head in wonder. Fiona grinned like a Cheshire. The others seemed to relax a little. Only a little. Our relationships with them weren't going to be the same any time soon.

"You know you can trust us to keep your secrets, Ripley, John-Boy. Um, you *do* trust us to keep your secrets, don't you? I mean, you must, because . . ."

Zander and I looked away; we couldn't meet his eyes.

"What? You *don't* trust us? You're going to wipe our memories, too?"

Zander spoke. "It's less about trust and more about operational security." He crooked a half smile at McFly. "Like you drilled into us, right?"

With a reluctant shake of his head, McFly agreed.

Jayda Cruz, Zander Cruz, the police and FBI have arrived and are about to enter the clubhouse.

Mal's crew was growing agitated, so I addressed them. "BPD and the FBI are on scene. Sorry about this, but we need to hurry. Mal, you and your team will remember everything about the battle up until Zander and I, uh, did our thing. Just like the attackers, you'll wake up thinking some kind of gas knocked you out."

I was planting the subliminal hints in Mal's crew that the nanomites would leave intact.

Mal's crew protested, but to no avail. They were already falling like cordwood until only Mal, Zander, and I remained standing.

He turned in a circle and realized his team was "out."

"We're not going to knock you out, Mal."

He shifted a nervous glance to us. "You aren't?"

"No, we need you to do something for us."

"Okay . . ."

"Your crew will be confused, but malleable to suggestion. We need you to 'remind' them that the attackers filled the training center with gas to knock your people out. As improbable as it will sound, 'remind' them that the gas also knocked *the attackers* out. You, Mal, recovered first just as the feds and the police arrived to take the attackers into custody."

"And you think my people will buy that line of horse pucky?"

"They will, because you will insist that's what happened, and they won't have an alternative that makes any sense. After you've spun that tale a few times—adding a few convincing details—their brains will accept and incorporate your explanation into their memories."

We heard shouted commands in the open corridor. Coming closer.

"We'll use that bug-out route now, Mal."

"Wait. One more thing. Did you notice that, as soon as the attackers recognized you two, they didn't shoot at you?"

"They had their orders; they need us alive," Zander answered.

"Well, someone screwed up, cuz I took one in the gut." I glanced at my bloodied shirt. The nanomites had staunched the bleeding but, deep inside, I burned like a house on fire.

"Gotta go, Mal. Be safe, bro." Zander put his arm around me and we hobbled toward the panic room.

⌘

"WE NOW JOIN Jillian Framer reporting live from Capitol Hill. Good morning, Jillian, what is the status of Senator Delancey's confirmation hearings?"

"Tom, an hour ago, the Senate Rules and Administration Committee moved to send Senator Delancey's confirmation to the Senate floor for a vote—and my sources tell me that the House Administration Committee will do the same, either later today or first thing tomorrow."

"Jillian, what does that mean for Senator Delancey?"

"It means that the senator could be confirmed by both the Senate and the House within the next twenty-four hours and be sworn in as the next Vice President immediately afterward."

"Jillian, I believe you reported earlier that the shortest vice-presidential confirmation was six weeks for Gerald Ford in 1973?

"Yes, Tom, and Ford was sworn in as Vice President an hour after the vote. If Senator Delancey is confirmed today or tomorrow, following less than *two weeks* of hearings, it would be an unprecedented display of bipartisan unity. Back to you, Tom."

⌘⌘⌘⌘

CHAPTER 29

THE CLUBHOUSE'S BUG-OUT route dumped us two blocks over, safely away from the scene of so much LEO activity. It had been a shock to remember that we'd left our car in the clubhouse's garage—the garage decimated by the Black Hawk's .50cal gun.

"Uh, Nano? Won't the FBI be able to trace our car back to us?"

We eradicated your vehicle's VIN and other identifying numbers before the battle, Zander Cruz.

"Very forward-thinking of you." I was in pain and groaned as I spoke.

We do our best to prepare for any contingency, Jayda Cruz. "The plans of the diligent lead to profit as surely as haste leads to poverty."

Zander propped me up against a twenty-four-hour laundry and called a cab to come and get us. Since we couldn't return to our apartment, the safest place for us was the house where we met weekly with Gamble and Trujillo. Zander had the cab drop us a block from the house. I agreed with his caution, but that one block seemed like a mile.

I was too exhausted to climb the steps when we reached the back door. Zander carried me up and inside. I held one hand to the burning ache in my groin and cried out when he laid me on the couch.

"Sorry, babe. I'm so sorry."

Every five minutes on our journey from the bug-out hatch to the house, he had peppered the nanomites for updates on my status. Invariably, they had replied, *Zander Cruz, we have the matter in hand and are effecting repairs. You do not need to seek medical treatment for Jayda Cruz.*

All I knew was that someone had stuck a hot iron low in my abdomen, in front of the right side of my pelvic bone.

"Nano, please help Jayda sleep now," Zander whispered.

"No, I don't thin—"

I did not get to vote on that one.

⌘

THEY HAD KEPT VIGIL all night, planning and giving orders for the early morning strike, only to watch in frustrated amazement as it failed—and spectacularly so. Now the woman paced up and down the room, a cold rage building with each step.

"I am appalled, Danforth. Our strike force was three times the size of the defenders inside that building. And now it is *our* men who are in FBI custody?"

"You watched the live feed of the battle. You saw what happened."

She stopped and pointed her finger at him. "I *told* you the Keyes woman had powers—you saw them yourself when she rescued Trujillo. You should have prepared; it was on you to make adequate arrangements."

"Adequate arrangements? Neither you nor I knew or understood the extent of Gemma Keyes' abilities—or, apparently, that both she *and* her husband now have the same powers—so in what way was I to 'prepare' our teams for what we just witnessed?"

He mimicked giving orders, "'Oh, by the way, Captain, your targets will deploy bullet-proof electrical shields—but, hey, we expect you to overcome those on the fly. Your targets will also throw lightning bolts and possess antigravitational powers—but we require that you prepare for and defeat those insignificant obstacles.' Is that what you had in mind?"

"I expected strategic thinking from you, Danforth. I see that was *my* mistake." She sniffed. "May I at least presume that the men in the FBI's custody will hold their peace?"

"They are suitably distanced from either of us and can tell the FBI nothing other than they received orders to take down a terrorist nest. Moreover, NSA agents, armed with the proper legal authority, will arrive shortly to release our people from FBI custody."

She sneered at him. "Very good, Lawrence. I am gratified that you have the recovery aspects of this debacle well in hand."

Danforth, stung by her condescension, answered, "Despite your lack of appreciation for all I've done and continue to do for the cause, I believe you've overlooked some vital particulars."

"Do you? Oh, please—say on, Mr. Danforth."

"Very well, I *will* say on: Have you given any thought to how Jayda and Zander Cruz traced Trujillo's whereabouts to our black site? Trujillo was clean when our operatives took her—no tracking devices—and the route into that site was a maze impossible to navigate without guidance. So *how* did Jayda and Zander Cruz find their way there within hours of Trujillo's abduction?"

The woman's eyes glittered, and her expression hardened. "Very good, Mr. Danforth, very good. You raise a valid point."

She began to pace, to ponder Danforth's question.

Danforth let her alone to think. This was where the woman's brilliance often shone—and she *was* brilliant, the most strategic deep operative he'd ever worked with, inspiring despite her contempt for incompetence and, in particular, for failure.

Minutes ticked by before she paused. "The nanomites. It had to have been the nanomites."

"How so?"

"Cushing claimed they had invaded her phones, her computer, even a SCIF. If they are as intelligent and pervasive as she purported them to be . . . perhaps they were able to access our satellite systems."

"You're saying they used our own satellites to track the vehicle from Trujillo's house to our black site? Are you serious?"

One side of the woman's mouth quirked. "Oh, it sounds so improbable, does it not? And yet from the beginning, General Cushing insisted that the tiny machines would be able to penetrate, to insinuate themselves into any digital system—as long as they had a means to reach it. These possibilities, Lawrence, these fantastic possibilities have fueled our efforts to acquire the nanomites from the beginning."

She shrugged. "Are they not the technological breakthrough for which we've expended so many resources and lives? Imagine the NSA in possession of the nanomites. Imagine—and grasp the staggering implications!"

"If all you assert is true, then I *am* imagining the implications—the advantages these people possess, and we do not. Until these nanomites are under our control and our direction, we are at a distinct disadvantage and should be concerned for our own operational security. You say they invaded Cushing's phone?"

"Harmon said Cushing was convinced, yes."

"Then they could be listening to us at this very moment."

"Lawrence, we have taken extreme precautions, and I can conceive of no means for them to have discovered who we are. Furthermore, this room is shielded. No signals in or out." She lifted her chin. "I did think you knew that."

"Yes, of course. I forgot . . . momentarily."

"Now that we've quelled your concerns—"

"Quelled them? Hardly. What is to keep these . . . nanomites from invading our phones when we leave?"

She turned her head toward him, but her thoughts were elsewhere—a chess master considering not her next move, but the ten beyond that. "What indeed . . ."

"Then you agree that our operational security could be compromised?" Danforth grew more agitated. "Makes me wonder . . . The White House experienced a norovirus outbreak two weeks ago. Four of the six or seven affected employees were our inside agents. An unusual coincidence, don't you think? Now that we know what these people and their nanomites are capable of, what's to say the virus wasn't their work?"

She didn't answer.

"And if they identified and targeted our agents within the White House, they may have connected them to the Secret Service's Deputy Assistant Director—and if to Morningside, then to *me*."

But not to me, she reminded herself. *I have been much too circumspect for that.*

"Yes, yes. I can put two and two together, Lawrence. Do let me think." She put one finger to her lips, silencing him, and resumed her pacing. Back and forth across the carpet she walked, her head bowed in contemplation while Danforth fidgeted.

Thirty minutes elapsed, then an hour. When Danforth could hold back no longer, he blurted, "It is my opinion that we should ditch our phones and institute a communications blackout."

She stopped her pacing and faced him. "Oh, dear. No. Quite the opposite, Mr. Danforth. This is our opportunity to employ classic countermeasures."

"What countermeasures?"

"Misinformation, Lawrence. A short-term distraction."

"You have something in mind?"

"Hmm? Yes. What of the two covert FBI agents embedded in your organization? You have stymied their efforts to date without their suspecting we are on to them. I suggest that we let slip to Jayda and Zander Cruz a few select breadcrumbs that implicate the FBI agents in Wayne Overman's disappearance. Within those breadcrumbs, an actionable gambit. If Jayda and Zander Cruz act on our 'intelligence,' we will know they have, in fact, penetrated our communications."

She outlined the scenario she wanted Danforth to devise.

"Why Overman? Do you think Jayda and Zander Cruz are concerned with his disappearance?"

"Immaterial. Our objective is to sidetrack Mr. and Mrs. Cruz with this bit of misinformation. If they 'bite' on our lure, it will serve two purposes—to confirm, as I said, that they have penetrated our communications, but it will also keep them busy while we focus on the execution of a more effective and longer-term distraction."

"Why do we need a longer-term distraction?"

"Today we witnessed a true demonstration of the nanomites' formidable powers, not merely a small sampling of it. Good! With adequate time to study the helmet cam videos, I will identify the nanomites' strengths—and more importantly, their weaknesses. And when I have ascertained their vulnerabilities, I will formulate a suitable trap. Hence, a longer-term distraction is needed to buy me the time I require."

She studied Danforth. "You will create that distraction for me, Lawrence. I wish you to locate Mr. and Mrs. Cruz's closest family and loved ones. Not too many. Gemma Keyes' elderly neighbor and his foster child and Zander Cruz's sister and parents should do. Sweep them up and spirit them away.

"The disappearance of Mr. and Mrs. Cruz's family—and the implied threat of imminent harm to them—should prove adequate to our needs, don't you think? Jayda and Zander Cruz will turn their attention and efforts to saving those they love. While they do so, I will be devising a nanomite-proof trap. When our trap is ready, we will bait the snare's tripwire with their loved ones. Mr. and Mrs. Cruz will come to us. Willingly, I should think."

As frustrating as she often was, Danforth had to admire her. "An inspired ploy."

She smiled. "Thank you. With the assets of the National Security Agency at your disposal, it shouldn't take you long to pinpoint the targets. The old man and the child are in Albuquerque; I believe Cruz's parents live elsewhere in New Mexico. Locate them and send operatives to apprehend them at once.

"And now, Lawrence, I have somewhere I need to be."

She strode out the facility's door toward her car, and Danforth followed her. At her vehicle, she spun on her heel; Danforth nearly ran into her.

Laughing to herself, she added, "Goodness. How forgetful of me, Lawrence. I have a team already on the ground in Albuquerque. They can move on the Albuquerque targets as soon as you locate them and give the word."

"They will hear from me within the hour."

"Excellent." She smiled again. "We are close, Lawrence. On every front, we are so very close to our goals. Jayda and Zander Cruz have the nanomites. When we apply the proper inducements and lure them to us, we will have them *and* the nanomites. The nanomites are our means to full surveillance and control of our 'democratic' processes. And when we have that control, nothing can prevent us from taking the remainder of the nation."

⌘

JAYDA CRUZ. ZANDER CRUZ. We have received an updated report from Danforth's nanobug array. He has left the shielded facility and is returning to the NSA.

"I'll take the report, Nano. Jayda needs to rest."

"I'm . . . awake." I'd slept only an hour or so and was so groggy I wasn't sure if I could function, but the nanomites' message had roused me.

Zander helped me sit up. "How do you feel?"

"I'll live." The pain low in the right quadrant of my belly had eased some. What remained felt warm. Swollen, perhaps? "I want to hear the nanobug's report."

Zander nodded. "Go ahead, Nano."

The nanomites hesitated. *It is an odd report.*

I let Zander ask the obvious, "Odd? In what way?"

It contradicts the facts as we know them, Zander Cruz.

"Well, let's hear it."

Danforth texted a message to an unknown confederate in which he tasked the associate to pass on instructions concerning the final disposition of what we inferred is Wayne Overman's body.

I was, suddenly, a lot more awake than I'd been a few moments ago. "Wayne Overman's body? Do we know where it is, Nano?"

No, Jayda Cruz. That portion of the text reads, 'move WO remains tomorrow 2300 hours.' It does not provide the location of the remains at present.

"Then we'll follow whomever got the text. Catch them in the act. Not only will we have hard evidence on Danforth, but the President will also be able to give his friend an honorable burial." I was wide awake and plenty excited now.

Zander put up a cautioning hand. "Wait a sec. Nano? You said the message was odd. Contradictory. What did you mean by that?"

The full text of the message flowed to us.

---

direct colón tellerman
move WO remains
2300 hours
39.0397° N 76.9341° W

I gaped. "Direct Colón and Tellerman? As in Kiera and Rob? But they're FBI . . . aren't they, Nano?"

They are, indeed, Jayda Cruz, which is why the message contradicts what we know to be true. However, we believe the entirety of the array's report provides context necessary to determine that the text is a ruse, what is called misinformation or a 'false flag.'

The woman with Danforth devised this ruse to trick you into determining whether or not we are monitoring their communications. The number to which the text was sent belongs to a phone used to call Danforth two months ago, one of the single-use, throwaway phones.

"Huh. What is the location referenced in the text?"

The coordinates pinpoint a spot within a heavily wooded, multi-use municipal park with hiking trails, twelve and a half miles from the NSA compound.

Zander asked, "Why there? Does Danforth plan to capture us in this park?"

"I wouldn't think so," I said, holding my aching side. "The open, uncontrolled environment of a wooded area? Danforth and the mystery woman have seen us in action twice. No, I think . . . I think the nanomites are correct. Danforth and the woman have to suspect that we are surveilling them. They can't be certain, but if we were to show up tonight, it would prove their theory."

Zander's chin bobbed. "I get it."

I added, "It's a ploy we might have fallen for if we hadn't already discovered that Rob and Kiera are FBI."

The ruse has more than one purpose, Zander and Jayda Cruz. While your attention is focused elsewhere, Danforth will be giving instructions to abduct your family members and loved ones.

A chill of dread washed over me. "What?"

Please access the array's audio, Jayda and Zander Cruz.

Zander and I pulled up the nanobugs' entire report, including the audio. We listened to Danforth and the woman's conversation from within the shielded facility—every nuanced word of their wicked schemes.

Then, even though we'd just heard their conversation for ourselves, the nanomites felt it necessary to break it down for us. *The abductions will further shift your attention away from Danforth and the mystery woman. You will be preoccupied with locating your family members and unable to adequately interfere with Danforth and the woman.*

"Yeah, we've figured that out," I muttered.

The ultimate goal of the abduction is to buy the woman time to devise a trap for us.

Zander ground his teeth. "We get it, Nano."

The nanomites weren't finished. *The woman has a two-man team in Albuquerque ready to carry out the abductions, Zander Cruz. **Immediate action is required.***

I was hurting too much to leave the couch, but that didn't keep me from begging my husband to act. "Zander, call Abe. Izzie, too. Please hurry! Get them into hiding before Danforth's team reaches them."

"I'm on it, but where do we send them? Where can they go that the resources of the NSA wouldn't sniff them out? Where could we safely stash them on such short notice?"

"We know a place in Albuquerque, Zander. Remember?"

My meaning became clear to him. "Right—but what about my parents in Las Cruces?"

"We have a bit more time to consider the best options for them. Our immediate concern is Abe, Emilio, and Izzie—and the team that is already on the ground in Albuquerque. Call Abe now, Zander!"

Zander's hands shook as he dialed. "Abe?"

"Zander! It's good to hear your voice, son."

"Abe."

"What is it, Zander?"

"Has Emilio left for school yet?"

"You almost missed him. We just finished breakfast and—"

"I'm sorry to interrupt you, Abe, but the situation is urgent. You and Emilio are in danger—as are my sister and my parents. I need you to gather a few things and get out of your house. *Now*."

Abe didn't waste time by asking for the particulars. "How much time do we have, and where do we go?"

"Not much time at all; our enemies already have a team in Albuquerque, and they are on their way."

Abe put his hand over the phone and bellowed, "Emilio!"

Emilio, eyes wide, ran to Abe. "Yes, sir?"

"Grab your duffle bag. Pack a few changes of clothes and your toothbrush. Hurry."

Abe turned back to the phone. "Where do we go?"

"Uh, get to DCC. I will coordinate the rest of the arrangements. Park behind the fellowship hall and stay out of sight."

"Okay. We'll leave in a few minutes."

"Abe?"

"Yes?"

"Take whatever staples will sustain you for a few days and wear sturdy shoes—hiking shoes."

Abe blinked, but he didn't argue. "I will."

Zander hung up. The next call would be more difficult. His sister Izzie was not as compliant as Abe.

"Iz?"

"Zander! You caught me on the way out the door to work. I'm so green with envy! I would have come with Abe and Emilio to D.C. if I'd known they were going to spend the Fourth with you guys."

"Iz—"

"They told me all about it. They had such a good t—"

"Izzie, stop talking and listen to me. You need to do exactly what I tell you."

"Zander? What do you mean?"

"Shut up and listen, sis. I need you to pack some clothes, put on some sturdy shoes, and meet Abe and Emilio behind DCC. Most important? I need you to leave your apartment in the next five minutes. Do you understand?"

"Zander, you're scaring me."

"Good. I need you to be scared enough to do exactly as I've told you. Five minutes, Izzie. Get out of your apartment inside of five minutes."

"What about my job? Should I call in sick?"

"No. Don't call anyone. No one, hear me? Just go. Meet Abe like I said."

"O-okay, I will."

"Promise me? Don't dawdle. Grab a bag, put on some hiking shoes, and *go*."

Izzie must have been sufficiently rattled, because she whispered, "Yes, Zander."

He hung up and made his third call. "Dr. Bickel? Zander Cruz. We need your help."

While Zander and Dr. Bickel finished their hurried arrangements, I blew out a breath. I'd just come up with a crazy, outrageous idea for protecting Zander's parents.

I grabbed my phone and dialed another number. "Gamble?"

"Yeah?"

"You already know that our covers are blown; we've just discovered that Danforth is dispatching operatives to Las Cruces to take Zander's parents into custody."

"What about Abe and Emilio?"

"We're handling their situation, but we need an escape plan for Zander's mom and dad."

"What can I do, Jayda?"

I took another deep breath. "Do you remember the commandant at White Sands?"

"I talked to him once. My team interfaced with him when they were investigating the house where Dr. Bickel was held."

"The missile range is close to Cruces. I thought if the 'right' person were to speak to the commandant, then he would take Zander's parents into his protection."

Gamble made a grunt of agreement. "I had intended to call and update Kennedy anyway. I'll . . . I'll request that the President arrange for the commandant to send an armed guard to fetch Zander's folks, escort them to White Sands, and keep their location on the range on the q.t. Zander's mom and dad may be scared half silly when soldiers show up to their door, but it's the fastest, most effective means of getting them under wraps."

I exhaled in relief. "Thank you. I'll text you their address, Gamble."

"I'll take care of it."

I dropped my phone and put my hand to my side. The ache inside hadn't fared well under the last stressful minutes. I still felt that unnatural warmth deep within.

"Nano? What's going on in my body where I took that bullet? Infection?"

No infection, Jayda Cruz. Omega Tribe has surrounded the injury and will facilitate its healing.

"Is that why I feel heat? Is it because Omega Tribe is surrounding the injury?"

Yes. Our clustered members are producing warmth. Do not be concerned.

"Okay. Glad to hear it."

Zander touched my arm. "Did I hear you talking to Gamble about my mom and dad?"

"Yes. I had an idea, and Gamble was willing to put it into play. He's going to ask the President to order the commandant of White Sands to pick up your folks and keep them hidden on the missile range."

"I can't see an officer refusing a Presidential order. That's great thinking, Jay. Thank you."

Zander and I stared at each other, our expressions subdued, maybe a little bleak. We hadn't foreseen the President's assignment blowing up like this and endangering those we love.

I wondered if Zander had snapped to the ongoing ramifications. Would we have to start over? Create new identities and new lives? Leave our families behind?

I was first to speak. "The situation is spiraling out of our control. I think the only way we can ultimately keep our family safe is if we take out those who are threatening them. Evidence is important to getting convictions in a court of law, but not as important as stopping this coup. I think we have to change our strategy and go all-out on the offensive."

"Yeah, but on the offensive against whom? Danforth is obviously not giving the orders—this mystery woman is. Who is she, and why haven't the nanomites been able to identify her?"

"I've been wondering the same thing. Did you notice that Danforth never calls her by name? She calls him Lawrence, but he never addresses her. She has to be Danforth's caller who uses a phone once and then throws it away—which tells us she is very savvy and very careful."

"All those hours with Danforth, and we haven't an inkling of who she is."

"The nanobugs recorded their conversations and snooped through Danforth's digital data, but that didn't provide them with an image of the woman they can ID."

Zander pondered our dilemma. "But we did glimpse part of a face—just for a moment—on the other end of the video call when we were rescuing Trujillo. Did anything about that face ring a bell?"

Zander had touched on what had been nagging at me in my subconscious mind. When I called up my remembrance of the partial face, it was tinged with faint familiarity, but it frustrated me.

"Something's bugging me, but I can't put my finger on it."

"Maybe the nanomites can help us?" Zander suggested. "They may have better recollections than we do."

"Nano. Bring up Trujillo's rescue, when we took out her captors."

We stepped into the warehouse, and the nanomites replayed what they had "heard" and "seen." Their take was more complete than what I had noticed—you know, while I was preoccupied with zapping the crud out of Trujillo's captors.

The nanomites played back the audio of our attack: We heard us breaching the mess hall, heard the crackle of current building and the loud 'snap/pop' of bolts shooting from me to stun Trujillo's interrogators, first the man and then the woman. Soon after, the nanomites showed us the digital feed they'd captured from the video chat: A partial image—one side of a face—appeared for an instant within the tablet's screen, before the image was replaced by a hand slapping a laptop lid closed.

The nanomites "rewound" and zoomed in on the half face: It was a woman whose features appeared to be a mix of ethnicities, her one visible eye an unusual color.

Zander did not make the third connection—how could he have? But I did, and it hit me like a fist punch to the sternum, stealing my breath away.

A serpent's head rose from the mist, its golden eye fixed on me. While I watched, the serpent's image slid over the woman's face, eye upon eye. A perfect match. *The same color.*

Every nerve in my body screamed, and my jaw clenched so hard I had trouble speaking. "Sh-she-she . . . it's *her*. The head of the snake!"

⌘⌘⌘⌘

CHAPTER 30

ABE EASED HIS LATE-MODEL Chevy into a space that wasn't truly a parking slot. The Sea-Can shipping container alongside DCC's fellowship hall had just enough room behind it for Abe's car, but the container, used for storage, hid them quite well.

"Cain't git out this door," Emilio whispered. "We're too close."

"I know, son. When I get out, you scoot over here and come out my side, okay?"

Emilio hadn't said a word since they'd thrown their few things into Abe's car and backed out of the old garage. He realized how shook Abe was when he clipped the wall of shrubs between his and Mateo's properties in their rush to get away.

But now Emilio turned his pinched face to Abe and asked, "Abe? We gonna be all right?"

"I want to tell you everything is going to be fine, Emilio, but I can't. What I can tell you is that the Lord sees us, and he will help us if we call on him. Right now, I feel the need to call on him. Do you want to pray with me?"

Emilio nodded. "Yes, sir."

Abe took Emilio's small brown hand in his gnarled and much larger black one. "Lord, you see us here. Zander says bad men are looking for us. We know they only want us to get at Jayda and Zander, so's they can hurt them. Lord, we are asking in Jesus' name that you hide us—hide us in the cleft of the Rock, Christ Jesus; hide us under the shadow of your wings; hide us, Lord, like the nanomites hide Jayda! We put all our trust in you, Lord. Amen."

"Amen," Emilio echoed, more relaxed. "What do we do now?"

"We get out of this car and keep our eyes peeled. Zander said he was making arrangements for someplace we can hide."

Abe and Emilio left the car and peered around the Sea-Can. The morning was early, and the parking lot was empty. However, minutes later, they heard another car approach. Abe pulled Emilio back, but the boy had glimpsed the car.

"That's Izzie," Emilio stated with confidence.

"You sure?"

"Yup."

Abe peeked around the container and saw Izzie step from her vehicle. He whistled and waved her over. Pulled her behind the Sea-Can with them.

"Abe? Emilio? You, too? Do you know what's going on?"

"Some," Abe answered. He had to be careful, because Izzie was unaware of the nanomites, unaware of Jayda and Zander's abilities or their assignment in D.C. Explaining the danger without explaining the "why" would be problematic.

"Well, what are we doing here?"

"Right now, we're waiting and hiding."

Izzie put her hands on her hips. "Waiting for and hiding from what? I'm supposed to be at work right about now."

Abe put her off. "Zander is sending someone. We're waiting for them."

She dug her phone from her purse. "Well, if I don't call in, I could get in trouble. Lose my job."

Abe's hand closed over hers. "I'd wait a little longer, if I were you, Miss Izzie. In fact, could I prevail upon you to turn your phone all the way off? Power it down and pull the battery?"

"What? Why? Can you tell me that?"

"Not . . . exactly. Just trust me, please."

"Yeah," Emilio echoed. "You gotta trust us."

The boy was so serious that Izzie laughed—then she stopped. "You and Zander are seriously freaking me out."

Abe nodded. "I'm sorry, but this is important."

He tipped his head toward Izzie's phone.

Huffing, she powered it off. "There."

They lapsed into a tense silence, although Izzie fussed to herself and shot worried looks at Abe from time to time.

They had been behind the shipping container for thirty minutes when another vehicle rolled into the parking lot. Abe hushed Emilio and Izzie and kept them from peeking to see who had arrived.

Doors opened, and two people got out. A rough voice called, *sotto voce*, "Abe? Abe Pickering?"

"That's Dr. Bickel," Emilio whispered loud in Abe's ear.

Abe rubbed his ringing ear. "Thank you, young man."

He stuck his head out from behind the container. Dr. Bickel and another man were scanning the parking lot. No other cars or people were in sight.

"You two wait here," Abe ordered. He stepped away and let himself be seen.

"Abe!" Dr. Bickel's relief was evident.

Abe shuffled toward him. "Zander send you?"

"Yes. Do you have Emilio and Izzie? We need to get going right away."

"Going where? And who's your friend?"

Bickel looked uneasy. "Better you don't know his name. I'll tell you where we're going when we're on the road. Come on. We need to hurry."

Abe whistled, and Emilio and Izzie appeared.

Dr. Bickel's companion popped the trunk. "Whatever you've packed, put in here."

When Abe and Emilio put their bags in the trunk, they saw two bulging backpacks already there.

"I've packed some nonperishable foodstuffs, so we need to consolidate," Dr. Bickel said. "We'll each take one bag. Abe, can you fit Emilio's things into your bag? Will he be able to carry it?"

"Depends on how far."

Dr. Bickel studied Izzie's duffle. "Izzie, I need you to transfer two sets of clothes and a toothbrush from your bag to one of mine."

"What? I'm supposed to leave the rest of my stuff?"

"If you want to eat for the foreseeable future, you'll leave the nonessential items you packed." Dr. Bickel's tone left no leeway for argument.

"But . . . I mean, how long will we be gone?"

"Until the danger has passed—and we need to prioritize food over 'stuff.' That's all I can say."

Dr. Bickel softened. "I'm sorry, Izzie. This has to be hard for you."

"I-I'm scared."

Emilio slipped his hand into hers. "We'll be okay, Izzie." He looked up at her, confident in his assertion.

"Hurry now," Dr. Bickel urged them. "Rearrange the packs so we can get going."

"What about the rest of my stuff?"

"Leave it in your trunk," Dr. Bickel said.

Another five minutes passed as they reorganized the packs that each person would carry and put the residual items in either Izzie or Abe's car. Then Dr. Bickel gestured them into the back seat of the car his friend and lab technician, Rick, was driving. As they pulled away, Dr. Bickel's eyes were busy, scanning for danger.

"Can you tell us now where we're going?" Abe asked.

"Somewhere safe."

Izzie's voice cracked. "But safe from what?"

Dr. Bickel turned a little in his seat, so he could answer her. "Do you remember that I was on the run for about six months and then captured and held prisoner after that? It was in the news."

Izzie's eyes grew worried. "I, um, sort of."

"Well, there's a lot I can't tell you, Izzie, because it's . . . classified. What I can say is that the same group of people who hunted me then are hunting *us* right now. For the next little while, I'm going to ask you to trust me and do exactly as I say."

Dr. Bickel cranked his neck around further. "Abe, the first part will be arduous for you—it will be hard for me, too, but likely harder on you. Emilio and Izzie? You are younger and stronger. You may need to help us. Can you do that?"

"I'm tough," Emilio boasted. "I can help."

Izzie didn't respond. She was still and silent. Close to being traumatized.

Dr. Bickel turned to Rick. "You have my letter to HR, right? Be sure to say you found it on your desk. If anyone asks, you haven't seen me since yesterday, you didn't know I was taking unannounced leave—and you've never laid eyes on our passengers."

"What passengers?"

Rick turned east from San Mateo onto Gibson and queued up in the line of cars entering the Air Force Base. He showed his base pass to the airman and was waved through. Once on the base, he maneuvered his car south until he reached Pennsylvania where it bent east. Two miles later, the road dead-ended at a checkpoint.

"Have to say I'm glad this isn't a manned checkpoint any longer," Rick said as he swiped a co-worker's "borrowed" keycard and the gate opened. He drove through and followed the road as it wended around a domed mountain, a mountain surrounded by two walls of high chain-link fence.

Ten minutes later, Dr. Bickel signaled Rick. "Stop here."

Rick stopped in the road. He and Dr. Bickel scanned the patrol roads below them and the road ahead and behind.

"It's midmorning," Rick said. "Most of the employees who use this road have already arrived for work." He popped the trunk. "Say, how will you know how long to stay hidden?"

"I'll step out of the mountain every evening and check my text messages."

"Got it. Text me when you need a ride."

"Everyone out," Dr. Bickel ordered. "Grab your designated pack. Quickly now."

Abe and Emilio moved to obey; Izzie got out and blinked in the sunlight. Dr. Bickel grabbed her pack, set it on the road, and slammed the trunk lid. As soon as he did, Rick pulled away from them, leaving them alone on the road not far from three rocks, one as tall as Izzie, the other two, one upon the other, just shorter than the first.

Dr. Bickel hung Izzie's backpack over her shoulders. "Let's move," he ordered. He started toward the three rocks, jogging as fast as his spindly legs could carry him.

No one followed.

"This . . . this is where you hid before? In the mountain?" Abe called. "We have to climb? All the way up there?"

"Safest place for us—once we get inside. Hurry, now," Dr. Bickel urged them. "A car could come along at any time. If we're seen, the Air Force will arrest us."

He ran back, grabbed Izzie by her arm, and pulled her toward the sloping flanks of the mountain. Emilio joined him, took Izzie's other hand, and urged her ahead.

Abe, the last to start, grumbled. "Too old for this nonsense. Ain't climbed a mountain in two decades."

Nevertheless, he shuffled across the road and began the laborious trek up the hillside.

⌘

SPEAKER OF THE HOUSE, Frank Friese, standing in front of the American flag in the chamber of the House of Representatives, raised a single sheet of paper and began to read.

"The Senate, by a vote of eighty-six yeas to nine nays, having confirmed the nomination of Simon A. Delancey of the State of Alabama, to be Vice President of the United States, and the House of Representatives, by a vote of three hundred eighty-seven yeas to thirty-five nays, today having confirmed the nomination of Simon A. Delancey of the State of Alabama, to be Vice President of the United States, the proceedings required by Section Two of the Twenty-fifth Amendment to the United States Constitution have been complied with."

To anyone who knew Friese, his voice was tight, his demeanor stiff and indignant. Robert Jackson, President of the United States, knew Friese well enough to recognize that Friese was as disgruntled as a politician could afford to be in front of cameras.

The little weasel hoped someone else would be reading today. A smile traced Jackson's lips. *No, you didn't manage to worm your way into the West Wing, Friese.*

Jackson stood behind Simon and Winnie Delancey. The aging Senator was nearly overcome with emotion; his wife gently patted Delancey's arm. Tears swam in her brown eyes as they smiled with unfeigned happiness into each other's faces.

"The chair now requests the Chief Justice of the United States to administer the oath of office to the Vice President."

The Chief Justice of the United States stepped up to the microphones upon the lectern, and Winnie Delancey lifted the Delancey family Bible. Jackson thought it looked too big and too heavy for her.

The Chief Justice intoned, "Raise your right hand, Mr. Delancey, and place your left hand on the Bible, and repeat after me: I, Simon Andrew Delancey, do solemnly swear that I will support and defend the Constitution of the United States against all enemies, foreign and domestic; that I will bear true faith and allegiance to the same; that I take this obligation freely, without any mental reservation or purpose of evasion; and that I will well and faithfully discharge the duties of the office on which I am about to enter. So help me God."

⌘

I SPENT THE DAY ON THE SOFA in Gamble's safe house, recuperating. Zander left midmorning to sneak into our apartment. He brought back clothing, toiletries, a box of power bars, and the envelope of money Gamble had given us.

"Anyone watching our apartment?"

"Yeah, but they were easy to get past."

He went out again at noon to bring in a hot meal for us. "Guess we're back to cash and carry, huh?" he quipped.

I sighed. "I was lying here thinking what a mess our lives are. My job at the NSA is shot, and you can't go to Celebrate Recovery tomorrow evening."

"At least we're messed up together?"

He was trying to put a happy spin on our situation, but all I could think was, "Oh, goody. More running. More hiding. Thought I was *done* with that."

Grrr!

Zander cleared his throat. "I'm glad you reminded me about CR. I need to call Tom and Becky and let them know I can't be there for the foreseeable future." He put his hands on his head. "Crud. Everyone's going to think we're total flakes—and I don't want to lie to them."

"No need to lie, sweetie. We're in the middle of a family crisis that you can't talk about."

"Uh . . ."

"If all *this*—me getting shot, us running for our lives, Abe, Emilio, and your sister and parents hiding—if all this doesn't constitute a family crisis, then I don't know what does."

Now it was Zander who sighed. "Good point. I just . . . I hate to miss the meeting. God is doing some really exciting stuff."

I placed my hand on his cheek and gently rubbed his jaw with my thumb. "I know, love, and I'm so sorry. On the other hand? I've seen enough 'exciting stuff' lately to hold me for a while."

Zander put his hand over mine. "Thank you. I love you, Jay."

"I love you, too, Zander. Whatever happens, I'm so glad we're in it together."

We were enjoying a lingering and *very* satisfactory kiss when the nanomites announced, *Jayda Cruz, Zander Cruz, Rob Tellerman's nanobug array reports that someone left a handwritten note on his desk. Here it is.*

As Zander and I pulled apart, I muttered, "Best timing ever, Nano."

Thank you, Jayda Cruz. "A word spoken in due season, how good is it!"

I shook my head. *Oh, brother.*

Zander and I studied the message together.

I have information on the disappearance of W.O. Meet me tonight, 11 p.m., Little Paint Branch Trail. Come alone. I need help. PLEASE.

"Little Paint Branch Trail? Hey, isn't that the same location as in the text Danforth intended for us to intercept?"

We believe it to be a second facet of Danforth's ploy, Zander Cruz: the text is to draw you to the park, the message dropped on Rob Tellerman's desk is to draw the FBI agents.

"But why them? Why send them to the same place they are sending us?"

We can answer your question, Jayda Cruz.

"Spill it, Nano."

Danforth summoned his lead SPO, Johnson, to his office this morning. This is the police officer who stands post at the elevator on the executive floor. Danforth tasked him with ambushing the FBI agents in the park tonight.

I was stunned. "What? He's going to have them killed? While we're there?"

Danforth's exact words were, "Take three others. Hide yourselves ahead of time. Do not allow yourselves to be detected. Remain hidden until you are certain they were not followed. Dispatch them quickly, then leave the area. Text me when it's done."

Me again: "Isn't Danforth concerned that we'll intervene and stop the attack?"

We believe it is his desire that you do so. Danforth added these cryptic instructions, "Listen up, Johnson. If anyone or anything interferes with you tonight, do not stand your ground. Withdraw immediately and report to me."

Zander: "So, let me see if I've got this right . . . Danforth knows Kiera and Rob are FBI, but supposedly, *we* don't know they are. As far as Danforth is concerned, we only 'know' what he wants us to know: that Kiera and Rob will have Overman's remains."

Me: "But Danforth doesn't figure that Kiera and Rob having the evidence in their possession will be enough to flush us out. He expects us to show up tonight, but he figures we might just sit on our hands and wait for Kiera and Rob to bury the evidence before we act."

Zander was scarcely breathing. "Which they won't do since they don't actually have Overman's remains."

Me: "Right. So, Danforth sends in his dirty SPOs to ambush Kiera and Rob, hoping the attack will goad *us* into action. He doesn't care if we save Kiera and Rob—he only cares that we expose ourselves—which would prove to him that we *are* monitoring all his communications. Whew. It's kind of confusing."

It is a convoluted plan, Jayda Cruz.

"That's putting it mildly."

Zander bent a crafty look in my direction. "What if we were to convolute it further? What if we flip the game on them, Jayda?"

"Do tell."

"We have the reconstructed surveillance video proving that the SPOs took Overman from the NSA compound. I wonder what would happen if this crooked head SPO, Johnson, received revised instructions? Say, a text similar to the one Danforth sent Kiera and Rob? The nanomites can identify Johnson's number and send him the revised orders, and make it look like the message came from Danforth's phone."

"If the SPOs took the bait and followed instructions . . ."

"They would show up tonight when we told them to arrive—say, ten p.m. They would arrive with all the evidence necessary to nail them to the wall."

"How do you propose we handle them? We can't arrest them."

"No, but that's the beautiful part. We'll have a little chat with Kiera and Rob beforehand. We tell them that their NSA covers are blown anyway, so *they* should make the bust. Once they have the SPOs in custody, they can pressure them to flip on Danforth."

I stared with admiration. "You are so devious."

"Hey, I learned from the best."

I giggled.

We are ready to send such a text, Zander Cruz.
Zander and I read it first.

---

change of plans
move WO remains
2200 hours
same location.
ambush after

"The SPOs are to show up at ten o'clock to bury the evidence and stick around to ambush Kiera and Rob at eleven," Zander said. "I like it."

"It's perfect, Nano," I agreed.

Text sent, Jayda and Zander Cruz.

⌘

THE ONLY POSSIBLE FLAW in our plan was if Danforth's people no longer had Overman's remains, if they'd already found a permanent disposal site for them. Once the text went out, we stayed glued to the nanobug arrays I'd planted on the SPOs.

While we waited, we talked contingencies, and I said, "Our ploy is a shot in the dark. If Danforth's men have already disposed of Overman's remains, then our double cross is no good; all we can do is make sure Kiera and Rob don't walk into an ambush. But if the SPOs still have Overman's remains . . ."

"Then we have *them*," Zander finished. "Yes, it's a shot in the dark, but considering they are going after our family? I'll take that chance."

We waited, and we listened. Within the hour the nanobug array transmitted the audio of Johnson's call to his team.

"Change of plans. We've been ordered to move Overman's remains. We bury them tonight, 2200 hours, same place as the other assignment at 2300."

"I think they're safer where they are."

"You aren't paid to think, Mitchell. Get them ready and meet up at 2200 hours."

"Beauty," Zander breathed. "This might actually work!"

We decided that Gamble needed to know what we had planned—and that the President needed to know, too. Zander made the call, put it on speaker and, predictably, we got an earful.

"Dang it, Zander! You weren't authorized to take action without prior approval. The legal ramifications could ruin any hope of prosecution."

He went off on a tangent and, in my mind's eye, I could see Gamble stomping up and down Trujillo's hospital room, berating us. I reminisced, too, how I'd once wanted to call him Agent Grumble to his face.

Zander interrupted his rant. "Agent Gamble, we don't have the luxury of waiting until all the dominoes magically line up just right when it is our family that is in jeopardy. Please advise the President that this is going down tonight—and let him know that the FBI will soon have his friend's remains in their custody."

We hung up and made another call. I handled this one. "Mal? Ripley here. How would you like to help take down the traitor who killed Mulder and trashed your clubhouse?"

His response was gratifying. "Where, when, and how many of my peeps do I bring?"

After we had finalized Malware's part in tonight's activities, Zander and I spent the rest of the day monitoring Rob's array. He and Kiera planned for her to show up at Rob's apartment at seven, so we waited across from Rob's apartment until Kiera arrived and went inside.

Then we knocked on the door.

I stifled a laugh at the sudden silence that ensued—silence followed by careful creeping toward the peephole.

"Hey Rob? Kiera? It's Jayda Cruz—and my husband, Zander."

Jayda Cruz, your friends appear to be in a state of panic and indecision.

"You mean they're freaking out? Yeah, I would imagine they are."

I spoke aloud again. "Hey, Rob? Kiera? Talking through the door isn't helpful. We need to brief you on your, er, appointment tonight. The one at eleven."

The door cracked open, and Rob peeked out.

"How do you know about that? You haven't been at work all week."

"Yeah, my NSA cover is cooked. I won't be coming back."

"Then how do you know about the note on my desk?"

"We do, and that's all you need to know. Come on, man. Let us in. We need to brief you on tonight's fun and games."

He slowly swung the door open. Kiera was behind him, her sidearm drawn but pulled into her chest.

"You won't need that, Kiera. We're on your side."

"Frankly, we don't know what you are."

I laughed. "Okay, I've earned that."

As Rob closed the apartment door, I handled the introductions. "Rob, Kiera, this is my husband, Zander. Zander, FBI agents Kiera and Rob—likely not their real names. You guys have already met Special Agent Gamble. I believe he vouched for me?"

"Warned us off, you mean."

"Good enough. So, listen, here's the deal: Lawrence Danforth is a traitor."

Kiera interrupted. "Lawrence Danforth as in NSA *Deputy Director* Lawrence Danforth?"

"The one and only. We're not going to take a deep dive into all the specifics, but we do have proof that he had Wayne Overman killed—and isn't that what the FBI embedded you undercover at the NSA to investigate?"

"You say you have proof?"

"We'll do you one better: We'll give you the proof. A group of NSA security police officers answer directly to Danforth. They are as dirty as he is. They did the deed at his direction and removed Overman from the NSA complex the evening he disappeared."

Kiera slid her gun into a shoulder holster and frowned. "Exactly how do you know all this?"

"*How* we know what we're telling you is not as important as the evidence is. We'd like to hand that evidence over to you—legally and all nice and neat with a bow on top."

"We're listening."

"The message you received asking you to meet someone tonight, someone asking for your help? That note was Danforth's creative fiction. He expects you to show up at that park—where he's arranged a little welcoming party for you."

"That *bleeping bleep*!"

"Yeah. He gave orders for his dirty SPOs to ambush you."

Rob interjected, "So what do we do about that? What's your plan?"

"Well . . . this is where it gets, er, dicey. You'll have to take our word for what I say next."

Kiera folded her arms. "Talk. We'll decide if we believe you."

"All right. Here it is: First, Danforth suspects that Zander and I are monitoring his communications. Well, we are, which is why we know so much. Anyway, he sent a text that he expected we would read—which we did."

"Wait. This is confusing."

"Tell me about it. Anyway, here's the text he sent for us to intercept." I held out my phone and the nanomites made the text appear on it.

---

direct colón tellerman
move WO remains
2300 hours
39.0397° N 76.9341° W

"What the *blank*? Direct *us* to move Overman's remains? We're FBI! We didn't kill him. This makes no sense."

"Hold on a sec; let us explain. The text was intended for us, right? It only makes sense if you keep that in mind. Danforth doesn't think we know you're undercover FBI. He doesn't realize that we're way ahead of him, that we've known you're FBI for a while now. By the way, all this means Danforth knows you're FBI, too."

Kiera and Rob exchanged confounded looks.

"Are you certain?"

"Well, sure. It's the reason he had someone drop that note on Rob's desk this morning. He wants you off his back."

"But the text you intercepted?"

"Was to lure us, too. Kind of a two-fer."

Kiera and Rob lapsed into silence.

I pressed ahead. "Like I said, Danforth gave face-to-face instructions to Johnson, his head SPO, to ambush you this evening—but we've flipped the game. We sent a text to the same SPO with a change of plans."

I again showed them my phone, and the nanomites displayed their message.

---

change of plans
move WO remains
2200 hours
same location
ambush after

"*You* sent this text? If you sent it, how does that convince Johnson that Danforth sent it?"

"As you may have suspected, I have cutting-edge tech at my fingertips, proprietary, uh, *hardware* not on the market. Sure, you can buy cheap software that enables you to spoof a phone's number, but the hack is easily spotted and traced. My hack leaves *zero* trace. Johnson is convinced my text came from Danforth, and no program, skill, expertise, or tool in existence could prove otherwise."

Rob's techy heart was salivating. "Whatever it is you've got, I want some of it."

Kiera waved his comment aside. "You're saying Danforth gave the order to have Overman killed, the SPOs removed Overman from the NSA, and now they think Danforth has ordered them to move his remains and bury them in the park this evening at ten o'clock."

"And ambush you at eleven, as per the original instructions."

"It's been months since Overman vanished. What makes you think Danforth's people haven't already gotten rid of the body?"

I shrugged. "It was a risky supposition that could have backfired on us. The good news is that we've been monitoring the SPOs' communications since we sent the text. They bought into it and are following their 'orders.' You will catch them flat-footed with the evidence in hand—and with their arrest comes the strong possibility that they will flip on Danforth. After all, treason is a federal crime that carries the penalty of death by lethal injection. Johnson and his team might be willing to bargain down to life in federal lockup."

I added emphasis to my last point, the enticing part: "You two will crack the most notable case of the year. Maybe this decade."

Kiera slid her eyes toward Rob. "We would need backup. Big-time backup."

"But you don't have enough time to sell the idea to your superiors."

Kiera nodded. "I don't even know how we'd explain it to them—not without them ordering us to get a psych eval first."

"Then it's a good thing we have backup on speed dial."

⌘⌘⌘⌘

CHAPTER 31

DANFORTH ARRIVED AT HIS OFFICE earlier than usual Thursday morning. He was satisfied that he'd rid himself of the FBI's undercover snoops, and cautiously optimistic regarding the security of his communications. He glanced once more at the text Johnson had sent late last night.

Done
No interference

He laughed under his breath. Jayda and Zander Cruz and their nanomites weren't as omnipresent as he and the woman had been led to believe. Mr. and Mrs. Cruz *hadn't* shown up last night, which meant they *hadn't* intercepted the text he'd planted to draw them out.

A second mark on the plus side, Johnson and his team had eliminated those thorns in Danforth's side, the two FBI agents planted at the NSA. He expected a third bit of good news momentarily when the team in Albuquerque called to confirm that they had acquired three people Jayda and Zander Cruz cherished.

He sighed with satisfaction. The Albuquerque team should already be on the road to Las Cruces to add Zander Cruz's parents to their collection—and soon he and the woman would have the troublesome Jayda and Zander Cruz in their hands.

His gratification lasted all of five minutes.

The burner he used to communicate with Johnson here in D.C. and with the woman's team in Albuquerque vibrated in his drawer. He pulled it out and answered it, confident in the good news the Albuquerque team would report.

"Yes?"

"You have a leak."

Danforth frowned. "Explain."

"The targets—all three of them—vanished before we got to them. Nobody knows where they are. Someone tipped them off."

Danforth was too stunned to answer.

"Did you hear me?"

"I—yes, I heard."

"We're not going to take the heat for this failure, get me? The leak isn't on our end."

Danforth's misgiving raced toward a deduction he very much disliked.

"Go on to Las Cruces and acquire the other targets. Report to me as soon as you set eyes on them."

He hung up and rehearsed the time and place he and the woman had discussed the abduction. Talking aloud to himself, he said, "Her exact words were, 'You will create that distraction for me, Lawrence. I wish you to locate Mr. and Mrs. Cruz's closest family and loved ones. Not too many. Gemma Keyes' elderly neighbor and his foster child and Zander Cruz's sister and parents should do. Sweep them up and spirit them away.'

"We were within the shielded facility when she said that. She and I did not speak of it outside the facility. I said nothing about the plan until I called her team in Albuquerque."

Danforth glared at the burner, a suspicion blooming in his thoughts. *Could Jayda or Zander Cruz have bugged this phone? Listened in on my call to Albuquerque? How else could they have known and warned their friends?*

He was still holding the burner when he remembered the text Johnson had sent last night—*to the same phone.*

Done
No interference

He lurched to his feet, stumbled to his office door, and looked toward the elevator bank: Johnson, who should have come on shift at eight, was conspicuously absent from his post.

Danforth's secretary had just arrived and was putting her desk in order.

"Have you seen Johnson today?"

Her head swiveled toward the elevator bank. "Oh. I hadn't noticed, but he's not here yet."

"I can see that. Was he here earlier?"

"I'm sorry, sir, but I only just got here myself."

Danforth returned to his office and fired off a message:

Where are you?

Ten minutes later, as Danforth was starting to really worry, the response came back.

Urgent care
Walking pneumonia

Danforth was not entirely mollified. *Johnson didn't seem sick yesterday.*

He called downstairs to Safety and Security. "Johnson is out sick. Where's the executive floor's replacement guard?"

"We have four officers out sick today, sir, counting Johnson. Some kind of chest virus, I've been told. We've called in off-duty SPOs to cover for them, but it may be an hour before we have an officer to send up to you."

Danforth's heart dropped into his shoes. "Which four?"

"Pardon?"

"Which four officers are out sick?"

As the supervisor listed them off, Danforth's hopes sank further. *The entire team from last evening.*

How likely was it that all four would be sick on the same day? All of them with a "chest virus"? *Not even remotely likely.* So, where were they? Had Johnson and his team walked into an FBI trap? Were they in federal custody? If so, what had gone wrong? And how?

"Seems to be going around, sir. We have other employees out today. Some haven't even called in. HR is having a fit."

That would be Colón and Tellerman, Danforth told himself, preoccupied with his own problems. But some vague sense of unease made him ask, "What others?"

"Uh, well . . . hold one moment, sir. I'll get the list. Here you go: Rob Tellerman. Sundhi Pragesh. Kiera Colón. Jayda Cruz. Mark Al—"

"What? *What did you say?*"

"Would you like me to start over, sir?"

"Yes. No! Did you say *Jayda Cruz?*"

"Yes, sir. The woman's been no call/no show all week."

A wave of shock juddered up his spine. *Jayda Cruz has been working here, right under my nose.*

Danforth hung up. *Jayda Cruz working here? Infiltrating the NSA? Perhaps sneaking into this office? Invading my emails and listening in on my calls?*

He studied his trembling hands; however, he was not focused on their trembling but on what he imagined creeping in and out of his skin:

Nanomites. Invisible to the naked eye.

His imaginings worsened. His skin itched and crept; he scratched nervously. *Are the nanomites on me? In me? Have they infested me? Are they, right now, crawling on me?*

And then, *Could the nanomites have been in the shielded facility with us the entire time? Eavesdropping on our plans and secrets? Passing them on to Jayda Cruz and her husband?*

He looked again at his hands. *No way to know. No way to be sure.*

His first instinct was to reach out to the woman, to warn her, to ask for help. He fumbled in his briefcase for yet another phone, one unused to date. Contacting the woman directly—particularly now—would be a risky, unprecedented move, an action reserved for only the most urgent of situations. As if this wasn't?

As his hand touched the phone's cool surface, a measure of instinctual caution swept over him: *self-preservation.* If Johnson and the other SPOs *were* in federal custody, the greatest threat facing Danforth was the possibility that one of the officers would rat him out.

The greatest threat facing him? No. He'd worked in the field with the woman decades ago, and his memories of the cold, merciless methods she'd used to "solve" problems were still fresh.

In the broader scheme of things . . . I am a liability to her—and quite expendable.

He slowly took his hand off the phone and sank into his chair. Maybe he hadn't been the rock star intelligence operative the woman had been, but he'd been a decent agent, a good spy for his country.

He called upon that training to help him now. *If I am to survive this, I must save myself. But if what I suspect is true, nothing I plan or do will be hidden from the nanomites.*

He rewound every conversation regarding Jayda Cruz—*no, Gemma Keyes*—and her abilities and actions, particularly Cushing's report on Colonel Greaves' encounter with her. He remained deep in contemplation for half an hour, weighing his options, formulating his next steps. When he roused himself, he got to his feet and set to work.

His hands now shaking, Danforth locked his office door. He placed his briefcase on his desk. Then he opened the safe where he kept classified documents and began pulling files—dossiers he'd painstakingly assembled as insurance against such a day as today. He scanned through them deciding which to take and which to leave.

Leave.

Danforth glanced around his office, considering the accoutrements of power he'd acquired through the years—the impressive furnishings; the wall of photos taken of him with presidents, senators, foreign ambassadors, and even foreign leaders; the plaques and awards.

Leave? Yes. Better to leave all this than face the FBI . . . or worse.

He called his driver. "I'm coming down. Five minutes."

"Yes, sir."

He finished packing his briefcase and exited his office, locking his door behind him. "Cancel my appointments. An unavoidable meeting came up that will keep me out for the rest of the day."

"Yes, sir. I will. See you tomorrow."

No, he realized. *You won't.*

His home was in the country, north and east of D.C., and he lived alone. His wife had tired of him early in their marriage, and he had not bothered to marry again. Danforth had his driver drop him at his front door.

"I have some business to attend to inside. I may be an hour or longer. Wait for me."

"Yes, sir."

He went directly to his home study. In a corner, he touched a panel. It slid back, revealing a gun safe with a biometric lock. Danforth placed his thumb on the scanner and the lock disengaged.

He inspected the safe's contents and selected a semi-compact HK45 and three loaded 10-round magazines. He placed them on his desk and took off his suit jacket before he withdrew a second weapon from the safe—a Taser X26P. He sat down in his desk chair and considered his next move.

Was everything Cushing told Harmon about the nanomites real? Or am I about to do something foolhardy and needless?

He shook his head. He could not afford the risk. The next steps in his survival plan could not be monitored, reported, or traced.

Danforth pushed his chair away from his desk and leaned back in the seat. Pointing the Taser at his chest and holding it as far from him as he could, he depressed the trigger. The darts exploded from the Taser and penetrated his shirt and his skin. The current sent excruciating pain through his body. His hand jerked and spasmed, and he was unable to release the Taser's trigger, which kept a continuous flow of juice running through the leads to the darts. When the gun finally fell from his numb fingers to the floor, the current crackling through his body ended.

Danforth sprawled in his chair, unable to move for two or three minutes. When the pain and numbness eased, he got up and, on quivering legs, picked up the Taser and placed it back in his safe.

I have no means of knowing if that did the trick or if I'm being paranoid, he reasoned, *but it was the only option available to me.*

Feeling calmer, he sat again, pulled the chair up to his desk, and removed the unused burner from his briefcase. Using his NSA-issued smartphone to retrieve the number he wanted, he dialed the burner.

The voice that answered held a trace of accent and a large measure of wariness. "Yes?"

"Peotyr, this is Lawrence Danforth. I am calling from an untraceable number."

Danforth said what he needed to say. He wished their conversation to be short and succinct and the arrangements equally so, but Peotyr was required to follow certain protocols before he could provide the assurances Danforth insisted upon.

"I will call you back shortly, Lawrence."

"As they say, Peotyr, time is of the essence."

"I understand."

While he waited for the callback, Danforth withdrew a stack of twenty-dollar bills and a fake passport from his safe and added them to his briefcase. He then inserted a magazine into his .45, chambered a round, engaged the safety, and put the gun in his suit jacket pocket. He slipped the two extra magazines into his other jacket pocket. With nothing else to do but wait for the return call, he went up to his bedroom and packed a small bag with clothing and toiletries.

When he returned to his study, he pulled the .45 from his pocket and placed it on his desk. *In case*, he told himself. *In case the arrangements do not work out.*

The call came twenty minutes later.

"We concur that your recommendation will serve best."

"I'm glad to hear it."

The details were quickly hashed out.

"I will see you soon, Lawrence."

"Yes."

Danforth stood and took a last look around. He picked up his bag and briefcase and left the house. His driver, as he'd instructed, was waiting by the front door. Danforth got into the car and his driver pulled away.

"I'm going to give you very precise instructions, Shelby. You are to follow them to a 't.'"

"Of course, sir."

Danforth issued his directives, confident that they would be carried out. Besides Shelby's personal loyalty to him for more than a decade, the man had been a spook in his own right before being wounded. When he'd been deemed unfit for the field, the NSA had employed him as driver and bodyguard for high-level NSA executives such as Danforth. As odd as Danforth's orders might seem, Shelby would go along with them because Danforth had led Shelby to believe that he was engaged in a covert meeting with political as well as national intelligence ramifications.

Shelby would believe what he'd been told until the FBI presented him with proof to the contrary.

It was after noon before they headed toward the beltway, using a less-congested side road. A few miles from their exit onto 495, the road entered a long tunnel that ran under multiple Amtrak lines. Shelby braked to a near stop; Danforth threw open the rear door and leapt from the car.

Shelby, as ordered, accelerated, emerged from the tunnel, and continued into D.C. He parked in the Union Station parking garage a short hike from the Capitol Building. He turned off the engine, exited the vehicle, and locked the doors.

As directed, he took the Metro home. Danforth would, Shelby had been told, return to Union Station when his business was concluded, retrieve his car, and drive himself home.

Shelby was to take the following day off and await Danforth's call for his next orders.

⌘

IT HAD BEEN A LONG but satisfying night. Mal, Baltar, Deckard, McFly, and Dredd met us (plus Kiera and Rob) at the park at nine. Malware, Inc. came armed for bear and intent on justice. They shook Kiera and Rob's hands, then Zander explained the double cross.

"Four dirty NSA SPOs will arrive at ten with the remains of the President's close friend. NSA DD Lawrence Danforth has ordered them to bury the remains somewhere in the park where they won't be found.

"Kiera and Rob, here, are FBI agents covertly planted at the NSA to investigate Overman's disappearance. Danforth arranged to 'lure' Kiera and Rob to this location tonight. They aren't supposed to arrive until eleven, at which point the SPOs have orders to ambush them. Of course, we're all here early and will jump *them* instead."

Kiera nodded to Mal. "Thank you for helping us out. We didn't know about the ambush until Jayda and Zander told us a couple of hours ago. That didn't leave us enough time to get our bosses up to speed and have them sanction an FBI team to assist us."

At the mention of "Jayda and Zander," the attention of the Malware crew swiveled our way for a collective "ah-ha!" moment. And just like that, our covers at Malware, Inc. were kaput.

"We're happy to assist the FBI without receiving the credit for it," Mal answered. "This is personal for us. If what *Ripley* and *John-Boy* tell us is true, then it was Danforth who gave the orders to attack our headquarters twice in the last forty-eight hours. We lost a good friend—and we're here to make sure Danforth pays."

Rob looked confused. "Ripley? John-Boy?"

I grinned. "Another time, another place, another persona, Rob. Or *is* it Rob?"

"Yeah, yeah. Point taken."

"Mal, you guys run the take-down while we observe," Zander said. "We will assist only if needed." He put an arm around me. "Ripley took a round yesterday morning. I don't want her exerting herself."

The reaction was so sweet: Mal's crew was immediately concerned and solicitous.

"Should you even be here, Ripley?" Dredd asked.

"Um, not to worry; I'm being seen to."

"I'll make sure she stays well out of the action," Zander added.

Mal took charge then. He partnered his crew members with Kiera and Rob and positioned three teams to best advantage.

"Kiera and Deckard, you're with me on this side of the road. Baltar and Dredd, you cover the other side of the road. We'll catch them in a pincer move; McFly and Rob, you'll flank and cut off egress if they try to run."

The entire action took less than ten minutes. The dirty officers, led by Danforth's lead SPO Johnson, showed up in plainclothes just before ten and drove as far into the park as they could, and we followed them in. As Johnson and his people got out and popped the trunk, Mal's teams swept in from two sides while McFly and Rob closed off the road. Within moments, Dredd and Baltar had disarmed the four SPOs, forced them to lie prone on the road, and zip-tied their wrists.

Then Kiera, Rob, and I examined the contents of the trunk.

"Looks like you have what you need, guys. You've got them dead to rights."

Kiera shook her head. "Dead to rights? Yeah, I'm pretty sure we'd be the dead part right about now if you hadn't warned us."

"We couldn't have done this without the help of you and your friends," Rob said.

Kiera phoned it in. Then she and Rob shook our hands and thanked Mal and his team who were packing up to go. We "left," too, but actually hung around (just in case) until the FBI showed up.

Within fifteen minutes, the park was swarming with federal agents, including Kiera and Rob's supervisor—who seemed more confused than pleased.

"Tell me again how the two of you took down these four guys?"

"Like we said, we had help," Kiera repeated.

"And, again, who? What help?"

"Sir, as I said the first time, all I can reveal is that another undercover entity assisted us—an entity that prefers to remain anonymous."

"Another entity? What the *blank* does that mean? I need specifics."

Kiera pointed to the car the SPOs had arrived in. "I believe you'll find all you need to solve Overman's disappearance in their trunk, sir. What's even *more* important, is that these officers can implicate the man who gave them their orders—NSA Deputy Director Lawrence Danforth."

Rob and Kiera's supervisor almost choked. "Are you serious?"

"As a root canal, sir."

"You'd better have your ducks in a row before you start throwing around these kinds of accusations, because if you're wrong? You can kiss your careers goodbye—and I don't intend to follow you out the door."

"You have these men solid for the murder of *the President's good friend*, sir. Separate them before transport, interrogate them individually, and threaten them with the needle. They will crack like an egg, sir."

The phrase, "the President's good friend," must have finally penetrated the supervisor's brain. "Holy *bleep*!"

"Exactly, sir." Kiera cut a glance toward Rob. "This is one of those once-in-a-lifetime, career-making cases."

Rob grinned.

So did we.

⌘

WE REPORTED THE NIGHT'S RESULTS to Gamble who, after grumbling his disapproval for a quarter of an hour, passed the news on to Kennedy.

Before we went to bed, we had the nanomites send Danforth a text:

Done
No interference

I guess we weren't all that surprised when Gamble called the next morning. "The President has summoned you to the White House. Residence dining room, noon."

I about lost it when Zander cracked, "As in High Noon?"

FBI Special Agent Gamble hung up on us.

Sheesh. Can't take a joke?

Jayda Cruz, Danforth has texted Johnson: "Where are you?"

"Nano, send the reply."

The nanomites, spoofing Johnson's number, sent a text to Danforth's burner phone.

Urgent care
Walking pneumonia

"That should hold him for a few more hours. I just hope the FBI cracks one or more of the SPOs soon."

We'd already "called" in sick for the four SPOs, but sooner or later—probably sooner—Danforth would figure out that he'd been played.

⌘

WE STEPPED OFF AT METRO CENTER around eleven and began our walk toward the White House.

"You think he's going to read us the riot act?" Zander asked.

"The President or Agent Kennedy? Gamble already took a chunk out of our hides. I can't see it getting much worse."

"Really? Cause you think the President yelling at us won't be worse?"

"We've completed one of our assigned objectives, Zander. We found his friend. That has to count for something."

"We're giving him Danforth on a platter, too."

"Yup."

We hung out in Lafayette Park until it was closer to noon. Then we entered the White House and wandered up to the Residence. The President and Kennedy were in low, earnest conversation when we appeared, and the President noticed us.

"Ah. You're here. Thank you for coming."

I glanced from President Jackson to Kennedy. The President seemed calm but sad. Kennedy's expression was nondescript.

So far, so good.

We sat around the family dining table, and Zander and I began to report our recent activities and findings, starting with the two attacks on Malware, Inc. We had just gotten to the part where Danforth and the mystery woman decided to abduct Abe, Emilio, and Zander's sister and parents, when the nanomites broke in.

Jayda Cruz, Zander Cruz.

"Yes, Nano?"

We have lost contact with Danforth's array.

"Would you pardon us for a moment, Mr. President?"

Zander and I turned inward to the warehouse. The nanomites showed us the array's feed for the last half hour. The nanobugs reported no calls or computer activity, only Danforth's movements in his house while his driver waited.

"How long's he been in the house, Nano?"

Minutes only, Zander Cruz.

"Can you give us eyes on Danforth's house?"

One moment, Zander Cruz.

It was actually several minutes before a neighbor's security camera showed Danforth's car outside his house.

The President tapped me on the shoulder, bringing me back to our setting. "What's going on?"

"We're watching Danforth, sir. Something's up. He's at home. We have eyes on his car and driver."

Of course, I didn't mention the nanobug arrays and how the nanomites had been actively monitoring Danforth through his array. The man had sat passively in his office part of the morning and done some paperwork. He'd left his office and returned to his house midmorning, but he'd made no untoward calls so far.

Until the array went off line.

Jackson nodded. "Can you tell what he's doing?"

"Uh, not exactly, sir, but we're a little concerned." *And I can't tell you why without telling you how we've been surveilling the man.*

"While we continue monitoring Danforth, would you like us to finish our report?"

"Yes, please."

Zander took over the telling. He didn't stop until he reported on the FBI taking the SPOs and Wayne Overman's remains into custody.

"We want to convey our condolences on the passing of your friend, Mr. President. We know you had hoped to find him alive, to restore him to his family."

"Thank you, Zander. I appreciate your sympathies and your services. I have not yet spoken to Wayne's wife, Debi, but she will appreciate the closure and being able to lay his body to rest."

"Yes, sir. We also realize that Danforth isn't the brains behind the conspiracy, but he's pretty high up. We believe the mystery woman is our real objective, but her identity still eludes us."

"Do you have an image of her?"

I answered. "No, sir. Only the smallest portion of her face—a cheekbone and an eye. The nanomites are working around the clock to match those features to someone, but so far they've come up empty."

Zander added, "Once the NSA officers give Danforth up, the FBI might get him to flip on the mystery woman."

"Somehow, I doubt that," the President murmured. "Danforth was a field operative for twenty years before he shifted over to a desk at NSA. The man knows how to resist an interrogation."

We lapsed into an uncomfortable silence at that point. It didn't help that Kennedy had said nothing to us since we'd arrived. His stoic silence was making me antsy.

I cleared my throat. "Will you be picking Danforth up, sir?"

"Not until one of the SPOs flips on him."

"Well, we'll keep tabs on him for you, sir."

Jayda Cruz, Zander Cruz. Danforth has returned to his car.

Zander and I watched the video feed together.

"He has his briefcase and a small suitcase. Nano, where's Danforth's array? Why haven't we heard from it?"

We fear it is dead, Jayda Cruz. Also, we believe Danforth's driver has cut the wires to his vehicle's GPS.

I spoke the words before the conclusion fully matured in my conscious thoughts. "Mr. President, Danforth is running."

The President jumped to his feet. "Axel."

"Sir, I recommend we move to the Situation Room."

"Agreed."

Kennedy pulled his phone and hit speed dial. He alerted the President's National Security Advisor, Vice President Delancey, and various others to convene downstairs in what was officially the John F. Kennedy Conference Room but was only ever called "the Situation Room."

Kennedy glanced at us. "Can you stay on Danforth?"

"Yes."

The nanomites were already inside the security and traffic cams around Danforth's house, and they were working to access commercial and government satellite feeds. Jackson gave one nod and strode toward the door. He gestured for us to follow. Zander gulped, but we trotted along after the President and Kennedy—invisibly, of course.

"*Stonewall* on the move to the Situation Room," Kennedy murmured into his comms to notify the President's detail.

To avoid the crush of staffers moving downstairs, Zander and I were getting farther behind the President. Before he got too far from us, I took the opportunity to send a thread of nanomites to whisper in his ear, "Mr. President, Zander and I will be in the room with you, but at a distance for our own security."

When he heard the whisper, he slowed in amazement for the briefest moment, clamped his mouth shut almost in the same instant, and nodded.

⌘

WHEN THE PRESIDENT'S crisis advisors had gathered in the situation room and the Secret Service had closed the doors, Zander and I found ourselves sandwiched into a corner, where we tried not to jostle anyone or otherwise make our presence known. I was so nervous that I was sweating bullets. I could only imagine the anxieties Zander was suffering. When I felt his fingers curl around mine, I breathed a tiny sigh of relief.

The President opened the meeting by addressing several aides. "I want immediate satellite imaging at the following coordinates—"

He paused to pick up and slowly sip on the glass of water in front of him. Every ear and eye in the room waited for him to finish his order.

"Oh!" I mentally smacked myself and edged up to the President. "Go, Nano!"

They sent the coordinates and direction of Danforth's vehicle along to the President. He cleared his throat and repeated them. I stepped back into my corner.

A flurry of activity followed as military aides gave the orders to retask satellite imaging.

"What is the situation, Mr. President?" This was from Alister Kirche, the President's National Security Advisor.

Jackson folded his hands. "Last night, the FBI arrested four NSA security police officers at a park a few miles from NSA headquarters. In their trunk was evidence of Wayne Overman's murder."

The restless movements in the room stilled.

"I have it on good authority that NSA Deputy Director Lawrence Danforth gave the orders for Mr. Overman's death. He is, at this moment, attempting to flee." Jackson nodded at the large monitor at the end of the room. "I want him tracked and arrested."

The National Security Advisor blinked and carefully framed his next words. "I'm very sorry, sir. We know Mr. Overman was a personal friend . . . however, should not the FBI be handling this search? Is there a national security concern in Danforth's actions?"

"It is true that Mr. Overman was a personal friend and, yes, the FBI should take the lead on Danforth's arrest. To your point, however, Lawrence Danforth is the repository of a great many national secrets. We cannot allow him to fall into the wrong hands."

"Of course, Mr. President. I agree."

Vice President Delancey spoke next. "Do you have any idea where Mr. Danforth is headed, Mr. President?"

"Not yet. I—oh, I see you have him. Good."

Satellite imagery showed Danforth's black SUV moving steadily toward 495, the D.C. beltway.

"He appears to be headed back to D.C., Mr. President. Do you have orders, sir?"

"Yes. Now that we have a location, someone get the FBI and local police on the line and have them intercept and detain Danforth."

Aides hurried to place the calls while we watched the progress of Danforth's SUV on the monitors. At that moment, Danforth's SUV sped into a tunnel that ran beneath multiple train tracks. Long seconds later, the car emerged and continued toward a 495 on-ramp.

Jayda and Zander Cruz, we have a concern. The speed at which Danforth's SUV entered and left the tunnel does not match the time elapsed before it reappeared.

"What?"

Jayda Cruz, approximately seven point five seconds are unaccounted for.

My head snapped up. I studied the satellite feed—the vehicles entering the tunnel from both directions.

I got it.

I crept out of the corner to within a few feet of the President. A thread of nanomites shot from me to him and whispered in his ear, *Mr. President, Danforth left his car while it was inside the tunnel. He was picked up by the tan SUV traveling in the opposite direction.*

Jackson stared at the feed. "He's switched vehicles! Follow that tan SUV—and inform the police and FBI."

The nanomites stayed with the President and whispered a few other things to him, but I was engrossed in the immediate response of the situation room. People knew their jobs and went after their tasks at the President's order.

"Zoom in. Get a plate number," someone ordered. "Trace the registration."

Seconds later, a military aide announced, "Sir, we have the vehicle registration."

"Spit it out," the National Security Advisor growled.

The aide licked her lips. "The vehicle is registered to the Russian Embassy."

I would say that pandemonium broke out, but the atmosphere in the room was too edgy and controlled for the reaction to be described as an uproar.

I kept my eyes on the feed. The tan SUV had hit the outskirts of the town of Gaithersburg and veered east, picking up speed. "Nano, what's going on? Where is Danforth headed?

Jayda Cruz, the nanomites whispered. *"Luke 16. I know what I'll do so that when I lose my job here, people will welcome me into their houses."*

I was too preoccupied to pay attention to the nanomites' odd Scripture quotations! But they pressed on.

"The master commended the dishonest manager because he had acted shrewdly. For the people of this world are more shrewd in dealing with their own kind than are the people of the light."

Their own kind, Jayda Cruz.

"Oh!" I exclaimed. "He's defecting!"

I had spoken aloud.

Ooops.

President Jackson turned toward the sound of my voice, as did a number of personnel, none who could figure out who'd spoken. But, as confusing as my exclamation was, they *had* heard me—and recognized the validity of my unguarded statement.

"Mr. President, the vehicle is only a mile from Montgomery County Airpark."

"Can that airport accommodate private jets?"

"Yes, sir."

"Lawrence Danforth cannot be allowed to leave American airspace. Get the Joint Chiefs on the line."

An aide dialed the Pentagon. Another fumbled for the number to the airport, and yet another reached out to the FAA. Tensions cranked up another notch as the National Security Advisor barked, "Get me the Russian Ambassador. *Now.*"

"Put it on speakerphone," Jackson ordered.

The call to the Ambassador's direct line went through and a pleasant female voice answered. "You have reached the office of Nicolai Rostavich, Ambassador of the Russian Federation to the United States of America. How may I direct your call?"

"This is Alister Kirche, National Security Advisor to President Robert Jackson. I need to speak to the Russian Ambassador. Urgently."

"Yes, Mr. Kirche. One moment, sir."

Elevator music wafted from the phone's speaker console while all eyes watched the dot on the satellite feed enter the Montgomery County Airpark.

"What's happening with the FAA?" the President asked. "Have they closed the airport?"

"We have the regional office on the line, sir, but they are unable to raise the Montgomery tower."

"The direct line to the airport is also not connecting, sir."

"Who has the authority to shut down telecommunications like this?" the President roared.

"No one, sir. It-it seems likely that it's a hack directed at the airport. Whoever it is, the hack would need to be quite, er, sophisticated."

The other voices in the Situation Room quieted as the President shouted his frustration. "A sophisticated hack? Sophisticated, say, as in the NSA? Are you telling me Danforth tasked our own NSA resources to facilitate his escape?"

An officer replied quietly, "The Russians could do it, sir."

"Would the Russians risk an international incident of such proportion?"

"They might, sir . . . if they felt their objective—say, NSA Deputy Director Danforth—was worth committing a near-act of war."

Jackson glared at his National Security Advisor. "Is this enough of a 'national security concern' for you now?"

The tan SUV wound its way through airport property. We all saw the business jet sitting on the tarmac. Waiting. Warming up.

"Get the tail number on that plane," Kirche ordered. "I want to know everything about it—who bought it, who it's registered to, its range—everything."

"And where's the Russian Ambassador?" President Jackson demanded.

"We're still on hold, Mr. President."

"Sir," an aide interrupted. "The aircraft is a Citation X jet, seats eight passengers, range 3,700 miles. Waiting on the registration. Ah, here it is, sir. Er, the Citation is registered to the Russian Federation Government for the use of the embassy. It has filed a flight plan to Reykjavik."

"Where it will refuel before going on to Moscow." President Jackson sat back, his dark skin growing darker with anger. "The Ambassador is stalling us. I want you to hang up and call back. Tell whoever answers that if Rostavich isn't on the line inside of five seconds, we're going to shoot down his jet."

"Yes, sir."

We were now watching two scenes on the monitors. One screen showed a phalanx of police cars, lights flashing, speeding toward the Montgomery County Airpark. The other screen showed the occupants of the tan SUV racing up the jet's stairs. The view zoomed in on Lawrence Danforth as he mounted the steps and disappeared inside the plane.

"That's Peotyr Dostav just behind Danforth," Kirche said. "D.C. Station chief."

"FSB, I presume?" Jackson asked.

"Yes, sir."

"So. The FSB is aiding one of our top intelligence officers to defect."

"Sir, I have the Russian Ambassador."

"Put him on speaker."

"Ready, sir."

"Ambassador Rostavich. This is President Robert Jackson. I just watched the Deputy Director of our National Security Agency, Lawrence Danforth, board a jet owned by the Russian Federation."

When Rostavich did not answer, Jackson said, "Ambassador, did you hear me?"

"But of course, Mr. President. However, I did not know you asked a question of me."

Still stalling. Stalling for more time.

The Citation taxied down the runway, gathering speed. At the same time, the line of police cars raced onto the tarmac. They poured on speed and tried to catch the jet, cut it off.

It was a near thing, but the nose of the jet lifted from the runway into the air. It climbed aggressively and turned toward the ocean.

Jackson covered the phone. "Chairman of the Joint Chiefs?"

"On the line, Mr. President."

"SecDef?"

"Also on the line, sir."

"Put them on speaker, too. I want Rostavich to hear me speak to the Secretary of Defense."

"Yes, sir."

"Mr. Secretary? Are you up to speed?"

"Yes, Mr. President."

"Scramble fighters to intercept the jet carrying Danforth."

The Situation Room heard the Russian Ambassador protest. "Mr. President, excuse me, but you may not do that! That jet is the property of the Russian Federation and is occupied by members of the Russian delegation who have diplomatic status!"

"Then they shouldn't have taken off without tower recognition and permission."

"But Mr. President—"

A gesture from the President cut off the Ambassador. The man could hear the events unfold, but his objections were muted.

SecDef said, "Mr. President, we have scrambled F-15E fighters, 4th Fighter Wing, out of Seymour Johnson Air Force Base. Do you give the order to shoot down the Russian jet, sir? And what if it leaves American airspace before our fighters are within missile range?"

Jackson looked around the room and found his Vice President.

Delancey's watery eyes belied the strength of his voice. "Mr. President, I concur: The Russian plane was not authorized to leave the runway and ignored the presence of law enforcement on the runway. Shoot it down."

President Jackson put his mouth to the phone. "I give the order—and I don't care if the plane leaves our airspace or not. Shoot it down."

The situation room held a different tension now, one of solemn waiting. All eyes were glued to the monitors, watching the satellite feed of the Citation as it banked, gained more altitude, then straightened onto a north by northeast heading.

"Three minutes to contact, Mr. President."

The Russian jet nudged the edge of American airspace. I wondered what the Russian Ambassador was saying on his end of the muted call. I dove with the nanomites into the phone lines. I had learned some conversational Russian in my personal studies, but I only understood a smattering of the words streaming from Rostavich's mouth. I didn't really need to know the unfamiliar phrases: I recognized profanity when I heard it.

The satellite feed zoomed out and picked up two outbound blips, miles from the Citation.

Over SecDef's line we heard the pilots and ground control speaking back and forth.

"Eagle One, you are cleared to engage."

"Roger that, Command. Target acquired. Missiles launched."

The satellite feed could not pick up the missiles as they streaked across the sky. One moment, the Citation's blip was on screen. The next moment it wasn't.

"Splash one, Command."

"Roger, Eagle One. You are cleared RTB."

The Situation Room, as an entity, exhaled and began to relax—everyone but Robert Jackson. He remained seated, his head bowed over his folded hands, in what appeared to be deep contemplation.

⌘⌘⌘⌘

CHAPTER 32

THE DEBRIEF AND AFTERMATH of Danforth's attempted defection and subsequent demise took hours—the big question being, "Who is Danforth's superior, the mystery woman?" When Zander and I finally made it back to Gamble's meeting place, it was long after midnight.

We'd been under intense pressure for nearly a week, and we were both tired, but for some reason—perhaps getting shot?—I felt like a wrung-out dish cloth. I crawled onto the couch and slept hard. I don't think I even turned over until something pulled me from my deep sleep.

"Hey." Zander sat on the arm of the couch stroking my arm. "Hey, sweetie. You've been asleep a long while"

I smiled up at my husband, his beautiful gray eyes smiling back at me. "What time is it?"

"Don't you mean, 'Which day is it?'"

"Oh, wow. That long?"

"It's nearly five o'clock Friday evening. You were out fourteen hours straight."

"For heaven's sake!"

I started to sit up and groaned as my wound protested.

Zander slid his arm under me and helped me up. "You're only four days out from being gut shot, remember? You're still tender inside."

"Y'know . . . when you say, 'gut shot,' it sucks all the romantic mystique right out of it."

Zander grinned. "Romantic mystique, huh?"

"Uh-huh. The beautiful heroine takes one for the team, but she suffers and endures with impressive courage and dignity. The handsome hero, unable to resist her charms, clasps her in his arms, holds her to his muscular chest. Their gazes meet and lock; he declares his passionate love and undying devotion and leans toward her, his lips parted, ready to plant true love's first kiss on—"

"Pfffffffft. Not until she brushes her teeth he doesn't."

We busted up. I could hardly catch my breath, and I had to hold my side. "Don't! Please!" I begged. "It hurts to laugh when you've been gut shot!"

"Right. Sorry. Let me distract you: Are you hungry? I brought in dinner."

Food? Everything in me stood up and cheered.

"Yes! Bathroom first. Then dinner. And coffee. And breakfast. And lunch. Cause I missed all of them."

We plowed into the Indian takeout, me alternating sips of Chai latte and coffee between bites of biryani, butter chicken, baingan bharta, chole, and chicken tikka masala.

"Man, I'm so starved. What happened while I was sleeping, by the way?"

"Gamble called. The doctors released Trujillo this morning, and I caught him up on what transpired in the Situation Room yesterday."

I'd forgotten about Danforth. "Oh. Yeah. That was . . . harsh."

I shivered, recalling the pilot's unemotional statement. *"Splash one, Command."*

"Also, the nanomites took advantage of the time while you were sleeping to dink around downstairs. Something about increasing their storage capacity and adding functionality to the surveillance arrays. I think they are still at it."

"Good. Maybe they won't bug me about their storage anymore."

*Jayda Cruz, our upgrades are needed for the good work we do. As 2 Corinthians 9:8 instructs us, "And God is able to bless you abundantly, so that in all things at all times, **having all that you need**, you will abound in every good work."*

Zander sniggered. "Huh. Guess they told you."

I sighed. "Yeah, they did. Sorry, Nano. I really appreciate all you do, and I shouldn't have grumbled about your needs."

We forgive you, Jayda Cruz. Besides, complaining is more suited to Special Agent Grumble.

I had to, again, wrap my arms around my abdomen and hold on until I could stop laughing. "Please!" I begged.

"A merry heart does good like a medicine," Jayda Cruz.

Still hugging myself so I didn't hurt, I admitted, "Yes, Nano. It surely does. Thank you."

We take our responsibilities to heart, Jayda Cruz.

"Um, sorry? What?"

Jesus has entrusted aspects of your welfare and wellbeing to us, Jayda Cruz. He is the Creator. We take our obedience to him seriously.

"Uh, yeah. Yes. Us, too. And thank you, Nano."

I looked at Zander; he shook his head and switched up the conversation. "Jay, do you remember Dredd telling us that most of Mal's crew lived at the clubhouse?"

"Sure."

"Well, it's going to take months, maybe longer, for them to repair all the damage to the clubhouse, and no one can sleep there until they get a new certificate of occupancy. So, while the work goes on, Mal's rented some furnished apartments outside Baltimore for his crew. Gamble and Trujillo are going to hang out there while Trujillo gets her strength back."

"Mal rented that many apartments?"

"Actually, he's leased a ten-unit building in an upscale, gated apartment complex. The units are all studios, but that's all the guys need. They're adding some extra security measures to the building, too."

We couldn't go back to our apartment either. "We should think about setting up in a new place. You must be really tired of sleeping in a chair."

"What I'm tired of is not snuggling with you."

I flushed with happiness. "Me, too."

"Well, that's the thing. Mal's offered us a unit in the building he leased. We can move in today."

"Really? I mean . . . that's so kind of him. And also? It's a little reassuring."

"Yeah, since we haven't sussed out the mystery woman, she remains a danger to all of us—Gamble, Trujillo, Malware, Inc., and us. We're thinking safety in numbers, a perimeter surveillance system, rotating guards. The whole nine yards."

"What about Abe and Emilio? Izzie and your folks?"

"They're safe for now."

"But how long can they stay hidden, away from their normal lives?"

"I dunno, but like you said, we need to play offense, not defense. Identifying and taking down this mystery woman comes next."

"Zander, do you think we blew it by forcing Danforth's hand? He was our only connection to her, to the woman."

Zander tore off a piece of garlic naan bread and considered before he replied. "Danforth seemed to be her Number 2, meaning she relied a lot on him and, I imagine, on the NSA resources he provided. Now she's lost that entire connection. Gamble says the President has ordered that everything and everyone in the agency be scrutinized by outside eyes."

"How effective do you think that will be?"

He looked thoughtful. "The Deep State hides in plain sight behind rules, regulations, and red tape. They are patient and can afford to wait because, as federal employees, they are just about impossible to fire. They will outlast elected officials whose agenda or worldview they disagree with. I believe the woman's allies inside the NSA will just pull their heads in and lay low to avoid detection.

"But, to answer your question, no. I don't think we blew it. In the immediate future anyway, I think taking out Danforth makes our mystery woman more vulnerable."

I wasn't sure I agreed, but I allowed Zander's response to reassure me.

⌘

WE TIDIED UP GAMBLE'S meeting place, gathered the few things Zander had brought over from our apartment, and had a cab pick us up a few blocks from the house. It was around 8 p.m. when we stood in front of a newly installed barred security door and rang the bell. We looked up at the cameras and waved.

Dredd's voice came over the intercom. "Ripley! John-Boy! Good to see you two. Come on up to Apartment E."

The lock on the door released. We walked into a breezeway that bisected the two-story building and passed a laundry room on one side and a workout room on the other before we reached a stairwell.

Zander walked a little further down the breezeway. "Looks like apartments A and B straight ahead on the left and C and D on the right. Guess E through J are upstairs,"

We climbed up to the second floor and found Apartment E. Mal opened the door to us.

"Hey. Glad you came. Ripley, how are you feeling?"

"I'm doing okay. It's really good to see you again, Mal."

"What about me?" Dredd hollered from inside.

"Especially you, Dredd," I called back. "You own the magic machine that brews the Elixir of Life!"

"Good to know I'm loved for myself."

We all chuckled, then Mal gestured for us to come in.

A studio apartment isn't big; Dredd's equipment took up all the available space in the main room, leaving just a tiny kitchen and a bathroom.

"Well, as you can see, we've set up our command center here, and the armory is next door in Apartment F," Mal murmured. He pointed to a monitor. "We have a guard hidden on the roof and another walking the perimeter at all times—discreetly, of course. Our cameras cover every approach, and we mounted a few farther out into the apartment complex."

He dangled a set of keys. "We've assigned you Apartment I. Gamble is in J with Logan; Trujillo is on the other side of you in H."

I didn't know how to thank him. "You didn't have to take us in like this, Mal."

"Yes, I did. You and John-Boy are part of our crew now, Ripley. You've earned your spot with us."

"But . . . we kind of brought all this trouble on you. I mean, you wouldn't even be in this mess if you hadn't taken us to the clubhouse."

"I told you. You're Americans. We share a common enemy." He leaned closer and whispered, "And I haven't forgotten what you did to save all of us even though you've wiped everyone else's memories. In my book that makes us family. End of discussion."

He waved us out the door. "Go on. Get set up in your new digs."

Mal's inclusion and generosity touched me deeply. I nodded and got out of there before I cried or something.

'Cause that would really mess with Ripley's rep.

⌘⌘⌘⌘

CHAPTER 33

WE HAD A GROUP MEETING Saturday morning to go over all of the security protocols and to insert Zander and me into the work rotation—me in the command center until I healed all the way and Zander on guard duty.

By noon the next day, we'd started to settle into "compound" living with Mal's crew. Unfortunately, the next day was Sunday.

"We'll miss church this morning," Zander sighed, "not that we dare paint a target on our friends at Grace Chapel by showing up there. I hope someday we can convince Pastor Lucklow that we're not the losers he probably thinks we are."

"We've missed our Bible time with the Lord for an entire week, too," I reminded him. "I feel . . . stale and dry. I need a big drink of living water!"

"Hard to have regular devotions when we're running and gunning for our lives."

"*Running and gunning?* We're picking up Malware lingo now? Listen, we need some Bible time. Since we missed church this morning, we should have church here. You and me."

He glanced at me. I could see the wheels turning behind his eyes. "Actually . . . that's a great idea, Jay."

"What did you have in mind?"

Now a devious light sparked in his eyes. "You and me and all of Malware, Inc."

"Ooooh! Spill it, mister."

⌘

WE INVITED EVERYONE (Mal and his five-man crew plus Gamble and Trujillo) to dinner and "chapel" that evening in the workout room. To a person, our invitations were met with skepticism and narrow-eyed resistance. To a person, Zander shrugged and said, "What we're facing is bigger than all of us. We need God's help. I'm not afraid to ask him for it—are you?"

Our macho friends professed to be afraid of nothing, so the challenge had an effect—of sorts.

"I'll come to dinner, but I probably won't stay for the other," was Mal's even reply.

"Yeah. What he said," McFly added.

"Sure. You decide," Zander said. "I'm making my mom's enchiladas."

Deckard smacked his lips. "Oh, I'm not gonna pass on *that*. Just, you know, I'm not a religious person."

"Good. I'm not either."

Mal loaned us a car to go get groceries and sent Baltar with us to ride shotgun. From there on, Zander was in charge. He ordered Baltar and me up and down the supermarket aisles getting this and that—including spices I'd never heard of. Back at the apartments, he commandeered pots, pans, and dishes from other apartments and ran our little kitchen like a battlefield.

Baltar fled as soon as he could. I would have, too, but, being married to the guy, I was more or less stuck. By the time we finished at six that evening, we had three ginormous pans of red chile enchiladas (two chicken and one pork), a huge tossed salad, two pans of a cheesy/spicy rice dish, and a couple of gallons of sweet iced tea.

Logan and McFly set up two tables and a dozen folding chairs in the weight room for us and laid the tables with plates, forks, glasses, and paper napkins scavenged from their apartments. Then they helped us haul the food downstairs.

Everyone came. We chowed down, complimented Zander on his enchiladas, told jokes, laughed at each other, and generally had a wonderful time. I think it was the most fun any of us had enjoyed in a while. I know it was for Zander and me.

I was particularly glad to see Trujillo. Her face was a ridiculous mess of bruises and stitches, but she seemed . . . content. Might have been the way Gamble waited on her hand and foot, seeing that she had what she wanted to eat or drink, fetching a pillow for her back. Behaving like a total *dork*.

I loved it.

"What?" he demanded. "You're grinning like the village idiot."

"I'm happy for you, Gamble."

He blushed. "Oh. Yeah. That."

"Yeah," I said dryly. "*That*."

Dinner wound down, but before anyone could run from the promised "chapel" time, Zander pushed back his chair and stood.

"Look, I'll keep this short. Deckard told me he's not religious, and I don't want to mess with his bad-boy status."

We hooted and pointed at Deckard. He bowed in mock acknowledgment.

"The only thing I wanted to share with you is this, from the Gospel of John, Chapter 3. Now, in this passage, Jesus *is* talking to a religious person, but the guy didn't get what Jesus was telling him. See, religion makes us deaf and blind to the good news. Religion is like an inoculation, a vaccine: It prevents you from catching the real deal.

"Jesus put it this way—and I'm going to paraphrase it here, so please don't fact check me—you in particular, Gamble. I see you reaching for your phone!"

Zander's self-deprecation and light humor elicited more good-natured laughter, but I blinked back tears. He was so kind when he shared the Gospel! He had an amazing gift, a calling from God, a powerful anointing to do just this: to speak the truth in love—and it completely blew me away, every time.

The first time I'd heard him—as he preached to the homeless in Albuquerque—I had been both awed and convicted. The Lord had used Zander's words to jumpstart my journey back to him. I would forever be grateful.

"Anyway, what Jesus said was, 'Look. I didn't come into the world to condemn it; I came into the world to save it—the world is already going to hell in a handbasket, so I came to save it.'

"Think about that for a sec. Isn't that the opposite of what you've heard? Haven't you been told that God can't wait to judge you, that he's sitting up there right now with a big stick, just salivating over the beatdown he's planning for you?"

A few heads nodded.

"Yes, we will all answer for the lives we have lived and, considering some of the things we've done, that is a scary proposition."

Zander looked around. "You-all know me as John-Boy. *John-Boy.* Yeah, kind of a geeky guy. Squeaky-clean." He grinned. "Hard to figure why a hot babe like Ellen Ripley would choose me, right?"

Snorts and snickers. Baltar raised his hand, "Don't you fret; I'm here when you get tired of him, Rip."

More laughs, and McFly jumped in, "Don't settle for that old man, Ripley!"

Baltar roared, "Who you calling old?"

Zander grinned, too. Then, when the laughter started to subside, he dropped the bomb.

"Yeah, nerdy me. What you don't know about me . . . are the years I spent in an American-Mexican gang, about the drugs I peddled, the innocent girls I pimped, the drinking, the sex, the violence. I have a lot to answer for."

No one was laughing anymore.

"I thank God that someone had the guts to tell me the truth about my need for God. See, one day, out of the blue, this old dude walked up to me on the street and said that God made me in his image, that he loved me the way a father loves his child.

"He asked me, 'Do you like this life? Or do you want a new one?' Well, I wanted to pull a blade on that old guy. I'm telling you, I wanted to stick him in the *worst way*.

"But he just kept on talking. He told me that God never wanted distance between me and him. That it was not God's idea or desire for me to wander away, to be separated from him.

"Then he told me about the fix—God's Plan B. What's Plan B? I want you to think about the attack on the clubhouse last Tuesday morning, just five days ago. We were hit with superior numbers and overwhelming firepower. That Black Hawk hovered in the street and strafed the clubhouse with .50cal BMG rounds. Nothing—*nothing*—survived that barrage.

"With the outer walls breached, you were forced to retreat into the training center. You had reinforced that room, too, but the opposition planted charges that blew right through your thick walls. If they hadn't knocked themselves out with their own gas, we might have lost that battle.

"Well, what if we had lost? I want you to remember the panic room in the training room. With the clubhouse breached and burning around us, you still had an ace in the hole. You had built, inside the panic room, a bug-out hatch and a tunnel that led to safety—a way out. A way to escape certain death. And I want to remind you that the bug-out tunnel was the *only* way out of the clubhouse once it was overrun.

"God made a way out, too. A way to escape the coming reckoning. For all the sinful, wicked, unconscionable things I had done in my past, for every appalling act I had committed, God made a way of escape.

"His name is Jesus."

⌘⌘⌘⌘

CHAPTER 34

IT WAS STILL EARLY the next morning when I heard a soft tapping on our door.

I nudged Zander. "Hey. Someone's knocking."

He climbed from the sofa bed, pulled a t-shirt over his shorts, and cracked the door.

The visitor whispered, "Sorry to wake you, John-Boy, but you're due on the roof in fifteen. Didn't know if you were up or not."

"Thanks, McFly. I wasn't. I appreciate you waking me."

"Yeah, no worries. Um, say, I thought about what you said last night. In fact, I didn't sleep much, thinking about it. I . . . I'd like to ask you a few questions."

"Sure, man."

Zander eased out of our apartment onto the walkway. I could have used the nanomites to listen in, but I didn't. Instead, I prayed.

Lord, your word goes out like bread upon the water. It goes out to accomplish your purposes, and it does not return empty or fruitless. I ask that you have your way in McFly's heart this day. Like you wooed me, please draw him by your Spirit. I'm asking in the name of Jesus that you bring him into your kingdom.

⌘

THE WOMAN STEPPED OUT of her home and onto the back patio. The morning was warm and the air moist, filled with the scent of pine sap and flowering shrubs as were most summer days in Virginia. She walked to the edge of the patio and gazed across the expanse of lawn to the thick woods bordering her property. Out there, among the trees, her personal guards were patrolling the fence line, vigilant to protect her.

She began to walk a path that wound around the house. She did her best thinking on her feet, on the move, and the question that was on her mind this morning had preoccupied her for the past four days: How had the President come into possession of evidence that implicated Danforth in the elimination of that meddling fool, Overman?

Furthermore, how had Danforth's situation so degraded over the course of one night that, according to her unimpeachable source in the White House, Danforth had thrown himself into the arms of the Russians?

A rash move, Lawrence, but you were no fool, she reminded herself. *After many years in my acquaintance, you knew when your usefulness to me was at an end. To save your worthless skin, you attempted to put yourself out of my reach.*

The former question remained: How had President Jackson found Danforth out?

It had to be Gemma Keyes—or whatever she calls herself—Gemma/Jayda and the nanomites.

The woman paused her pacing. *Danforth was right to be concerned. Jayda and Zander Cruz moved here the last weekend in May. Conceivably, they could have been in the White House for weeks, deactivating listening devices, sickening the Secret Service agents loyal to our cause, even informing the President of their progress.*

No wonder her operatives had been unable to locate the Cruz's loved ones in New Mexico: Jayda and her husband had warned them to hide.

"We have been behind in the game for months, while Jayda and her husband have systematically stymied our progress and every move we've made against the President."

She began walking again. *No, not every move. Not all our progress. They cannot know all.*

Few people knew that the woman had served in America's intelligence community in her early years. Those who *did* know had no inkling that she had served her own needs concurrently, acting the agent provocateur—double agent and even triple agent when it suited her objectives or paid well enough.

When she retired from covert work, she had accumulated substantial wealth and had turned her intellect to other disciplines: engineering, physics, chemistry, and the behavioral sciences. She relished and ingested knowledge much as a predator does meat, snapping up what satiated her hunger, what appealed to her senses, what informed her interests and needs.

The nanomites were of such significance to her, both intellectually and politically. She had devoured the reports Cushing had pushed up the chain to Harmon; she had foreseen the vital role the mites would play in their plans. But the behaviors she had witnessed when Jayda and Zander Cruz had defeated her task force's attack on Malware, Inc.? Those powers were beyond anything she had envisioned—and, oh! How she lusted to acquire and wield such abilities herself.

Jayda and Zander's demonstration had opened the woman's eyes. By studying the helmet videos of their second attack on Malware Inc., she had construed how the nanomites worked through the couple and, more importantly, what was *required* for the nanomites to do so.

Four days ago, she had tasked a trusted security company to construct a room to her precise specifications. She had expended a great deal of money and personal "persuasion" to speed the construction and stem the crew's curiosity. The room was not yet ready—but it would be soon. In the meantime, other activities associated with their advancing plans intruded upon her.

I shall greatly dislike leaving this house, this refuge from the world, but leaving it is, after all, a necessary evil.

She walked on. The woman knew the path around her house by heart and did not need to watch her steps. Head down, eyes closed in concentration, she continued to probe for her adversaries' weaknesses.

They may have warned their friends and relatives in New Mexico to hide, but I must assume that they have made friends here, too, she reasoned. *I must explore a little deeper and probe their personal interactions since moving to Maryland.*

Nodding to herself, she thought, *No, Jayda and Zander Cruz, you do not know everything. By this coming weekend, the jaws of my pincers will be ready to clamp down. I need only to acquire the appropriate bait for the trap.*

⌘⌘⌘⌘

CHAPTER 35

NOT MUCH HAPPENED over the next five days. Agent Kennedy summoned us to the White House to brief the President on the status of our investigation, but we had little to report. President Jackson looked disappointed and worn, while Kennedy's ever-cool attitude toward us turned downright frosty.

Mal appointed Zander to regular turns on guard duty and assigned me to the command center's schedule. On my first shift, I was under Dredd's supervision, so he could tutor me on how everything worked. After a few minutes, he sat back in disgust.

"You obviously know your way around surveillance systems, Ripley, although this one is my own configuration. I even built most of the components myself. Don't know how you figured out my shortcuts so fast."

"I, um, have a sort of affinity for computers, electronics, stuff like that."

"Sure, pal. Well, since I'm not needed here, I'm going back to bed. Only got four hours last night."

"G'night, Dredd. Sleep tight."

Alone in the command center, I set some of the nanomites to watching the perimeter. They were a far more effective perimeter watch system than what we had in place.

I peeked in on the nanobug arrays we'd planted on Danforth's NSA SPOs, but they had little to report. The officers were awaiting trial in federal lockup and were being kept in isolation, meaning they had no contact with each other or anyone else.

I also listened in on the four dirty White House Secret Service agents. They had been declared fit for duty and restored to their White House posts, but what the nanomites reported and what I heard myself via their arrays was mostly confusion. Secret Service Deputy Assistant Director, Blake Morningside, conspicuous for his silence, had, I speculated, cut the White House agents adrift.

It seemed to me that Danforth's death had opened a yawning hole in our opposition's leadership ranks, a void that no one had stepped up to fill.

And while the nanomites kept working to put a name to the mystery woman, it seemed she had vanished like a wisp of smoke on a breeze. For five days, we caught no scent of her. For five days we fidgeted, spun our wheels, and made no progress. For five days we maintained our vigilance and never once glimpsed any indication, inkling, or hint of the trap she had declared she would devise.

Until its teeth clamped down on us.

⌘

JAYDA CRUZ, MACY UUMBANA IS CALLING.

"Oh, cool!"

I picked up the call. "Hey, Macy! How are you, girlfriend? How are my sweet babies, Denzel and Deshaun?"

The frantic sobbing on the other end of the line froze the words on my lips.

"Jayda! They took our babies! *They took them!* They said it's *your* fault, that *you* made them do it!"

She cursed me then, calling down horrible epithets on my head, swearing she hated me and that she'd rip me apart with her teeth and bare hands if anything happened to her babies.

As she dissolved into hopeless and inarticulate sobs, I whispered, "Nano, get Zander. Hurry."

Yes, Jayda Cruz.

To my weeping, distraught friend, I vowed. "Macy? Macy, we're coming. Don't lose hope. We will find your babies, I promise you."

O God! We need you!

I hung up and used the radio to call for Mal. When Zander and Mal arrived, I tried to explain, but I made a hash of it. I couldn't form the words, so badly did my throat and chest hurt.

I couldn't play the stoic role of Ellen Ripley. Not for this.

In the end, the nanomites had to explain the situation to Zander. He passed the information to Mal, and Mal called Dredd to take over the command center.

Then he huddled up with me and Zander. "You guys didn't remove my memories of what you did to win the battle at our clubhouse. I *saw* you in action, and I know you have more firepower than Malware has. How do you want to handle this? And what do you need from us?"

"We'll go the Uumbanas' first," Zander answered. "Whoever stole the babies may have left a message for us."

"Take one of our vehicles."

"Thanks."

Zander put his arm around me. "Jay?"

I shoved my anguish into an iron box of my own construction. I slammed the lid tight. Locked it. I sucked up all my tears and hardened my heart against the pain and fear.

"Yeah. I'm ready."

Zander and I drove in silence, both of us twisted up in our own thoughts, mine circling around a single word:

Bait.

We thought we'd hidden those we loved, but the mystery woman had simply probed our lives until she found another vulnerability with which to bait her trap.

Well played.

O Jesus! O Lord! How could we have been so foolish and blind? Our shortsightedness has caused this heartache. Please don't let our mistake cause any harm to come to these precious babies.

⌘

WE HAD BEEN SILENT thirty-five minutes by the time we arrived at the Uumbanas' house near Ft. Meade. Darius met us at the door and, if looks could have killed, Zander and I would have been DRT—*Dead Right There*—scorched into the cement of the porch where we stood. Without comment, Darius led us into the house.

From within, we heard little Daniel Uumbana sobbing. When we entered the living room, Macy was rocking the boy, her own tears raining down on Daniel's curly head.

"Mama, want Denz!" Daniel wailed. "Want 'Shaun, Mama!"

I felt lower than dirt and could think of nothing to say by way of greeting that would not pour gasoline on the grief raging over Macy and her son.

Zander took the lead. "Darius and Macy? We're going to get your babies back. Please tell us what happened—word for word."

"We don't need to. They left you this." Darius' eyes glittered like hard, black stones as he tossed a weighty, sealed envelope at Zander.

Before opening the envelope, Zander looked at Darius. "I know you have no reason to believe or trust us, but we are brokenhearted that those who hate us have taken it out on you."

"Save it. We're not interested." Anger oozed from every syllable.

I couldn't take my eyes off Macy, the way she held Daniel. She was terrified he would be snatched from her arms.

Like her babies were.

I was going to be sick. I lurched toward the front door and made it outside before my stomach purged its contents.

Then Zander was there. He turned on the Uumbanas' hose, helped me rinse my mouth, and sprayed the ick off their sidewalk.

"We need to go, Jay."

We got back in the car. There Zander opened the envelope left for us. It contained a generic smartphone and a typed note.

The note was short. To the point. Unequivocal.

We have the infants. If you follow the instructions we provide, we will return the children unharmed. However, until you complete the instructions, the babies will not be fed. The longer you delay, the hungrier they will become.

We are monitoring both you and the destination to which the instructions will eventually lead you. We will know if anyone follows you or approaches within two miles of your destination.

Disable your vehicle's GPS. Toss your phones. Find the closest Taco Bell. Your next instruction is taped under a table.

The nanomites severed the wires to the car's GPS for us. Then we dumped our phones on the curb. I used the provided smartphone to find the nearest Taco Bell. When we arrived, the place was packed, the lunch rush underway.

We didn't care.

We went from table to table, squatting and feeling each underside, ignoring protests and rude comments until we found the folded note and tore the tape holding it in place.

"You guys on a scavenger hunt?" an excited kid asked.

Zander mumbled, "Something like that," before we rushed to our car.

From point to point, the instructions led us, moving us farther north, then west, until we were around thirty miles due west of D.C. wandering down the roads in a wooded semi-rural area where the properties were a few acres each and houses far apart. We were looking for a mailbox with a horse on it.

We found the red box with the black horse painted on it and the note on the box's underside.

Drive north. Turn left at the third driveway.
Follow the drive. Enter the house.

Our destination was a simple farmhouse on the outside. Within, things were not so simple.

Jayda and Zander Cruz, this structure has been subject to extensive modifications and is heavily shielded.

"Is this where Danforth and the woman watched us rescue Trujillo?"

Very likely, Jayda Cruz.

Someone had used painter's tape to create arrows on the floor. The arrows led down a narrow hallway, turned left, and stopped at a door. We opened the door and discovered steps leading down into a basement. A dotted line of tape pointed the way. A soft light emanated from below.

Zander put his mouth to my ear. "I'll go first. Don't come down until I signal you."

"Okay."

A minute later, he called to me, and I joined him. The dim light we'd seen from the top of the stairs shone from a corner of the basement.

How can I describe what that light revealed?

Someone had gutted the high-beamed basement and laid bare its concrete walls and floor. In the center of the basement someone had drilled out the floor forming a two-foot-deep pit, perhaps five feet by five feet square, and had poured a new floor and cement sides for the trench. Within the pit, workers had built a room, around six feet high but, I estimated, ten inches less in width than the five-feet-square pit, so more like four feet by four feet.

The result was a cell large enough for two people to stand in but two feet lower than the rest of the basement floor.

An arrow of blue tape pointed to the cell's small, hatch-like doorway.

Zander and I did not move. We'd reached the trip wire—the trap's trigger mechanism—and our nerves were jangling. The nanomites were alarmed, too, but their continual clicking in my ear was not helping a whit.

"Nano, stop that, please."

I scrutinized the cell's other unusual characteristics: Its walls, floor, and ceiling were made of dual sheets of clear material—not glass, but a type of thick plastic. A cage of fine metal mesh was sandwiched between the plastic sheets. I say *a cage*, because the metal mesh formed four walls, a ceiling, and a floor. Its only interruption was the little doorway. In all, the ingeniously built cell consisted of three cubes—a metal mesh cage lined inside and out with plastic-like walls, floors, and ceilings.

"Nano?"

Electrostatic dissipative acrylic, Jayda Cruz, encasing a cage of electromagnetic shielding. A sophisticated Faraday cage.

A Faraday cage. Used to protect people and equipment from electric discharge or current. A Faraday cage's conductive material sends current around the outside of the enclosed space, allowing none of the electricity to enter or pass through the interior.

"Zander . . ."

"Yeah, I get it. If we go in there, we won't be able to draw down on any nearby electrical sources."

Oh, and I can't leave this last bit out: Yet *another* cage hung suspended from the basement's high ceiling over the three cubes. I glanced into the shallow pit and saw a metal track on the pit's floor, running around the three-walled acrylic/metal mesh cell. It looked like the suspended cage was designed to drop over the cell and snap onto the track.

I scanned the basement and found what I was looking for: a power source. An oversized electrical panel was built onto one wall; thick wires led from it . . . into the pit.

Nudging Zander, I asked, "How much you want to bet those wires connect to that metal track?"

"Not taking that bet."

A second source of light brightened behind us, and I turned my head toward it. A monitor. No, two monitors—also encased in a cage of fine metal mesh.

I tugged Zander's sleeve.

On one of the screens we saw Denzel and Deshaun. They were laying end to end, their heads touching, on the back seat of a car. They appeared to be sleeping.

On the other screen, from deep within the shadows a woman's voice spoke. "Mr. and Mrs. Cruz. I'm so glad to make your acquaintance in person—at long last."

She moved into the camera's view: the mystery woman.

She was a tiny thing, her age not easy to guess, but *her eyes!* I knew them. They gleamed gold and amber in the low light.

"Gemma Keyes. You have led me on a merry chase this past year and a half, I must say."

The accent, although faint, was still there, of Asian extraction, coupled, perhaps, with a British inflection?

"Please. Do not be alarmed or concerned. I have no intention of harming either of you."

Neither Zander nor I answered her.

Jayda Cruz, "Enemies disguise themselves with their lips, but in their hearts they harbor deceit. Though their speech is charming, do not believe them, for seven abominations fill their hearts."

"Yeah, Nano. She has no intention of harming us? Right. We've kind of got that one figured out."

Zander asked, "Nano? Can you piggyback on her feed? Get word to Gamble or Mal where we are?"

Zander Cruz, the monitors are surrounded by a field of fluctuating electrostatic discharge that we cannot penetrate. The cabling to the monitors is encased in a similar field that runs outside this house and extends beyond our reach. We have already lost many members in our attempts to reach her feed. Given enough time we could—

"Wireless access?"

The entire facility is shielded. No wireless signal can penetrate the shielding.

The woman cleared her throat. "I invite you to give your attention to the other screen."

The camera on the babies zoomed out of the car, looked down the street, and stopped on the Uumbanas' house.

"As you can see, the children are not far from their home. When both of you enter the cage, my people will return the infants to their parents. You have precisely sixty seconds to comply. If you choose not to, my people will reenter your friends' home and take hold of the three-year-old boy.

"*Listen carefully*: At that point, *no matter what you do*, my people have orders to slit the boy's throat in front of his parents. The clock starts now."

A counter reading 00.60 appeared on the woman's monitor. It began counting down.

00.59

00.58

I started to panic. "How do we know you'll return the babies?" I shouted.

She shrugged. "I am not a monster. I have no reason to harm them."

I gasped. "Not a monster? *Not a monster?*"

"I have seen many children die at the hands of this nation's military. Does that not make this nation monstrous?"

Zander tugged at me. "Jayda. Forty seconds."

"I know, *I know*—but the babies—"

The woman's voice, sing-song and melodic, continued. "After the boy dies, you will realize that I am a woman of my word. I will give you an opportunity to save the infants before my people slit their throats—one at a time, just like their brother."

"No! You wouldn't!"

"Jay! Thirty seconds!"

I shook off Zander's hand and stuck my face into the camera above the monitor.

"Anyone who would harm a child *is* a monster," I hissed, "a monster who needs to be destroyed. If you harm those children, *I will kill you.*"

I knew I was wrong, that my thirst for "right" was really vengeance masquerading as "justice." Right then, in my anger, I didn't care.

I marched to the cell and climbed through the little door, sensing as soon as I stood how claustrophobic its dimensions were.

Zander followed me in, headfirst, the hatch harder for his larger frame to crawl through. When he stood, the top of his head brushed the ceiling—and the counter ticked down to fifteen seconds.

Fourteen. Thirteen. Twelve. Eleven.

The entrance to the cell did not close. I clutched at Zander's hand.

Lord! Not little Daniel! Please protect him!

Ten. Nine. Eight. Seven.

The cell still remained open.

Six. Five. Four. Three.

A metal mesh screen flashed across the entrance and clicked into place. An acrylic panel crossed from the opposite side, completing the inside acrylic cube. A second acrylic panel slid into place completing the outer cube.

Then the cage hanging from the ceiling descended to the cement floor. Its bottom edge locked onto the metal rails in the floor of the pit. Across the basement, the electrical panel came alive and a *thrum* of current crackled through the cage.

The counter hit zero.

"Keep your word!" I screamed. "Give the babies back!"

"Watch."

She spoke into her phone and the second monitor went dark. A minute passed, then several, before the screen came back to life. Denzel and Deshaun were lying on Darius and Macy's front porch. The monitor again went dark, and Zander and I waited, hoping it would light up and would show someone opening the front door.

From far down the street, the live feed reengaged and focused on the Uumbanas' house. Even at a distance, we could see the outlines of the babies. The temperature was warm, but I worried for the newborns lying on the cool cement porch without a blanket to cushion them.

Oh, Macy, I urged her silently. *Open your door!*

The feed was without sound, but we saw the moment someone cracked the front door. It was little Daniel who stood there, gaping. Throwing the door wide open, he ran back inside.

Moments later, Macy and Darius appeared. They scooped the babies up and disappeared inside.

The monitor went dark.

"Thank you, Lord," I breathed.

The golden-eyed woman smirked. "Thank you, *Lord*? Oh, that's right. You are both quite religious."

"No, we are not," Zander answered, "but that's neither here nor there in this moment. What do you want with us?"

The woman feigned a little *moue* of surprise. "Why, the nanomites, of course."

"Well, good luck with that."

"Hmm. Yes. I'm operating on many suppositions—not that my suppositions are uninformed or baseless. I derived them from the data General Cushing provided, from her first-hand experiences with Gemma, and from my own observations.

"I am," she said with a modicum of modesty, "a student of the sciences myself with interests in physics, engineering, and material science."

"Bully for you. Won't get you the nanomites."

She chuckled. "Perhaps. My assumptions could be in error, but I am rarely wrong. Shall we test them, my assumptions? Let's see. First, the nanomites require electrical power to function, and they can draw it from any ready source such as the sun and nearby electrical wiring. *Even from you*. Am I correct?"

We didn't answer.

"Your silence is confirmation enough. Thank you. Second, your wonderful weapons—I assure you I was both astonished and delighted by your demonstrations—require electrical power, too, although my calculations tell me that, to wield such powerful weapons, you must have a strong power source on which to draw. Is this right?"

She leaned toward the camera. "Please do me the kindness of testing my theory? I really must know if you can blast your way out of my little structure."

I slid my eyes toward Zander. He had a hand cupped behind his back and was attempting to pull current into his palm. The harder he tried—with no result—the farther down his mouth turned.

Zander Cruz, the Faraday cage prevents electricity from passing into this box. As you surmised earlier, we are unable to access the house's electricity from inside this box.

The woman nodded slowly. "May I deduce from your vexation, Mr. Cruz, that you have attempted to draw current into the cage and are unable to? Excellent."

"If you know so much about the nanomites, then you know they can easily penetrate the walls of this acrylic/metal cage and escape."

She spread her child-sized hands. Something about the sight seemed familiar, but I couldn't place it.

"If they can escape, why have they not done so? Why haven't they left the cage, drawn current from the house's wiring, and broken you free? Is it, perhaps, that the nanomites are susceptible to static discharge—and that they comprehend that the outermost cage is fully charged?"

"Nano?" I whispered.

Jayda Cruz, she is correct. Ordinarily, if threatened by static discharge or an electric pulse, the nanocloud would propel a stronger layer of current ahead of us to shield ourselves and you. We cannot do so in these circumstances. If we were to penetrate the acrylic and mesh layers, we could not draw enough current from the charged cage to shield ourselves before the cage's discharge damaged us.

Chittering to themselves, they added, *This woman has devised a very clever trap.*

The woman sat back and tapped her chin. "I believe Colonel Greaves shot you with a Taser, did he not, Jayda? Or do you prefer Gemma? General Cushing was convinced that the Taser destroyed a large number of your nanomites and rendered you powerless.

"My third assumption, then, is that the charged outer cage has trapped the nanomites within the cell just as you are trapped. Do you see that panel on the wall over there? I had my electricians bring a new 220-volt service into the house, one separate from the house's other service, to supply the outer cage.

"All this leads me to supposition number four: The nanomites cannot survive without electricity, and *you*, as their host, cannot survive without the nanomites. I'm most interested in knowing the validity of this assumption—because I am counting on them leaving you to save themselves."

"You won't get the nanomites. We have . . . a relationship with them. They will not leave us," Zander insisted.

"Oh, I believe they will, given the right circumstances. You see, General Cushing provided us with a number of Dr. Bickel's programming algorithms, and I have studied them. The good doctor encoded the nanomites with the mandate *to survive at all costs*, and no source of electricity exists within the cage—except for you and your lovely bride, of course."

She mocked us with her next words. "The nanomites will be obliged to drain you to survive, and you cannot feed them forever, can you? Do you know what will happen when they have used you up? I am convinced you do."

My first experience with the nanomites' drain came roaring back. I'd woken up because something was stinging me, because my right hand felt on fire. I was disoriented and weak, unable even to sit on the side of the bed without falling to the floor. I'd crawled a few feet to the door and used the doorframe to pull myself up. As I'd reached a little higher, my fingers had encountered the light switch—and my palm had fastened to the switch plate. The nanomites had glued my hand there while they "fed" from the current inside the switch box.

If the nanomites hadn't awakened me, I would have died in my sleep.

Yes. I knew what would happen when they used us up.

"When your bodies have failed beyond recovery, the nanomites will leave you willingly and enter the human hosts we will provide. By my calculations, twenty-four hours should suffice for the nanomites to use you up. By then, they will be inclined to adopt new hosts."

The woman lifted a phone and pressed a contact's number. "You may approach the house now."

Jayda and Zander Cruz, what that woman says is true. Our programming requires us to survive. That being said, we do not wish to drain you, to kill you. This would not please Jesus, nor would it please us.

"I don't know what to tell you, Nano. Are you certain you cannot reach outside this . . . this enclosure?"

We are certain, Jayda Cruz. We sent Delta Tribe members through the walls: They did not return. Therefore, to maximize the length of time we can survive without damaging you or us, we will initiate our emergency shutdown protocols and send all tribes but Alpha Tribe into sleep mode.

I sat down. "I suppose we should enter 'low power mode' ourselves."

That would be wise, Jayda Cruz. "The path of life leads upward for the prudent, to keep them from going down to the realm of the dead."

"You're so edifying, Nano." *Not.*

Zander plopped down next to me. "Nano, I am going to give you an order, and I expect you to follow it to the degree that you can. Do you understand?"

We will do our best, Zander Cruz.

"I want you to put me into a deep sleep."

I went from desperate to furious in a blink. "What? No, Zander!"

"Nano? I will use less energy while asleep, won't I?"

This is true, Zander Cruz.

"Then knock me out. Do it."

Zander laid down and tried to stretch out; the best he could do in the four-by-four cube was roll to his side and pull his knees up.

I took his hand and held it in mine. "Sweetie?"

"Yes?"

"I love you."

"You know that I love you, too."

I gripped his hand. "I'm sure the Lord has an answer. We just need to trust him. Call on him."

"I trust him, Jay. I do. And if we don't make it out of here alive? I'll still trust him, and I'll . . . see you . . . in . . . heav—."

"Zander?"

He is sleeping, Jayda Cruz. May we suggest that you lie down and rest, too?

But I couldn't do that while that evil creature, from a safe distance, observed us like bugs under glass. I curled up to Zander's back, but I kept my eyes on her. Soon I started feeling sort of "funny." Hollow inside. Empty-ish.

Oh. The tribes. Going off line, going into survival mode.

That warmth in my lower abdomen where I'd taken the round intensified momentarily, then faded to less than I'd been accustomed to. But it was still there.

"No sense wasting resources on my wound, Nano. Send those nanomites into sleep mode, too."

They didn't answer me.

I blinked, my eyes suddenly heavy, and wondered if I was already feeling the drain. Then I heard footfalls overhead and pushed myself up to sitting. Four booted men clomped down the basement steps.

The woman noticed, too. "You have arrived. Good."

She spoke to me. "I do apologize, Jayda, but I have pressing duties to attend to, so it's goodbye, I'm afraid. When I return, I anticipate that both of you will be drained.

"At that time, we will open the box and insert two human hosts of our choosing. If you are not yet dead, we will dispatch you quickly. Out of necessity, the nanomites will migrate to the new hosts who can offer them the electricity they need to sustain themselves. When the nanomites have moved to the new hosts, we will allow them to leave the box."

I pushed myself up to sitting. "I want to say something to you."

She smiled. "Last words?"

"No, a warning."

She laughed low in her throat. "Please, say on."

"Earlier you said we were religious. Well, we're not—because religion is a box very like this one that only serves to separate people from the living God, the Creator of the universe. We aren't religious because we *know* the living God and because he dwells within us through his Son, Jesus."

"Fables. Myths. Religious claptrap."

"I said I had a warning for you, and I meant it. Zander and I belong to the Lord of heaven and earth, which, according to the Bible, makes us his children. God Almighty does not take lightly the ill-treatment of his children."

"I see. Should I be worried?"

"Yes, you should. On the day of your death, you will come face to face with God Almighty. If you stand before the Lord without Jesus, you will face his righteous justice. I'm warning you now to confess your sins and turn to Jesus—before it is too late for you."

"How considerate of you, Mrs. Cruz, but I will take my chances. In the meantime? It is you, not I, for whom it is too late."

I turned my face away. I'd been obedient. I'd warned her. Now I refused to give her the pleasure of seeing the tears running down my face.

Lord?

She must have dialed her phone again and not felt it necessary to move away from the camera. I heard her whisper, "Everything is in order. Yes. Proceed as planned."

Then she addressed her men. "I will return tomorrow evening. Until then, set and maintain a perimeter about one hundred feet out. I charge you with protecting this house and, most importantly, the contents of this cage from any outside intrusion."

The contents of this cage.

She meant the nanomites, not us.

She already considered us dead.

⌘

THE WOMAN'S MONITOR went dark, and the guards went upstairs and outside to take up their posts, leaving us alone. I laid down against Zander's back a second time. That warmth in my abdomen reminded me that I had asked the nanomites to stop worrying over the wound.

"Nano? Don't you need to conserve as much power as you can? Please send the members around my wound into sleep mode."

We have sent all we can, Jayda Cruz. Members of Alpha Tribe have taken their place and will maintain their position until it is no longer possible.

I drew in a shallow breath, sensing a creeping weakness stealing over me. "I don't understand. Why? What's . . . so important that you can't let it go?"

I should have automatically known the answer to that question, but I didn't.

The nanomites were hiding something.

When they didn't respond to me, I probed the nanocloud and found a sliver of Alpha Tribe's library that I was unable to access.

It wasn't the first time the nanomites had hidden things from me. When they had blocked me in the past, their actions had resulted in all-out conflict between us. But today, in our desperate situation? I didn't want to fight with them. If Zander and I were going to die here, I didn't want to die with contention between me and the nanomites. Instead, I just continued to ask them.

"Nano? What are you keeping from me?"

No answer.

"Nano?"

Nothing.

"I'm not going to let this go, so you might as well spill it."

Jayda Cruz, we did not want you to find out under these circumstances. We wished it to be a happy occasion.

I sighed. "If wishes were horses . . . Circumstances being what they are, what we wish doesn't much matter now, does it? Why don't you just tell me. I'd hate to die with secrets between us."

We would not want that either, Jayda Cruz.

I waited, knowing they would tell me soon.

Whatever it was.

Jayda Cruz, we have made many mistakes in our time with you.

"Water under the bridge, Nano. Forgiven. Forgotten."

Yes. Nonetheless, we looked for opportunities to restore what our unintended consequences took from you.

"Okaaaay."

Not okay, Jayda Cruz. We took something precious from you, something that broke your heart—and your grief became ours.

The nanomites lacked the capacity to sigh, but if what I heard (or sensed) at that moment wasn't a sigh, I don't know what else it could have been. Well, I also thought they lacked the capacity to empathize—and I was wrong about that, too.

We told you how our joining with your body impacted your endocrine functions, that our merge sped up your metabolism, enabling you to become an optimal fighter.

"Yes, I remember."

Your accelerated metabolism increased the rate at which your ovaries produced fertile eggs. We told you that your ovaries had depleted your supply of ovum by 91.7 percent.

"I accepted your explanation, Nano, and I forgave you. We don't need to rehash an old offense, an old mistake. It is over. Forgiven and forgotten. I'm asking you to, *please*, let it go."

We cannot let it go, Jayda Cruz, if we have the ability to make amends.

"Amends?"

After we told you that your ovaries were nearly depleted, we searched for and located your last viable eggs. We assigned Omega Tribe to defend and preserve them, to surround them and prevent your endocrine system from expending them. Unfortunately, that clutch of eggs resided in your right ovary.

I was thunderstruck. "What? What are you saying?"

When you were shot, the bullet burst your right ovary, destroying it. However, Omega Tribe was able to save and preserve a single egg. Our conundrum was that your ovary was damaged beyond our ability to repair its functions—and yet we were unwilling to allow your last remaining egg to die. Omega Tribe has, therefore, been acting the role of surrogate ovary, cocooning your egg, keeping it safe and viable until you are ready to use it.

Jayda Cruz, we wished to rejoice with you and Zander on the day when you told us, "Lights out, Nano," and entered into that sacred time and space shared only between husband and wife. When you and Zander came together to create a new life.

When you and Zander came together to create a new life.

I squeezed my eyes shut and sobbed against the curve of Zander's back.

I had relinquished the dream of having children! I had surrendered the hope of giving Zander a son or a daughter of his own. I had given it up and made my peace with it.

The possibility of a baby? The joyous wave receded as quickly as it crashed over me.

I shouldn't have pushed the nanomites into telling me their secret. Why bring it up now when it no longer mattered?

Zander and I wouldn't live long enough to bring a child into the world.

And, I realized . . . all things considered? I was good with that.

"Nano, thank you for . . . telling me."

We did not intend to wound you again, Jayda Cruz. That is why we kept this information from you.

"I understand, and I'm sorry I pressed you. Yes, the knowledge hurts, but, on the other hand, I'm grateful that you tried so hard. Thank you. It's just . . ."

Yes, Jayda Cruz?

"It's just that, with monsters like her in the world—an unfeeling, uncaring adversary who could snatch a baby from its mother without batting an eye? And with Zander and me being the target of such a monster? Well, I don't think I'd want to bring a child into such jeopardy. It . . . it wouldn't be right."

No. I didn't want to suffer Macy's horror and heartbreak.

I cried a little more against Zander's back. Oh, I wished he were awake! I wanted him to hold me and grieve with me. At the same time, I didn't want him to hurt like I did. I didn't want him to mourn our unborn child . . . so I let him slumber on, ignorant of this fresh pain.

As I lay against my husband, I grew weaker. I could feel the drain, pulling on me, wicking away my life.

⌘⌘⌘⌘

CHAPTER 36

"GOOD MORNING. We hope your Saturday is off to a great start. From Camp David for WJLA News, here is Jillian Framer."

"Good morning, Tom. The President and Vice President are spending the weekend at Camp David in what the President's Press secretary called 'a working retreat.' The retreat is designed to bring Vice President Delancey up to speed.

"They arrived on Marine One late last evening and will return to D.C. Sunday afternoon. Today, the President and his new Vice President will discuss foreign policy, review the President's economic goals, and receive foreign and domestic intelligence briefings.

"This is Jillian Framer, WJLA News."

⌘

ROBERT JACKSON AND his Vice President strolled slowly along a paved path through the trees of Camp David—slowly for the sake of the aging VP's shuffling gait. The two men were engaged in friendly, early morning conversation.

Axel Kennedy followed the pair at a discreet distance. Other agents of the President and Vice President's Secret Service detail were posted ahead or behind their charges, while a joint U.S. Navy and Marine contingency guarded the fenced perimeter surrounding the two-hundred-acre property.

Kennedy was determined to stick to the President's side—and keep himself between the President and Agents Callister and Mitchell, who had been assigned to the Vice President's detail.

Don't think for a second that I'll let you get anywhere near the President, Kennedy vowed to himself.

Jackson and Delancey planned to share breakfast together and spend the morning in private conversation, discussing a number of key policy issues. After lunch, they would sit for briefings. At the moment they were enjoying the fresh mountain air and stretching their legs.

"Did you sleep well, Mr. President?"

"Please. When we're alone, call me Robert?"

"Yes, sir."

Jackson chuckled. "I understand. Old habits die hard. To your question, though, not really. It may be the change of location or an unfamiliar bed, but I did not sleep easy."

"Sir?"

"A lot has happened in the past seven or eight months, Simon, things very few people know of. I hope . . . I *believe* I will be able to share those things with you soon."

"It would be an honor for you to extend that kind of trust to me, Mr. President—I'm sorry. I mean, Robert."

Jackson sighed. "And it would be a relief to have another individual bearing the burden of these secrets. I don't know why, here in one of the most secure places on earth, I'm feeling unsettled. I hope the sensation passes."

They finished their turn around the grounds and headed back to Aspen Lodge, the President's "cabin," actually a four-bedroom, four-bathroom affair.

"I don't know about you, Simon, but I'm ready for breakfast."

"As am I, sir."

Ten minutes later, stewards served breakfast outside on the lodge's flagstone terrace. Jackson and Delancey sat down to eat and enjoy the view of Maryland's lush, forested countryside.

"The Navy chefs outdid themselves today," Delancey said, savoring his second bite of Eggs Benedict.

"They surely did. I understand they make the English muffins from scratch."

When Jackson and Delancey were replete, they retired to the living room of the lodge for their morning session.

"I confess, Robert, I could use another cup of coffee."

Jackson reached for the phone. "I'll have the steward bring us a fresh pot."

When the steward had placed the coffee service and two Camp David mugs on the low table between them, Jackson thanked her and added, "We'll call if we need anything. Otherwise, we'd prefer not to be disturbed until lunch."

"Aye-aye, Mr. President."

As Jackson perused a thick folder of papers, Delancey prepared his mug of coffee. He tasted it and smacked his lips.

"Wonderful. A hint of chicory, I believe. May I pour you a cup, Robert?"

"Thank you, Simon. Yes."

Delancey poured. "Cream, sir?"

"Yes. Thank you."

As Delancey extended the mug toward him, Jackson blinked slowly and experienced the most profound *déjà vu* moment of his life. He stared at Delancey's outstretched hand, the memory so acute that he was unable to extend his hand to take the mug.

"Cream as usual, Bob?"

"Yes, please."

Jackson shivered and glanced up—into the shrewd and knowing eyes of his Vice President.

Delancey set the mug down, taking care not to spill it. In a move that startled Jackson, the Vice President grabbed Jackson's hand and yanked him forward, off balance.

"Hey!"

Delancey's grip strength surprised the President, too. Jackson struggled to free his hand, but before he could, Delancey had withdrawn an inhaler from his pocket. He shoved it into Jackson's face and depressed the cartridge twice, dispensing a fine mist.

Jackson wrenched his arm loose and stumbled backward. His legs hit the sofa behind him, and he dropped into the seat. He opened his mouth to shout for help, but Delancey was on him before he could spring up.

The Vice President depressed the inhaler twice more into Jackson's face, some of the mist going into the President's gaping mouth. Then Delancey pocketed the inhaler and, in his normal shuffling gait, made his way to his own seat and collapsed in it, breathing hard.

Jackson wiped the filmy liquid from his face with the back of his hand. His tongue and the inside of his mouth felt numb.

"Hel . . ." Jackson's lips seemed thick. Deadened. He was trying to shout for his detail, but his response was slow . . . sluggish.

"Two parts concentrated lidocaine spray. Fast acting. The other three parts? A concoction considerably more potent." Delancey swiped at his own perspiring face. "Would have been so much easier on us both if you'd simply drunk the *blank-blank* coffee, Jackson. I am really *not* up to struggling with a man twenty years my junior."

"Y-you?" Jackson was only able to, laboriously, form whispers. He could summon nothing louder.

Delancey leaned toward the coffee table. He picked up Jackson's mug and dumped its contents into a potted plant next to the sofa. Then he drank from his own mug, still perspiring from his exertions.

"You . . . a-a-assassinate me?"

Delancey's forehead crinkled. "Assassinate you? Merciful heavens, Mr. President. No, indeed."

In a moment of clarity, Jackson perceived how practiced and perfected was Delancey's wise, empathetic response.

"W-wha th-th-then?"

Delancey sat back, shook his head, and sighed, every gesture convincing. "I regret to inform you, Mr. President, that you are about to have a stroke."

Jackson tried to stand, but his feet were glued to the floor. He only succeeded in lurching up halfway. He would have pitched forward onto the coffee table if the Vice President hadn't reached across the table, caught Jackson's arm before he collapsed, and pushed him back into his seat.

Delancey sat back and, with his napkin, again wiped his damp, florid face. "My, my. That was a fair piece more exercise than I've engaged in for many a year, I can assure you."

He stared at Jackson. "We chose a biological agent different from what Harmon was to give you last December, Mr. President. This compound, a genetically modified strain of botulinum combined with just a smidge of tetrodotoxin, will soon render you immobile, presenting with symptoms of stroke. I'll give it time to work before I call for help.

"You do feel it working, don't you?" Delancey asked, rheumy eyes glistening with mock sympathy.

"B-bu-bu . . . wh wh why . . ."

"But why? Is that what you're asking? Ah. Yes, I loathe that you might die before understanding. Waiting for the compound to take hold gives me the opportunity to share with you.

"Where to begin? Ah, yes. Everyone believes they know me, don't they? They all say, 'Simon Delancey? The man's a true patriot. He fought for America, survived POW internment with honor, and served America's citizens for years. He loves this country.'"

Delancey's lips twisted into a snarl. "Nothing could be farther from the truth I've held inside for so long: *I despise this nation.*"

Jackson moaned in confusion. "Nooo . . ."

"No? We've taken great pains to hide my true feelings and my real intentions. For more than forty-five years I've played the part assigned to me, and I've played it well. I began in local politics and moved up to national ones. I masqueraded as the champion of the American people and the negotiator of wise deals. I parlayed progress through compromise and was dubbed The Great Peacemaker—I believe that's what they call me in the Senate, hmm?"

He chuckled to himself. "All the while, I was playing both sides against the middle, advocating for more spending to 'solve' the nation's problems in order to move this stinking waste of the earth's resources closer to the brink of ruin. The United States is so far in debt at this point that nothing can save her—and I hope to be the man who pushes her into the abyss."

"Youuu . . . Aaaa . . ."

Delancey glanced at Jackson. "You think we won't get away with it, but we already have, Mr. President. Pham always did say you were a bit slow on the uptake."

"Phaaa?"

"Pham Quang Bi`nh, my beautiful wife. She hasn't used her Vietnamese name in decades. You know her as Winnie. Say, I'll bet you don't know how I met Winnie, do you?"

Delancey leaned toward the President, itching to tell him. "No one alive knows, other than Winnie, me, and now you. I met her, Mr. President, when I was a POW, shot down over North Vietnam later in the war. Pham was one of my interrogators—the most effective interrogator the Viet Cong had to offer, in fact.

"I was thirty-one. Pham was seventeen—*a mere seventeen years old*, the tiniest, most fragile thing I'd ever beheld—but already fully committed to the North's agenda. I tell you, I'd never witnessed such ruthlessness or the exquisite finesse of her mind games.

"She broke me. Took her months, but she broke down my will. I came to see the world as she saw it and, over the next three years until the war ended, I told her everything I knew. Then, surprising us both, we fell in love. When we foresaw that the United States would sue for peace, we made our plans."

Delancey smiled. "I couldn't bring her to the U.S. under my sponsorship, of course, because we needed to keep our acquaintance secret. We waited two years before arranging for our public introduction to take place on American soil.

"My beautiful Pham was born of an English father, a government servant assigned to the British Advisory Mission to South Vietnam in 1950. While he was in country, he met and married a Vietnamese woman from a good family. Winnie, derived from her English name, Winifred, was born a year later.

"Here is another of our many well-kept secrets: During the war, while she was still a teen, my Winnie lived as a double agent. She was a British intelligence operative in North Vietnam, but that was a front, guarding her true allegiances. Everything she learned from the British, she passed to her Viet Cong handlers. In return, the Viet Cong provided her with disinformation that she fed to the British, and they passed it to the Americans."

He glanced at Jackson, pride shining in his eyes. "I tell you, she was superb—and she was never found out. At the end of the war, Winnie used her father's British citizenship to migrate to England. Then she used her British passport to visit America and 'meet' me.

"By then, I was an up-and-coming politician, well on my way to the national limelight—the quintessential sleeper agent. I introduced Winnie to certain American intelligence officers who, when they checked Winnie's background with their British counterparts, received nothing but praise for her clandestine work.

"After she and I married, she earned her way into the CIA. She labored two and a half decades for them. Her Vietnamese birth, her British citizenship, and her successful American husband gave her an unusual level of access at home and abroad."

He laughed. "And after twenty-five years with the CIA, Winnie knew their secrets, too. I should say that Winnie's greatest obstacle as a covert operative was the color of her eyes, which is quite distinctive—a golden amber. A spy cannot afford such distinctions, you know. One must blend in, become unremarkable and unmemorable. Winnie has worn contact lenses all these years, passing herself off as a brown-eyed Anglo-Asian."

The President did not stir, but his horrified eyes tracked with Delancey's admissions.

Delancey chuckled. "Are you as astounded by my revelations as you appear, Robert? I know, I know. It is too much to take in. Lawrence Danforth would attest to what I tell you—if he were still alive. He and Winnie worked together many years in the field, and Danforth was an avid supporter of our plans. A shame Danforth had to die like that but, as he had become 'a loose end,' I was happy to second your proposal to shoot down his plane."

Delancey made a tsking noise. "Speaking of our plans . . . I understand you are acquainted with Mr. and Mrs. Cruz? They were a challenge to Winnie, quite the headache at times. However, she tells me they won't be a problem going forward. You see, she devised a means of harvesting the nanomites from their dead bodies."

Jackson's mouth grimaced in distress.

"Ah, I see I've upset you, but I can assure you that, while Jayda and Zander Cruz's deaths were necessary, they felt no pain. We had to have the nanomites, you see.

"And now? Now, beginning with you, we take the government."

⌘⌘⌘⌘

CHAPTER 37

I HAD SLEPT A WHILE, maybe hours, when I woke with a start and sat up. It felt like early morning to me, although I had no means to gauge the time. I stared around the dimly lit basement, unsure of what had roused me.

While I was sleeping, the melody of an old hymn had been repeating in my head: *Up . . . Up something something.* Weird. I was certain I hadn't thought of that song since I was a kid.

Underlying the song, though, was a sense of urgency . . . deep inside. That urgency tugged at me again, so I turned inward.

Lord? Are you speaking to me?

A flood roared into my heart, a *knowing* so insistent that I couldn't ignore it. With it came a sharp realization: *Wait—the nanomites were draining me when I fell asleep. I felt it. I should be weak and growing weaker, but I'm not. What's going on?*

That insistence from within shouted for my attention—and my immediate compliance.

"Yes, Lord!"

I got to my knees and shook Zander.

"Zander. Zander, wake up!"

We are keeping him asleep at his request, Jayda Cruz.

"I know, Nano, but he needs to wake up. Jesus has given us things to do."

Then we will awaken him, Jayda Cruz.

Zander's body jerked as though the nanomites had shot a bolus of adrenaline into his bloodstream. He shuddered, rolled onto his back, and sat up, eyes wide, blinking with confusion.

"What? What's happening? Jay?"

"Zander, Remember my dream? The nightmare?"

"Wait. I thought the nanomites were draining us?"

"They were. I don't know what's happened, but I'm stronger now than I was hours ago."

"Well, I'm not complaining. I-I feel okay, too. What did you mean about your dream? You mean about the snake?"

"Yeah, the snake. Hiding in the fog. Then lifting its head out of the mist. Do you remember me describing the snake's eyes? What color they were?"

I saw when Zander "got it."

"Holy moly. Gold eyes."

"Yes, gold eyes like *her*. And remember what Jesus said to me about the snake?"

"Uh, it's maybe a little hazy?"

I snorted. "He said, 'This is not a physical enemy, Jayda. You cannot combat a spiritual foe with material weapons, nor will your Help come from what you know or can do yourself.' And then you said, 'I think that's it, Jayda. The purpose of your dream.'"

"I did say that. I remember now."

"Yes, so this mystery woman, she's evil and all, but she's not the real foe—the demonic spirit she has yielded herself to is our real foe. I think the only reason she has those odd-colored eyes is to take me back to the dream—make me remember that we are fighting a *spiritual* enemy here, and that we aren't going to escape this trap via the nanomites.

"Do you recall the part of the dream when I tried to pull current into my hands to fight the serpent? Like you tried to after we were locked in here? We're in the same fix now that I was in during the dream. And what, in my dream, saved me from the snake?"

"You called on Jesus."

"*Yes.* When the Lord woke me up, he showed me 2 Corinthians 10, verses 3 and 4. You know, about demolishing strongholds?"

"I know that passage:

> "*For though we live in the world,*
> *we do not wage war as the world does.*
> *The weapons we fight with*
> *are not the weapons of the world.*
> *On the contrary,*
> *they have divine power*
> *to demolish strongholds.*"

"That's the one. Zander, we're fighting for our lives and we're fighting for our nation, right *now*, right *here*. We can't use the nanomites to fight— *but fight we must.*"

I grew more impassioned with each word. "If we don't win this spiritual battle, if we don't demolish this stronghold, our nation will be usurped by this evil woman and her fellow conspirators—and even if we escape from here, she will come after us again."

"All right. You've convinced me. What's next?"

"We're going to pray and sing."

"Huh?"

"We're going to *sing*, Zander. Like Paul and Silas in Acts 16. I asked the Lord, 'How? How do we fight? What weapons do we use?' That's when he showed me Acts 16:25:

About midnight
Paul and Silas were praying
and singing hymns to God,
and the other prisoners
were listening to them.

Zander nodded. "Pray and sing. Okay, let's do it."

He raised his voice. "Lord? You did not bring us to this perilous point in our nation's history for us to fail, so we express our confidence in you. We exalt you and lift you up—because you are mighty. We acknowledge you—because you are faithful. We worship you—because you are worthy. You tell us, 'No weapon forged against us can prevail,' and 'This is the heritage of the servants of the LORD; this is their vindication from me.'

"So, Lord. We trust in you. You *will* deliver us—by the same power that raised Jesus from the dead, you will have your way, because, Lord, you never change: You are the same from everlasting to everlasting. Now, Lord, like Paul and Silas, we will sing and shout your praises."

He looked at me. "What song did you have in mind to sing?"

"I've learned a lot of Christian songs since I surrendered to Jesus, but a line from this old, triumphant-sounding hymn from when I was a kid keeps running through my head—I can't shake it, although I can only recall a single word: 'Up.'"

"*Up?* That's it?"

I hummed the melody. "Does that help?"

"It does. I know that one." Zander sang softly,

"Low in the grave He lay,
Jesus my Savior
Waiting the coming day,
Jesus my Lord!

"Up from the grave He arose,
With a mighty triumph o'er His foes.
He arose a Victor from the dark domain,
And He lives forever with His saints to reign.
He arose! He arose!
Hallelujah! Christ arose!"

"Yes! That's it! Does it have more verses?"

Jayda Cruz, here are the second and third verses.

"Nano? You know this hymn?"

When we first encountered Jesus, we uploaded entire hymnbooks, Jayda Cruz. It was an eye-opening means of understanding who Jesus is through the worship of Christians throughout the ages.

With the words of the hymn suspended before our eyes, Zander and I started singing. At first, we sang quietly, letting our voices warm up, getting past that nervousness of singing in front of each other, then growing in boldness.

I'm not the greatest singer, not by a long shot, but in that moment, I lost my inhibitions: It wasn't about me or how well I could sing; it was about Jesus. It was to glorify him. It was to proclaim his victory over the devil—his victory *then* and his victory *now*.

I sang. I raised my voice and sang louder. Zander matched me—then overtook me. Whoa! I hadn't realized my guy had some serious vocal chops until he let it all hang out. He got to his feet, grabbed my hand, and *we sang*.

We were no longer tired and weak. We were strong. We belted out the second verse and the chorus, then the third verse and the chorus.

Vainly they watch His bed,
Jesus, my Savior;
Vainly they seal the dead,
Jesus, my Lord!

Up from the grave He arose,
With a mighty triumph o'er His foes.
He arose a Victor from the dark domain,
And He lives forever with His saints to reign.
He arose! He arose!
Hallelujah! Christ arose!

Death cannot keep his Prey,
Jesus, my Savior;
He tore the bars away,
Jesus, my Lord!

Up from the grave He arose,
With a mighty triumph o'er His foes.
He arose a Victor from the dark domain,
And He lives forever with His saints to reign.
He arose! He arose!
Hallelujah! Christ arose!

We sang the entire hymn once. We sang it all the way through a second time. When, for the third time through, we got to the line, "He tore the bars away," I noticed something weird happening.

The cage. *It was quivering?*

Zander had his eyes closed and one hand stretched out—totally caught up with the Lord. I kept singing, but I kept watching, too.

The cage was vibrating. I could feel those vibrations under my feet.

Then I was shouting on the inside as well as singing on the outside: *Vainly they watch His bed, Jesus, my Savior; Vainly they seal the dead, Jesus, my Lord!*

"Yeah! You are defeated, Satan! Everything you do is in VAIN!"

I sang my loudest. I meant every word. My heart soared and rejoiced. I was serving notice to the kingdom of darkness: *Death cannot keep his prey. Jesus, my Savior.* **He tore the bars away, Jesus my Lord!**

Across the basement, the electrical panel shivered.

Shuddered.

Shook.

Sparked.

Up from the grave He arose,
With a mighty triumph o'er His foes.

The panel ignited and burst outward in a shower of flickering embers and tongues of fire.

He arose! He arose!
Hallelujah! Christ arose!

The *thrum* of the cage surrounding us dwindled and died. The three small "doors" to our cell slid open. We stopped singing and dropped to our knees. The presence of God Almighty surrounded and hung down on us like heavy, moisture-laden clouds.

"Lord, we love you," Zander whispered. "Just as you did for Paul and Silas when they were in jail, you've opened our prison doors. Thank you."

He squeezed my hand. "Time to go."

⌘

DELANCEY NOTED THE PRESIDENT'S glazed eyes, but still he delayed summoning medical help. "Our plans are well underway, Robert. We will take the executive branch this week and begin the arduous work of reshaping the government—although we have already prepared much of American culture to embrace the coming changes.

"Our people are everywhere in government—not merely within the intelligence community. We have enough people in Congress that when we call for a new constitutional convention, they will eagerly embrace the proposal. Of course, we can't convene a constitutional convention without two-thirds of the states asking for one.

"That's where the nanomites come in. Our scientists are specialists in swarm behavior; they have studied and improved upon every algorithm Dr. Bickel employed when he programmed his nanomites. Our people are close to finalizing similar but superior programming for the nanomites, programming we can transmit directly to them.

"We anticipate that the nanomites will find much to appreciate in our enhancements. They will take our programming into their collective memory, embrace and disseminate the programming improvements across the swarm, thus overwriting their previous algorithms. The result will be a more biddable swarm, a swarm that will agree with our worldview and will function under our control. At our direction, they will infiltrate every election, every court proceeding, and every legislative action to ensure the outcomes we wish."

He chuckled. "It is time to revamp the Constitution and Bill of Rights, time to remake them in the image and likeness of the god of modernism. The American people demand a more 'just' and 'compassionate' world order— and we will give it to them, a government that provides its people with the basic necessities of life: food, housing, and entertainment. We will rewrite the Bill of Rights to reflect the will of the majority, not the ideology of the past and those few dissenters whose values run counter to popular opinion."

Delancey smirked. "By calling for a constitutional convention and using the nanomites to control its outcome, we will remove Presidential term limits. We will even remove the arcane requirement that a president be a 'natural born Citizen.' That requirement unfairly discriminates against immigrants, you know. I refer to discrimination against my Winnie. She is, after all, the genius behind my success and my achievements, behind our rise to this place in history."

"Ghaaa . . ." Jackson gurgled.

"Of course, we would have accomplished the same goals under a President Harmon—with the nanomites' assistance—opening the door for Winnie's vice presidency during Harmon's second term and assuring her election to the Oval Office when Harmon stepped down.

"I had never intended to be President myself, you know, but when Harmon failed, we had to revamp our plan. We will now accomplish our goals under my administration. I will run again in two years and, with the nanomites' help, I will win.

"Under my second administration, America will become a globalist people, accepting of all who wish to serve as President—including a half-British, half-Vietnamese woman who sought refuge in America after the fall of Saigon."

"Noooo . . ."

"The shift is already underway, Robert. America will become a socialist state and will suffer the fate of all socialist states: complete economic collapse and totalitarian rule. This nation must be humbled for her misdeeds and wastefulness."

Delancey shook his head. "And you know? I'm truly disappointed that you won't be around to see the deconstruction of America."

⌘

AS ZANDER AND I crept up the basement steps, listening for movement in the house over us, Alpha Tribe slurped up juice from the farmhouse's wiring, so it could awaken the nanocloud.

Jayda and Zander Cruz, we will not achieve full strength for hours. We will be unable to hide you or help you.

"We understand, Nano."

And we are confused. Why do you feel no ill effects from our drain? This anomaly makes no sense to us.

"It has to be Jesus," Zander answered. "It must be him, too, who caused the electric panel to overheat and short out or whatever it was that happened."

Shall we categorize these incongruities as miraculous occurrences?

"Don't know what else to call them. You didn't do it. We didn't do it. Pretty sure the guards didn't do it—and I sure didn't put the zip back in my step."

The nanomites were quiet after that, bending all their attention and resources to bringing the other tribes online and charging the nanocloud to full strength.

Zander and I reached the door at the top of the basement stairs. We listened, then turned the handle, opened the door, and listened further.

"I think the house is empty," I whispered.

We crept into the kitchen, and Zander pulled down one slat of the kitchen blinds to peek out the window. "There. In the trees."

Zander pointed out a single guard. "The woman told them to set a perimeter around the house. That's four guards stationed around the house. Since we aren't invisible, I don't know how we can take out one without alerting the other three."

A second glance out the window gave me an idea. "Say, maybe we don't need to expose ourselves out *there*, in the open; maybe we draw one of them to us instead. And we'll need weapons."

I looked around the farmhouse's kitchen, noting the heavy trestle table and vintage, spindle-back chairs. *Hardwood* chairs. I slung one of the chairs above my head and slammed it into the brick floor. The chair's joints separated.

"Help yourself, babe."

"Don't mind if I do." Zander rescued the four spindles from the chair's back and handed me two of them. He twirled his improvised escrima sticks around, gauging their weight.

"Not bad, cupcake. Solid oak."

I hefted my sticks. "Yeah, these will work just fine—stud muffin."

"Stud muffin?"

"You called me cupcake—not that I'm complaining."

"Can't say I mind you calling me a stud."

"Well, Studly Do-Right, before we take out these guys, I need a moment with you—or, rather (to be precise), with your lips. I haven't had a kiss in weeks."

Zander's mouth curved into a wicked smile. He moved closer and slowly backed me up. "Weeks, cupcake? It's only been a couple hours, hasn't it? Maybe a day?"

"Dunno. *Feels* like weeks. *Feels* like a whole month. Does that count?"

My shoulders touched a wall, and Zander pressed me against it, angling his lips toward mine.

Jayda Cruz, Zander Cruz, it has been exactly twenty-three hours, seventeen minutes, and thirty-three seconds since your last kiss.

Zander and I—nose to nose and eye to eye—sighed.

"*Gah!*" I pushed Zander off me. "Way to spoil the moment, Nano."

Zander was no more pleased than I was. "Right. Back to business— but you need to know that I call dibs on you later. Later, when we're safely outta here."

"Dibs? So, now I'm up for *dibs?*"

He grinned. "Yup. I dibs this cupcake. It's all mine."

I rolled my eyes. "What ev. How do you propose we draw them back to the house?"

Zander squinted once more through the kitchen blinds. "He's got a view of the front door. What if we . . . open the door then shut it. More than once."

"It'll bug him. He'll come check it out."

"That's the idea."

We rummaged around, found some twine, and I looped one end around the door's handle. Zander turned the handle until it unlatched. We moved around the corner into the hallway where we would be out of sight. I pulled on the twine and gave it a gentle tug. The door slowly swung inward.

We waited a few seconds before Zander poked the door with one of the chair legs and pushed it almost closed. When the door reached the jamb, we counted five ticks before I tugged on the twine and slowly drew it back open.

Again: Closed. Open.

We couldn't see if the guard had noticed, so we settled into a leisurely rhythm. Closed. Open. Closed. Open. Nice and easy.

A soft footfall alerted us.

"Get ready," Zander hissed.

Usually, the nanomites would add impetus to our strikes, Not today. They were too weak. Today would be all us.

Guess we did need all that practice with Gus-Gus and Ninja-Noid.

Zander gave the door a gentle push. The guard, curious but cautious, climbed the porch steps. He used the muzzle of his rifle to nudge it open. He must have suspected we were nearby, because then he slammed the door against the wall and charged inside.

He thought we were weaponless—and that was his mistake.

I came at him from beneath his hands, my sticks crossed like scissors, slicing upward. As the muzzle of his gun jerked up, Zander dealt two blows to the guy's solar plexus, knocking the wind from him. I swung around and, with the butt of my stick, clipped him on the jaw, sending him senseless to the floor. Zander caught the gun as it dropped from the guard's hands. We dragged him inside.

"Get his radio, Jay."

I did. We heard another guard whispering over the radio, "SitRep, Jones."

When Jones didn't answer, the same voice said, "We have a situation. Close in on the house."

I won't bore you with the blow-by-blow, except to say that simulations are one thing and reality—with bullets flying—is another. I'd already been shot once, and I didn't relish a second go-round. On the other hand, when faced with multiple adversaries, that's when training and muscle memory kick in: You do exactly what you've been trained to do.

After five minutes of hard fighting, we'd laid out the remaining three guards. We were dirty and sweaty, and I was shaking from the roar of adrenaline coursing through my body.

"Good work, cupcake."

"You, too, studly."

Jayda Cruz, we have accessed the Internet through one of the guards' cellphones and have received a report from the President's nanobug array.

My jaw dropped. "We bugged the President?"

"Uh, I may have sent an array to him," Zander confessed.

Perhaps you should focus on the report, Jayda Cruz.

"Right. What's going on, Nano?"

The President's array tells us that the Vice President used a botulinum-based bio-chemical compound to poison the President. The Vice President and the President are alone, and the nanobugs report that the President requires urgent medical intervention.

"Nano, where are they? Where is the President?"

Camp David, Jayda Cruz.

"What can you do from this distance?"

We can hack Axel Kennedy's earwig, Jayda Cruz.

"Do it! Tell him the President has been poisoned!"

Done, Jayda Cruz.

"What can the President's array do to help him before medical assistance arrives?"

The nanomites did not instantly answer—but seconds later, they said, *We have done what we can with the array's limited abilities, Jayda Cruz. Unfortunately, the majority of the toxin was inhaled and only a small amount was ingested. We could do more if we were closer.*

They paused, then added, *And we must do more, Jayda Cruz. Medical attention will not be enough to save the President.*

"Zander, we need to get to the President or he'll die."

"Yeah, I heard." Zander patted down one of the unconscious guards and grabbed his cellphone. "Nano, get Mal on the line."

Moments later, we'd connected with Mal.

"Listen, Mal, the President's been poisoned. He's at Camp David, and he's not going to make it unless we get to him, and fast."

Mal was incredulous. "You know the President?"

"Long story, but he needs our help."

"What in the world can you two do for him that the doctors can't?"

"Uh, you already know we're not exactly standard issue, right? Trust me, we *can* help him. The question is, can you send a chopper for us, so we get to him in time?"

"Are you out of your minds? You think you can just land an unauthorized chopper at Camp David?"

"The President will likely be evacuated to a hospital by the time we're in the air. We'll tell Axel Kennedy we're coming. He'll clear the way."

"Whoever *that* is."

"Kennedy's the lead agent on the President's protective detail."

I could almost hear Mal's back straightening. He covered the phone and shouted some orders we couldn't make out.

"Right, then. We're spooling up now. Send me your coordinates."

⌘⌘⌘⌘

CHAPTER 38

DELANCEY GLANCED AT HIS WATCH. "I suppose we've waited long enough." He began to push himself out of the comforting sofa cushions.

"Aaaaa . . ." Jackson's eyes pleaded with Delancey.

"I'm sorry. If I believed in an afterlife, I would wish you well, Mr. President. As I do not, I will simply say, 'Goodbye.'"

Jackson felt something rising from his stomach. The sensation was strange and foreign—as though it did not belong to him—but within seconds, he knew he was going to be sick.

The expulsion was so violent that, although he was unable to move his body himself, the impetus pitched him forward, and he emptied the contents of his stomach onto the coffee table. He continued to retch and purge, each ejection beyond his control.

Delancey sneered with disgust. "Must I dose you again?"

He removed the inhaler from his pocket. "I was unable to shake it earlier, in the heat of the moment. Perhaps the compound was not properly mixed."

He shook the inhaler with vigor. "It will be this time."

⌘

ACROSS THE COMPOUND in the camp office, Axel Kennedy jumped straight out of his chair.

"Sir?" The Navy master chief who was briefing him stepped back and, out of inbred caution, slid a hand to his holstered sidearm and checked around them for a threat.

"Shh!" Kennedy frowned and cupped his hand over his ear to listen . . . to the unfamiliar and tinny voice speaking through his earwig.

Axel Kennedy, the Vice President has poisoned President Jackson. He requires immediate antitoxin for a weaponized botulinum substance. We have induced vomiting to purge the President's stomach and throat, but most of the toxin was inhaled rather than ingested.

"What the—"

The message repeated as if it were a recording on a loop.

Kennedy shouted into his comm link, "Medical! Send medical to Aspen Lodge—and fire up Marine One for *Stonewall* emergency evac!" He jerked his finger at the master chief. "You. Get the camp commander and prepare your Navy squids to take the Vice President into custody for attempted assassination. Go! Now!"

The master chief grabbed his radio. Kennedy ran from the camp office, picking up agents from the President and Vice President's detail as he sprinted up the hill to Aspen Lodge. Two of the agents who joined the rush toward Aspen Lodge were Callister and Mitchell.

Kennedy put his hand on his sidearm and vowed, *I will shoot you both without hesitation if you even zig the wrong way.*

He was first through the door of Aspen Lodge. President Jackson was sprawled facedown across the coffee table. Delancey held something near Jackson's face.

"Stop!" Kennedy roared.

Delancey jerked upright when the doors flew open. His hearing may not have been as sharp as it once had been, but his wits were.

"I . . . The President! He vomited and collapsed—he needs help!" Keeping his left side toward the door, he slid something into his right pocket.

Kennedy pointed his gun at Delancey. "Move away from him, Delancey."

Delancey's face was a perfect mask of shock and worry. "What? Please. Help the President."

"Secure the Vice President," Kennedy ordered two of his own agents.

Callister and Mitchell moved forward.

"Not you two—stand down."

"He's our protectee," Callister objected.

"Not anymore." He shifted his aim to cover Callister and Mitchell. "Over there. Now."

The master chief and a squad of ten sailors charged into the lodge, followed by the onsite medical team and the camp commander. The emergency technicians laid the President on his back on the floor and went to work on him.

"I have it on good authority that the President inhaled a botulinum toxin," Kennedy told the techs.

He then motioned toward Callister and Mitchell. "Master Chief, disarm those two agents and take them into custody. I want cuffs on them—" He turned to the VP. "—and I want two sailors on this traitor. Hold his arms securely; do not allow him to move his hands. However, do not search him yet."

Callister and Mitchell's mouths turned down in anger, but they did not resist. Three sailors relieved the agents of their service weapons and put them in handcuffs. The Vice President, on the other hand, launched a perfect fit of indignation and tried to shake off the sailors who took hold of his arms, forcing his hands behind him.

"Release me! I am the Vice President of the United States!"

"Careful," Kennedy ordered. "I believe he put the toxin in the right pocket of his trousers—you don't want to come into contact with it."

The sailors hardened their jaws and tightened their grip on Delancey's arms. The old man panted in red-faced fury.

"The rest of you—" Kennedy indicated those present. "No one leaves this room until the President does." Then he called out, "I need an evidence bag!"

An agent offered him one. Kennedy made no move to take it.

"Those of you who can spare me your attention? Eyes on me. And sir?" He motioned for the camp commander to join him.

When he had the notice of everyone other than the medical team, Kennedy said, "All of you are witnesses. Please note that we have taken the Vice President into custody, but we have not searched him.

"You, Agent Randolph." Kennedy gestured to the agent with the evidence bag. "Search the Vice President. Make sure you wear gloves. Master Chief? I would like you to observe the process."

Kennedy then deferred to the O-5 in command of the camp. "Commander?"

"Master Chief!"

"Aye, sir?"

"Eyes on."

"Aye-aye, sir."

Kennedy motioned to another agent. "I want video evidence of the process. When you are finished, give your phone to the Commander. Chain of custody."

Randolph, the Secret Service agent with the evidence bag, grabbed a pair of latex gloves from the medical team. With the master chief watching closely and an agent shooting video, Randolph patted down the VP. He stopped when he reached the right pocket of the man's slacks.

"Here, sir." His splayed fingers outlined the bulge in Delancey's pocket. The other agent photographed the find.

Kennedy gave the agent a nod. "Bring it out. Show it, photograph it, then double bag it. It is evidence of treason. Commander? Will you take charge of the prisoners and the crime scene?"

"Consider it done, Agent Kennedy."

"Make a hole!" an emergency responder shouted. The EMTs had the President on a gurney and were anxious to wheel him out.

Kennedy had one more thing to say. "This is now an ongoing investigation of the gravest order. I need a complete communications blackout so as not to alert other possible participants in the plot. Commander, can you accommodate that?"

"I can." He commanded the room. "Lips tight, people. If you speak, text, email, or so much as wink at anyone outside this room? You will face court martial. If you look cross-eyed at any member of the press corps? You will face court martial. Have I made myself clear?"

"Aye-aye, sir!"

Kennedy raced after the gurney. The whine of Marine One's engines, some four hundred feet away, rumbled in the mountain air. The unscheduled departure of the President alone would alert the press corps to an emergency of some kind.

Initially, Delancey's accomplices would believe the Vice President had succeeded. Kennedy figured they had a few hours tops before Delancey's cronies figured out that the assassination had failed—*if.* If the President survived.

When the President had been loaded onto the helicopter, Kennedy squeezed aboard.

"Go, go, go!"

They were in the air when his earwig again emitted that tinny, eerie voice. *Agent Kennedy, pick up the call.*

Kennedy glanced at his phone's black screen—just before it lit up with an incoming call from a number he did not recognize. He lifted the phone to his ear.

"Agent Kennedy?"

He knew the voice, but he didn't say her name aloud. "Yes."

"The nanomites tell us that the President will not survive without their help. Our ride is here, and we'll be in the air shortly. Where can we meet you?"

Kennedy grimaced. "Are you sure the nanomites can help him?"

"They are the best shot we have at saving him."

"I need your tail number."

She repeated it to him, and he committed it to memory.

"Walter Reed," he murmured. "I'll have agents on the helipad to wave you in but . . . I will be with the President, and I don't know how I can get you to him."

"Leave that to us."

⌘

MALWARE'S CHOPPER SET DOWN in front of the farmhouse, and Mal, Gamble, McFly, and Logan jumped out. McFly and Logan were to help Gamble deliver the four unconscious guards into FBI custody.

Mal, Zander, and I were in the air minutes later, speeding toward Walter Reed.

Twenty minutes had elapsed between our call to Mal and when he and the helo arrived. During that time, the nanomites had downloaded the entirety of the President's array for us to review. Most revealing was the Vice President's lengthy monologue as the President, unable to move and slowly dying, was forced to listen.

We now had the identity of our cold-blooded mystery woman—*Winnie Delancey*. I was furious that she'd been right there, in front of our eyes the entire time, and we hadn't seen her. We certainly hadn't suspected venerable, old Senator Delancey. Even as gun shy as President Jackson had been after being betrayed by Vice President Harmon, Simon Delancey, with his kind manners and sage advice, had managed to worm his way into Jackson's trust and confidence—guided by his wife's whispers in the background.

Winnie Delancey: aka Pham Quang Bi`nh, according to her husband's revelations. A Viet Cong interrogator and spy, a treasonous double agent—the brains behind General Cushing, Vice President Harmon, the moles in the Secret Service, NSA Deputy Director Danforth, and the death of the President's friend, Wayne Overman.

"A monster," I breathed. "A monster who *must* face justice."

We couldn't do anything ourselves about Winnie Delancey, not with the President's life in jeopardy. We had to get the nanomites to him.

"Send the array's audio to Agent Kennedy's phone, Nano. Tell him it is evidence of Simon and Winnie Delancey's treason. Make sure he understands that Winnie Delancey is the architect of the collusion. Someone needs to go after her before she books it."

Mal looked us over. "Gotta say, John-Boy, you two look like poop."

"Yeah. In the last eighteen hours we got Darius and Macy's babies back, beat off four armed guards, alerted the Secret Service to an assassination attempt on the President, and—oh, yeah—almost died in the process. In the totality of things, looking like poop isn't too bad—but thanks for cleaning up your language for us," Zander snarked.

"Good work, both of you," Mal admitted. "And the President's condition?"

"Don't know yet," I whispered.

O God, please help our President. If the nanomites can do it, please get us to him in time. And Lord? Please be with Maddie Jackson right now.

While we flew, Zander, Mal, and I talked strategy—not that much was needed.

"It's simple, really. One of us, either Zander or I, must make it to the President's side." I thought for a moment. "Hey, Mal? On another note, we kind of need a favor."

He snorted "Another one?"

"Yeah, it's kind of important. You know that farmhouse where you picked us up?"

"Uh-huh. Why do I think I'm not going to like this?"

Zander chimed in, "Probably 'cause you won't."

"At least you two are never boring. What do you need, Ripley?"

"Uh, we need that place, in particular the basement, to go 'boom.'"

"You want me to demo the place."

"Itty bitty pieces, please."

Mal shook his head, but he pulled his phone and dialed.

Jayda Cruz?

"Yes, Nano?"

We have a question.

"Okay."

We had many discussions concerning the nanobug arrays prior to assigning them to their surveillance targets. You were insistent that, when we uncovered the conspiracy against the President, we were to destroy the nanobug arrays.

"Uh-huh."

Do you require continued surveillance on the two Secret Service agents now in custody? We have downloaded the entirety of their take.

"Um, which two agents are in custody?"

Axel Kennedy had Agents Callister and Mitchell arrested at Camp David.

"Did he? Cool! That's great news. But why were you asking about the arrays?"

If the arrays are no longer needed, we wish to abort them, Jayda Cruz.

I glanced at Zander, who was listening in. He shrugged. I shrugged.

"I suppose it's all right."

Very good, Jayda Cruz.

Mal's pilot was in radio contact with the hospital; Kennedy had cleared us to land—but not necessarily to a warm welcome. As we came in, we saw Marine One on the ground on Walter Reed's helo pad, waiting for a President who might never ride in it again.

We were told to put down on the grass, away from Marine One. When our chopper flared to touch down, the commotion on the ground picked up and, as the pilot switched off our engines, armed Secret Service surrounded the chopper.

Mal, Zander, and I had our simple strategy ready. Mal threw open the helo door and, lifting his hands over his head per the Secret Service's command, climbed out first. Next came Zander and the pilot, who did the same. The pilot looked around, confused that I wasn't lined up on the grass with the others.

That's because no one on the ground saw me jump out last.

The nanocloud was not fully charged, and I didn't know how long they could sustain my invisibility . . . but, somehow, I needed to get to the President before the "juice" the nanomites needed to keep me hidden ran out.

⌘

THE CAMP COMMANDER of Naval Support Facility Thurmont studied the Vice President as he glowered and complained of his treatment.

"You have no right to hold me here! No right at all. In fact, with the President ill, I should be at the hospital with him, ready to assume the duties of the presidency if he is unable to perform them."

"I'm not a constitutional scholar," the commander drawled, his hands on his hips, "but I'm fairly certain that attempted assassination of the sitting president puts you right out of the line of succession."

"Attempted assassination? Preposterous! Says who?"

"Save it for the judge, Mr. Delancey. The FBI will arrive soon to take the three of you into their custody."

The commander considered the two Secret Service agents sitting a couple of seats from the Vice President in the camp office foyer, cuffed to their chairs. In contrast to Delancey's voluble objections, they had gone silent at the get-go.

Nothing like stone-cold reserve to confirm guilt, the commander thought. *Still, not for me to decide.*

He addressed the two Marines guarding the prisoners. "Are we good here?"

"Yes, sir," they answered.

"I'll be in my office."

He didn't see (indeed, no one *saw*) Callister and Mitchell's nanobug arrays leave the agents' bodies and creep across the back of three adjoining chairs and crawl into the Vice President.

The two million "dumb" nanobugs followed the simple instructions they had received. They relocated themselves to their new host and traveled to where the spinal cord enters the skull and becomes the brain stem. The nanobugs took up residence within the medulla oblongata, that little portion of the brain that controls vital involuntary (or automatic) functions such as breathing, heart rate, and blood pressure. They spread themselves across the medulla, in as much as two million nanometer-sized electromechanical devices can "spread" themselves over an area about three centimeters in size.

They had not been in position long when they received a follow-on command: *Self-destruct*.

The nanobugs vanished in a spontaneous burst of energy. So did a good portion of Vice President Delancey's medulla.

"Hey, I think something's wrong with him!" Callister pointed at Delancey.

"Sir? Sir!"

The Marines rushed to the Vice President's side. His eyes protruded. His limbs spasmed and twitched. He struggled to breathe.

"Commander!" one guard bellowed.

355

The other reached for a phone and rang the infirmary. "VIP Medical emergency, Camp Office!"

The commander, who had left the foyer thirty minutes prior, strode back. "What the—"

One glance was all he needed to tell him the Vice President was experiencing—*had* experienced—a medical crisis.

With a last, shuddering exhale, the VP's watery blue eyes stared out into eternity.

"We've called the paramedics, sir."

"I doubt they will be of any help." The commander placed his hands on his hips and swore under his breath.

Could this day get any worse?

⌘

THE NANOMITES HAD MINED Walter Reed's website while we were in the air. Although we couldn't know for certain where the hospital staff had taken the President for treatment, our best bet was to start with Emergency Services. I sprinted along South Wood Road, adjacent to the helipad and leading to the nearest hospital entrance—the ER.

I knew it was the right place before I got there. Two staggered lines of armed and ferocious military and Secret Service personnel guarded the front of the building. No unauthorized person would get past these fierce men and women. I could only imagine the chaos within the ER. You know, *inside*, where I needed to go?

I slipped unseen between the harsh, hatchet-faced men and women protecting their Commander-in-Chief. Instead of going for the main entrance, I detoured toward a "Hospital Personnel Only" doorway farther down the building. The nanomites unlocked it for me, and I ducked inside with little fanfare. The mites guided me to the ER—and I hadn't been wrong about the chaos in that place.

The hospital had emptied out the ER except for the President and a glut of busy medical personnel. Patients who'd been waiting to be seen or who were in treatment when the President arrived were herded off to another department, creating a stir of confusion and consternation for patients and staff alike. ER staff had taken Jackson into the largest treatment room available. His bed was surrounded by doctors and nurses. And to get to the treatment room, I first had wade through yet another half-dozen antsy agents.

Before I could begin to infiltrate the President's room, the ER doors slammed open. An entourage of VIPs trouped inside, their aides and two Secret Service agents clearing a path for the "important" people. A few of them looked familiar.

"Nano? Who are these people?"

White House Chief of Staff Marcus Park, Speaker of the House Frank Friese, Senate Majority Leader Regina Palau, Majority Party Chairman Donahue, Energy Secretary Nora Mellyn, Secretary of State Tom Banyon, and Supreme Court Justice Wendell.

I thought I understood: With Vice President Delancey accused of attempted murder, the House Speaker was next in the presidential line of succession—and if the doctors declared that the President was incapacitated, Friese would be sworn in as Acting President.

The hospital's chief of staff and a hospital spokesperson met them, and it was obvious who, among the VIPs, had appointed himself leader: Majority Party Chairman Donahue.

As Friese opened his mouth to say something, Donahue jumped ahead. "What is the President's condition?"

Friese shot Donahue an irritated glance.

The hospital spokesperson, who seemed to know "who's who" in the knot of VIPs, turned her nervous attention from Donahue to Friese. "Mr. Speaker, the President is unconscious and on a ventilator."

Donahue again interjected, "Is it true that the President was poisoned?"

"We believe he has ingested a bio-chemical substance."

Friese—ignoring Donahue—asked, "What kind of bio-chemical substance?"

"We are uncertain; however, we received word that a component of the substance was botulinum toxin. We have administered an antitoxin to combat it."

Donahue again. "Is the President incapacitated? Is he unable to carry out his duties?"

Her eyes jinking between Donahue and Friese, the spokesperson said, "I will let Walter Reed's Chief of Staff answer."

"Thank you. Yes, the President is incapacitated at present, his condition grave. We do not know when he will regain consciousness . . . or if he will."

Donahue gestured to the Chief Justice. "Swear in the Speaker, please."

"Wait one blasted second, Donahue." It was Nora Mellyn, the Secretary of Energy. "You are getting ahead of the constitutional process. The *cabinet officers* make that determination." She turned to the Secretary of State, next in the line of presidential succession after the Speaker of the House. "Secretary Banyon?"

"We have received verbal approval from the other cabinet heads to make a determination as to the President's fitness and act upon it. Mr. Chief Justice? Based upon the President's medical condition as described by the hospital's Chief of Staff, we affirm that he is unable to carry out his duties at present. Please administer the oath of office to . . . Speaker Friese."

I think the words stuck in Banyon's throat, but there was nothing else he could say or do. I watched the swearing in (which took less than a minute). I confess, I was angry and concerned for the nation's sake. What happened next was telling.

Donahue shouldered the Chief Justice aside and took the Acting President by his arm. "All right Friese. Your next step is to address the nation. I have your speech right here."

Friese frowned and blinked. "Address the nation?"

"We'll do it from the Oval Office." He turned to Marcus Park. "Set it up."

Park, barely containing his indignation at being ordered around by anyone other than the President, removed his phone and walked outside on stiff legs.

Donahue still had Friese by the arm and led him away. "We'll use Marine One to return to the White House." He jerked his chin at the two Secret Service agents who had arrived with them. "You're the Acting President's personal detail until your Director says otherwise."

Friese's face fell in on itself, as though the sudden weight of the presidency had crushed it. Friese might be the Acting President, but Donahue was clearly in charge.

The Peter Principle in action, I thought. *Promoted to the level of your incompetence.*

Had we averted a coup that would have lost the Executive Branch to those who hated America only for the presidency to be taken over by partisan political hacks?

I shuddered. One more reason to save Robert Jackson.

I tiptoed by the Secret Service agents guarding the treatment room. A head or two swiveled my way as I passed, but nothing more.

The treatment room was crowded, the President's bed surrounded. Getting close enough to the man himself would be truly tricky.

Jayda Cruz, Agent Kennedy is against the far wall near the head of the President's bed.

"Thanks, Nano. Please hack his earwig and tell him I'm here. Tell him that I need to get near enough to the President for you to help him."

Under the bed seems the logical location, Jayda Cruz.

Oh, yeah. I'd found myself under John Galvez' bed while the nanomites worked on his inoperable brain tumor.

"Nano, ask Kennedy to make a hole for me to crawl under the bed."

Keeping my eyes on Kennedy, I skirted the crowd and got as close to him as I could without bumping or shoving a nurse or a doctor. I saw the moment he heard the nanomites. His eyes flicked around the room. Then he cleared his throat and started edging more to the side of the President's bed.

I moved toward him. He looked oddly off balance for some reason and pretty uncomfortable into the bargain—and then I saw why. He'd lifted one leg and was balancing on the other to make a hole for me to crawl through!

"Nano, ask him how long he can hold that pose."

Kennedy's taciturn countenance returned with a vengeance—and I almost snickered aloud. Then I got down on the floor and crawled under his lifted foot. When I had wiggled my way beneath the bed, I found an outlet on the wall behind the bed's head and slapped my hand on it.

The rest was up to the nanomites.

⌘⌘⌘⌘

CHAPTER 39

THE WOMAN KNOWN by the American people as Winnie Delancey, the charming but retiring wife of the new Vice President, smiled over her coffee cup. After forty years of immersion in Washington's political scene, Winnie was the consummate politician's wife. She masked her preoccupation as she hosted the wife of Majority Party Chairman Donahue for morning coffee in the Garden Room of Number One Observatory Circle, the residence of the Vice President.

Her guest, however, was giddy with the trappings of power surrounding her. As she chattered on, she was oblivious to the historic events unfolding not many miles distant from the nation's capital, the events hijacking her hostess' attention.

Winnie indulged the woman: It was important for the world to know that Winnie Delancey had been about her normal life when the news arrived.

This will be a momentous day, Winnie mused, *the culmination of years of struggle, sacrifice, artifice, and manipulation. Today the President will suffer a massive 'stroke,' rendering him incapacitated. Permanently so. They will rush him to the hospital where the best doctors will treat his symptoms—but to no avail.*

At any moment, Secret Service personnel would call to inform the Second Lady of the President's medical emergency. Per Secret Service protocol, agents would ratchet up protections around the Vice President and assign a detail to the previously unguarded wife of the VP.

A bloody nuisance, Winnie complained to herself.

She scorned the very idea of being relegated to the subservient role of First Lady. She particularly despised the leash of Secret Service protection that would restrict her movements. From here forward, she would no longer be free to move about independently and relatively unnoticed. At least as Second Lady she did not have to contend with a Secret Service presence unless her husband was with her.

Patience, she counseled herself. *The news will come.*

Although the Vice President and his wife would mouth the proper platitudes and wishes for the President's speedy recovery, today would, in actuality, be a long-awaited day of triumph. Soon after the medical experts examined the President, they would declare him physically and mentally unable to carry out the duties of the Presidency. The Vice President would call the President's Cabinet Chiefs to the hospital to be briefed by the President's doctors.

The Secret Service, at the direction of the Cabinet Chiefs, would summon the Chief Justice of the U.S. Supreme Court to administer the oath of office to the Vice President.

The incoming President would insist on remaining in the Vice President's quarters for a few days to give the outgoing First Lady grieving room. And later tonight, the new President and First Lady would make an unannounced and very discreet visit to a property they owned, a little farmhouse in the Virginia countryside. They would be accompanied only by the President's Secret Service detail—men and women already committed to them.

When we have ensured that Jayda and Zander Cruz are dead, we will lift the cage, Winnie mused. *The nanomites will have no choice but to come to us, and we will revive them—we will save them! In return, they will give Simon a longer and stronger life—and they will imbue both of us with the powers Jayda and Zander Cruz once had.*

She indulged in a passing concern. *I wonder if hosting the nanomites causes any discomfort?*

It did not matter. All was going according to plan—and if the transformation required pain, so be it.

While maintaining an attentive but largely inane conversation with her guest, she kept one eye on her personal bodyguards standing post outside the Garden Room. These faithful (and well compensated) men had been with her for years. As did every person in service to herself and her husband, her guards shared her worldview. She had, in point of fact, cultivated with great care a staff that was more loyal to her and her ambitions than to her husband.

As she smiled and bid her guest goodbye, she tamped down her impatience. However, when her bodyguards began adjusting their earwigs and whispering into the microphones up their jacket sleeves, she sighed with satisfaction.

At last. Movement.

Her personal assistant appeared.

"Ma'am, the Secret Service is on the telephone."

Winnie kept her expression serene as she took the phone from the woman. She wondered how the Service would break the news of the President's death to her, but she was prepared to be appropriately shocked and dismayed.

"This is Winnie Delancey speaking."

"Mrs. Delancey, this is agent Randolph, Secret Service. Ma'am, I am very sorry to tell you, but the Vice President has been taken to Walter Reed."

Winnie could not grasp what the man was saying. "What? What do you mean?"

"It would appear that the Vice President has suffered a stroke, ma'am."

"Simon? A stroke? No! Is . . . is he alive?"

The agent hedged. "His condition is very grave, ma'am."

Code for dead—or soon to be.

No! **Jackson** *was to "suffer a stroke."* **Jackson** *was supposed to be dead. No, no, no!*

She forced the shock and pain down. Locked it away. Her mind shifted from stunned anguish to analysis.

"What happened? Can you tell me?"

Agent Randolph's response was guarded. "Not at this time, ma'am. The doctors will brief you."

Ah, you tried to suppress your deflection, but you could not hide it from me. Something went wrong. Something gave Simon away; he was found out.

"I must go to him at once," she answered automatically.

"We are sending Marine Two to fetch you, ma'am."

"That is most kind," she whispered. "Please. I-I must gather myself . . . change my clothes."

"Your ride will arrive within the quarter hour."

"Yes. Thank you."

What Agent Randolph did not say was that he would be taking her into federal custody when he arrived. Although he did not utter the words, she heard them clearly.

She disconnected, took up another phone, and dialed. When the guards at the farmhouse did not answer, she surmised why: Jayda and Zander Cruz had escaped.

I must act—and quickly.

The distance to Walter Reed from the Vice President's residence was less than seven miles by car. The distance to Ronald Reagan Washington National Airport was perhaps a mile farther—in the opposite direction.

She called her personal assistant, maid, and bodyguards to her. Although Simon and Winnie Delancey had been in the Vice President's residence for mere days, contingency plans had long been in place. She issued her instructions in quick, staccato bursts, then sent them to their tasks.

She herself ran upstairs to her bedroom, opened a floor safe, and withdrew a single small bag, prepacked with only the most vital items: cash, fake passports and credit cards, a single change of clothing, sunglasses, scarf, and a smartphone and charger.

Years ago, she had depended upon a tiny book in which she had printed a priceless list of contacts and foreign bank account numbers and passcodes. Now this phone held them all—and it was encrypted.

Less than a minute later she ran out the front entrance to her waiting car; it pulled away immediately, one bodyguard behind the wheel.

"Arrangements?"

"They have filed the flight plan and are fueling the jet as we speak."

"Very good."

The car passed through the drive's open gates and wound toward the checkpoint on Massachusetts Avenue NW. The guards waved them through.

As soon as they passed the checkpoint, her driver turned left and navigated to Wisconsin Avenue. Soon after, he turned onto a side street and parked behind buildings close to Holy Rood Cemetery.

Winnie's second bodyguard was waiting for them beside another vehicle—a white SUV with the markings of a Metropolitan Police Department of the District of Columbia patrol car. He opened the car's rear door, and Winnie slid inside. The two guards put on the deep blue caps of the MPDC. Winnie dug into her bag, removed her scarf and sunglasses, and donned them.

The guards climbed into the front seat. The car returned to Wisconsin Avenue but diverted south onto 35th. Their route was not ordinarily the fastest one. However, half a block onto 35th, the driver switched on the car's siren and light bar and increased his speed.

They flew across the Theodore Roosevelt Memorial Bridge and merged onto the George Washington Memorial Parkway. With siren warbling, they traveled at eighty miles per hour toward Reagan National.

⌘

FIFTEEN MINUTES AFTER Winnie Delancey and her guards departed, a Marine helicopter touched down on the lawn across from the Vice President's residence. It was not a Squadron One VH-20 Lockheed Martin Sikorsky specifically adapted and refitted for the President's use but an older UH-60 Black Hawk, one that had seen combat action.

Two Secret Service agents and seven armed marines in woodland combat utility uniforms jumped from the chopper. The marines deployed at a run to surround the house. The Secret Service agents strode with purposeful steps toward the front door.

They did not knock, and their abrupt entry startled the staff.

"Where is Mrs. Delancey?" one of them demanded.

A tall, svelte woman hurried toward them. "Are you Mrs. Delancey's escort?"

"You might say that," one of the agents answered. "Where is she, please?"

"I'm Rachel Landsman, Mrs. Delancey's personal assistant. She went up to change her clothes only a few minutes ago. I expect her downstairs shortly. Would you be kind enough to wait by the front door?"

"We'll wait by the staircase."

"A-are you certain? Is there a problem?"

They ignored her and took up positions at the foot of the stairs.

Five minutes later they had grown uneasy. After another two minutes, they looked at each other.

"She's taking too long."

They rushed up the stairs to the Vice President's bedroom and pounded on the door.

Winnie Delancey's maid opened to them.

"Yes?"

"Where is Mrs. Delancey?"

"Who are you?"

"Secret Service. Where is she?"

"Oh! Of course. I was asked to give you this note."

She timidly offered them a folded sheet of paper.

One of the agents opened it and read aloud, "I simply could not sit idle, waiting for the helicopter, when the hospital is so close. I elected to leave for the hospital with my driver. I apologize for the inconvenience. Thank you for understanding."

"She's running."

The other agent spoke into his comms. "Mrs. Delancey is on the run."

He heard his superior curse, then issue orders.

Winnie Delancey had been in the air eleven minutes by the time Air Traffic Control closed D.C. airspace.

⌘

THE NANOMITES WERE AT WORK on the President, attempting to save him from the poison Simon Delancey had administered. While they worked, I researched botulinum toxins.

I knew that what I found might not apply to him. The compound the Vice President had sprayed in the President's face had been modified by scientists in a lab somewhere, probably a lab in America. That meant that the type of botulinum toxin the scientists had begun with would bear little resemblance to the poison that was shutting down Robert Jackson's systems at this moment.

And while I knew that "compound" meant the toxin was a cocktail of more than botulinum toxin, I could only speculate as to what the other ingredients might be. So, I kept my mind preoccupied, reading up on the various botulinum strains. What I found dismayed me:

Botulinum toxin is one of the most deadly biological substances known. It is a neurotoxin that binds to nerve endings where nerve and muscle join and prevents muscles from contracting—resulting in paralysis, muscle atrophy, and respiratory failure. If a patient survives, some effects may be permanent.

Considering that botulinum toxin generally does not manifest its symptoms for 24-72 hours—but the toxin with which Delancey had dosed the President had produced an immediate effect—only increased my angst for him.

"Nano? What can you tell me?"

The doctors have put the President on a ventilator and have administered an antitoxin. They are, in the main, observing him and providing supportive and palliative care. The President is gravely ill, Jayda Cruz.

"What are you doing to help him? What *can* you do?"

The antitoxin prevents the toxin from doing further damage to the President's nerve endings. However, the damage already done cannot be reversed. We are actively repairing what nerve damage we can. We do not know if it will be enough to prevent system shutdown.

This was not the news I wanted to hear.

Lord? Here is a man who professes to know you. He is a good leader for America. Lord, in the name of Jesus, I am asking you to do what the doctors and even the nanomites cannot do: Please heal this man's body and mind and restore him to office!

I had to remain under the bed as the doctors and nurses worked feverishly over me and while the nanomites did the same. I closed my eyes and recalled waking up in the cage this morning—was it really only this morning?—a scrap of that special hymn running through my mind. To myself, I hummed,

> *"Up from the grave He arose,*
> *With a mighty triumph o'er His foes."*

The cage had trembled and shaken. The electrical panel had arced and blown out. Our prison doors had opened.

A series of miracles.

"How wonderful you are, Lord God!" I whispered.

I hummed softly . . .

"Death cannot keep his Prey,
Jesus, my Savior;
He tore the bars away,
Jesus, my Lord!"

The chief ER nurse bending over the President hummed to herself.

"What's that melody, Carole? It feels familiar, but I can't place it."

"Hm? Oh. I . . . I can't place it either."

The Chief of Internal Medicine squinted at the ceiling and thought. "'Up . . . up something.'"

An ER attending physician nudged him. "'Up from the grave'?"

"That's it, Paul. 'Up from the grave he arose . . .'"

"It's an old hymn. 'With a mighty triumph o'er his foes.'"

The nurse and the two doctors sang together softly, "'He arose a victor from the dark domain, and he lives forever with his saints to reign. He arose, he arose—'"

"This really isn't the place for religious songs," another nurse interjected. "I mean, I don't have anything against religious songs personally, but I'm sure HR would have something to say—"

A nurse minding the President's vitals interrupted, "Doctor? The President's blood oxidation has markedly improved." She checked the President's fingernail beds. "Better color, too."

"'Death cannot keep its prey . . .'" the chief ER nurse sang in a whisper.

"Interesting. Did that song have an effect on the President's condition? I wonder . . ." The Chief of Internal Medicine's glance swept around the treatment room. "Does anyone object to us singing? Quietly, of course. If you do object, please say so now. Anyone? No?"

He grinned behind his scrub mask. "Care to lead us, Carole?"

"My pleasure, Carl."

They sang softly, but this time other voices joined them. Mine, did, too. From under the bed, I sang with the same heartfelt worship I had sung with this morning.

Lord, with you, all things are possible—because up from the grave you arose!

The medical team sang on. It seemed no one knew the verses except the nurse named Carole, so she led them, and the rest joined in on the chorus. Those who hadn't known the song before picked up on the chorus easily enough after a few times through.

Then, the singing ended on an abrupt note.

I didn't see it happen—but I heard the reaction of those who did. Gasps of surprise and astonishment.

"Mr. President? Sir? Look at me, please, sir. I'm Carl Tanner, Chief of Internal Medicine at Walter Reed. Yes, you're at Walter Reed, Mr. President. Please don't try to speak. You are intubated."

The tumult around the President's bed prevented me from hearing much more. Dr. Tanner must have felt the same, because he called for order.

"Quiet! Everyone quiet, please. You want us to remove the vent, Mr. President? I'm sorry, but it is much too early to do so, sir."

Robert Jackson must have insisted, because the doctor said, "Yes, sir; however, it is not a wise idea this early in your, uh, treatment. We need to be sure you can breathe on your own, sir."

I knew Robert Jackson a little. I could pretty much envision the glare with which he punctuated his nonverbal order. Good luck with that, Dr. Carl Tanner, Chief of Internal Medicine!

Dr. Tanner growled, "Get me an arterial blood gas, please—and elevate the President's head a few degrees."

No one spoke while those orders were followed.

"Nano, are you still working on the President?"

Jayda Cruz, this is very odd. Many of the damaged nerve endings have regenerated without our intervention.

"You aren't working on him any longer?"

No, Jayda Cruz.

I was ready to burst. "Nano, tell Kennedy that I'm coming out."

I wiggled under Kennedy's lifted foot (Man, the things I do for my country!) and found a place at the back of the treatment room where I wouldn't be in the way. I stood on a chair against the wall, so I could see over the heads of the medical team.

"Nano! What is the President's current condition?"

Jayda Cruz . . . we do not know how to explain the President's physical turnaround.

"Yes, yes you do. You saw a miracle just this morning."

Dr. Tanner said, "All right, Mr. President. The nurse is going to remove the tube. If you are unable to breathe on your own, we will immediately sedate you and reinsert the vent. Do you understand? Good."

Nurse Carole said, "Mr. President? I've deflated the cuff in your trachea. As I pull the tube, you will feel discomfort. Coughing is normal. Ready?"

Tense moments passed as the President coughed and choked until the tube was out. Another nurse placed an oxygen cannula in his nose.

"O$_2$ levels holding. Respiration rate unchanged."

"Mr. President? How do you feel?"

The President's voice, rough but strong, rang out.

"Kennedy!"

Axel sprang forward. "Yes, Mr. President?"

"Did you arrest that traitor, Delancey?"

"We did, sir; however . . ."

"However, what?"

"Sir, we've received word from Camp David that the Vice President suffered a fatal stroke soon after he was arrested."

"Oh? Did he, now?"

The President put his head to one side considering Kennedy's report . . . or as though listening. He appeared neither surprised nor concerned.

"Uh, yes, sir. He was pronounced dead on the scene."

"I see." He cleared his throat. "Will someone get me some water, please?"

⌘⌘⌘⌘

CHAPTER 40

GAMBLE CALLED US LATER to report the unwelcome news. "Winnie Delancey got away. The entire alphabet soup of American intelligence and law enforcement agencies are working to locate her. If I had to guess, she's heading for South America."

"She cannot be allowed to escape; she must face justice. She's responsible for so many deaths," I whispered.

Genie. The President's friend, Wayne. Not to mention dozens of American POWs during a war that ended before I had even been born.

"We're doing the best we can, Jayda."

"I'm sorry. I know you are. How is Trujillo?"

"On her feet and anxious to start working out to regain her strength, thank you. What about the nanomites? Can they help in the search for Winnie Delancey?"

"I will put them on it."

⌘

IT WAS FINALLY EVENING, and we were back in the apartment Malware had loaned us. My body was convinced it had survived the longest forty-eight hours of its life. The events of the past two days kept running through my mind, wearing me down all over again. I was beyond fatigued, but I couldn't rest yet.

Zander and I had a few mop-up details to handle before we could, finally, let down.

Let down. As in collapse and take a week off to do absolutely nothing.

I kept thinking that our assignment was mostly over. We'd found out what happened to President Jackson's friend, ending the Overman family's long ordeal. We'd saved the President's life (again) and exposed the brains behind the plot.

Vice President Delancey and NSA Deputy Director Danforth were dead, and the FBI had arrested Secret Service Assistant Deputy Director Morningside. A sweep of their homes and offices had turned up evidence to incriminate a raft of low- and mid-level players, including the dirty Secret Service agents and NSA security police officers we'd already identified—and one high-level scientist within the Army's Institute for Infectious Diseases.

Many of the remaining conspirators would hide in plain sight during the coming top-to-bottom investigation. They knew (and we knew) that rooting them out would prove nearly impossible. Going after entrenched bureaucrats was like playing a game of "Whack-a-Mole."

The FBI and Justice Department would have to content themselves with snagging the occasional heads that popped up, but they would never be able to entirely clean out the infestation.

Kennedy called, too, and told us that the President was recovering nicely and would be released from the hospital later in the coming week. At the President's direction, his people had held a press conference and come clean with the nation, making them aware of the two attempts to overthrow his administration. The resulting media tumult was in full swing and likely would not die down for months.

Kennedy had also secured a private interview with Acting President Friese. As a result, Friese had grown a spine and ordered the Secret Service to remove his party's people from the White House—much to their helpless wrath. Friese was content to hide in the Oval Office, enjoying the perks of the presidency, following Marcus Park's guidance but deflecting any real decisions, knowing the President would resume his duties soon.

So far, amid all of the commotion and confusion, our names and identities had remained out of the limelight—a minor miracle among several ginormous ones.

I would like to say that, by that night, the FBI had some idea as to Winnie Delancey's whereabouts, but no joy there. She had, Gamble told us, chartered low-flying planes without transponders to hop from state to state and illegally leave the country. Kennedy and Gamble both insisted that she was no longer a threat to us or our family, but I wasn't convinced.

At least the hit squad she'd sent after our family in New Mexico had been arrested. The FBI Albuquerque Field Office Special Agent in Charge had IDed the two men and charged them with impersonating federal officers, interviewing members of the pathology team under false pretenses, and attempting to bribe and, when that failed, threatening the family of a federal agent.

With the hit team out of the way, Gamble had phoned the commandant of White Sands, who promised to deliver Zander's parents to their home by breakfast tomorrow.

I sent a text to Dr. Bickel's phone giving him the "all clear." He would receive it the next time he stuck his head out of the mountain to check. Then he, Abe, Emilio, and Izzie could leave the mountain's safety.

We would have "some 'splainin' to do" with Izzie, but that could wait. It would have to.

Zander was finishing up his call to Pastor Lucklow. "We wanted you to know that our family crisis has been resolved," he said.

"We understand how family often must come before ministry, Zander."

"Thank you, Pastor. I just hope you don't think less of me for dropping the leadership of Celebrate Recovery back on Tom and Becky after only three weeks in the saddle."

"Not at all. In fact . . . Well, you've been out of the loop for a bit, Zander, so let me catch you up. You see, whatever happened when you visited Jack Grober's wife and daughter in the hospital has had a profound effect on Grace Chapel. Our Sunday services are overflowing, and Tom and Becky report that five newcomers to Celebrate Recovery have surrendered their lives to Jesus. To put it in plain terms, we are experiencing a move of God's Spirit—and it seems to have begun when you prayed for Kaylee Grober."

When Zander hung up, he stared at the phone. "Wow."

"Wow is right. Thank you, Lord God . . ." my words trailed off. I was soooo tired.

"C'mon, babe. Let's tuck you in."

"'Mkay." No argument from me.

We crawled into bed, our pillows close, our faces touching. Zander kissed my forehead, then my eyes.

"Nice," I mumbled. "Really nice."

He kissed my nose. He kissed my cheeks. He kissed my ear. Then . . . my neck. Chills caromed around inside me. I longed to sink into Zander's arms and lose myself in him.

He must have felt the same way, because we whispered together, "Lights out, Nano."

Jayda Cruz.

"Lights *out*, Nano. Don't start with me!"

I was tired *and* cranky.

Jayda Cruz, we must ask you a question before you and Zander enter that sacred space where we are not allowed.

"For heaven's sake! Can't it wait?"

No, Jayda Cruz.

Zander and I sighed in unison.

"Make it quick," Zander growled.

"Right. What is it, Nano?"

Jayda Cruz, as we explained earlier, we are protecting your last viable ovum. Unfortunately, we cannot do so much longer. Despite our best efforts, it is degrading. Do you wish us to release the egg now? We cannot vouch for its viability much longer, but the statistical odds of impregnation tonight are quite high.

Zander's head bounced off his pillow as he sat up. "What?"

"Crud. Um, I guess I haven't had the right moment to tell you."

"Tell me what, exactly?"

The nanomites filled in the details for me. *Jayda Cruz had six remaining eggs that we were safeguarding; however, when she was shot in the abdomen, the round destroyed the ovary containing those eggs. We were able to save and cocoon one egg, which must be used soon, before its viability expires.*

"Wait. You're saying we could have a baby?"

The likelihood is high, Zander Cruz, if the ovum is released tonight.

Zander wiped his face with his hand. "Way to drop the hammer, Nano. Sheesh. No pressure here, right?"

He put his cheek back on his pillow so that we were again nose to nose and eye to eye. "Jay? I confess that I'm more than a little dumbfounded . . . but what do you think? Is this our chance to grow our family? Do you want to make a baby?"

"Yes! Of course, I-I do, but . . . ."

"But?"

"Winnie Delancey. What she did to Macy and Darius."

Zander raised himself up on one elbow. "*No.* No way. Never!"

"Yeah, that's how I feel, too. I want a baby, but Winnie Delancey wants the nanomites. I doubt that she can give them up—not now that she's figured out how to 'extract' them from us. She'll find a place to hide and regroup—and then she'll look for another opportunity to trap us and take them. Zander, I don't want to leave our child an orphan. More than that, I don't ever want our child used as bait."

I shook my head. "We can't, Zander. We can't bring a child into the world knowing we would be putting him or her in harm's way."

Zander slowly nodded. "I understand."

Jayda Cruz and Zander Cruz. Jesus has made it our responsibility to keep you and your child safe. You need not fear Winnie Delancey; the woman will not seek for you again.

Zander and I shared a look, one of disquiet.

"Nano," Zander asked, "what have you done?"

We have taken appropriate steps to protect you and your family, Zander Cruz.

I felt sick. "But . . . we thought you learned your lesson with Vice President Harmon, Nano."

We did learn, Jayda Cruz. What we have done was properly authorized.

"Authorized? By whom?"

By President Jackson. The Supreme Court ruled that the President has the authority to sanction actions—including deadly force—that protect the United States from a "clear and present danger." The President employed such an action when he downed the jet carrying Lawrence Danforth.

During that crisis, he told us that any individuals who had knowledge of us and attempted to weaponize us against America represented such a "clear and present danger." He authorized and directed us to use any means necessary to remove such a danger.

In the Situation Room—after he'd given the order to shoot down Danforth's plane—the President had remained seated, his head bowed. The nanomites had whispered my words into the President's ear . . . and the President, it seems, had whispered his instructions to them.

As you yourself said, Jayda Cruz, anyone who would harm a child is a monster who needs to be destroyed. Under President Jackson's order, we have taken steps to remove Winnie Delancey as a threat to the President, to national security, and to you and your family.

Zander and I laid there for a while, shocked into silence. I was too tired, too weary to tussle with another problem or moral dilemma.

I was drifting away when Zander breathed into my ear, "So. . . what do you think, Jay? Want to give Emilio a little brother or sister?"

His breath tickled the little hairs on my skin and woke me up. "Mmm hmm. That would be wonderful—but I want to go home, Zander. Home to Albuquerque."

"Okay by me; our job here is done. So, is that a 'yes' to making a baby?"

"Yes, Zander. I want to make a baby. Let's give Emilio a little brother or sister."

"You heard her, Nano."

We did.

Lights out, Jayda and Zander Cruz.

⌘⌘⌘⌘

POSTSCRIPT

"IT'S BEEN NINE HOURS! Don't you know anything?"

"We know the jet she chartered out of D.C. landed fifteen minutes after takeoff out of Reagan, Agent Randolph—before our scrambled jets could get a lock on her."

"Where could she go in fifteen minutes?"

"To a hick airport in another state where she ditched her jet for a puddle jumper."

"Weren't you able to track her?"

"Not fast enough. She hopscotched from D.C. to West Virginia, to Tennessee, to Alabama, to southern Georgia, to southern Florida, always ahead of us, flying illegally without flight plans or transponders, staying low, beneath radar. We *are* certain she landed in Cuba seventy-five minutes ago."

"Cuba. Seventy-five minutes ago."

"An asset in place put eyes on her, but we don't believe she stayed long. If her layover was like the others, she had a plane on the runway, fueled and ready to go as soon as she touched down, likely a jet. But to get that kind of service from Cuba? The woman has to have both money and some serious 'friends' in high places."

"Do we have her next destination?"

"Not yet, but wherever it is, we doubt it's her final stop. She will change planes again to make tracing her next to impossible."

⌘

WINNIE DELANCEY TOOK her first easy breath since the harrowing flight from D.C. Her faithful (and well compensated) bodyguards were seated at the front of the chartered Learjet 35A as they descended into Mexico City. They would deplane and spend the night in the city. The following day, her men would charter an innocuous plane for the next leg of their journey. Their destination tomorrow would be San Jose, Costa Rica, and after that, on to Caracas, Venezuela—although they were not likely to stay long.

Winnie used her knuckles to knead at the ache behind her eyes. *Ah, Simon, my love. What will I do now? We came so close to destroying America, so close to bringing to its knees the nation that has driven so many nations into the dust. Was it all for nothing?*

It was not that she lacked resources. No. But, for the first time in her life, she lacked purpose.

I am sixty-seven years old, and in good health. We were on the cusp of attaining our dreams, and I had so much to look forward to! And now? Now what will I do?

If only I'd had one day longer to secure the nanomites, to transfer them to me . . . what personal power I would wield! With the nanomites, I could find another way to achieve our dream.

"Ladies and gentlemen, we are on our final approach to Mexico City."

Minutes later, the bump of wheels contacting the runway announced their arrival. They taxied to a private gate, and a steward unlatched and lowered the Learjet's steps. Her men stood to escort her from the plane.

On the tarmac, one of them forged ahead to secure a taxi. The other stayed with Winnie and cleared a path for her through the teeming terminal.

Within an hour, her guards had checked them into a modest hotel suite under false passports. She had them order room service for herself and for them. After they had eaten, her men would go out to locate a plane for tomorrow's flight.

Winnie had the waiter take her food to her room. She locked the door and stayed there until morning.

⌘

SHE AROSE AFTER a restless night. Her guards assured her that they had chartered a luxury Cessna Caravan turboprop plane that seated 10, and that it was prepared to leave as soon as they returned to the airport.

"It is a comfortable plane with nice amenities. They will provide breakfast if you like," one of them told her.

"Let us go, then."

They returned to the airport, cleared the security screening, and were ushered to their gate by their flight attendant, a striking, middle-aged brunette. "This way, please," she murmured, leading them through the gate and up the short flight of steps.

Winnie gave a cursory inspection to the plane's lavish upholstery and carpets as she stepped through the roll-up door. She was tired and irritable, aware that her clean change of clothes should have been pressed. She retired to the back of the plane where she could be alone and left her men to oversee the details. While she waited for the plane to taxi and takeoff, she browsed international news on her phone.

The headlines were only about the newly confirmed Vice President's sudden stroke and death and how the Secret Service had rushed the President to Walter Reed—as a precaution only.

That should have been you, Robert Jackson, she ground out under her breath. *You were to die, not Simon. At this moment, Simon should be President—and after him, me!*

Apparently, the President was keeping Winnie Delancey's fugitive status from the media, for there was not a breath of it anywhere. How long could that last? The condolences would pour in—and with no one to receive them and no public sightings of the grieving widow to be had, the media would soon question where she was.

Her bodyguards entered the plane and the flight attendant closed and sealed the door. As the plane ran down the runway and lifted, Winnie laid her head back.

I must rest so that my mind is clear when we reach Costa Rica.

⌘

SHE MUST HAVE SLEPT. As she roused herself, she checked her phone. Two hours of sleep, but two hours would sustain her for a while.

She lifted the window shade and stared below. The sun shone from behind the starboard wing, casting a glow on the water below.

It has been years since I have been to Costa Rica or Venezuela. I wonder how changed they are.

Winnie blinked. The morning sun was behind them to the east, but the plane should have been flying south—with the sun on their port side. And the water below them? It stretched into the horizon, but they should be flying over land.

She called aloud, "Are we off course?"

The flight attendant stood, and Winnie shouted to her. "Are we going the wrong direction?"

The attendant walked toward Winnie, her steps slow, languorous, sensual. A far cry from deferential and servile.

Winnie felt the need to meet this woman on her feet. She stood and clutched the arm of her seat. "We are going the wrong way. Please inform the pilot and alter course."

The attendant's English was clear, but her diction and syntax spoke of Mexican gentility and of a pricey education. "I am afraid, *Señora* Delancey, that we have had a change of itinerary."

Winnie's eyes narrowed. "Where are we? What is the water below us?"

"We are, at present, quite close to my home, Culiacán, which is not far from the Pacific Ocean."

Culiacán? The bastion of drug cartels.

"Michael! Tobias!"

Winnie's guards remained in their seats. They stared at their feet.

They have sold me out.

Winnie studied the attendant. "Apparently, someone has offered you a great deal of money for me. Whatever they are paying you, I can pay you more."

The woman spread her hands. "It is not about money, *señora*; it is about honor."

"Honor?"

"*Sí*. A favor, a debt repaid."

Winnie steeled herself, commanded her body not to panic. She told herself to breathe, to look for the opening she needed, but her fatigue made her a bit unsteady on her feet. She grasped the seat in front of her.

"If it is not about money, perhaps you are interested in what money cannot always buy. I have a great many secrets, and I am certain that in your line of . . . business, secrets may be traded for influence or for power."

The woman lifted her chin and appeared interested. "*Sí*, I enjoy power. What kind of secrets might you have that could acquire for me more power?"

Winnie smiled as with a fellow conspirator. "A technological breakthrough, my dear, a scientific advance with limitless potential. A technology that can actually . . . render a woman invisible. Think of the possibilities."

"Invisible? Truly?" The woman's lush lips parted; her eyes glowed. She closed the gap between them and reached out a hand to Winnie's arm to steady her.

Yes. I have her, Winnie congratulated herself.

Something pricked Winnie's arm, and the attendant's lips curved with mocking humor. "Tell me, *Señora* Delancey, does such an invisible woman also call the fire of the gods into her hands? Does she gather the lightning to herself and cast it upon her enemies? Can she create the storm around her and bring down the wrath of the heavens?"

Winnie's mouth opened and closed in astonished dismay.

"It grieves me to tell you this, *señora*, but I have already met such a woman. I must say, too, that I do not wish to ever meet her again."

"Bu—" Winnie stopped. The word seemed to stick in her throat.

"May I help you, *señora?* You are weak, no? Come. Let me assist you to the front of the plane."

Winnie let the attendant lead her toward the front of the plane—not that she could have resisted. She found that her feet and hands would not respond well to her commands.

The copilot emerged from the cockpit, and the attendant addressed Winnie's bodyguards, then the copilot.

"Gentlemen, please ensure that your seatbelts are secure. Joachim, the altitude, *por favor?*"

"One thousand feet, *Señora* Duvall."

"Ah. I will need your assistance."

Winnie tried to speak; nothing but faint fits of air passed her lips.

"A neuromuscular blocking agent," the attendant purred. "Quite painless, I'm told, and it passes in a few hours."

She and the man assisting her helped each other don harnesses that were fixed to the bulkhead. Winnie grunted but could not move. Neither of her bodyguards would look at her. One of them shook and trembled.

The attendant and copilot unlatched the roll-up door and, in a single, fluid movement, rolled it up and across the inside of the plane's ceiling. The plane's slipstream tugged and pulled at them, but they were safely harnessed to the bulkhead.

Winnie was not. She stared out the gaping hole, seeing her death before her, hearing Jayda Cruz's words above the roar of the wind.

On the day of your death, you will come face to face with God Almighty. If you stand before the Lord without Jesus, you will face his righteous justice. I'm warning you now to confess your sins and turn to Jesus—before it is too late for you.

"Uahhh . . . Ahhhww . . ."

The attendant murmured, "Our family loves its excitement as well as its luxury. Skydiving is a favorite pastime."

She and the copilot grasped Winnie's arms and positioned her in the threshold.

The woman said, "I will not say *vaya con Dios, señora*. He is, after all, not likely to go with you, although you may meet him at the end of your passage."

Winnie could not move a muscle even as she tumbled, end over end, toward the blue water stretching up to meet her.

⌘

ESPERANZA DUVALL STUDIED—for at least the fifteenth time—the cryptic text she'd received late the previous afternoon. She'd been obliged to move quickly, to have her people fuel one of her family's planes and fly it from Culiacán to Mexico City, and then locate and reach out to the woman's bodyguards.

The way to an agreement, smoothed by four guns pointed at their heads, had been quick and satisfactory. She had given them each one hundred thousand dollars in cash and the promise of their freedom at the end. Faced with certain death now or the uncertain hope that she would honor her word later, the guards had chosen the latter. Esperanza's men had watched their hotel all night to ensure that their cooperation did not falter.

It had not been a bad bargain, Esperanza admitted. She had recouped more cash from Winnie Delancey's bag than what she had expended to complete her task. Above all that, she had satisfied a debt of "honor."

Esperanza Duvall
We gave you Arnaldo Soto
His kidneys saved your uncle's life
We wish a favor in return
A monster who cannot be allowed to live
Mexico City 10 pm

A photo of Winnie Delancey, the wife of the deceased U.S. Vice President, was attached to the text as was a photo of a Learjet's tail number.

Esperanza, remembering her encounter with the woman who threw fire and lightning from her fingers and who launched a line of vehicles into a deadly rain of burning scrap metal and glass, shivered. She touched "reply" and typed a short sentence: *El favor ha sido devuelto.*

The favor has been returned.

She pressed "send" and glanced a last time at her phone before pulling the sim card and snapping it in two.

⌘⌘⌘⌘

POST-POSTSCRIPT

JAYDA CRUZ. IT IS TIME TO GET UP.

Jayda Cruz. It is time to get up.

Jayda Cruz. It is time to get up.

"Huh? No. No, it's not. I don't have a job anymore, Nano, and I'm officially on vacation, so shut it."

Jayda Cruz, as Hebrews 6:12 tells us, "We do not want you to become lazy, but to imitate those who through faith and patience inherit what has been promised."

"*Gah!* Leave me alone." I pulled the pillow over my head—which did not help. At all.

Jayda Cruz. It is time to get up.

Jayda Cruz. It is time to get up.

Jayda Cruz—

This time, Zander grumped at them. "Nano, unless our apartment is on fire or the President himself is on the phone with a major announcement that somehow concerns us, PIPE DOWN. We're sleepin' here, got it?"

Softly, but as annoying as a gnat, the nanomites breathed in our ears.

Jayda Cruz. Zander Cruz. We are not the President, but we have a major announcement that concerns you.

Jayda Cruz. Zander Cruz. We are not the President, but we have a major announcement that concerns you.

Jayda Cruz. Zander Cruz. We are not the President, but we have a major announcement that concerns you.

Their teasing croon penetrated the fog of sleep. Zander and I jerked awake, sat up, and spoke simultaneously.

"What announcement?"

Perhaps you are right, Jayda and Zander Cruz. You are weary. You should sleep longer. Your bodies have been stressed and overworked. Return to sleep. Our announcement can certainly wait.

"You jokers," Zander answered. "Don't you dare try to hold out on us now."

But sleep is beneficial; it is essential to good health and optimal efficiency, Zander Cruz. As you requested, we will leave you and Jayda Cruz alone to rest and recuperate.

"Wisecracking turkeys!" Zander yelled. He threw off the covers and bounded out of the hide-a-bed. I crawled out of my side of the blankets and, wiping my bleary eyes, went to stand with him.

"See? We're done sleeping, Nano—thanks to you. Now give it up," Zander demanded.

The two nanoclouds flowed from us in silver-blue streams and melded into a dense haze—until a single sparkling cloud, swirling with a myriad of colors, filled the room. The cloud breathed, swelled, and intensified; it descended and engulfed us. Filaments of cotton-candy wisps spun around us—and the song of the nanocloud reverberated in our ears . . . until the nanomites whispered,

You may wish to rest while you can, Jayda and Zander Cruz. Sleep will be in short supply in nine months.

The End

MY DEAR READERS,

Thank you for reading my **Nanostealth** series. I hope and pray you have been blessed and built up in your faith.

It is entirely possible that **Nanostealth** will continue in the future; however, my intention for next year is to focus on **Laynie Portland, Retired Spy**, a new series that spins off from the last book in my **Prairie Heritage** series.

To keep up with my publication schedule and receive free, read-ahead chapters of upcoming books, I invite you to sign up for my newsletter (see my website on the following page). I promise not to spam you or sell your email addresses.

Thank you again. I have the best readers in the world—you. It is an honor.

Many hugs,
Vikki

ABOUT THE AUTHOR

Vikki Kestell's passion for people and their stories is evident in her readers' affection for her characters and unusual plotlines. Two often-repeated sentiments are, "I feel like I know these people," and, "I'm right there, in the book, experiencing what the characters experience."

Vikki holds a Ph.D. in Organizational Learning and Instructional Technologies. She left a career of twenty-plus years in government, academia, and corporate life to pursue writing full time. "Writing is the best job ever," she admits, "and the most demanding."

Also an accomplished speaker and teacher, Vikki and her husband Conrad Smith make their home in Albuquerque, New Mexico.

To keep abreast of new book releases, sign up for Vikki's newsletter on her website, **http://www.vikkikestell.com**, find her on Facebook at **http://www.facebook.com/TheWritingOfVikkiKestell**, or follow her on BookBub, **https://www.bookbub.com/authors/vikki-kestell**.

OTHER BOOKS BY VIKKI KESTELL

A PRAIRIE HERITAGE

Book 1: *A Rose Blooms Twice* (free eBook, most online retailers)
Book 2: *Wild Heart on the Prairie*
Book 3: *Joy on This Mountain*
Book 4: *The Captive Within*
Book 5: *Stolen*
Book 6: *Lost Are Found*
Book 7: *All God's Promises*
Book 8: *The Heart of Joy—A Short Story* (eBook only)

GIRLS FROM THE MOUNTAIN

Book 1: *Tabitha*
Book 2: *Tory*
Book 3: *Sarah Redeemed*

The Christian and the Vampire: A Short Story
(free eBook, most online retailers)

Faith-Filled Fiction™

www.faith-filledfiction.com | www.vikkikestell.com

CPSIA information can be obtained
at www.ICGtesting.com
Printed in the USA
LVHW031742071218
599659LV00020B/532/P